TOAST

The Ride to Hell

Rick Allen

A catalogue record for this book is available from the National Library of Australia

First published 2021 by Rick Allen

Copyright © Rick Allen 2021

This novel is entirely a work of fiction. The incidents and some of the characters portrayed in it are the work of the author's imagination.

All rights reserved. No part of this publication may be reproduced, stored in a retrieval system, or transmitted in any form, or by any means, electronic, mechanical, photocopying, recording or otherwise, without the written permission of the author.

This book is sold subject to the condition that it shall not, by way of trade or otherwise, be lent, re-sold, hired out or otherwise circulated without the author's prior consent in any form of binding or cover other than that in which it is published and without a similar condition including this condition being imposed on the subsequent purchaser.

Publisher:
Inspiring Publishers
P.O. Box 159, Calwell, ACT Australia 2905
Email: publishaspg@gmail.com
http://www.inspiringpublishers.com

National Library of Australia Cataloguing-in-Publication entry

Author: Allen, Rick

Title: **Book One: TOAST - The Ride To Hell**/Rick Allen

ISBN: 978-1-922327-59-8 (Print)

The Author

Rick Allen lives in Woodsdale, Tasmania, with his wife Lesley. Rick is a, 'born and bred' Tasmanian (1956), with a keen interest in naval history, military horses, saddlery, long equestrian journeys, and the history of his profession; that of a saddler. He started his education at Cosgrove High School, and with his father a merchant seaman and professional fisherman, grandfather a master mariner tug skipper in London, and his great grandfather a master mariner Thames Barge sailing captain, it was a natural progression for Rick to join the Navy at the age of 15 and complete his education at HMAS Leeuwin.

Rick then went into the Electronic Technical Weapons branch of the Navy and served on many ships and support depots. Upon discharge from the permanent navy, Rick then served another 8 years in the reserves on a patrol boat. Some of the hats that Rick has worn since those navy days include those of qualified electrical fitter, workplace trainer and assessor, ship's master, marine engine driver, saddler, and horseback tour guide; just to mention a few.

Rick's passion to write comes from a desire to pass knowledge and stories on to others.

Table of Contents

Dedications

I dedicate this book to my loving wife Lesley, whose support during the writing of this book was unsurpassed.

Acknowledgements

COVER DESIGN

Original design by my great mate from West Texas, the late Lee Schultz, 'Wannabee Cowboy,' 'Old Curmudgeon,' and gifted poet, and featuring his beloved Quarter Horse, Zen.

Photo on the back cover of me riding Bob by Cynthia Larner.

Other photos used in this book were copied by me from my photographs.

'No copyright infringement is intended.'

*Statistics, where appropriate by Wikipedia.

Those people in my life who inspired the main characters in this book

Even though this book is fiction, it is based on real life characters. Their names have been changed to protect their privacy, and I would like to formally acknowledge them here.

INITIAL EDITING TEAM

I would like to formally recognise my other half of my editing team, Lesley Allen.
Thank you for your many long hours of dedicated work.

Prologue

In the year 2000, after ten long years spent designing and re-designing it, an international law was eventually passed to help combat climate change. All vehicles manufactured from that point on were to have the E1 (Engine 1) modification; a device which successfully reduced emissions to less than 1%.

This revolutionary device was an accumulation of twenty years of painstaking research, involving scientists from all major countries. The device was eventually perfected in 1996.

It took four long years before all nations world-wide would agree to its instigation; this was largely due to concerns over who would manufacture the device and who would get the profits. Eventually China won the rights to produce the E1, and it was agreed that the profits would be split between all those countries that had a hand in its design.

The E1 was considered to be the one major coup for mankind since the beginning of time. To assist with emission reduction, every country in the world agreed to get rid of all pre-2000 vehicles. This type of world-wide co-operation in itself was a never before heard of event. At the time of this world-changing legislation there were untold numbers of pre-2000 vehicles in operation; it was left up to each individual country to develop its own unique way of dealing with the problem. In Australia alone, there were literally millions of pre-2000 vehicles in use.

Vehicle owners were given two years in which to make a decision, they could either sell their pre-2000 vehicle to the government for bugger-all coin, or they could choose to have them modified. To choose modification was not an easy option, the cost was exorbitant, and most governments were against the idea anyway. It was easier for governments to simply turn these vehicles into scrap.

The, 'Dob in a Dirty,' program was introduced in Australia in 2002. Service station proprietors, mechanics, panel beaters and everyone employed in vehicle related industries were, 'encouraged' to advise the authorities when a customer brought in a vehicle with a pre-2000 manufacturing plate for repair, refuelling or re-registration. The reward for this was a $1000.00 bounty paid to the, 'dobber'. Once advised of its existence the authorities would simply confiscate the rogue vehicle and scrap it. In return, they would recoup the scrap metal price, and on top of this the owner of the vehicle incurred a hefty fine of $1000.00. As you can imagine, this was a very popular program which had the potential to generate large amounts of money for those who chose to, 'Dob in a Dirty.'

Within a couple of years this program alone had seen the destruction of nearly three million, 'dirty vehicles,' throughout Australia. By 2005, statistics gathered world-wide showed that all engines remaining in use were in compliance with the less than 1% emission output ruling.

The world was a different place following the events of 9/11 and the consequent, 'War on Terror.' ISIS had become without doubt the most well-known participant in terror activities world-wide. There were multiple suicide bombings in most terror-threatened countries on a daily basis, resulting in the formation of an elite sub-committee of the United Nations for the sole purpose of dealing with this problem. The heavy-handedness of the major powers was seen as an excuse for some of the more extreme nuclear equipped countries to sit up and take notice. While the rest of the Western world was thoroughly engaged with the, 'War on Terror,' they focused their efforts on planning their revenge against the major powers.

Unbeknownst to the rest of the world, in 2012 North Korea, Indonesia, India, Pakistan, Turkey and Iraq banded together to form an alliance. Although invited, China was reluctant at first to become involved. However, after much deliberation, and believing that the Alliance would eventually achieve global domination, China joined in 2013. None of the other major non-Alliance players were aware of what was going on.

In mid-2014 a united push against ISIS took place, with all the major countries throwing everything they had at the, 'War on Terror.' After more than a decade of terrorist activities, the United Nations sanctioned a show of force which it hoped would finally annihilate the enemy once and for all. The one stipulation was that only conventional weapons would be used.

At the highest level it was agreed without doubt that there would be collateral damage; however, this was considered acceptable in light of the ultimate aim of ridding the world of terrorists. In essence, all non-Alliance nations, (including the United States of America, the United Kingdom, Russia, France, Germany, Australia, Japan, New Haka, Saudi Arabia, the African Nations Group, Italy, the Scandinavian Group and Canada), agreed to deploy 95% of their ground troops; backed up with 95% of their navy and 100% of their air force, to get rid of the menace once and for all. It was decided that the only way to rid the world of these constant threats was to simply kill them all.

In August 2014, Iran accused the United States of spying on their nuclear facilities, this made world-wide headlines after Iranian forces confiscated two US Patrol Boats and their entire crews after catching them out. This was the catalyst that convinced Iran to stand alongside the Alliance against the Western powers, and especially against the United States of America. In November 2014, North Korea added fuel to the fire by testing its own nuclear capabilities; a nuclear device was deployed as a 'test', in preparation for possible world-wide conflict. This action in itself stirred the old feud between themselves and the United States.

With 90 to 100% of the military might of the world's major countries focused on Syria, Iraq and the Middle East, it wasn't long before tensions reached boiling point. Too late, it was discovered that it was a monumental mistake to place all your eggs in one basket, so to speak.

With the, ' War on Terror, at its peak, tensions boiled over on the 17th of December 2014. North Korea pushed the button to unleash its nuclear arsenal on Central Europe and the United States. Simultaneously, all other countries within the Alliance did the same; targeting all strategic satellites, including the E1 Master Satellite that controlled the E1 components, along with many non-Alliance nations, including the Middle East, United Kingdom, and U.S. Bases in Northern Australia and Russia. Needless to say, the Western world had been expecting action of some sort and was not caught entirely with their pants down. Swift retaliation came within thirty minutes.

Unbeknownst to the majority of Alliance members, a small number of countries within the Alliance had predicted this retaliation and had secretly formed a pact to identify a safe haven where they could start again if the world as we knew it was obliterated. North Korea, Indonesia and India were the three break-away Alliance members who shared this vision. It was obvious that, in the event of a world-wide nuclear disaster, all countries in the Northern Hemisphere would be wiped out in a very short space of time. After meticulously working out the global weather patterns, and predicting the areas where they believed the majority of the nuclear fall-out would settle, the break-away Alliance agreed that the only two possible regions in the Southern Hemisphere where a new start could be made were New Haka and Taswegia.

Within twenty-four hours of the first strike, all digital E1 compatible electronic components world-wide were rendered totally ineffectual. Every aircraft world-wide simply fell out of the sky; the E1 device in every post-2000 vehicle exploded and disabled the unit, all digital satellites were destroyed, and all digital transmissions became non-existent. The world, as we knew it at that point in time, simply ceased to exist.

In Taswegia, this catastrophic event occurred at 0235 AEST. The flow-on effect was extreme, with no transport, power, planes, or combustion engines of any description able to continue to operate. The most immediate impact on the local inhabitants was that within two days all supermarkets ran out of fresh produce. Those people who were able to access grocery stores on foot or by other means went into panic mode, and within five days, this resulted in the stocks of tinned and dry goods being almost totally depleted. The roads were littered with abandoned vehicles and trucks. Displaced people could be found everywhere, trying desperately to get home, and all business was stopped in its tracks.

All pleasure and commercial vessels ceased to operate, and the main passenger ferry between Devonshire and Millburn was rendered powerless and left to drift with the tides. On the positive side of things, (if it could be considered positive), because the effects of the strike hit Taswegia in the early hours of the morning, only a few freight planes fell out of the sky, however, all aircraft on the ground were immediately rendered unusable.

In the majority of northern hemisphere countries, the impact of losing all modes of transport was the least of their problems. The citizens of these nations were either killed outright in the blasts or were dying due to radiation fall-out. Within 24 hours life had ceased to exist on mainland Australia, and even the Boss Strait islands just north of Taswegia suffered limited fallout.

In Taswegia itself, within a few weeks of the first strike, the new Alliance invaded the State with an unwritten mandate to annihilate every Taswegian, with the exception of the doctors. The invasion date was Friday, 2nd January 2015. This was part of their plan to re-populate Taswegia and New Haka with their own people, and to eventually rebuild their empire. There was simply not enough room for the native Taswegians and their invaders. It was literally, 'them or us!'

Twenty purpose-built super tankers powered by old steam and fuel oil engines had been filled with the invading force some six weeks before North Korea pushed the button. The first ten tankers held over two million North Koreans who, along with their accompanying troops, were planning on becoming the new inhabitants of Taswegia. They brought with them countless quantities of aging machinery, which, being non-E1 compliant, would enable them to spread out and occupy their new country of residence.

The first four super tankers started departing Haeju Bay on 5th November: with regular sailings every week. Fights for survival broke out when loading the last two tankers, every person there was desperate to be among the privileged few to board. The President, his family and his North Korean naval escort were included as part of this last convoy; it was felt that the first four convoys would have drawn too much attention if escorted. No-one was certain on which date this last tanker sailed.

During this time, a second fleet of ten tankers were sent to New Haka with the same plan of action.

In addition to the fleet despatched by the North Korean invaders, Indonesia despatched one tanker and four old navy vessels containing 275,000 invaders. In the end India was not able to finalise loading their forces in time and left it too late. Although they finally set off on 15th December, in the ensuing blasts their fleet of vessels and the one million invaders aboard were ultimately destroyed.

Upon reaching Taswegia, knowing that their own medical staff would not arrive until the landing of the third convoy, Alliance skirmish parties quickly rounded up all the medical doctors they could find. They also started their push to gather up all remaining fuel. This was needed to run the antiquated generator sets and their aging military hardware, as well as keeping essential buildings such as the hospital and headquarters operational. All their military vehicles were pre-2000. In a well-thought-out plan, the Alliance forces landed simultaneously at Kings Town, Bull Bay, and Devonshire.

With all conventional communications lost across Taswegia, the few news broadcasts still running post-holocaust could only be heard on the old UHF radio band through the repeaters around the island State; although the prevailing atmospheric conditions meant that even these were intermittent ...

Chapter 1
Here is the News!

Friday 2nd January 2015 ... Dick and Patch Mann's property outside Twaddle.

Richard and Beth Mann, better known to their friends and family as Dick and Patch, were in their workshop finishing the last of the repairs for some locals. Because there was no power, they were using the old Pearson sewing machine, (hand operated), to mend some canvas roo bags. The locals used these when out shooting kangaroos, putting the carcasses in them, and carrying them on their backs. It was no good flashing up their little generator set to run the heavy industrial sewing machines because they drew too much current, so they only used it for running the water pump for showers.

Following the holocaust, Dick and Patch had started switching the old UHF base station on at 10 a.m. each day so they could listen for any updates. This set was left over from the trekking days when they had used UHF communications for emergencies and contacting their guides and back-up vehicle. The head and tail guide had hand-held units and the back-up 4 x 4 had a vehicle mounted set, and with a base station back at the motel they were able to keep in touch. Well, sort of, because UHF was pretty much line of sight, not much good out in some of the hilly terrain that they rode in. Sometimes they would switch over to the repeater, channel 1 and hook up that way because it gave a greater range. This set was 12V and charged by solar power.

Things for the pair had been pretty tough since the holocaust; no vehicles, no supplies and no word on the rest of the world whatsoever. Well, that wasn't quite true, they did have a vehicle … their trusty 1998 Hilux Flat Tray. This was kept on the property and only used for taking rubbish to their personal rubbish tip some 500 metres away from the house. They had got away with it because no-one knew it was there. Well, maybe a few friends did, but they weren't about to dob in Dick and Patch.

People were now mainly living out of their cupboards and gardens, most folk who lived in Twaddle and surrounding areas were used to having full pantries just because of the distance to the nearest supermarket, which was in the town of Soothe, some two hours away. Most of the transport was provided by their two horses left over from the trekking business, Bob and Zen.

It all seemed a bit surreal living as they did within the tranquil setting of the bush, with its familiar smells and the animals. Then came the looters. This became a problem. On one occasion looters came up the drive shooting at the house; probably to try and scare the inhabitants so they could scrounge what fuel was around, along with food and alcohol. They too were driving a pre-2000 vehicle; this time it was an old Bedford truck which looked like the one Sarge and Annie had on their farm, only it was red instead of green.

They could hear the old bomb from halfway along the road, even before it turned up the driveway. This gave Dick time to get the 9 mm Browning pistol out of the gun safe. When they pulled up, he simply shot 3 or 4 rounds into the truck's windscreen and scared them off. They were just kids with .22 rifles and a skin-full of grog.

Dick called out to Patch, "Hey Chook, it's nearly 10 a.m. can you turn the UHF set on please? We might get an update."

A few minutes later the familiar sound of ...

Beep ... Beep ... Beep ...

"Here is the news for Friday 2nd January 2015, Alex Brand reporting.

As I speak, we have reports that forces, calling themselves, 'The New Alliance,' have landed at all major ports in Taswegia.

In Kings Town, commander of the invasion force, General Jun Lee Sung, has summoned all the members of the Taswegian Parliament on to the lawns in front of parliament to discuss our surrender details!

This is crazy, who do these people think they are. Surrender? Why? And to who?

Wait. I have more reports coming in. They're systematically executing everyone. Oh no! They have beheaded the Premier! People are running for their lives. People are being shot down by the Alliance force, which is at least fifteen hundred strong. Some return fire now by local police but this seems insignificant. What a mess!

More news ... in his statement, the General reiterated the only personnel safe from this slaughter are the doctors attached to hospitals.

This is madness! I can't believe that this is happening!

Wait! I have more reports coming in from our man on the ground, Bill Green on portable ..."

"Thanks Alex," said Bill Green as his voice took over the commentary. *"The city is in chaos. More troops are arriving from what looks like two old tankers docking at Macquarie Street Wharf. This looks like something out of the Second World War, with old trucks and jeeps disembarking more troops."*

"Thanks Bill ..." Alex Brand's voice returned, *"What? Oh no! We'll have to shut down this broadcast. Troops are approaching*

the building! Stay tuned f ... Shit! They're coming up the stairs! If we can get another ..."

Bang, Bang ... Schhhhhhhhhhh ... Only static ...

"Shit! Did you hear that Love?" Dick asked.

Patch was in shock, she couldn't believe what she just heard. Was it all some sort of joke? Maybe a radio play of some sorts? Both of them sat in stunned silence, trying to take in what they had heard in the short broadcast. It all seemed a bit surreal; outside the birds were still chirping, and the bloody kookaburras were laughing their heads off, (maybe the birds knew something they didn't!) Dick wandered outside to take in some fresh air. As he headed down to the house he kept going over and over everything in his head.

"Fuck! Fuck! Fuck!! Glad I recorded that broadcast; might come in handy!"

Opening up the old football locker that was hidden in a linen chest bolted to the floor, and also doubled as his gun safe, he found what he was looking for. Returning to the workshop he could see Patch crying. Dick hugged her with one of his famously strong bear-hugs that everyone loved and said "It'll be all right Chook." Although deep down he knew that this was far from the truth.

Having retrieved two pistols and spare magazines from the gun safe, he strapped on a webbing holster for the 9 mm and got Patch to strap on the other.

"What are these for?"

Dick explained that things were going to get a lot rougher from now on and that they should be prepared. He suggested they break with protocol and drive the Hilux around to Twaddle to catch up with Jack and April, and then maybe Sarge and Annie. At this time there had to be safety in numbers.

Patch, who was still not functioning 100%, slid into the cab of the aging Hilux. Turning the ignition on to pre-heat, Dick waited for the indicator light to go out, and then hit the start. The engine fired on the first rotation, with a bit of diesel smoke puffing from the exhaust. The old girl was extremely reliable, considering she only got used about once a fortnight and driven 500 metres to and from their private tip. Driving down the one-kilometre driveway, as always, the overhead canopy of trees took their breath away, as did the occasional roo hopping across in front of them. Usually the bloody potholes were a real pain, but today, with all that they'd heard over the radio, they didn't even notice them.

Not many people were around, although they passed the occasional abandoned vehicle, guessing that's where they'd all stopped on the 17th, along with an old man feeding a cow, who did give a bit of a look at the sound of the vehicle; something that was a rarity of late. They made the journey in half an hour, pulling up in Jack and April's yard. Dick could see April feeding the chooks. She looked up and saw them, then nodded in the direction of Jack's man-cave as she headed inside to put the kettle on, closely followed by Patch.

Dick entered Jack's man-cave and found his mate doing what he seemed to spend most of his time doing, reloading cartridges. The walls were covered with memorabilia of Jack's navy days; mainly ship's crests, which seemed to be the norm for sailors to purchase and end up as dust gatherers on lonely shelves. Or they would give to the sailor's parents as a memento of the ship or depot they were serving on, only to inherit them back again after they died. All around the man-cave were boxes of brass casings, and steel safes with open doors exposing boxes full of gun powder. There was also a fridge full of whiskey mixers and a few beers for when Jack had company.

The cave was about four metres by four metres square, with Colorbond walls and roof and a cement floor covered with some old carpet. The walls were half lined and insulated; this seemed to be one of those never-ending stories that Jack had never quite got around to finishing off, although he reckoned it didn't matter as long as it was functional.

Dick bought his mate up to speed with what had transpired on the broadcast. The two aging Pussers stood and looked at each other; Dick knowing that at this precise time Patch was probably doing the same with April inside the house. Jack told Dick that when they'd pushed the button, it had made the news for the few short hours before the satellites were knocked out. He and April had been watching television, and got the gist of what had happened, as well as the effects it was going to have, predicted fall-out patterns etc. Then ... zip! No more TV! Of course, there had been no mention of the Alliance at that time because no-one knew about it.

"Well that's torn it," Jack said, with real concern in his voice. "What do you reckon is their next move?"

Dick pointed out that if he was running the show, he would send troops out to the outlying areas to round up all the food and fuel they could find, as well as kill everyone they found. After all they wouldn't want to share Taswegia with anyone, especially the former inhabitants. Sure, they'd let a few doctors and some of the specialists live, and possibly their families, just to keep them happy, and perhaps keep a few nursing sisters alive to train their own medical staff, but gradually over the coming months they would no doubt work out who was, "dead wood," out of them as well.

"My estimation is it will take them about four or five days to find their way up to where we live. It looks like the UHF repeater is probably down, but we could try to transmit and see if anyone is listening maybe. The thing is, the Alliance could be listening, and that would bring them right down on top of us!"

"Coffee's ready!" yelled Patch from the back door.

Jack and Dick made their way inside to where the girls were. Sipping his coffee, Jack asked April whether she had heard the news from Patch. Obviously upset, she nodded her head in acknowledgement, then started crying.

"What's going to happen to us all? Are we just going to be hunted down and shot like wild dogs or something?"

"Not bloody likely!" Dick and Jack blurted out together, as if they had rehearsed it for days.

"We need to make a plan. Patch, we might go and see Sarge and Annie, and fill them in with what's going on. Then we'll head home. Jack, can you and April ride out to our place tomorrow morning first up? I'll get Sarge and Annie to do the same; see what we can come up with." Jack nodded to his mate and put his arm around his sobbing wife, lighting up another cigarette.

Dick and Patch found Sarge in the shed at his place, tinkering with a chainsaw. They could see Annie down the back riding a horse, giving it a workout.

"Hey Dick, Patch," called Sarge as he saw the ute pull up. "Geez, must be a special occasion for you to bring the wheels!"

Annie rode up, and with a cheeky grin asked if they had found out what had happened to the world yet.

"Not quite," returned Dick, "but we do have some news, although it's not good."

Driving back home Patch was very quiet, Dick asked her what was on her mind? This was the usual question they'd used to ask each other when they were out driving; it helped stimulate conversation and pass the time. As she often did, Patch was worrying about the kids; they had no idea what had become of each of their five children, who were scattered about the mainland, just going about their own lives. At least they had been up until a few weeks ago. Three of them were in the military, and to be honest, both Dick and Patch had suspected that they were deployed to fight, 'the War on Terror', which would probably have meant their demise.

As far as the other two went, one had been living in Millburn and one in Darwin; nobody knew what had happened, to them. Patch had tried to call them just after they heard the news but got no answer. She tried not to think of them too often, knowing that to get through this, whatever happened she would need to be strong. Even if their worst fears came true, then she knew they were with God, so there wasn't any point in dwelling on it all.

Continuing past their drive they called into another neighbours' place, Vince and Laurel. Laurel had been a security guard and Vince worked for a communications company as their IT whiz-kid. Both were ex-Pussers. When the E1 devices blew, Vince was at work and Laurel was asleep, having just come off night shift. The good thing was that Vince was only working a couple of hours away and had walked home. Pulling into their driveway Dick and Patch could see no sign of the pair.

"They're probably out for a horse ride," said Dick. "We'll catch up with them later. I need to pick Vince's brain."

Saturday 3rd January 2015 ... Dick and Patch Mann's property outside Twaddle.

Patch was finding it hard to sleep, which wasn't unusual even in 'normal' times. She found herself wondering whether she had what it would take to survive. Normally a passive person, she really couldn't see herself fighting, and certainly not shooting someone. Dick had taught her to use the .22 Rifle and she had used the pistol a couple of times. They used to set up a target at the tip where no-one could hear them, and she'd shot off a few rounds. But this was different. For the first time since the holocaust, Patch felt afraid. Really afraid!

Dick woke at 2 a.m. and found his wife huddled up on their red leather couch in the foetal position, quivering with fear. He couldn't sleep, and whereas he would normally just lie and design something in his head or plan the next day's work, he sensed that Patch was not right. Sure, in the past she would get up plenty of times and get a cup of tea, then work at the computer or read a magazine for a while and then come back to bed. This was different. They sat on the couch and hugged each other, and talked about the kids, the good times, the bad times, the ups and the downs. They had faced many barriers in their life together. Patch had lost her mum ten years earlier to a brain tumour, and her father had died twenty years before that. Dick had lost both parents; first his mother then his father, they'd almost gone bankrupt at one stage after years of dwindling business and had to sell off a lot of their assets. Then there was the PTSD after Dick came back from Vietnam; something he still struggled with constantly. On the upside they had five great kids and a business that, up until this point, had provided a living. All those years running the trekking business didn't give them much money, but it sure gave them a fantastic life. They'd met a lot of great people and ended up with some really good friends. Yes, they'd been through a lot in the past; but this was really going to test them.

Dick was out at the barbeque. He could hear the horses, Bob and Zen, calling out from where they were tethered; it was 8 a.m. and it looked like the first of their friends were arriving. The unmistakable call from the horses when another horse was approaching was normal, after all, Bob and Zen didn't get to see many other horses these days. Not like back in the trekking days when they'd had a fleet of 18-20 horses at any one time. Dick often pondered on the thought, "Does Bob really miss the other horses?" There was no way of really knowing. After tying up their mounts Sarge and Annie knocked on the sliding glass door that led into the lounge. Patch beckoned them in and put the kettle on.

"Dick's out the back, cooking sausages on the barbie," said Patch. Sarge gave the thumbs up sign and wandered off. Annie said with a smirk, "The others will be about twenty minutes behind us I reckon."

Patch got the idea that there might have been a little bit of competition on the way out. Annie was always out to show up her riding skills and Sarge wouldn't have wanted to upset Annie. Patch looked at Annie. "How are you feeling?"

"Don't really know Patch. Everything's sort of not really sunk in yet."

Sarge and Annie knew Jack and April, but not that well; this would certainly be a challenge for them all coming together as a close-knit team, because in the past the only catalyst was Dick. It was always Dick, Patch, Jack and April, or Dick, Patch, Sarge and Annie. Never the six together. Sarge and Dick went way back to the start of the trekking days when they had been introduced to each other by Dick's farrier. Sarge had needed a place to stay and was very helpful with building the motel in the wilderness, eventually becoming the back-up driver and roustabout on the treks. Annie was a young local girl who'd just wanted a job with horses, so she trained under Dick and became a trekking guide. That's how she'd met Sarge.

Jack came along later. He'd shown a real interest in saddlery and had eventually built his own saddle under Dick's guidance; with so much in common they'd became great mates. Jack had introduced April to the group some years later after another trip abroad, and then a second catch up with her in France; she came from a small village south west of Paris called Chevaigne-du-Maine. It had taken a while, but Jack was finally able to convince her to migrate to Taswegia, and now she was doing great work with transforming the long-time bachelor, (following the failure of his first marriage) into a functioning, albeit half-hearted, farmer.

Sarge wandered out the back where Dick was doing what he loved best, cooking!

"Good ride mate?"

"If you like everything to be a bloody race!" Sarge replied. "I don't know why she has to be the best and the fastest at everything she does!"

But he did still love her all the same, after all Annie's competitive attitude was what had attracted him to her in the first place … that and the fact she was under-aged the first time he slept with her. He'd been seeing another guide at the time, trying his luck, as he did with all of Dick and Patch's guides, when Annie took a shine to the ex-army Sapper and said to Dick, "I want him!" Well, the rest was history.

Patch called out, "Jack and April are here, drinks are ready!"

Dick yelled back, "Snags are done! We might as well have it outside."

Good thing they'd converted to gas a few years back or they might be boiling the billy on the barbie. The back patio was well used, it was a great spot out of the weather, with a waist high retaining wall running the length of the patio and housing the barbeque. A couple of large wood storage boxes doubled as bench seats and there was a bar fridge, sink and cupboard which held all the utensils they needed for outdoor eating. Two six-seater outdoor tables with comfy chairs had set the scene for many good times in the past.

April gave Patch a hand to bring out all the drinks, while Dick put the snags on a plate, saying, "These need to be eaten before they go off."

They were soon downed with bread and sauce by the hungry group. Then there was a silence while they sipped their coffees, all feeling a little shell shocked and not really knowing where to start.

Now whether it was Dick's age, his leadership skills or a little of both, he couldn't be certain, but somehow, he'd always find himself in charge of most things. Not that this worried him, he was a born leader and had risen quickly through the ranks as a clearance diver, normally a hard branch to climb the ladder in. He made it to the rank of Chief Petty Officer, and was always being pressured into changing over to Officer, but he'd always refused because he didn't want to lose the rapport he had with his troops.

"Well, we've got to start somewhere, let's go over what we know," suggested Dick. "Someone started a nuclear war ... in all probability it was North Korea. Most of the world as we knew it is probably fucked, because we heard that just about every country that had nuclear capabilities also pushed their buttons. If they didn't disintegrate immediately, the poor bastards will die from the fallout anyway. It looks like the invaders made plans to come here well before pushing the button, but how many, when and what they brought with them, who knows? There are no vehicles operational, apart from an aging fleet of pre-2000 vehicles that weren't turned in; it looks like the Alliance, as they call themselves, uses these vehicles as well. There's no digital system, the last reports we heard before the last satellite crashed and burned told us that all communications are dead. The only thing we have left is the old UHF band through a repeater; that's if that's even safe!" Dick made sure he made eye contact with everyone, as he continued.

"We think the Alliance chose our neck of the woods because they would have known there'd be no fall out, and also because we've been generating our own power from hydro schemes. Plus, it's a great place to live. We're pretty sure they want to kill everyone, give or take a few medical staff, to enable their own people to reinhabit our state. This is probably a ploy and as soon as their medical people get up to speed, I suspect they'll do all of ours in. They have really old WWII trucks and jeeps; so they'll want to round up all the fuel they can. Power generation will be paramount. Unfortunately, our water reserves are down to 5%, and we were running on diesel generation anyway. I know this has been systematically shut down over the last week, hence the need to use the meat before it thaws out. Our only sustainable mode of transport right now is horseback … with little fuel left, I want to keep the Hilux for emergencies. I think that just about sums it up," Dick said with a sigh. "Anyone care to add any more?"

"Sounds pretty bleak," agreed Jack. "I think we have about three to four days of frozen meat left before that goes off."

Annie added, "We've got about ten days' worth, but only because we bought in a killer two weeks ago; just before the bang. I reckon we have about two days tops before the kill squads get here … although I can't see them making a fuss over little old Twaddle. Mind you, that depends on a lot of things," she added. "If they think we are loaded in fresh produce and fuel we could see them here faster than we think!"

"What's our weapon's arsenal?" asked Dick with a very wide smile, making Patch wonder what he knew that she didn't!

Sarge started … "Well our tally is a pump action shotgun with 100 cartridges, a .22 rifle, not much ammo (don't use it much now), and a selection of machetes and boning, skinning and hunting knives.

Jack added … "Add to that one .19 target rifle with 200 rounds, a .243 deer rifle with 100 rounds, a 9 mm pistol and a couple of boxes of ammo, a .45 pistol and 50 rounds, a 50-calibre sniper rifle with only about 10 rounds, various empty cases of mixed calibre, four bags of gunpowder and my reload press."

"Fucking hell!" exploded Sarge. "What the fuck were you packing all that for?"

Jack answered soberly, "I guess for today, Sarge."

Dick, with a bit of a grin added his bit. "Well, you ain't seen nothing yet! Not that I've been to the container lately, but off the top of my head it goes something like this ... two Bren Guns with two boxes of .303 ammo, two SLR Rifles with two boxes of 7.62 ammo, six Claymore mines, twelve grenades high explosive, one box of dynamite, six 9 mm Browning Pistols with 200 rounds, one .22 rifle and 50 rounds, a crossbow and six bolts, a pump action shotgun and 50 cartridges, two old .303 Lee Enfield rifles, ammo to go with them, a mixed bag of side arms (most with no ammo), one RPG Attachment and ten grenades to suit and one F1 Sub Machine Gun with 100 rounds of 9 mm. Oh, and I nearly forgot, about fifty navy ration packs!"

Well you could hear a penny drop! The silence was deafening! After what seemed like a REALLY long time, Patch blurted out "What container?!More to the point, where is this container?"

Jack piped up, "You sly dog!"

Dick explained that, apart from the two 9 mm Brownings that were in the gun safe in the spare room, along with the .22 and the crossbow, the rest of the arsenal was in a twenty-foot container buried up near the tip.

Patch didn't know whether to kill Dick or kiss him! "How could you keep this a secret for this long?" she asked.

Dick explained that his accumulation of weapons went back to when he was still in Pussers and serving on patrol boats. Every year they'd had to expend all their ammo, or they wouldn't be allowed to draw new stuff from the store, so he 'helped' the weapons officer out a few times. It had been easier whenever the boat came to Kings Town, then he'd just unloaded the haul and bring it up to the block where he'd hoped someday to build the motel in the wilderness and run the trekking business. He had the opportunity to bury a container there; when the old guy dug the first tip for him, Dick had told him it was going to be a wine cellar. Slowly over the years he'd added to the stash. A few times he'd thought about telling Patch about it, but the longer it went on the easier it was just to forget about it.

"I reckon the last time I ventured inside it was about five years ago. Now I know what I've been saving it for!"

The five of them followed Dick as he made his way some 500 metres from the house, and up an overgrown track that eventually ended at the tip. He'd had to act fast a few years ago; when the excavator operator came to clean out the drains. Patch had asked whether they needed a new tip dug. Dick had had to think fast, "Bloody hell! What if he tries to dig it where the container is ... wouldn't that be a surprise!"

Dick walked some twenty metres past the existing site, and past the previous two sites, then bent over and pushed aside a log sitting on the ground, revealing the hidden handle to the trap door. There was an old piece of carpet covered in leaf litter over the top of the door which he brushed aside with his boot. He needed Sarge's help to raise the rusty door, then led the way down a few steps to the entrance of a twenty-foot container.

"Fuck! Well I never," snorted Patch. "Oops, sorry! I never knew. I've been past this a hundred times!"

Just inside the door on a shelf was a bank of 12-volt car batteries and when Dick hit the switch, the whole container lit up, revealing shelf after shelf, along with large military style box-like containers. He opened them up one at a time, revealing the weapons he'd told them about. Dick issued the SLR's to Jack and Sarge, dividing all the ammo between them, and gave Annie, Sarge and April their own 9 mm pistols in webbing holsters, saying, "Better take one of these, just for the time being."

Jack and Sarge decided to leave the SLR's at Dick's house, agreeing it would draw too much attention to the group if they rode back through Twaddle with weapons like that slung over their backs. After closing up the container again and disguising the entrance, they all went back to the patio and sat around the table.

Looking around the group, Dick said to them, "Now we need to think about what we should do next." After a fair bit of discussion, they agreed that the goal was to set a plan up within the next two days. They knew this meant that they would probably have to move, and maybe keep moving, just to keep in front of the Alliance. With one accord they agreed that their creed should be, 'To the death if need be; to get to where we can communicate with any other survivors.'

"We'll meet back here same time tomorrow to work out the finer details." Dick warned them not to tell anyone else what they were doing; even though everyone was in the same boat and would eventually be killed, it would be harder for them if the group was larger; much more of a challenge to move around without being seen.

"Patch and I have an idea, but we need to check out the logistics first." He didn't want to say too much more yet, but he could tell them that it involved the analogue phone system. "From what I can work out, it seems the analogue satellite is still orbiting the Earth, although it is at a really low trajectory."

Maybe if they could find a spot to access this signal and make contact with others who still kept their, 'brick phones,' it might just work. The plan was to make contact with others and hopefully put together a force to make some serious trouble for the Alliance forces; if there was any of their navy still out there, they might also be able to help. Sounded a bit like, 'pie in the sky' type of stuff, but it was all they had.

Chapter 2
Richard Mann (Dick)

Richard Mann, better known to his family and friends as Dick, was born in 1954, and grew up in Kings Town, Taswegia. Dick was the only child of Eddy Mann, fisherman and Lilly Mann, confectioner. After his birth, Lilly had firmly declared that one child was more than enough!

There was nothing all that exciting about his upbringing, except for his inherent love of the sea. With his Dad being a fisherman Dick soon became immersed in the seafaring life, learning from a young age all about boats, ropes, nets, engines, seamanship, and navigation. He would spend many weeks at sea with his father fishing for crayfish and scallops and filling in the seasons with the gill netting of other species and trawling for barracouta. He learned to row a dinghy before his fifth birthday and could tie twenty knots and do an eye splice before he turned six.

Dick had a passion for diving and started before he could even swim properly. He was given a set of fins and goggles for his eighth birthday and never looked back. His best mate, Gordon, was also from a diving family and they tried to fit in as much time in the water as they could while growing up. Dick saved up and bought his first boat at the age of thirteen, and whenever the families were away camping together, the two boys would spend all day off in the boat, skindiving for abalone and trying to spear a trumpeter or two.

It didn't come as a surprise to anyone when Dick declared after school one night that he was joining the Navy. He entered as a boy sailor at the age of fifteen, commencing training in Western Australia's HMAS Leeuwin in 1969.

After that came seamanship school at HMAS Cerberus, with Dick graduating as a WM (Weapons Mechanic) before doing twelve months at sea on the HMAS Sydney and then passing CDAT (Clearance Diving Acceptance Test). Because of his previous diving experience, he found the diving component easy enough, but because of his heavy build and being 6' 6" in height, he struggled at times with the general fitness side of things. The smaller trainees definitely had the upper hand there.

The following is a snapshot of Dick's life as a Clearance Diver (CD) in the Royal Australian Navy ...

Clearance Divers were the Australian Defence Forces' specialist divers. Their tasks included specialist diving missions to depths of fifty-four metres, surface and underwater demolitions, and the rendering safe and disposal of conventional explosive ordnance and improvised explosive devices. During their careers, CDs were usually rotated through a variety of sea and shore positions.

Huon Class Mine Hunter Coastal (MHC) vessels employment for CDs posted to these ships included upper-deck seaman part-of-ship duties during sea service within Australia and overseas. Specialist diving duties involved the use of self-contained mixed gas equipment for mine-counter measures tasks, these types of missions focussed on the prosecution and disposal of sea mines. The ships were based at *HMAS Waterhen* in Sydney.

Clearance diving teams were employed to carry out a number of operational duties, including maritime tactical operations (MTO). MTO missions included diving on 100% oxygen and using self-contained, closed-circuit re-breather equipment that doesn't give off tell-tale exhaust gases for specialist operations underwater and ashore. They also undertook mine countermeasures (MCM). The CDT MCM missions were similar to MHC MCM missions but were focussed more on specialist shore-based operations.

Then there were the underwater battle damage repair (UBDR) missions. UBDR missions included diving on surface-supplied and self-contained air equipment, primarily for the maintenance and repair of ships' underwater fittings. These missions often involved the use of underwater electric, explosive-power, hydraulic and pneumatic tools for major repairs and salvage operations.

Explosive ordnance disposal (EOD) missions included the rendering safe and disposal of improvised (home-made) devices, military ordnance, and obstructions both on land and underwater. These missions often involved the use of remote operated vehicles (ROV), portable x-ray devices and high-powered disruptors. Tactical Assault Group (East), referred to as TAG(E) CDs, were employed in special forces roles at the TAG(E), which was part of 2 Commando Regiment. TAG(E) maintained a short-notice capability to conduct special military operations, using a variety of specialist skill sets that included the extensive use of small arms.

After completing this extensive range of specialised assignments, Dick was attached to CDT 3, and towards the end of the Vietnam War assisted the US Navy Explosive Ordinance Disposal Units and carried out other specialist insurgent work.

Over his time in the Navy, Dick saw service in Vietnam, Somalia, and the Gulf War, eventually paying off after his twenty-two years in 1991.

Dick met his wife Patch while training with the SAS in Western Australia, back in 1984, and over the years their family expanded as they welcomed five children into their lives.

One of his passions was leatherwork and saddlery, so eventually Dick started his own business in the high country of Taswegia. They could have lived anywhere in Australia, but he chose his home state because of the fond memories he had of growing up there, along with the slower pace of life and less people. Taswegia was pretty well as far away from the world's problems as possible.

Riding horses came naturally to Dick, and in a very short time he became a master horseman ... something to do with being trained by an old mountain stockman in the old bush survival ways. Ryan's methods were simple and to the point; he would say there are only three rules. "Number one ... Don't fall off! Number two ...Always make the horse do what you want it to do! Number three ... It's never the horse's fault!"

Now this may seem too simple, but old Ryan reckoned it had always worked for him, and it certainly worked for Dick.

Dick and Patch started to build the, 'Motel in the Wilderness,' in the mid 1990's. He'd acquired a hundred-acre bush block during the time he was still serving, buying it from the neighbour, who'd wanted to sell his back block off for some extra cash.

Dick had fallen in love with the place the very first time he saw it. Wandering into an old log landing, he'd sat down on a stump to take in his surroundings, and almost straight away the idea of his, 'Motel in the Wilderness,' started taking shape in his mind. After many months of hard work, his dream eventually became a reality. From there they ran a horse trekking business, catering for clients, locals and international travellers who wanted to experience the remoteness of that beautiful part of Taswegia.

The treks ranged from one day, through to fourteen. Early on Dick realised that the business could not run with him doing all the guiding on his own, so he started training horseback trekking guides in 2002, eventually running eleven courses and training nearly thirty-five guides. Some of these continued to work for Dick and Patch at the end of their training, while others would move on and work for other operators in the state and in Victoria. Between 2003 and 2012, Dick had an average of four guides working for him at any one time on a roster system. Many of them worked at other jobs in Kings Town during the week and could only do weekend work. The only local guide was Annie, and she made herself available for any weekday work as well as her share of the rostered weekend stuff.

Dick's mate, Wayne, known as Sarge, was the backup driver and general dog's body; his ex-army and bushman skills were a vital part of the business.

Sadly, the trekking business closed in 2012 after the cost of public liability insurance became too expensive, and after that Dick and Patch settled down to a more sedate life of mending and manufacturing saddlery in their workshop just above the motel.

Chapter 3
Skirmishes

Dick and Patch spent the rest of the day trying to come up with a list of the things they would need for their survival. The real problem was not knowing where they were going to hide, or how they were going to get there.

Every time they had a list started, one of them would say to the other, "How on earth are we going to carry all this stuff?" They talked about using pack horses, and about maybe using the Hilux as a one-way back-up vehicle like in the trekking days, although the main flaw in this plan was that they didn't have much fuel left.

"Everybody would have to lead a pack horse to make this work Patch."

So back to the drawing board they would go, trying to work out what to take and what to leave behind.

Giving up for the moment, Dick started the generator and went to take a shower. As he dried himself off, he yelled out, "Shower's ready Chook, soon as you're done, I'll kill the gen set."

He sat on the bed, and just as he did every night, opened his little black bag and took out his nightly medication. Taking prescription drugs had become a fact of life as he'd grown older, he used the usual blood pressure and cholesterol medications plus a couple of tablets for his type two diabetes.

"Oh shit. I've got a BIG problem!"

Patch, who'd been just about to step into the shower, ran back into the bedroom, expecting to find Dick in some sort of pain, or maybe collapsed on the floor. But instead she found him sitting on the bed looking frantically through the bag.

"WHAT?" Patch was feeling just a little bit frustrated as there didn't seem to be too much wrong with him.

"I'm going to run out of medication in about seven days, clean forgot all about it!" he snapped back, feeling a bit annoyed at her obvious frustration.

Ever since the button got pushed, they'd been somewhat preoccupied about everything else and had forgotten to stock up on meds. This was normally done as stocks got low, and they rarely ran completely out. They used to get six months' worth at a time, just in case they had to go to the mainland to visit family, but what with no vehicle and the events of the past few weeks, they'd simply forgotten.

"How's your supply going Love?" Dick asked her in a quieter tone of voice. He couldn't really blame her for not being as patient as usual, they were all under an immense amount of stress right now.

Patch, also realising the seriousness of the situation responded, "Sorry Dick didn't mean to get angry with you."

Sitting on her side of the bed, she opened the drawer which held her medication, she was thankful that she didn't need as many as Dick … only two tablets a day, but they were still needed to control her blood pressure. Counting carefully, she saw she had ten days' supply still, but then realised she had no prescriptions left.

Dick realised that this meant they'd have to get to a chemist and try and source what they needed. Even if they could just drive into Lakeside or Soothe, the chemist wasn't going to just cough them up without a script ... that's if there was even a chemist around these days.

He thought about it, sharing his thoughts out loud with Patch. If the place was locked, they'd just have to break in and then try and find the appropriate drugs if they could recognise them. The trip either way would just about exhaust the fuel in the Hilux, and there was no telling if they could find any more fuel along the way. Then there were the Alliance troops to deal with.

Patch sighed, and said as she headed back to the shower, "Hold that thought!"

After turning off the little generator, Dick went back to the bedroom, finding his wife sitting naked on the side of the bed, drying her hair. After all these years, Dick still found the sight a turn on.

He continued on from where he'd left off.

"I've been thinking. I reckon we should go on horseback, if we leave before dusk it will take us around five or six hours to ride to Lakeside. We should be able to keep out of sight most of the way by keeping to the back tracks, it's only over the last couple of clicks that we'll be out in the open, and by then it will be after midnight."

"It's a pity we don't know the chemist personally," Patch added. "If we did, she could just let us in and there wouldn't be any problems. I don't even know where she lives ... I wonder if Annie knows."

Dick thought it might be better if he and Sarge went on their own, leaving Patch with Annie, or even maybe take Jack with them as well. However, that would leave the women unguarded. It was hard to decide what to do.

They decided to get some sleep and discuss the problem the next morning when the others came back. Dick was pretty sure Sarge and Annie didn't need to take medication at their age, but it was possible that Jack or April might need drugs as well, and they only wanted to make one trip in these dangerous times.

Sunday 4th January 2015 ... Dick and Patch Mann's property outside Twaddle.

It had been another restless night for Patch; she was not coping with all the possible scenarios.

"Surely we could try and reason with someone from the Alliance Dick?" she said after Dick found her on the red couch again. This time it was around 5 a.m. and nearly light outside.

She had been awake for a few hours and had managed to move out to the couch without waking him.

"Chook, unfortunately I don't think they'd be in that."

He went on to clarify that as far as he could tell, they were out to clear the population so they could repopulate with their own people, and take over the existing housing. Taswegia's population was only about five hundred thousand; if the Alliance was to bring in one or two million it was going to get a bit crowded.

He knew his wife couldn't understand how or why anyone could do such a vile and ungodly act. With her Christian upbringing, the events that were coming up were not going to be to her liking or comprehension.

Patch walked over to the window, and stood there, thinking about all that had happened. Dick used to call this a, 'companionable silence,' the one where two people in love do not have to be verbal to communicate.

Asking his wife to put the kettle on broke the silence and gave her something else to think about.

"I feel like bum nuts for breakfast Love," he added, knowing that eggs were her favourite breakfast meal always, favourite any time meal for that matter!

"Yummo!" she responded, shaking free of the negative thoughts that had been dragging her down.

The rest of the troops arrived as the pair were finishing their poached eggs on toast.

"Didn't make us any!" Jack exclaimed jokingly.

"Shut up and make the drinks," said April, elbowing the ex-CD in his side.

Dick, who was feeling considerably older than his 60 years right now, explained their issue with the medication, and they agreed they would have to do something about it sooner rather than later, with only six days' worth of pills left.

He suggested that he make the horse ride with one of the boys that night. His thoughts were that they could all leave together around 7 p.m. and then two hours later, the three girls plus whoever wasn't going could peel off and go to one home for safe keeping ... it didn't really matter which one. If all went well the skirmish pair should be back around 6 a.m. the next morning.

He asked for a volunteer to go with him, and both boys raised their hands, both excited at the thought of a bit of action. After thinking about it, Jack offered to stay behind, suggesting that Sarge was the better horseman, and much younger as well, so it should probably be him who should go with Dick. This came as a bit of a shock to the forty-five-year-old ex-Sapper, who until this moment hadn't really thought about the difference in people's ages ... he tended to look at them all as just being the same.

Smiling, he said, "It would be a pleasure! Just like old times Dick!"

Now everyone in the room knew that Dick and Sarge hadn't actually served together, but they were all fully aware of the antics that the two of them had got up to while building the motel all those years ago.

There was one particular time when the pair had gone to the Bulldust Pub for a counter meal. Patch was staying elsewhere while they built that particular stage of the motel, and the two of them didn't feel like cooking. They stayed a while after the meal and headed back after downing a skinful of grog each. The two of them had been working on a lot of fencing at that time, and they decided to, 'collect ,' a few star pickets on the way home which would help with the fencing project.

So, there they were … Dick driving his dual cab truck along the dirt road, with Sarge hanging out the back-passenger window. They were targeting roadworks where the workers had used pickets to mark off certain parts of the road. Dick would slow down, and Sarge would lean out and grab the picket with a pair of old welding gloves, hoping it wasn't too deep in the ground, and relieve it from the dirt, throwing it into the back of the truck.

They managed to acquire around sixty of these all up, and might have added many more, if one of the locals hadn't, 'seen,' them while he was putting his trash out. It would be more accurate to say that he heard the bang when the picket hit the steel tray as it joined the other escaped fence posts. Dick put his foot down, and Sarge nearly fell out the window, but managed to hang on until they'd got clear. They headed back to the block, Sarge with sore hands and both with sore heads but laughing all the way.

Over the years there had been many such escapades and Sarge was looking forward to joining his mate for another.

It was agreed the rest would hold up at Jack and April's, and that Patch and Annie would bunk down there while they were gone.

They spent the rest of the day coming up with the pharmaceutical, 'shopping list,' Dick cut the labels off his and

Patch's meds, hoping this would help him find them, and Jack handed over his and April's order to add to the list. Jack's list was nearly as long as Dick's, but, seeing as he had been on an invalid pension after being wounded just before getting out of Pussers, that was fair enough. They also went over some of the problems Patch and Dick had been trying to work through the previous day.

Sarge and Dick first saddled up Bob and Socks ready for the escapade, adding a set of wither bags onto their two saddles; this was for a drink, snack, and spare ammo and somewhere to put the booty, when or if they succeeded in their quest. They then saddled the rest of the horses ready for the ride.

As always, the emergency bag was on the near side of Dick's saddle. After padding the sling to the SLR that Sarge had left at Dick's place, he slung it over his shoulder. He was also carrying four self-loaders of the 7.62 ammunition, (these were five rounds inside a clip and easier to reload than loading individual rounds).

Dick went back to the container and retrieved the F1 Sub Machine Gun and three spare clips; this was all the ammo he had for the weapon.

"That's the second time I've been to the container in five years," he grinned. Patch couldn't see the funny side of the comment, still feeling a bit peeved that he hadn't told her about it.

They made their way down the driveway, across the road and into the pine plantation, then continued on bush tracks until they emerged in the sleepy town of Twaddle. Dick and Sarge gave their respective partners a hug and a kiss. It was the first time that Dick had ever seen Annie and Sarge get passionate in public.

As he watched the girls and Jack drift off in the direction of Jack's place Sarge admitted, "You know, I'm a bit excited Dick!"

"So, the bloody hell am I Sarge!" was Dick's reply. It was good to have something to do.

They followed the trail, which took them back out of the town and through some fifteen kilometres of bush tracks and old growth forest. They had to cross some open fields every now and then, but thankfully they were nowhere near civilisation.

By now a slight breeze had started, and Dick gave a shiver as he started to feel the chill hitting his body; first around the ankles, then his neck and then as it worked its way through the heavy woolly pully he had chosen to wear. His feet were warm, but he realised he probably should have also worn the chaps for this ride.

The first settlement they came to, if you could call it that, was Mt Frost. It was more like a group of properties close to the road. As they made their way across the outside paddock they could see a light coming from one of the farm windows; however, with no generator noise, they wondered whether power had been restored or maybe even whether it might have been battery powered.

"Do you think it's worth a look Dick?" asked Sarge, secretly hoping for some action.

"Yes, I think we will Sarge; you never know what we'll find."

Something was not quite right, no dogs were barking ... in fact there were no animal noises at all. That didn't make sense, they both knew this bloke had a good herd of cattle. They stopped, both listening intently, but nothing!

Slowly moving Socks and Bob closer they rode up to the back yard. Without warning Bob baulked violently and backed away from the gate. Dick spurred him on so he could get close enough to reach the latch; he thought he knew the reason for Bob's behaviour.

Quite a few years ago while taking a group on a trek up to Mount Morris, he'd witnessed the same behaviour from his trusty friend, that time Bob had been spooked by a huge log on the ground. Upon closer inspection they'd discovered the carcasses of some fifty sheep dumped there by a local farmer during a particularly bad drought. He had realised then that Bob could smell death.

Quietening Bob, Dick leant down and undid the gate latch. Spurring the horse into the yard he drew the 9 mm Browning and indicated to Sarge to do the same. Sarge was ahead of him, he already had the SLR in the ready position. The uncurtained back window revealed a scene that resembled the inside of the butcher's shop.

The first thing they realised was that the inhabitants were dead, the second was that they didn't die quickly; or cleanly. Blood and body fluids were everywhere. Dick was glad he hadn't brought Patch with him.

Sarge went left and Dick right; after riding around the house, they met at the front door. Dick reported that through the side window it looked like the two women had possibly been viciously raped and then mutilated. Sarge said that, apart from the bodies in the back kitchen that they had first seen, there was one other older man in a bedroom, and that he'd been beheaded.

This was confirmation that there would be no mercy. They also realised that, if the Alliance had made it out this far from Lakeside, it meant they could reach Twaddle the next day.

"Better pull our fingers out," said Dick, still trying tc process what he'd seen, and vividly remembering some of the atrocities carried out by the Viet Kong that he'd witnessed during his time in Vietnam.

The last two kilometres into Lakeside were pretty exposed, after rapid discussion they'd agreed that if they were challenged at all they would shoot first and ask questions later.

They'd come across a few farms after that first one .. at every one all the stock was gone, and all the vehicles looked like they'd been sucked dry of fuel ... and there had been plenty of dead bodies.

Sarge was wondering who was going to come along and clean up all the mess. If they wanted to move in someone would have to do something about it, everything was going to be on the nose pretty soon if they didn't.

They could hear voices and laughter coming from one of the Lakeside homes, so they carefully skirted around the west side of the lake. It didn't take long to realise it was the Alliance troops occupying the home, not its original owners.

Monday 5th January 2015 ... Lakeside.

At 0010 down past the swimming pool, they spied the chemist shop over the other side of the main road. Making their way around the back, the pair had clear vision of the stock yards; they were chock-a-block with cattle.

They dismounted and surveyed the premises. They knew the pharmacy was usually alarmed; to set off the alarm would most certainly alert the enemy to their presence. That was the last thing they wanted. Dick decided to stand on the fence and cut the wires to the strobe light and siren; this was risky, as even doing this might set off the alarm. Both of them could feel their hearts beating rapidly, accelerating as he stretched out with his old Gerber in his hand and made the cut. Thankfully, there was nothing but silence.

"So far so good!" said Sarge.

"Nothing like that old adrenaline rush." snorted Dick, smashing the small window in the top of the door with the butt of the SLR, and gingerly reaching inside to undo the lock. They both held their breath after the sound of the glass smashing, but nothing.

"Phew!"

Using their torches, they worked their way to the dispensary. Having been in there a hundred times over the last fifteen years or so, Dick had a fairly good idea where his pills were kept and quickly cleaned out the shelf. Finding the rest of them was not so easy. He started working his way through the other shelves.

Suddenly Sarge turned off his torch and whispered to Dick that it looked like they had company. He thought he'd heard someone at the front door of the shop. Dick flicked his torch off too, just as the two troopers outside tried to open the door. Bugger me! It was open! Dick gave Sarge one of those, 'What the fuck' looks, as it turned out, they could have just walked in the front bloody door after all!

As Dick and Sarge crouched down behind the dispensary bench, a discussion erupted between the two troopers. It was an uncomfortable position to say the least. Dick was silently wishing his knees were in better shape. If only he hadn't come off that horse and snapped the main tendon that holds the joint together, same with the time he'd been kicked in the knee by Zen so hard that it had sounded like a shotgun going off. He tried to shift his position without drawing attention to where they were.

Too late! An Asian head suddenly appeared over the top of the bench. Who got the biggest shock no one knew, but in unison both Dick and Sarge levelled their 9 mm pistols, both shooting the two troopers at exactly the same time!

"Shit! Shit! Shit! Let's get the fuck out of here! Grab that garbage bag and clean out the whole shelf where we think Jack's meds are," yelled Dick as he quickly gathered up the medication from the shelf he'd been looking at.

Mounting quite quickly, and with the adrenaline pumping, Sarge missed the top step as he exited the pharmacy. There was a sickening *crunch* as his ankle twisted in a totally unnatural way. Dick helped his mate to mount Socks, and with no time to spare the pair urged their mounts east, away from the pharmacy and the house where they had heard the voices. After two minutes they started to back off speed, cantering alongside the lake and still heading east.

"Might have to go around the other side of the lake this time mate! How's the ankle?" asked Dick breathlessly.

"Sounds like a good plan! Pretty sure the ankle's not broken; just twisted and bloody sore!" answered Sarge.

They could hear noises coming from the town behind them; a vehicle had started up ... sounded like an old Bedford.

After a kilometre or so more they slowed to a walk.

Checking out the horses as they rode, Dick said to Sarge, "I think Socks has a loose shoe mate. Looks like you're both lame."

"Bugger! That's certainly not what we wanted," replied Sarge, knowing full well that he would have to stop and fix it. "Might get off and walk them for a bit now we are on this hard gravel."

Dick dismounted and checked all four of Bob's shoes. "All okay."

Sarge did the same with Socks.

"Bugger! Dick, it looks like he needs a couple tightened! Well, he probably needs to be re-shod."

Pulling the shortened down version of a shoeing hammer and a few nails out of the emergency bag, Sarge proceeded to put a couple of nails in Sock's hoof.

"Don't worry about cutting them off Sarge; just bend them over. You can do a pretty job when you re-shoe him later."

The pair continued around the back of the lake. Well, it wasn't really a lake, the bloody thing had been dry for years. Not really dry enough to traverse though; every time it rained it turned into mud and was quite boggy. From their vantage point they could make out vehicle lights moving around in Lakeside.

"Do you reckon they've found the bodies yet Dick?"

"Let's hope not, but ... fuck! It looks like they're coming this way!"

They had to make it through the swamp, but with Sarge sporting a rolled ankle and Socks now limping badly, this was turning into hell; a very hot and bloody one. In the back of his mind, Dick could hear the echo of his old Chief's words ... "Forward Mates. No Going back. NEVER going back!"

Being on foot, it was real slow going, but they eventually found themselves back on soft ground. Looking back, they realised they had lost the lights behind them, so they mounted up again and made good time back to the Mt Frost Farm. It was beginning to get light as they stopped just short of moving out of the bush.

"What time is it Sarge?"

"Daylight Dick! If you want to know the time, you're going to have to get yourself a bloody watch. It's 0530!"

Dick hadn't worn a watch for the past fifteen years or so, and even back then it was a fob watch which had been given to him by some Japanese clients he'd taken riding. He just didn't like anything on his wrist. The fob watch, finally stopped working after a few years of being used in the rough environment out there on the trail.

"That answers your question from last night Sarge."

Peering round the trees, they could see what looked like a clean-up crew at the farm. The old Bedford had barge boards up the sides, and it was filled with bloody and rotting bodies. It also sported what could only be described as some kind of snow plough fitted to the front. They could see the clean-up detail putting on gloves and masks.

"What do you think they use that for Dick?"

"Not sure Sarge, maybe to push the abandoned vehicles out of the way."

They dismounted, and after making sure that Bob and Socks were well hidden behind one of the outlying sheds, they carefully made their way over to the back yard, staying out of sight as well as they could. Dick gingerly opened the back gate, cringing as it creaked loudly. Stopping behind a small woodshed they discussed their options.

"I just want to kill the dirty little yellow bastards!" whispered Sarge.

"I know Sarge, me too. How's that bloody ankle of yours?"

It seemed they had two possible courses of action, provided Sarge could cope with walking on his injured ankle.

The first was to kill the four troops that were cleaning up. They'd have to check there wasn't another one sitting in the driver's seat first though. If the kill squad was in front of them the noise might alert them, and they could come back. If that happened, they'd just have to kill them all!

"Even if they don't hear the noise," Dick reasoned, "we could come across them as we get closer to Twaddle."

They figured their second option would be to leave now and try and work out whether the kill squad was in front of them. They could then ambush and kill them. The disadvantage of this plan was that the clean-up crew might hear the noise; if that happened, they would probably scarper back to Lakeside to get reinforcements.

By this time the crew had entered the farm and was bringing out the first two bodies. They were having trouble carrying them, so were moving pretty slowly.

Dick made the decision. "If you're up to it mate, let's kill these bastards!"

Sarge nodded with an excited grin; they took the same tactic as they had the night before, except that this time they were on foot.

Dick made his way round the right-hand side of the farmhouse. Looking carefully through the window where he'd seen the women, he could see the crew trying to clean up all the body parts; they were placing them on a sheet ready to carry them out to the truck.

He moved over to the hot water cylinder, which provided him with a place to stay out of sight. From there he had full view of the front door and of the other corner of the house, although he still couldn't see the cab of the truck.

Sarge made his way ever so gingerly along the left wall; from the corner of the house he could tell there was no one sitting in the truck. Good news! That meant they only had to deal with four of them.

He could see Dick on the other corner, and pointed to the truck, giving Dick the thumbs down signal. Dick replied with thumbs up and slashed his hand across his throat. Sarge knew what he meant, and carefully made his way back to the bedroom where the body of the old man was lying.

Through the window he could make out the pair, who were having an animated discussion while they rolled a couple of cigarettes. He knew they were probably doing what all soldiers do, whinging about the detail they had drawn.

Sarge briefly thought about using the 9 mm but at the last minute realised that the round might be deflected through the glass window. Not a good plan. That settled it ... time to bring out the big gun!

Dick heard the SLR let rip; being semi-automatic it meant that Sarge just had to keep pulling the trigger to get the five, (or was it six rounds off). It sounded very loud from where he was leaning against the wall.

There was the sound of a scuffle inside as the crew possibly dropped their load; then the two troopers came running out of the front door. Fortunately for Dick and Sarge, they were more concerned about what was behind them, and didn't see the ex-Navy CD standing in the open until it was too late. He nearly cut them in half with a long burst from the F1!

After a quick reccy the boys realised there were no vehicles coming. Obviously, the kill squad was either too far away to have heard, or maybe hadn't made it out from Lakeside that early in the morning.

Dick muttered to Sarge, "Lazy pricks are probably still in bed!"

As he mounted up again, Dick noticed his body was aching all over, and said to Sarge, "I'm too fucking old for this shit!"

Sarge just grinned, trying to hide the pain, but for both of them the incident had brought back memories of similar situations they had come across while serving their country.

By the time they reached the back paddock to Jack's farm, daylight had well and truly kicked in.

"I reckon it must be about 0730?" Dick asked, realising that they had both automatically drifted back into the military 24-hour clock way of thinking about time.

"Yep, spot on!" replied Sarge.

The pair had discussed whether to tell the others exactly what had happened, or whether to soften it and just say it all went okay. After some thought they'd agreed that if they did that it would give the others a false sense of security, so it was decided to tell all.

The plan was to meet back at Dick and Patch's place later on that day, with their saddlebags full with essentials for living on the run; essential things like dry food, weapons, ammo, a change of clothes and the emergency first aid kit plus whatever they thought was needed and could be fitted in.

As well as this, Dick asked them to pack up all the camping gear they would need for an extended time in the bush, just in case he could get the Hilux back to pick it up. He deciced to fill Patch in about what had happened while he'd been away as they made their way back home, hopefully calling in to Vince's to run a possible scenario past him and Laurel.

Sarge spoke to Jack and let him know how things had gone, then he and Annie headed for home, leaving Jack and April to pack. Dick decided that the quickest way to get to Vince's place was to take the risk and ride down the main street; if they heard a vehicle the plan was to move into the bush quick smart.

Chapter 4
Beth Mann (Patch)

Beth Macfarlane, who was later given the nickname of Patch by a close mate, was born in Carnarvon, Western Australia in 1960. Patch was a gawky kid, but soon blossomed into a stunning woman. As a child she seemed to be all arms and legs, and eventually standing 6' tall in her bare feet, was taller than most women. Although she was hopeless at sports, and had no ball skills whatsoever, she turned out to be really good at anything to do with admin and IT.

Her father, Alfred Macfarlane, was a mining engineer who worked away a fair bit of the time at Mount Tom Price, and her mother, Helga, was a radiologist. Patch was part of a large troop of kids, with five sisters and no brothers ... people reckoned it was no wonder her father spent so much time away in the mines with that many females at home!

Patch was born first, and was followed by Agatha, Christina, Helena, Angela, and Trish.

As well as all things computer-oriented, Patch was heavily into music, and was an accomplished pianist and guitarist, often performing at her local church.

A great friend and fellow musician reckoned that Beth was always around to patch him up when he felt bad, a lot like the celebrated doctor, Patch Adams. From that point on everybody called her Patch.

She'd learnt how to ride while still at school, using her friend's horses because her parents reckoned they just couldn't afford to buy her one. Patch secretly believed that this was more likely because if they bought one for her they'd have to do it for all of the sisters.

Her first job was selling shoes. Although she had a go at this, she hated it, mainly because her, boss was always trying to hit on her, but also because she was no good at trying to talk people into buying things they simply couldn't afford.

Patch ended up going to university, graduating with a Masters in IT. She was well on the way to a great career in the banking industry when she met Dick.

You know what they say, it was love at first sight. It was 1978. Dick was at the beach with a few of his SAS mates while on a training course, while Patch was just enjoying a day off at the beach, surfing with Agatha and her boyfriend. Well he wasn't really Agatha's boyfriend, he thought he was, but everyone knew he just wanted to get in Aggie's pants. This was why she'd asked Patch to come along and ride shotgun.

Everyone was having a good time frolicking around in the water until Dick, who'd been body surfing, was run over by Patch on her humongous surfboard. Dick reckoned it must have been 8' long!

Patch was really embarrassed and kept apologising; the only way Dick could stop her was to ask her to come to the beach café for a coffee. Aggie wasn't too happy at being left on her own with the dork she was with. Of course, he made a play for her, although it didn't end up well at all for him and brought their, 'relationship,' to a complete stop!

He ended up ripping her bikini bottom off in the surf. One of Dick's mates, hearing her scream for help, and seeing the drama unfold in front of him, came to her rescue, and broke the guy's nose. He escorted the dork out of the surf and retrieved Aggies swimming costume, or what was left of it. This was obviously not going to work, so after borrowing a rash vest off another mate he got Aggie to put her legs through the arm holes and pull the rest of the vest up above her waist. After using what was left of her bikini bottoms as a belt Aggie was able to exit the surf in a somewhat decent state.

While all this was going on, Dick and Patch were enjoying getting to know each other over coffee at the beach side café. Patch, who was worried about Aggie, had just decided to have a quick check on how she was going when she saw the dork running past the café with blood streaming out of his nose. She pointed him out to Dick, they both decided he must have been hit by a surfboard. None of them ever saw the dork again, but nobody minded that at all.

They dated a few times over the remaining two weeks of Dick's course with the SAS, it was pretty obvious to both of them and everyone else how they felt about each other.

Patch didn't see much of Dick over the following twelve months, but it must have been enough, because they were married on 23rd March, 1979. The first of their five children was born ten months later.

While Dick moved around with Pussers, Patch stayed in the west, raising the children best she could. The time came for Dick to pay off in 1989, this was a hard decision to make. The senior members of the clearance diving fraternity were putting a lot of pressure on Dick to stay in, at one stage they even offered him a huge bonus, which would be his if he re-enlisted!

Part of their decision revolved about what was best to do for their family. The kids were just getting settled in at school in Carnarvon. After a lot of discussion and weighing up of the pros and cons of paying off, the offer of the bonus won. It was just too good to pass up. The Navy wanted Dick to sign up for another nine years, but he screwed them down to six; eventually paying off in 1995.

The bonus money came in just at the right time to allow them to purchase the hundred-acre block just out of Twaddle, where it was their dream to eventually build their Motel in the Wilderness.

Bringing the kids up in this remote area of Taswegia during the time the pair were designing and building the motel was challenging to say the least. Because they were so far from civilisation, the kids thought they were hard done by; it was a cut lunch and a camel just to get them to the school bus pick-up point. As they grew older, all the kids took every opportunity to go and stay with their, 'town friends.'

Even though the bonus money brought about the purchase of the land, finding the dollars to build the motel was a real challenge. Their dream became a reality with the help of a navy reserve mate of Dick's.

Roger was an Ear Nose and Throat specialist. He'd met Dick while he was at Waterhen. Roger was attached to the Taswegian reserve boat; it was an ideal partnership ... he had access to the funds and Dick and Patch did the hard yakka!

By 2000 all the kids had finally fled the nest, this left Patch and Dick to run the trekking business on their own. It was about this time that business started to pick up, meaning that Dick was able to spend more time on horseback, and less time on repairs and manufacturing.

They started the Guides Training Course in 2001, with Dick training would-be guides to help him run the rides. These courses took in everything from emergency procedures to ride planning, shoeing, first aid, bush navigation, customer relations, minimal impact riding and emergency tack repairs.

The courses were run over a five-day period, with a task book to be completed during the next five rides following the completion of the course. The guides went along as back-up guide for the first three, then had to lead the next with Dick riding tail. Their final challenge was to plan and lead the last ride on their own.

By 2002, Sarge had come on to the scene and was a great help to both of them. Not too long after that a local girl started coming around looking for a job ... Annie.

Dick and Patch both loved living in the high country of South East Taswegia, and certainly enjoyed building from scratch a wilderness motel while running their little saddlery repair business.

Chapter 5
The Solution

Monday 5th January 2015 … Dick and Patch's property outside Twaddle.

Patch listened intently as her man went over the night's events.

After a few minutes thinking about it all, she asked, "Are you all right?" This was closely followed by, "how did you feel when you shot those people?"

The aging Pusser simply replied, "They weren't people!"

As they started to head up their driveway, Dick leaned over and removed the two property numbers from the post in the middle of the twin driveways, leaving only the Forestry warning sign, which stated that removal of vegetation was prohibited.

Patch was somewhat puzzled by this, but decided he probably knew what he was doing. She asked whether they were still going over to Vince's place or whether they should dump the saddle bags full of Jack's and April's stuff first. They'd taken the opportunity of sending some ammo and dry provisions out with Patch and Dick, as this would save them having to bring it all with them later.

Dick told her he thought they should head off across country, through the farm gate in the boundary fence between the two properties, just in case they got unexpected company.

As they got closer to Vince's, they could hear the dogs barking as they always did. After tying Bob and Zen up behind the dog kennels they made their way to the house. Through the open back door, they could see Vince sitting in his office, working on hooking his laptop up to the solar charger.

"Howdy neighbours!" Vince greeted them in his usual dry way. "What are you two up to?"

Dick asked Vince if he had heard the news lately, then, after Vince said he had heard nothing, continued on, briefly explaining the events of the last two days.

Patch pulled a USB stick out of her pocket and asked Vince to have a look at her data. He inserted it into the laptop and thoughtfully studied the info Patch had gathered, and what she'd written about her theory. She knew if anyone would know about the analogue system it would be Vince!

"You know Patch, you're bloody right! There's a chance that if you can get line-of-sight established with the satellite you will get a signal, which means anyone else that has one of the older brick phones will be contactable."

As an ex-navy communication technician, Vince's knowledge of this area was extensive. He told the pair that all Royal Australian Navy (RAN) ships still had analogue transmitting gear locked away in the comms centres on all ships. This was news to Dick, although that wasn't hard to understand, as the comms centre is the most heavily guarded part of a ship. Only the communicators and their technicians were allowed into them, with NO exceptions! Dick had never set foot inside one in all the time he was serving.

"Vince, where's your missus?" Dick asked, feeling just a little concerned she hadn't come to say hello. Usually whenever Patch and Dick came to visit, she would be the first on the scene to have a chin wag.

"Took the dog for a walk Dick. I told her she was a bloody idiot with all the uncertainty right now, and it's even worse than I realised!"

Dick warned Vince that he figured it would only take a day or two at the most before the kill squad made it there from Lakeside; it would take them a day to get to Twaddle, then by the time they worked their way down all the sideroads looking for residents, and out to Vince's place, it could be a couple of days more.

Vince reckoned he and Laurel were going to stay and hide, and simply come back after they'd gone.

Dick tried to make Vince understand the danger they were in, explaining that eventually more and more of the Alliance would be turning up and taking over everything.

Patch asked Vince if they wanted to join the group. Dick gave her a real dirty look, she hadn't thought that the fact Vince couldn't ride would be a big problem. He also didn't want too big a group. Patch was just being Patch, he knew this. She couldn't help herself, she would always go out of her way to help out those in need ... it was who she was.

"Pass!" said Vince. He told the pair that he and Laurel were going to try and get his motorbike going, he had a plan to rebuild the engine, and he figured this was a good time to get it done.

Dick told Vince about his plan to camp on top of Red Mountain. He knew the tracks and had a couple of good camp sites in mind. He reckoned they would be able to get a good signal up there, the only downside with the place was that there were too many access tracks to keep an eye on.

Vince disagreed. "Nope, that won't work! In this part of the world the trajectory on this satellite is just too low. To get a good signal you will have to get to an area where there's nothing between you and the satellite except water, and even then, it's only just going to pop its head above the horizon."

Pulling a map of Taswegia off the wall, Dick asked Vince to show him the best area where the plan might work.

"Hmmm," pondered Vince, thinking about possible locations. "Somewhere in this bit between the top end of Mary Island and Myrtle Bay might work."

Dick didn't like that option at all and explained to Vince that it would be suicide to base themselves on Mary Island. It would be all right for a short while because the Alliance would need a boat to get to them, but once they'd found one, the group would be trapped, like rabbits in the cross hairs.

"But ..." he continued, "I know the perfect place! Don't know why I didn't think of it before."

With a grin he pointed to a beach he knew only too well. "Hells Beach."

Hells Beach was a natural fortress, and in their trekking days, Dick had often used the small, isolated beach as a ride destination for the extended treks. They had to be extended, Hells Beach was nearly two hundred kilometres away.

Patch had never been to Hells Beach as she rarely went along on the rides. Her role had been to assist with the admin and all other aspects of the business, as well as to keep the repairs ticking over.

Suddenly Patch dug Dick in the ribs, making him jump. "Don't get too excited! I think I hear a truck."

She was right! What's more, after running to the window they could see Laurel and Killer, their German Shepherd, coming in the gate; not far behind them was an old Bedford truck coming from the other direction; from Soothe!

Vince was out the door before Dick could stop him, yelling "That's great! One of the neighbours has got their truck going."

"Bastards!" exclaimed Dick, "they fooled us by coming the other bloody way!"

Dick and Patch bolted out the back door, turned left and made a run for the kennels, with Dick yelling back to Vince, "It's the kill squad, you fuckwit!"

He had no idea whether or not Vince heard him, but he wasn't going to hang around to check. Mounting up, they took off across the back paddock towards the boundary gate. All they could hear behind them was rifle fire.

The rest of the gang were waiting for them. "Where the fuck have you two been?" Jack asked politely.

Dick told them what had just happened and warned them to prepare for visitors. He suggested they take the horses up the tip and then take up positions from where they could protect the house. They didn't have any choice; the buggers could be there in less than half an hour.

"All they have to do is go through the two other farms between Vince and us, then we're next!" Dick explained.

Patch had found the back bags and wither bags that fit Bob and Zen, so April and Annie quickly started helping her pack some things to take with them.

"I'll leave the ammo and guns to Dick," she said, not really wanting to think about what might happen next.

Sarge and Jack positioned themselves above the drive in a slightly elevated position. The spot was perfect for an ambush; by now the two were getting on quite well and were constantly re-living old skirmishes. Sarge had developed a lot of respect for the invalid Clearance Diver.

In the meantime, Dick was working through the container, sorting out what weapons to take. The problem was that they were all a bit too heavy to carry on horseback. Dick had an idea that might just work.

Jack heard rifle fire coming from the direction of the closest house.

"Looks like they found someone home at Ted's!"

Next came the explosive sounds of vehicles being destroyed, followed by the constant drone of a Bedford motor coming their way. Suddenly the drone stopped.

"My guess is that it's probably at the entrance to the drive." said Sarge grimly.

They heard the truck start up again, and got ready for action, but then looked at each other in disbelief as they heard the drone of the engine continue on along the road, and gradually fade into the distance.

Dick startled them both as he came up behind them, and said with a grin, "I know what you're thinking! Why didn't they come up the drive?"

He explained how he had removed the property numbers, hoping this would confuse them into thinking it was just a forestry track.

"Looks like we've bought ourselves some time, although there's no knowing how long we've got before they come back."

When they told the girls that the truck had moved on, they all looked relieved.

"Does this mean we don't have to move out?" asked April, hoping that now everything was going to be okay and that maybe they all could just keep living there unnoticed.

Dick shook his head, explaining that he was sure that, when someone with a brain came through, they would see the power lines heading up the marsh, and realise there were properties that had been overlooked by the initial kill and clean-up squads.

They spent the next two hours helping Dick and Patch pull out camping gear; placing this in the container out of sight. Because they'd kept most of the gear from the old trekking days; they knew they were in a great position as far as gear went ... there were solar panels, chargers for the batteries, swags, a camp shower and toilet, water containers, cooking implements, camp ovens and heavy frypans.

They loaded ration packs, changes of clothing, billies, water bottles and ammo into the saddlebags; it was a real test of just how much they could hold!

The weapons chosen for the ride were 9 mm pistols all round, Jack had his .50 Cal on his back, with its modified and padded sling, Sarge had the SLR as before and Dick also carried an SLR. Annie carried Sarge's 12 gauge, April had Jack's .243 and Dick gave Patch the F1.

It all became a bit too real at that point. April had a melt-down, and started crying bitterly, "Why is there so much killing? Why don't people run away? Why do they just sit and wait for them to arrive and kill them? Why don't they just fight back? Most farmers have got guns!"

Jack held his distraught wife in his arms, explaining that no-one knew exactly what had happened, and that they were just lucky that Dick and Patch were listening to the radio and worked out what was possibly going to happen next. They had to take things seriously because of what Dick and Sarge had seen ... the mutilations, the killings and the clean-up crews.

He reminded her that they were so much better off than so many other locals, who were just waiting at home for something to change. With no power and no vehicles, there was nowhere for them to go. "They're just sitting ducks and they'll be easy prey to the Slopes when they arrive in the trucks. Most farmers and their families will probably think it was someone coming to help them, not annihilate them!"

"Okay, maybe it's time to tell you about my idea," said Dick. "There's no guarantees it will work, but better than doing nothing,"

After explaining Patch's theory and Vince's answer, and the whole analogue signal and low trajectory thing he started.

"I'll take one of you with me in the Hilux to go and pick up all the camping gear you've got stowed away, as well as all the excess ammo and weapons. Then there's all the camping gear we just put in the container as well as all the weapons and ammo. We need to load all of that if we can, plus as much food as we can fit in. We'll also need gas bottles, barbeques, my saddler's repair kit, and anything else you girls want to take but thought there wasn't enough room for."

Annie asked hopefully, "hair dryer?"

Dick just stared. "No power Annie!"

"What we do need is Sarge's chainsaw and fuel. Pity there's not enough room to take the gen set; it's too big, and I'd rather use the fuel in the saw."

Dick continued. "The two of us can then make our way to Barracouta in the Hilux; then all we have to do is to borrow a boat and get to Hells Beach by sea. Easy!"

"I've been there" said Annie, "on the treks. It's a gorgeous place."

"Plus, it's well-fortified," Dick continued.

"I know an old fisherman, a mate of Dad's, who has an old thirty-six-foot cray boat; and I know where he hides his spare fuel. If the Alliance is as slack as I'm hoping they are, they'll only syphon off the fuel from the boat. Hopefully, they won't torch it after that, and hopefully they won't find the old fella's stash!"

"But surely the engine has to be stuffed Dick, right?"

"Nah! The old codger was cagy! He didn't want to get rid of his old inline auxiliary, so he just hid it."

Dick proposed that the other four should ride together to Hells Beach, using Bob and the other horse as pack horses. The big question was who the best person for Dick to take with him in the Hilux was going to be.

Someone had to lead the way on horseback, and that obviously was going to have to be either Sarge or Annie. Patch had never been on the trek to Hells Beach, so she couldn't help there.

Sarge said, "I'm pretty sure I can remember the way." He was fine with taking the lead there; what he wasn't so sure about was whether Annie would back him up.

Given the fact that the run in the vehicle had the potential to be quite dangerous, it was agreed that Jack should go with Dick, and that the pack horses would be Bob and Cowboy.

Sarge was eager to get going. "Better check all their feet first. Annie, if you can get them out for me, I'll go over them; might re-shoe Socks while I'm at it."

Dick went to check how much fuel was in the Hilux. Seeing there was just under half a tank, he reckoned that would probably be enough to get them to Twaddle and back here, and then on to Barracouta.

He wasn't anticipating a quiet journey ... some of it would take them a long way out of the way on forestry tracks, which was the safest option; however he knew that the most dangerous section was going to be where they had to drive into Oxford, which was the seaside town just before Barracouta. The only way in was on a narrow road alongside the river. This wasn't going to be easy for any of them ... whether they were driving or riding.

Chapter 6
Jack Smouch

Born on the first day of June 1965, Jack grew up in the Northern Territory town of Katherine. He was the only son of Terry Smouch, a long-haul truck driver, and Sarah, who was the local remote area schoolteacher. The other sibling making up the Smouch household was Helen, his older sister.

Jack grew up about as far away from the sea as you could get. Nobody knows why he wanted to join the Navy, but from a very early age this is all he ever wanted to do. Any time his father was taking a load anywhere near the ocean, Jack went with him, often without his mother's knowledge. He would wag school to join his father on journeys that sometimes kept him away for weeks. Terry didn't mind, he liked the company.

Fortunately for both of them, Sarah worked remote in the Aboriginal community of 'Yarralin', which meant she was usually away during the week. On Friday afternoons she would drive the four and a half hours back to Katherine for the weekend, then travel back in on Sunday afternoons.

Mind you, this only happened during the dry season. Over the wet season the roads were impassable, which meant she had to stay in community, away from her family for the duration. The wet season ran from late December until early April, with the only way out being by air on the mail plane. Passenger seats were limited, so most people chose to stay put.

The only other air service was the RFDS (Royal Flying Doctor Service) flights when they were requested, but there were no available seats on these.

Terry taught Jack how to shoot from an early age, and they would quite often break the return long-haul journeys with hunting or fishing trips. By the time he was in his teens, Jack had started competition rifle shooting, and over time he became a crack shot and made his way up the ladder to first represent his school, and later the Northern Territory in the Nationals.

Helen was five years older than Jack. To put it bluntly, she was nothing but the local, 'bike.' She was the talk of the school in Katherine, many a tale was told about what Helen and the boys were doing behind the scoreboard. One could say that she literally seduced her way through high school and then onto boarding school in Darwin, where she entertained the lecturers at college. Whether it was the lack of parental influence at home that sent her in this direction wasn't clear, but Helen really didn't seem to care, or maybe she'd stopped caring long ago.

Jack could tell that his parents' marriage was falling apart, but he never raised the subject with either his father or his mother. As for his relationship with his sister? There wasn't one!

After leaving school, Jack found work locally, working for a tour company as a hunting guide, and showing would-be hunters where to go to shoot wild pigs, kangaroo and bush turkeys. He put up with the work, even though he found it boring, he'd much rather be the one doing the shooting instead of having to deal with city folk who'd signed up for an adventure. He did his best to make sure they went home happy, with a pictorial trophy of something that they had shot, but to Jack it was just a job.

Things changed the day young Jack found himself taking out a group of navy divers. The four mates had decided to do something different to celebrate the impending wedding of one of their number. They figured it was a kind of buck's party with a twist of adventure in celebration of the groom's looming loss of independent living.

Jack couldn't get enough of their stories, he loved hearing about the camaraderie, the grog, the girls and the sea. They got to do all of that and be trained to shoot people as well!

All too soon the tour came to an end. Jack could hardly wait to wave them goodbye before heading off to Darwin to enlist. Leaving his never-at-home mother, and his whore of a sister didn't worry him, the only thing he would miss were the truck driving times with Terry.

HMAS Cerberus, situated at Westernport Bay, south of Millburn in the state of Victoria, was the main adult recruit training establishment for the Royal Australian Navy. This was where Jack was to receive his indoctrination into the Navy, and it was also where he would decide what branch of the Navy he would go into.

After listening to the yarns of the buck's party, he wanted to be a diver right or wrong! But he soon learned he couldn't go straight into the CD (Clearance Diver) branch; he had to serve his apprenticeship, so to speak, in another branch first. In the past, this had to be a seaman branch, but at the time Jack signed up the Navy was experimenting with something new. They knew Jack would eventually try out for CD but allowed him to train as a stoker first.

Stokers in the RAN were marine technicians, they operated and maintained the ship's engineering plant including the engine room, generators, pumps, freshwater distilling equipment and also the boat engines. They also looked after fuel stowage and transfer and ship's stability and had equivalent ranks to other branches.

Jack served his first four years well and made it up the ranks to Leading Stoker, serving on DDG's in the Gulf War. He had a chance to try out for CD in 1989, by then he was twenty-four years of age, and in perfect shape. The fitness test usually sorted the men from the boys, it was the equivalent of trying to get into the SAS or the US Marines, but also having to be able to swim three miles underwater before you started your assault on the enemy.

The selection course (CDAT) was murderous, but Jack loved every minute of it! Even though he woke up every morning on CDAT with his body screaming at him, *'Why the fuck am I doing this,'* he was up to the challenge, and knew it was what he was born to do. He passed with flying colours.

Then came the real test, the formidable thirty-seven-week basic training course that would eventually turn him into a clearance diver, provided he was still alive at the end of it.

He figured this would be a piece of cake when compared to the demands of the advanced clearance diver course and the clearance diving component of the mine warfare and clearance diving officer's course. Those pour souls had to endure forty-one weeks of pure torture. The demands placed on potential applicants to that category were not seen anywhere else in the Australian Defence Forces, apart from those training for the special forces.

Jack joined CDT 1 based at HMAS Waterhen, and saw service throughout the world, specialising in bomb disposal. At the pinnacle of his career he proudly served as a sniper with the TAG(E) as part of 2 Commando Regiment.

At some stage during his service, Jack became a married man, and the father of two children, but the marriage didn't last long under the strain of constantly having to move around. The divorce came through just prior to his last deployment to Afghanistan.

He was injured in 2005 whilst in a Black Hawk chopper being transported to Helmand Provence. The Black Hawk had come under ground fire and Jack took a round in the back, that pretty much ended his career right there and then. Being considered totally and permanently incapacitated, Jack was discharged later that year on a full TPI Navy pension.

Jack moved to Taswegia, thinking the slower way of life would be a change, he met Dick shortly after the move, while attending a training course Dick was running on saddle building. Over the next couple of years, he'd started riding under Dick's guidance and became a decent rider in time, settling down to his new life on the farm and helping Dick and Patch out whenever they needed a hand.

Jack had no intentions of ever re-marrying, but things happen. He'd first met April, his wife-to-be, while travelling in France following the end of his first marriage. They caught up again while Jack was convalescing after being discharged from hospital after being shot in the back while on deployment in Afghanistan. They kept the conversation going by snail mail and occasional phone calls for a couple of years, and Jack eventually talked April into paying a visit to Taswegia. The spark between them that had flickered into life in France continued to grow, and eventually April packed up her life in France and moved to the secluded island for good. She loved her new life and it didn't take long for Jack to ask her to be his wife. Much to his relief, she said "Yes!"

Chapter 7
Not Safe

The plan to get ready for the move to Hells Beach was starting to come together. Sarge had started working through the shoeing; not being particularly tall in stature was something he'd always found an asset when working under the large horses. Annie was helping Sarge sort through the shoes. Hoping Dick was within earshot she yelled out to him, "Dick! Do you have any more of the size five shoes anywhere?"

Dick and Jack were busy in the workshop, working on the list of gear they wanted to take with them on the Hilux. "Yeah!" he called back. "I'll bring them down to you. Let me know what other sizes you want."

Five minutes later they heard her yell out again. "Better find two sets of fours and one set of size threes as well!"

"Jack can you go through that box to your left, I'm pretty sure we've got some of the smaller ones left from the trekking days. Bob and Zen are both fives."

"No problems mate," answered Jack. Locating the smaller shoes, Jack volunteered to take them down to Sarge and Annie. Dick handed him the fives, then turned back to the rest of the gear he was sorting through as Jack took a wander over to where the horses were being shoed.

Patch was going through her list with April, meticulously working out whether they had enough cookware for what they'd need. "The two camp ovens will be fine for roasts," she said, pulling them out from the bottom of the pantry.

April added, "We've got a third one, and I know Sarge has one as well."

"That should be plenty," said Patch. "I think I remember Dick telling me there's a steel plate there they use for barbeques, and we can always use a frypan as well."

"What if we get a few more people joining us? Do you think we need more fire plates?"

"I reckon that's a great idea April, I'll tell the boys to put it in the Hilux."

"What about pots?" April was rummaging around in the pot drawer, thinking that they'd be better to take the bigger ones.

Patch replied with a laugh, "We have shitloads April! You've got to remember that we had to look after groups of up to twelve people at a time, plus four on the crew while out on the treks! Plus, we also have more tin mugs and cups than you can poke a stick at. We used to use them in the motel when we had school groups, saved us using the good crockery." She stopped what she was doing for a minute, caught up in memories of the trekking days. "Better get on with it," she said to April. "Now for the most important item of all. Toilet rolls!"

"I have a good two hundred rolls back home Patch. Jack always buys in bulk, reckons that way you won't get caught out."

"Well he was right this time April. I think Dick and I have about four packs of thirty-six rolls as well."

The pair worked their way through the list, deciding that they had ample supplies to supply, cook and feed up to thirty people for some time.

"How much tinned food did you pack for the boys to pick up April?"

"I've got two boxes of tinned food and dry pasta, rice, herbs, all of my spices, and also four boxes of preserves: all sorts of fruit and vegetables. Hopefully, it won't be too much to take with us."

Patch had always admired April's preserves and pickles. "Sounds great April," she said with a smile. "I'm sure they'll fit it all in somehow." The conversation seemed a bit surreal to the two friends, they both knew there was no guarantee that Dick and Jack would even get to where they were going, let alone be able to pick up the supplies.

"All we can do is pray," said Patch, not really knowing where the French woman stood as far as religion went.

"If it helps, I'll be in anything," was the reply. Still coming to terms with her own beliefs, she'd always considered herself a fence-sitter as far as God was concerned. She figured praying was worth a try though!

Dick opened the back door and came through into the kitchen. "Hon, I just realised we haven't seen our neighbours from up the road for quite a while. We usually see Steve or Heidi go past most days walking the dogs."

Patch realised he was right. "Maybe they're not at home," she said. "They could be staying with friends down the road."

"It's not likely, they don't have any wheels."

Patch was starting to feel worried. "Maybe I should go up and have a look, see if they're about."

Dick thought for a moment.

"Nah," he said, not wanting her to go on her own. "Jack and I will go, we've pretty much finished in the workshop. It will give us something to do while you finish off here."

After telling Jack where they were going, Dick grabbed the F1, and they started up the last kilometre to the end of the road to where the old motel Dick and Patch had built stood. After the business had folded, they'd decided they really didn't want so many rooms to look after, so some time later they'd sold it to Steve and Heidi, who'd had aspirations of continuing on with something similar to what they'd been doing. Unfortunately, their plans didn't work, Steve had dealt with constant depression for many years, and poor Heidi was just not used to the tough way of life in the remote Taswegian bush. They had great ideas, but nothing seemed to come of them. All they seemed to do was to accumulate more and more junk. Steve was a bit of a 'collector'; from cars to old toilets, he kept everything! It was that bad that Dick refused to go up there in the end, because it made him angry to see the way they'd let the place run down.

As they made their way around the last bend in the driveway Jack said in amazement, "Mate what a fucking mess! There must be at least thirty cars here."

"Yep!" was the terse response, "and if I know Steve there will be another twenty out the other side of the motel."

They could hear horses calling out as they drew closer. They knew Heidi had a couple of old ponies up there somewhere. The boys wandered over to the small holding paddock and discovered there was no water in the old bath which substituted as a water trough. Dick frowned; it was unusual for Heidi not to make sure her animals had plenty of water. "That'll be what all the commotion is about. They're probably thirsty." He turned on the poly pipe tap just a few yards away, and water trickled out into the trough. They watched as the two ponies almost knocked each other over trying to get to the water, it didn't take them long to pretty well empty the trough.

As they approached the end steps to the verandah that ran down past the ten double rooms outside the main building, Dick yelled out, "You about Steve? Heidi?"

Jack noticed that one of the rooms was open. He peered inside, but nothing seemed out of the ordinary. "No-one here Dick."

As he looked to the left, Jack could see a newish mountain bike leaning against the verandah post by the back door. "Maybe he's into push bikes now Dick?"

"I don't reckon he'd have a new one," responded Dick, with his mind only half on what Jack had said. Something was definitely wrong, he just couldn't quite work out what it was. The old tack room bar was on their right. As they approached Dick worked out why he felt so uneasy.

"They usually keep the dogs in here. So why isn't there any barking? And what's that awful smell!"

Gingerly he slid the sliding door open, and the full force of the stench hit them both, making them both instinctively back away. They'd both seen the remains of all four dogs on the floor of the bar.

"They've obviously been there a while," muttered Jack, covering his nose and mouth with the tail end of his jacket.

Without getting too close for comfort, Dick couldn't detect what had killed the dogs, and moved on to the back door, which was partly open. With the F1 on his hip he stepped into the back room which used to be the reception area. He knew that behind the folding screen of doors to his right was the laundry.

"It looks like a bomb's gone off," whispered Jack as he followed closely, with his 9 mm Browning drawn and ready.

"That's not all that unusual." whispered Dick, pointing to the yellow door of the women's toilets, and motioning Jack to check in there. Dick opened the blue door to check out the men's toilets. Both of them were on edge but emerged with thumbs down. Moving on through the next set of heavy glass doors into the main part of the building, they paused and stood silent for a minute, just looking around.

Back shoeing the horses, Sarge was not happy. "Bloody oath my back is killing me!" grunted Sarge after a while, standing up and stretching his back. "I agree with Dick ... I'm getting too old for this shit!"

"Is that what Dick reckons?" asked Annie, not really believing that Dick could ever be too old for anything. "He's a rock Sarge!"

"Yes Annie, but we all get older eventually, you've got to realise that he's ... well, not sure; but he's got to be around fifty-nine or sixty years old by now."

"No way! You reckon?"

The thought of Dick's age had never really crossed her mind, it was one of those things. To her he'd never changed.

"Who's left!" snapped Sarge, who wasn't really happy about getting no sympathy from his partner.

"Just Zen, Fannie and Tom," retorted Annie, not knowing why Sarge was snapping at her.

Dick, with Jack right behind him, quietly opened the first glass door on the right. Peering down the hallway, he could see doors leading into the rooms on the left, and just in front of him was the kitchen on the right.

Dick called out again, "Steve! Heidi! Are you about?"

There was a slight noise, sounding a bit like a muffled voice, it seemed to come from the direction of the common lounge room just up in front of them. They started to move forward quietly. As they passed the kitchen, Dick quickly glanced to his right, but there was nobody in there, just mess everywhere! He was thinking that there was maybe just too much mess even for these two. Turning to Jack, he put his finger to his lips, Jack responded with the thumbs up signal.

Dick knew the layout of the room well, although he could see there'd been a few changes made since he and Patch had lived there. At some stage Steve had replaced the huge barrel heater that had stood against the wall just around the corner to his right, in its place was a much smaller wood heater. From where he stood Dick could scan the whole room without moving anything but his head. A large dining table, which could seat up to forty people, and which was pretty well the width of the room in length, was against the front wall, and in front of that, around the fire, were three couches and five comfortable lounge chairs. There were a number of smaller rooms down the right-hand side of the common room, the end one had always been set aside for the owner's use. This is where he and Patch had lived. He knew from what Patch had told him that it was now Steve's room. Heidi had a room to the left of the common room, he could see that door clearly as well. Dick, wishing his knees were twenty years younger, slid down the wall to floor level. Jack followed suit and tapped Dick on the shoulder.

"Do you think we should ..."

Dooff! They both recognised the unmistakable sound of a .22 with a silencer!

Jack looked at the mark that had appeared at head height on the wall to their left. He stared at Dick with that, 'Oh shit!' look.

Dick made a twirling motion with his hand to Jack, knowing that Jack would understand he wanted them to take a forward roll into the room, and then shoot at whatever was in there. He was pretty sure the blast from the .22 had come from Steve's room.

Jack nodded, thinking that this maybe wasn't the work of the Alliance. With all the stuff that had been happening, maybe Steve had finally lost the plot, and had barricaded himself in the room. He didn't realise that Dick had already run through that scenario in his mind but was convinced it wasn't Steve because he didn't own a weapon. He knew this because on more than one occasion he'd had to put down sick animals for Heidi when they couldn't afford the vet.

Dick counted down, using his fingers … 3 … 2 … 1! On '1' both men rolled forward into the middle of the larger room. Almost without pausing, Dick was up on his knees, and pulled the trigger on the F1. Its fiery mass of 9 mm lead spewed out in the general direction of Steve's bedroom. At the same time Jack rose into a back-up stance from behind a chair. Holding steady, he waited until he was able to pinpoint the position where he thought the .22 had been fired from; slightly to the left of where Dick had been aiming. Jack fired twice, catching the intruder in the torso. Although they couldn't see what happened, they could clearly hear the thump of a body hitting the floor.

Dick got to his feet and ran to the doorway, F1 at the ready. "All clear!"

Wishing he was somewhere else right now, another place, and another time, Jack straightened up and followed Dick into the room. He examined the body, exclaiming in disgust, "He's just a bloody kid Dick! You got him with the first burst, I just finished him off. Geez, he's got no pants on!"

"Looks like that's not all I got!" exclaimed Dick. The sight of what lay before them left them both feeling a bit sick.

They were both looking down at Heidi, who was naked, and had been almost cut in half by the blast of the F1. In the corner of the room, Steve's body was draped over the edge of a chair; his head was hanging on an unnatural angle … it was obvious his neck had been broken.

"No prizes for guessing what the kid was doing to Heidi!" exclaimed Dick in disgust. "I reckon he was probably a looter; maybe one of the guys that came up the other night in the old truck. He must have come in the back way, thinking he wouldn't be heard, it must have given him a shock to come across the motel before hitting my place!"

"I've had enough! It's got to be beer-o'clock," exclaimed Sarge.

Annie wasn't going to let him stop there. "Come on Sarge. You've only got one to go!"

"Which one?" asked Sarge, sweat rolling off his bald head and dripping down through his moustache.

"Your favourite. Tom!"

Sarge swore. "Great! Forgot about him." Tom was Annie's favourite. Standing seventeen hands high, the big thoroughbred sported size seven shoes. The gentle giant hadn't been ridden much in the last six weeks, he just needed his shoes taken off, a bit of a trim, and re-shoeing with the same shoes. Sarge gave a weary sigh. The sooner he started the sooner he'd be finished.

"Annie, after you bring Tom down can you go and ask Dick to do a bit of a stocktake on the shoes, nails and rasps please?"

As she led the huge showjumper in for his re-shoe, Annie reported that Dick and Jack were not in the workshop.

"Don't know where they are."

Sarge looked at the love of his life standing there holding Tom. Her trim body looked good in blue jeans and a tee shirt. Looking over her shoulder, he started to laugh.

"What are you grinning at Sarge?"

Annie didn't see Dick sneak up behind her; the big man placed his hands around her waist and picked her up, nearly making her drop the lead.

"You bastard! Where did you come from?" she asked.

"We were just up the road checking whether the neighbours are okay."

Sarge noticed the F1 around Dick's neck. Not wanting to upset Annie, he just asked, "Everything all right Dick?"

"I'll fill you in later, when you come inside."

It was nearly dark by the time they all finished up and gathered together inside the house. If all went well, Jack and Dick would be staying there the next night, but they all realised that, for Patch, April, Annie and Sarge, this was possibly their last night there for quite some time.

Dick and Jack filled the others in about what had happened up the road, leaving out the distressing details of how Heidi was raped, or that it was probably him that had killed Heidi during the fire fight, They didn't want to upset the girls more than they had to; it was enough for them to know that Steve and Heidi were dead, as was the looter. Dick pointed out that it was just as well the looter had died, eventually the kid would have come down the road and paid them a visit. Patch made him promise to go back and bury the three bodies after they left.

Changing the subject, Dick turned to his wife and April asking, "What have you two been up to?"

"Well Dick," responded April, we've cooked all the roasts and chops we could fit in your gas oven and sorted out the dry provisions and the cooking equipment. We've been doing our bit; what have you two been up to?"

Jack pried his way into the conversation. "Well Hon, we've sorted out the shoes for Annie and Sarge, pulled out all the camping gear left over from Dick's treks, and then finished off the afternoon by going up the road and killing the bad guy!"

Sarge interrupted, asking how many shoes they had for the trip.

"Got around four sets of each size, as well as three boxes of nails and four rasps," reported Jack.

"Do you reckon that will be enough to get us through Dick?"

"We've got four sets of size sevens packed up at home to add to the list," said Annie. " I reckon we'll be right"

"Last supper?" suggested Patch, feeling hungry. "What do you all want to eat?"

Sarge looked at Dick, and they said in unison, "Steak, chips and eggs!"

Patch announced, "You're cooking dear, as usual. I've done enough cooking for one day!"

"With pleasure," said Dick, who loved to cook. "I'm not sure whether there is any steak. What was left in the freezer after you cooked the roasts April?"

"I think there's a few still there, although I don't mind eating a snag instead if there's not enough steak to go around."

"I'm the same," agreed Patch, "I'm happy to have a chop or a snag instead of a steak."

"Sounds like a plan," grinned Dick. "Three steaks, snags and a chop coming up; that's if I can round them up. Any other requests while I'm at it?" he added.

The three women looked at each other. "A shower would be great!"

Chapter 8
April Smouch

Chevaigne-du-Maine was situated at the heart of the old province of Maine, at the edge of Anjou and Brittany, some 206 km from Paris in the Mayenne (Pays de la Loire) region of central France. Mayenne's heritage was a complex and richly intertwined tapestry of such wonders as the medieval villages of Sainte-Suzanne and Saint-Denis-d'Anjou, the Gallo-Roman town of Jublains, the art and history of nearby Laval, the prehistoric caves of Saulges, the castles of Mayenne, Lassay and Craon, the Évron basilica and the Thévalles watermill. Chevaigne-du-Maine's small population of 195 residents was increased by one on a quiet night in 1955, which was when April Dupree entered the world.

April had the usual upbringing for a child of that era, attending the village school, then later going on to school in Laval. Eventually she travelled to Paris to study self-sustainability at the University there, graduating in 1978. With this degree under her belt, she quickly scored a job working for the French Government on a number of scientific and economic projects. She married Jacque in 1980, unfortunately finding out the hard way that this wasn't a good thing. Jacque was a drunk and a wife-beater of the worst kind, and even when he wasn't causing poor April physical harm, the mental abuse never stopped.

Initially, she had fallen in love with his typical French charisma. Jacque was a vintner, working for one of the boutique vineyards in neighbouring Laval. Over the eighteen years they were together he went through no less than twenty-seven jobs, all in various wineries. It was an ever-repeating pattern; he'd start well, but with easy access to wine he'd end up spending most of the day drinking. It would only be a matter of time before he would be discovered and lose his job. To avoid a scandal, the winery would say nothing of his sacking, which meant that he had no trouble finding another job at a different place.

Like many women who end up in an abusive relationship, April stayed with him; she kept on telling herself that it was all her fault, and that he really did love her. She just kept hanging in there, hoping that one day things would start getting better.

Over the years, Jacque's abuse had meant that April had to spend time in hospital half a dozen times, for injuries ranging from deep bruising of her ribs, to a broken nose. It seemed hopeless, the more he did it the more he seemed to get away with it. At one stage he invited his mates around to get drunk together. They'd been so drunk that they'd tied April to the kitchen table and taken it in turns to rape her. This should have been the catalyst for her to leave, but Jacque had broken down the next day, saying he was truly sorry, and begged her to stay. In the end April gave in, forgiving him once again.

Together they'd had one child, a daughter, Rachel. Rachel was growing up fast, and as the years went by April found it more and more difficult to hide what Jacque was doing. Terrified that he might take his frustrations out on his daughter, April used any excuse to let the girl stay with friends whenever she could. Rachel left home as soon as she was old enough to legally do so. Once she'd gone, April felt completely alone; she realised that nothing was ever going to change, and that the abuse would never stop. The very next time Jacque hurt her she made up her mind; she didn't have to protect Rachel any-more, so that night, once he'd passed out, April simply walked out the door and into the night.

Over the next five years she moved from place to place, gaining work wherever she could find it. This gypsy life continued until 2003, which was when she first came across Jack Smouch, who was on a well-earned holiday after the failure of his first marriage.

Jack had taken a, 'sit and relax ,' bus tour of Paris and was enjoying the care-free life of a tourist. As he was sitting with his fellow bus companions at a local restaurant on the outskirts of Paris, he caught sight of April, who was sitting on her own. It was her hair, adorned with a traditional headscarf, that first caught his eye; although plaited it hung down to her waist. Jack thought she was the most stunning woman he had ever laid eyes on.

After dinner, the rest of the tour group moved on to a show; paid for as part of their tour. Jack didn't go with them, instead deciding to stay where he was. It was obvious to him that April was lonely, and everything about him wanted to comfort her. It took him a few drinks before he plucked up enough courage to try and break the ice. His biggest fear was he couldn't speak French, he was pretty sure she would not be able to speak English.

Jack didn't usually have any difficulty in speaking to members of the opposite sex but for some reason this was different. His legs felt as heavy as lead, and he had to muster all the courage he could find in order to approach her, but he did it in the end, asking if she would mind him buying her another glass of wine. He must have looked a sight, with his usual cowboy hat on, not all that well-dressed, red faced, and more than a little bit awkward.

April was startled at first, but then thought, "What have I got to lose?" He was obviously part of the tour that had just left. What harm could come from a bit of safe company, and after all he would be moving on with his tour the next day.

She replied with a smile, "Oui Monsieur."

Jack was suddenly tongue-tied, he hadn't expected her to actually say yes! Seeing his embarrassment, April felt sorry for him, and putting him out of his misery she continued the conversation in English. They seemed to hit it off from the word go, and it didn't take too long for them to share their life's history with each other. Although it was not what she would normally have done, in the end April invited the Australian back to her apartment, and they spent the night together. It had been some five years since she'd left Jacque, but they'd stopped sleeping together two years before that, and if she looked at things honestly, she'd stopped wanting to sleep with anyone ten years before that. After leaving him she'd never trusted anyone else enough to allow them to become intimate with her, so it was a big decision for her to make.

They both were a bit surprised at the immediate bond which they felt, it was as if they'd known each other for years. The next morning Jack made a spur of the moment decision, and decided to not continue with the tour, but instead to stay with April. This came as quite a shock to April, although she did admit to herself that the Australian cowboy took her fancy.

April was an amazing cook, and Jack absolutely loved her culinary skills; he could now understand why people reckoned that the way to a man's heart was through his stomach. They would spend endless hours together fantasizing about a new life on a farm somewhere, enjoying a self-sustainable way of life. It had always been a dream of hers to live, 'off the grid,' outside the realms of society; not having to rely on the Government or power companies to survive. She knew she had the knowledge and skills to do this, but she'd never quite had the courage to make a go at it.

All too quickly Jack's leave was up, and he had to return home. He was due for deployment to Afghanistan, assisting in bomb disposal; this was one of the most dangerous jobs in the military, even more so with the increased use of improvised explosive devices (IEDs).

With over half of the recent Australian fatalities in Afghanistan resulting from blast injuries, authorities had redirected their focus to working on eradicating IEDs in an effort to better protect the troops. There were major concerns about the lack of explosive ordnance disposal technicians available for operations; but on top of this, recent experience on the ground in Afghanistan suggested the Taliban's use of IEDs was becoming more frequent, and also more sophisticated.

It was during this last tour that Jack was wounded in the back. After many months spent recuperating at HMAS Penguin Base Hospital, he was finally well enough to take another bout of leave.

Jack was never any good at email, so since last seeing her, they'd kept in touch through letters and occasional phone calls. April was eager to see him again, so Jack ended up flying to France for a bit of a convalescent holiday. This time, because of his injuries, he wasn't able to do much else other than force himself to make the most of being pampered by April while enjoying the wonders of her French cuisine.

By the time he had to return from leave to finish out his final few weeks, Jack had put on an extra ten kilograms in weight, but he didn't mind.

After paying off in 2005, he realised he had no ties to the Northern Territory and looked around for a small farm he could call home. The slower way of life, and cheaper property prices of Taswegia drew him to the island state. He decided that Twaddle was the answer he was looking for, and it didn't take him too long to talk April into joining him.

She emigrated in 2007.

Chapter 9
Red Mountain

Tuesday 6th January 2015 … Dick and Patch Mann's property outside Twaddle. Through Patch's eyes …

It was just past 6 a.m. or 0600 as I was learning to call it, trying to please Dick, with his love of all things military. I woke to the sounds of the belly-laughing kookaburras, remembering that Dick and I had just learnt this was actually a warning challenge to other intruding kookaburras. Most people thought they were laughing. It was pretty quiet outside, although I could hear the wind rustling through the trees above our workshop. We didn't hear it much from the house, being below the workshop it was pretty well protected from the wind.

Turning over, I gave Dick a cuddle, spooning into his back and feeling his hairy back tickle my breasts.

It had been a good last night together; the meal was perfect. As usual Dick had done a sterling job with the barbeque, ably assisted by Sarge and Jack, while April, Annie and I had made the wedgies and baked them in the oven. A few beers and a couple of wines to celebrate being alive, and with good friends.

Dick had thought of posting a guard but had elected instead to set booby traps above and below the house on the criveway. It was a pretty basic setup, a trip wire across the track which was attached to huge noisemakers. An old and simple trick, but quite ingenious.

Jack and April had peeled off to the spare room around ten, leaving Sarge, Annie and Dick still discussing the route we would be taking today. I'd had enough of it all for now, so had concentrated on trying to finish my jigsaw.

Annie and Sarge spent the night in the small bungalow out the back. It was good to have one last chance to be together, and sleep in our own bed. There was no way of knowing how long it would be before we would have the chance to do it again ... maybe never.

I could hear someone moving about in the kitchen. Then there was the familiar sound of the kettle being filled out of the water container on the bench, followed by the gas igniting. I thought to myself, "I bet that's Sarge."

Dick stirred, and turned to see me propped up, leaning on his chest, and looking at him with my big brown eyes.

"What's wrong Chook?" he asked sleepily.

"I love you," I whispered back.

"I love you too Chook. Who's up?"

"It sounds like Sarge, although it could be Jack, they're both early risers."

"My bet is that it's Sarge."

Pushing back the covers, Dick dressed quickly, and then turned to me, saying, "Do you want the generator on Hon?"

"Yes please. Another shower would be a luxury! Not sure when the next one will be."

"It'll probably be a camp shower at Hells Beach if we're lucky," he smiled at me, as he left the room, closing the door behind him.

Dick entered the kitchen and found Sarge sitting at the bench. All the coffee cups were lined up, ready for the water.

"Sarge!"

"Dick!"

"Annie still in bed?" Dick grinned, knowing this was a stupid question.

"No, she's out checking the horses, but you knew that didn't you?"

"Yep."

As he made his way out the back to put the gen set on, Dick ran into Jack, who was coming out of the spare room.

"Morning Dick!"

"Jack!"

He started the generator and yelled out that showers were now available, the solar hot water could probably stand one more round.

Sarge poured the drinks and put a couple of pans on the stove.

"Snags and bum nuts okay Dick?"

Dick realised how hungry he was. "Sounds great to me mate!"

Annie appeared, grumpily announcing, "Horses are all okay. Isn't April out of that shower yet.

"Nothing to do with me!" grinned Jack.

I finished my shower and went to tell Annie she was welcome to use our bathroom.

Breakfast over, we all enjoyed another round of drinks before going outside to tack up the horses.

Once all the horses were lined up outside the workshop Dick started going through the saddles and tack with a fine-tooth comb, not wanting any mistakes or anything to go wrong during the trek. Even though he knew it was best that he ride in the Hilux with Jack, I knew he must have been feeling just a little bit guilty about leaving the long ride to Sarge and Annie to oversee; normally he would have been the one to lead it.

Sarge and us three women had agreed that, as far as guard duty went, Sarge was the only one with real experience, so he would be doing four-hour shifts, with the rest of us doing two apiece. We thought this should give everyone enough sleep.

After checking each horse for sore backs, sole bruises and girth soreness, Dick declared they were ready. Annie tacked up Tom with her western saddle, (this is one that Dick had built for her late mother some years before). Because, of all her saddles, this one held the most sentimental value to Annie, she chose this one over one of her stock saddles. Tom was a ten-year-old 17-hands thoroughbred and was Annie's beloved jumper; once fitted out with front bags and twin back bags he really looked the part.

Dick had fashioned a heavy canvas bucket to help take the weight of Sarge's 12-gauge shotgun, this was the one that Annie would be carrying.

Socks, at twenty years of age, was slightly older. The Arab-Welsh Cob Cross was Sarge's mount and was kitted out in another of Dicks saddles, a traditional stock saddle, often called a, 'dog saddle,' that he also made on spec, and which was now owned by Annie. This was fitted with wither bags and a single back bag full of shoeing gear, along with the emergency first aid kit and fire lighting equipment.

Dick had fitted an old WWI rifle bucket to the saddle Sarge was using, modifying this with a large cut-out to accommodate the magazine for the SLR; a little different to the Lee Enfield it had been originally intended for.

Zen was a striking animal, a full Quarter Horse imported from one of Dick's mates in the USA some ten years earlier. He had been a very special birthday surprise for me, Dick reckoned it had cost a bloody fortune to get him here, but that the money had been well worth it.

I loved him so much! Zen had some powerful ancestors: a direct lineage to Three Bars, (the King foundation sire and an all-round racing and performance champion), Gay Bar King, (bottom and top-side grand and great-grand parents), and Poco Lena, (a world champion cutting horse).

It wouldn't have mattered to me what his lineage was, I absolutely adored him and could get him to do almost anything I asked. Luckily, I was not the competitive type, otherwise I would have had a big problem with Annie, who was green with envy over Zen. If she'd had her own way, he would have been hers.

I was planning on riding in the Syd Hill stock saddle that had been bought for Zen, and which had been used on the treks. This had also been fitted with wither bags and double back bags. Because of its unique shape and extremely long magazine I knew I would have to wear the F1 over my back using a padded sling.

April's mount, Fannie, was a Welsh Quarter Horse Cross around twelve years old; she was quite lively on her feet, and sometimes proved too much for the Frenchwoman. Fannie had been tacked up with an old, imported stock saddle which was left over from the trekking business; this saddle too had been fitted out with wither bags and single back bag. It was amazing just how much you could fit in those things! Dick had also made a heavy canvas bucket to take Jack's .243.

"Make sure all your surcingles are on," he reminded them.

Bob carried Dick's saddle, a set of wither bags full of ammo and two swags which were strapped to either side. Dick decided to add a folded-up groundsheet running down the middle, which could easily be deployed to cover the swags if it started raining.

The swags had been designed and manufactured by Dick to suit the cold Taswegian temperatures, especially in the winter. Back when we first started the trekking business, we'd found that the only type of swag you could get was what was called a Queensland Swag. This consisted of a flat sheet of canvas with a mattress clipped on one edge; you pulled it over you at night, but still gave you a way of keeping cool.

That might have been okay in Queensland, but it certainly didn't work here! So Dick decided to design his own, opting for a canvas, 'envelope' lined with wool, then a mattress inserted between the wool and the canvas. The swag was zipped up along the bottom where it was folded and then up the side to the top. He added a weather sheet which came off the top; you could either pull it right over your head or keep it off on a good night. The swags were supplied with a sheet bag, pillow and doona, the idea was to take your clothes off when you got in, folding them and placing them down the backline between the mattress and the side, while your boots and socks were placed under your head to elevate the pillow a little bit. Nobody had ever had a cold night when using one of Dick's swags!

We'd wrapped some spare clothing, a change of underwear, socks, toiletries and a towel in the swags before loading them on to Bob, better to do this rather than take up extra space in our saddlebags.

Cowboy was fitted out with the saddle that Jack had built at one of Dick's saddle building courses. Jack had always been proud of the fact that he could boast that he had made pretty well every single piece of saddlery that he put on his horse. Wither bags, and a set of double back bags were added to Cowboy's load and another two swags strapped to either side, along with a protective groundsheet.

All the horses wore a rope halter and lead rope done up around their neck and tied in a cavalryman's knot.

Annie and Sarge had their own swags, Jack and April were taking two out of the old trekking stock. Because of their extra-large size, Dick had decided to take the double swags in the Hilux.

We'd decided to take a full range of cooking gear with us, along with enough food for six days and water for two. Dick reckoned we'd be able to replenish the water at the creeks and rivers along the way.

We were hoping that most of the campsites would still have their steel plates and fireplaces intact.

"Its 0930. Time to mount up!" said Dick.

Annie, who was already mounted and eager to get going, yelled back impatiently, "Come on you lot, we're burning daylight!"

After a brief moment to say our goodbyes April and I mounted up, both of us had tears in our eyes, and after leaning down to give Dick a quick kiss, Zen and I moved off at the walk, following April on Fannie.

Turning back for a brief moment, I smiled, "See you in Hell!" I was trying to hide it but couldn't help shedding a tear at the same time; it wasn't easy to leave him. I was worried about everything, but most of all my own performance, it had been quite a few years since I'd tackled a ride this long.

Sarge bought up the rear. As he started off, he turned and gave Dick and Jack the thumbs up, his way of saying everything was okay.

As we left the property, we took a steep hill climb up the boundary until just before the corner, then turned left, punched through a short distance of dense scrub and out onto an arterial track in State Forest.

Annie, who was automatically in guiding mode, turned in the saddle and looked back.

"Everyone okay?"

April, next in line, responded, "De toute façon, tout est bon ici," meaning, *"Don't worry, everything's good here."*

"Yep!" was my reply. Sarge just grinned.

"You're not speaking that French shit are you April?"

Knowing that for once she had the upper hand over the younger woman, April couldn't help herself, replying, "Qu'est ce qui te fait penser ça!" (*"What makes you think that!"*)

Sarge chuckled to himself, thinking that this was going to be one hell of a ride.

They followed the track as it wandered for a little over a kilometre. This part of the ride had always been known as the D9 Waterhole Track, because it was dotted with waterholes used by Forestry workers to fill the fire-fighting tankers while fighting a fire. The terrain was very rocky, and you could hear the *tink tink* of the horses' hooves on the volcanic shale.

Forestry named all their forests alphabetically and each of the spur roads which ran off the main one was referred to by numbers, with odd roads leading to the right and even to the left.

Dick used to say it was just like a ship, compartments are numbered in the same way. He reckoned it was easy to remember … 'Port,' having an even number of letters was the left side of the ship, whereas 'Starboard,' having an odd number referred to the right.

Just before they dissected the main track, Sarge reminded them, "If we end up going down the main track, you'll all need to keep your eyes peeled for vehicle tracks. If they're fresh, I reckon we should exit onto the fire break. It might take a bit longer, but it will be a darn sight safer!"

Annie stopped and listened, looking up and down the D Road before giving the move forward signal. We moved off, I was leading Bob and Sarge was leading Cowboy.

Around four kilometres further on we descended a slope covered with a canopy of tall eucalyptus regnans. Also known as Swamp Gums, these huge trees often grew to be over 120 metres tall: they're the tallest flowering gum in the world!

Sarge cleared his throat. "The track coming up on the right is the D8. Any signs of tyre tracks Annie?"

Turning in the saddle she replied with a wicked smile, "Nah, tut bin Izzie, or whatever it was that April said before!"

"I wish I'd continued on with French while I was at school," I said to Sarge with a sigh, hoping Annie wasn't going to stir up too much trouble during the trip.

"Hah! I had enough trouble speaking English," replied Sarge with a wink.

We'd planned to stop for lunch down the D4 track, nearly to the end where they used to camp. I'd only been there a couple of times with Dick when he'd wanted to check how much water there was in the waterhole.

Studying the track, Sarge commented, "No-one's been on this since I drove down it last."

"Ya got that right Sarge," replied Annie.

The fresh air and early start meant we were all hungry. It didn't take long to down our feast of cold chicken, cheese, biscuits and carrots, all washed down with cold water.

"I think we should cut around the fire break next, at least till we get to the big tree."

Sarge agreed. "Good idea Annie."

"Is it going to be very rough?" April asked nervously.

Annie thought for a moment. "It should be pretty good going, a bit like a concertina ride up and down and in and out of the little gullies until we hit a boundary fence. Then we'll turn left and follow a track out to the D Road and end up coming out at what we call the big tree."

For some reason Zen and Fannie were just not getting on, so Annie suggested a change in order, with April leading Cowboy if she felt up to it, Zen and I following, still leading Bob, and Sarge continuing behind. As she'd anticipated, this worked well; Annie had counted on this, knowing that Fannie and Cowboy had lived together back home.

Looking at the majestic scenery I secretly wished I had been part of the treks. The man ferns were huge, with up to thirty and even forty in a cluster, some of them twenty foot high!

"What a lovely place this is."

Annie turned in the saddle. "Believe me, it gets better the closer we get to the boundary fence, even more rainforest-like."

Turning right at the 'big tree,' we rode around ten kilometres to the D2 turnoff; at one stage travelling close to the property known as Lion Point. We could see the homestead in the distance. As he rode, Sarge closely monitored the buildings through his binoculars, he knew it was possible that the Alliance had started occupying these homes, and he didn't want to risk a confrontation if he didn't have to.

He and Dick had a long conversation about it the night before, after Jack and April had gone to bed. Dick's theory was that the Alliance wouldn't wait too long before placing their own people in these farms, with all the local people dead, if they left the animals alive, these would need feeding and watering pretty soon. He figured they wouldn't have killed the stock animals because they would be needed for milk and meat.

We couldn't get to the D2 quick enough, and were tempted to trot; however, Sarge, remembering Dick's instructions to the, 'wannabe cowboys, during the treks, didn't agree.

"No! The horses have a long way to go yet."

Once we were away from the open ground, we all felt the tension ease for a bit. We next had to ride through a eucalypt plantation and join up to the Red Mountain Track. After that it could possibly get tricky again because the firebreak track after the plantation was going to take us very close to the back of the Fly Marsh homestead.

Annie still hadn't quite understood the danger we were in. As we approached, she called back, "I remember this place! This is where Boru shit himself and dumped his rider, all because he was scared of the two donkeys that lived there." The twenty-eight-year-old laughed out loud, as she remembered the looks on the faces of the clients that day.

Sarge put his finger up to his lips with a frown and shook his head. "Shush! We're within hearing distance of that house," he whispered.

As we drew level with the house Sarge saw an all too familiar Bedford look-alike truck making its way up the long driveway.

"Shit! It's time to skedaddle!"

Taking off at a trot, we soon cleared the ground to the Red Mountain Track and pulled up for a minute. Sarge wanted to make sure we were in the clear.

"You lot just keep going. Socks and I will go back and do a reccy and make sure they didn't see us. I'll catch you up."

We started the long upwards climb, winding our way over five hundred metres of zig zagging track, which took us up the side of the mountain.

"How far do you think we should go Annie?" I asked.

"And when do we stop and wait for Sarge?" added April.

"We don't! Just keep going till we get to the campsite." snapped Annie. She obviously wasn't too happy about Sarge staying behind.

Sarge carefully made his way back to the property known as Fly Marsh, tying up Socks out of sight. There was a lot of movement in and around the house, and he could see people moving in and out carting suitcases and bags.

Sarge could make out what looked like a man, a woman and two children, maybe aged around five or six years old.

"Looks like the new owners," he thought sarcastically.

He was more interested in the troops, trying to work out what they were doing, and whether they'd seen them. Maybe they'd been lucky this time; no one seemed to be looking in the direction of the mountain. He waited a while longer, just to be certain they were in the clear, then started to move back to where Socks was tethered.

Something caught his attention, and he stopped to check it out. "Well, this is very interesting indeed," he muttered to himself.

Annie was feeling really edgy. "If Sarge doesn't show up by the time we get the campsite set up, I'll go back and look for him," she snorted.

I started unloading the swags off the horses, and between us we de-tacked all but Tom. Setting off to gather some kindling for a fire, I turned to Annie and asked, "Do we feed them to settle them now or should we wait till you get back?"

"Leave it till I get back," she said, swinging up on board Tom. Annie cantered off back down the track, obviously too worried about Sarge's absence to sit and just wait for him as he'd said.

"Damn! I'm hanging out for a coffee," grumbled April.

I felt the same but wasn't sure whether it was wise to light the fire just yet. "We'd better wait till everyone's back before we light the fire."

April looked really exhausted. I knew that she had probably never tackled a long ride before, especially under these circumstances. I was wondering whether Fannie had picked up on the tension. I knew that when standardbred horses get stressed they revert back to their natural gait, which is a pace! No doubt that was why April had started speaking French.

"Let's put all the saddles and tack together under a groundsheet, in case there's a frost tomorrow morning," I suggested, trying to think of something we could do to distract her for the moment.

I was about to ask her how she was coping with it all, when noises coming from along the track startled us both. We looked at each other in trepidation; I grabbed the F1, and April quickly ran to pick up the .243.

"Hope I remember how to shoot the bloody thing!" I gasped.

"You'll be fine," replied April, pulling back the bolt and loading one up the spout.

"Well you two, if we were the bad guys you'd really be in trouble! Next time, get behind some fucking cover instead of standing out in the open like Annie-get-your-gun-Oakley!" Thankfully, it was Sarge who appeared around the bend, laughing as he rode, followed close behind by Annie, who, by the look on her face was more than happy to have her man back.

"Finally! Can we please light the fire now so we can have a cuppa?"

"Not till we've run the windbreak around it April," answered Sarge.

He went on to explain that an open flame could be seen for miles at night. It was 1930 and would be dark in just over an hour; with the wind break around the fire we wouldn't be seen, and because there was already a fair night breeze blowing, the smoke would dissipate before it could be detected. Dick and Sarge had made the wind break many years ago. It was a 3-foot canvas screen, which was placed around the fireplace, leaving enough room for the swags to go in between the fire and the screen. The other advantage with it was that it would keep us all a lot warmer during the night.

I was pleased that he had remembered to bring it along. "I'm sure glad you were a Sapper Sarge!"

We all got busy, the fire was soon flickering brightly, and the horses, after being hobbled inside a roped off makeshift yard, were munching happily on a handful of grain. April was feeling much happier, having finally got her coffee, and after thoroughly cleaning off the steel plate with salt water Sarge started to cook the hamburgers. April and I sliced up tomatoes, red onions, and cucumbers, all from her garden.

"Really appreciate the fresh stuff April," admitted Arnie, still not sure how to take the older French woman.

"Le plaisir était pour moi!" Annie couldn't help herself.

"There you fucking go again!"

"She's just pulling your leg Annie," I said" I know that one. 'The pleasure is mine.'"

Thinking about the long night ahead, Sarge let the fire die down a bit as he enjoyed his fourth cup of coffee.

"Patch can you do the first watch till midnight, then April's on till 0130. Annie you'll be on watch till 0300, then I'll take over until it's time to leave … at 0500. I'm giving April the short watch tonight, we can all take it in turns over the next four nights. If you don't have a wristwatch you can borrow mine."

As April and Annie climbed into their swags he added, "Don't build the fire up too much and don't wander off. If you hear ANYTHING wake me!"

I wasn't sure whether I'd drawn a good watch or a bad watch, but it was okay … I figured it would be easier to keep awake if I hadn't been asleep. As I stared out into the darkness, I thought over all the things that had happened over the past five days. Hard to believe, it seemed to be a lot longer than that. I wondered what Dick and Jack were up to, trying not to worry about them, something that was proving harder to do than I'd anticipated!

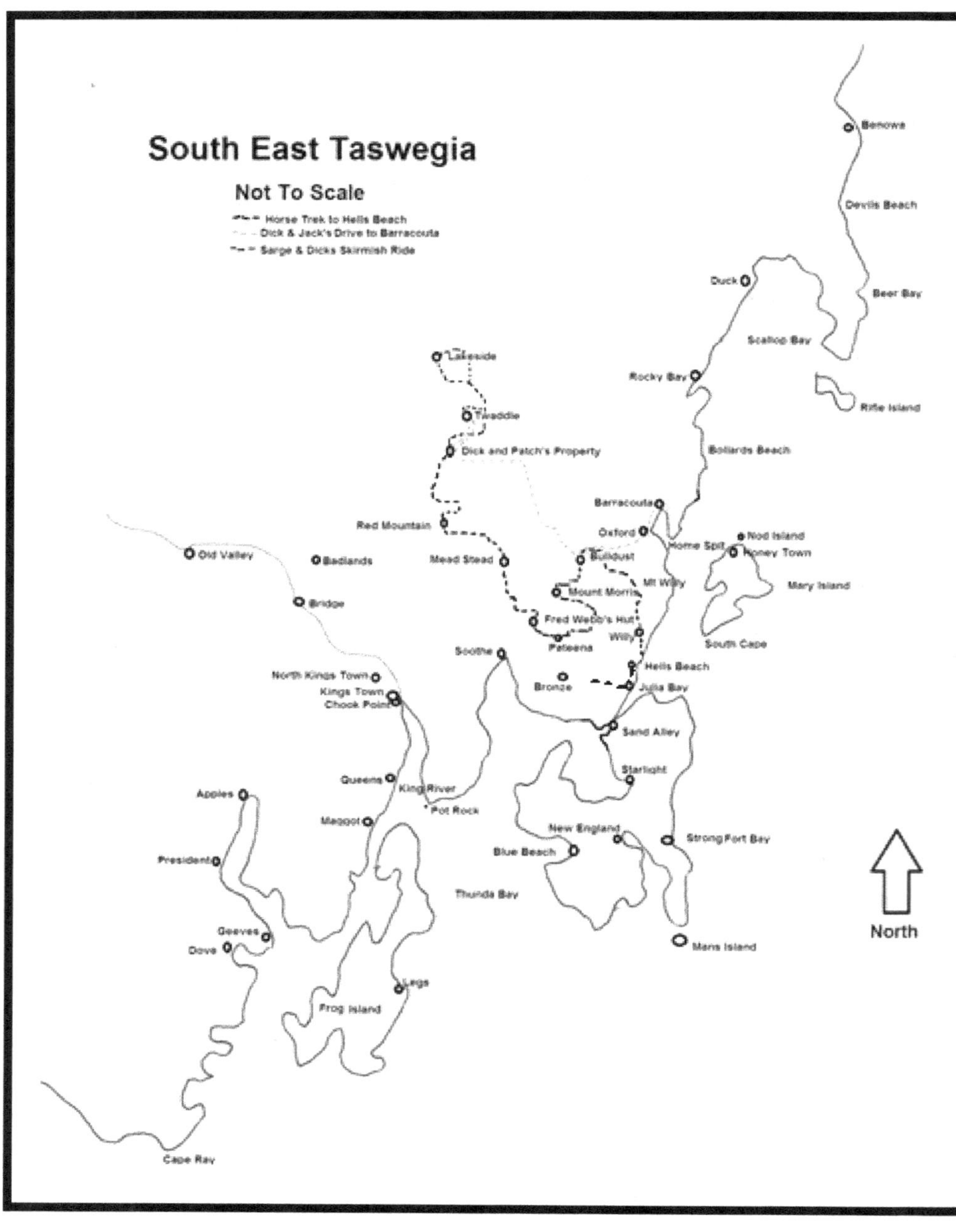

South East Taswegia
Not To Scale
Horse Trek to Hells Beach
Dick & Jack's Drive to Barracouta
Sarge & Dicks Skirmish Ride
Benowa
Devils Beach
Beer Bay
Duck
Scallop Bay
Rifle Island
Lakeside
Rocky Bay
Twaddle
Bollards Beach
Dick and Patch's Property
Barracouta
Nod Island
Oxford
Red Mountain
Home Spit
Honey Town
Old Valley
Badlands
Mead Stead
Bulldust
Mt Willy
Mary Island
Bridge
Mount Morris
Fred Webb's Hut
Willy
Pateena
South Cape
Soothe
North Kings Town
Bronze
Hells Beach
Kings Town
Julia Bay
Chook Point
Sand Alley
Queens
Starlight
King River
Apples
Pot Rock
Maggot
New England
Strong Fort Bay
President
Blue Beach
Thunda Bay
Geeves
Dove
Mans Island
Legs
Frog Island
North
Cape Ray

Chapter 10
Wayne Michaels (Sarge)

Sarge was an ex-Sapper RAA turned bushman. It was said he could survive on two red berries and a dirty puddle for a month!

He was Taswegian born and bred, coming into this world in 1970 in Kings Town, and was the son of Basil and Florence Michaels. Basil was a bulldozer driver who worked for a large civil contractor, his job often took him away from home and all over the state. Most of the time he'd camp away for the week, returning home for the weekend if he was lucky.

Sarge's upbringing was different to most, he wasn't a great scholar and pretty well hated his school days. Picked on by the hierarchy and branded dumb by his peers, most of the time Sarge just took off and spent time away with his father. Basil, a qualified bushman, taught him far more than he would ever have learned in the classroom, everything from how to drive a bulldozer to how to fall a tree.

Sarge thrived in this environment and by the time he was twelve years old he could out-cut most grown men with a chainsaw and could handle the O65 Stihl pro-saw with ease.

Basil realised the future wasn't going to be easy for Wayne and encouraged him to try out for the Army. Much to everyone's surprise he was accepted, given his lack of education one could only assume that Basil must have had contacts.

After completing his basic training at Kapooka in 1987, Sarge joined the Royal Australian Engineers. It was the perfect career path for him, being part of this corps would allow him to use all the skill sets his father had taught him.

Sapper Michaels attended the School of Military Engineering in Sydney and began his initial employment training as a Combat Engineer. Upon completion of his Combat Engineer course in August 1987, he was posted to the 2nd Combat Engineer Regiment in Brisbane.

As a Combat Engineer, Sarge belonged to the Royal Australian Engineers (RAE) Corps. RAE soldiers are known as, 'Sappers,' and were responsible for assisting their own forces to move, while at the same time denying mobility to the enemy. They were combat soldiers who held specialists in military field engineering, and held a very wide range of trade and technical skills; being trained in a broad range of tasks including wielding a chainsaw, bridge-building, clearing minefields, demolitions, field defences and road and airfield construction and repair. They were also highly skilled in using explosives to demolish a target.

Among other things, at different times during his military career, Sarge was called upon to assist in the construction of temporary roads, bypasses and fords, dig drains and construct culverts, erect bridges using both equipment and non-equipment components, construct and operate rafts and ferries, carry out concreting tasks, and construct field defences and wire obstacles.

He was experienced in laying, arming, neutralising, disarming, and removing mines and booby traps, conducting demolition tasks and producing potable water using water purification equipment. On top of this he could pretty well operate any field machine, boat or power tool imaginable.

Sarge saw extensive service in Iraq, East Timor, the Gulf War and Afghanistan. After paying off in 2008, he ended up back in Taswegia trying to start his own firewood cutting business.

To those who didn't know him, he seemed like a quiet, unassuming man, with not much to say. But Sarge didn't mind, he liked it that way.

It was Dick's farrier who'd originally introduced him to Sarge. Whilst home on one of his bouts of leave, Sarge needed a supply of wood to cut and a place to stay, and Dick and Patch needed someone to help them finish building the motel. There was still a lot of fencing, landscaping, clearing and general bush work that needed to be done. It was a natural progression for Sarge to end up with them, his skills had sure come in handy.

Not long after that the long treks kicked off, and Sarge offered to be backup driver. It was his job to prepare the campsite for the arrival of Dick and his customers, this often meant travelling through dense forest on small, and sometimes non-existent tracks. He was also happy to double as a tail guide whenever needed, as well as help with cattle musters and general work around the property.

The friendship between Sarge and Dick developed rapidly, they were a great team, as well as great mates, and the pair worked tirelessly at whatever had to be done.

Sarge was a single man, and he thought it was the best idea ever when they started training the guides, nearly all of the trainees were female and under twenty years old. This was right up Sarge's alley, and he proceeded to test them all out. By 'testing,' he didn't mean their horse-riding skills! He'd worked his way through to a guide whose name was Jan by the time the skinny local girl came onto the scene.

Fifteen-year-old Annie, who was an excellent horsewoman, took to Dick's training like a duck takes to water. She also took a shine to Sarge, but Dick was never certain whether this was initially because of the fun it would be to take him away from Jan or whether it was because of the feelings she had for the ex-Digger. Although there was a seventeen-year age difference, neither of them cared, it was obvious to everyone that this relationship was one that was going to last.

Eventually, after Annie's mother died, the pair settled down on her family farm at Twaddle. Her other siblings were happy for Sarge and Annie to pay them out, and the farm eventually became Sarge and Annie's place.

Chapter 11
Let's go Hunting

1000 Tuesday 6th January 2015 ... Dick and Patch Mann's property outside Twaddle.

"Was that hard or what mate!" said Jack with a sigh, thinking saying goodbye to April. He'd just realised that since they'd been married, he had never been apart from his wife, even for a single day.

"You're not Robinson Crusoe as far as that goes Mate!"

They backed the Hilux up to the workshop door and looked at the huge pile of camping gear that the pair had removed from the container, and that was now sitting in front of them.

"I think we're going to need a bigger ute!"

"Yeah Dick. Just wait till you see the stuff that's round at our place!"

The first step was to put the cage on the ute; this would help keep it all in place. Standing 900 mm off the tray it had a removable peak that went on top, and then the canvas canopy was added, covering the lot, and held down with shock cords. This kept everything protected from the elements. By the time they packed the trestle tables, the boxes of camping utensils, the twenty-man army tent, the toilet water containers, the sink, the camp ovens, a box of weapons, four boxes of ammo, the food boxes and Dick's double swag, the ute was starting to look pretty full. Then they added Dick and Patch's clothing and towels and toilet rolls.

"Bloody hell! I nearly forgot the whole reason for going to Hells Beach, the bloody brick phone!"

"I wonder how much stuff Sarge and Annie have," said Jack, amazed at just what the Hilux was able to hold.

"We'll do your place first Jack, if we have to go higher than the cage the canopy will hold it in place."

"Shit! We'd better not forget the RPG attachment and the grenades! I suggest we lay it all out in the workshop and load from there."

After cleaning out the cool boxes and freezer for lunch the boys spent the afternoon cleaning their weapons and reloading the 9 mm magazines.

"I'll leave the 50-Cal in the ute Dick, it's too big to lug around and no good up close."

"No problems Jack. What do you want to use?"

"I was thinking I'd take the pump action if that's okay."

Dick gave the thumbs up, saying he thought there were a couple of cartridge belts lying around somewhere, this would make things a lot easier than if they had to take a heap of loose shells. He realised he should have thought of that for Annie, although she should be okay ... as it was, she only had to get them out of the wither bags in front of her. Dick found the belts, and after loading twenty-five shells in each of them, he stored them in the cab of the ute, making sure that the six spare SLR magazines were in the glove box. Finished at last, they took some time to carefully go over the plan for the night, before heading over to the house for a quick bite to eat.

2100 Tuesday 6ᵗʰ January 2015 … Dick and Patch Mann's property outside Twaddle.

After dinner they cleaned up and locked up the house. They'd just started to move down the drive when Dick exclaimed in disgust, "I'm a bloody dickhead!"

After quickly reversing the ute up to the tip he jumped out and disappeared into the dark interior of the container. Jack scratched his head, not knowing what to think, or whether to fol ow him. What could he possibly have forgotten? As he sat there waiting, Jack realised that he felt nervous for the first time since leaving Pussers; well apart from the nerves he'd felt just before his wedding to April. The ex-CD thought through everything that could go wrong, then wished he hadn't done that … too many possibilities!

He could hear his mate rummaging around in the container. He figured they had more than enough weapons, maybe Dick had a tank hidden in there! He smiled to himself as he thought about April, by now they should be at Red Mountain. He wondered how she faired with the day's events, especially the ride, he was fully aware that she had never ridden anywhere near that distance before today. He was suddenly struck by the realisation that he hadn't ridden that sort of distance either!

Finally, Dick emerged from the gloom, with two camo bags dangling over his shoulder. "I knew they were in there somewhere!"

Jack smiled. "Why, you old dog! Of course! We're set now."

After putting on their night vision goggles (NVGs) they proceeded to move down the driveway again, but this time with the lights off. It seemed really strange to be driving with no lights, the roos they came across certainly did a double take. Jack wondered what they thought of it all. Looking at their native animals through NVG's was certainly different. The Old River Road was quiet, with the wind blowing in from the north they slowly made their way past a couple of farms to their left.

"Looks like there's someone in there," whispered Jack, looking out of the passenger side window. "There's smoke coming out of the chimney."

They were both glad of the NVG's. As they turned right onto the main road it was bloody obvious that all of the houses had people in them, smoke was coming out of just about every chimney.

"This is going to be a pain Jack. Too many chances of being seen by someone!"

"We might have to use the back-road Dick."

Nodding his head, Dick turned into the small lane that ran around the back of all the houses on the main road, they knew this would bring them out on Gum Tree Hill Road, which was where Jack and Sarge lived.

"Only two more properties to pass mate."

Dick turned left, driving through an open paddock gate, and cut across the paddock, then through the next farm gate and across the paddock opposite Jack and April's place.

"That was genius mate!"

"It's pretty obvious these people aren't farmers," observed Dick. "The old fellow would have had your balls for leaving a road gate open like that!"

After quietly reversing the Hilux into the garage they stacked the boxes of food, a bit of camping gear and the clothing on to the back. Dick stood back and surveyed their efforts. "I think we'll leave the barbeque Jack." They'd packed one already, and seeing as they were running out of room, they didn't really need a second one.

"We'll just take the gas bottle then." Dick gave Jack the thumbs up.

There was only one farm between Jack's and Sarge's places, they could see that it was lit up like a Christmas tree.

"They must have a bloody gen set Dick!"

The light pouring out of the front door made it difficult to be sure, but they thought they could make out two people standing there. With many of the houses around the area that wouldn't have caused an issue, however, in this case, with the front door only being six feet away from the road, they had big problems.

"What stupid bastard thought of building the house so close to the bloody road!" muttered Dick. Annie had told him that the house had originally belonged to her uncle, and that he'd later given it to his kids. God only knows what happened to them.

Dick brought the Hilux to a standstill some fifty yards from the house. It looked like they were cooking up a feed on the barbeque; one of them was obviously a trooper, carrying a weapon on his shoulder. Dick had been wondering whether the Alliance would simply deposit their people in the homes without protection; now he knew the answer to that one. It was obvious that every house would have a guard posted there to protect the new inhabitants. They could hear the gentle hum of a portable generator in the background. Jack pulled the .22 cut-down with the silencer out from under the seat. He'd taken it with him after they'd discovered Heidi and Steve's dead bodies. He figured the kid wouldn't need it anymore.

"Well done Jack!"

They quietly exited the vehicle and crept up to a huge pile of rubbish in the paddock alongside the front yard. There were old refrigerators, farm implements, building material, a kid's play set and an old swing. Both of them were thankful for the cover; they were literally only ten feet away from the pair standing in the doorway.

Dooff! Dooff!

Dick and Jack were on them before their bodies hit the ground. They quickly dragged them off to the left-hand side of the front door out of sight. With the adrenalin pumping hard, Dick motioned towards the inside of the house. Jack nodded, making his way in through the front door. With Dick covering him, they moved stealthily down the hallway towards the living room.

Dick had been in the house before and knew the layout well; the kitchen and living room were at the back of the house. Between them and the kitchen were the closed doors to the bedrooms. As he reached the entrance to the living room, Jack slid down to floor level and carefully peered around the corner. He turned toward Dick, holding two fingers up, then, after a quick look in the direction of the kitchen, turned and held up one finger, along with making a downwards motion with his other hand, indicating that this time he'd seen a third person in there; a child. There was no other way out; they had to do it! Jack moved left and turned ...

Dooff!

The child dropped to the floor. Turning again ...

Dooff!

He hit the mother square in the chest. The other person in the living room turned out to be an older child, a girl aged about fourteen years. Realising she was only a child, Jack was caught off guard and hesitated for a second as, without warning, she grabbed a kitchen knife and charged towards him.

Bang!

Dick let rip with the 9 mm browning, killing her instantly. Without stopping to think, they covered all the bedrooms in turn, just in case there were others.

"All clear mate," reported Jack. "Let's get out of here!"

They moved on to Sarge and Annie's place, thankful to find it was empty of invaders, and went over to the stables, where they knew their stuff was waiting. It was a strange feeling, knowing that, within a few days, Sarge and Annie's farm was going to be taken over by North Korean Nationals, living here, going through their possessions, and playing with their animals. Dick found himself wondering for a moment whether they ate horses in Korea! "Better not think too much about that," he thought to himself.

They loaded up the ute and made the return journey in silence; neither of them said a word until they were back on the Old River Road.

"That's a fucking bastard having to kill those kids Dick!" blurted Jack.

"Mate, they would have done us in at the drop of a hat." Dick felt the same, but it was no good dwelling on what had happened.

Reluctantly, Jack had to admit he was right, "I suppose."

Jack was still reeling from the action, it was okay to kill an enemy soldier, that made sense. Killing civilians was something new to him. He knew Dick would have had to deal with this while he'd been in Nam.

"Mate, how did you cope with having to kill women and children?"

"Simple mate. You can't think of them as people at that point, they're just the enemy!"

Jack understood what he meant, but he still didn't like it.

After resetting the booby trap, they parked the ute up behind the workshop.

"We'll sort the load out tomorrow Jack. Remind me not to forget to pack Patch's laptop, and all of the hard drives containing the backups. She'll kill me if I forget!"

It was nearly midnight. As he lay in his bed that night, Dick wondered how Patch was going. Hell! How all of them were going, and what danger they were all going to come across during the dangerous journey ahead of them. He could hear the heavy tread of a possum on the roof as it clumped its way from the back of the house to the front, and then waited for the usual *thud* as it jumped down on to the verandah, then scuttled off. He was going to miss this place! He didn't want to think too much about the fact that someone else might soon be living here, in the place he and Patch had called their own!

Jack was also lying awake, he missed April immensely. After a ride like the one she was on, boy was her butt going to be sore! He smiled to himself as he drifted off to sleep.

Wednesday 7ᵗʰ January 2015 ... Dick and Patch Mann's property outside Twaddle.

Bang! Clang! Bang! Clang, Clang, and Clang!
The awful commotion outside woke Dick out of a deep sleep. Jumping out of bed he rushed to the window, thinking a truck must have driven through the booby trap and set off the drums full of rocks and small tin cans.

He couldn't see anything from there, so, after grabbing the SLR he moved out onto the verandah, hearing Jack stumble out behind him. Realising it was too dark to see anything yet, Jack went back and grabbed the NVGs; passing one of them to Dick so that he could scan the area. The only movement out there was a couple of large kangaroos hopping past the corner of the house.

"Pew! They must have got tangled up in the trap for a moment ... could have been worse Jack!"

"You're not wrong mate! It's almost 0430. I don't think I could go back to sleep now, even if I wanted to. Do you want a brew?"

"A brew would be good. I'm the same Jack. You know, it's the first time in a long time that I've slept right through the night. Maybe I need to kill people more often."

They enjoyed a hearty breakfast, thanks to the efforts of Jack's chooks, accompanied by some of Annie's home-made bread, then, after firing up the generator for toilet flushes, the pair enjoyed a shower apiece.

Dick had been thinking. "Let's make up some canvas tarps Jack; I've got about thirty metres of camo canvas in stock still."

"What did you buy that for?"

"It was cheap. I've used it for saddle and tack bags in the past. It will be great for what I want to do with it."

Dick explained the idea he'd been dreaming about last night. As he often had in the past, he'd come up with the design as he slept. Each tarp would be 2.5 metres x 7.5 metres in size and would be made up of three smaller pieces sewn together. He planned to fold and eyelet the corners, reinforcing them with three greenhide triangles. The idea was to peg the end down near the edge of the double swag, then run it up two metres in height, and then horizontally so that it covered the swag area and basically created a form of tent, with a two-metre-high 'roof'. The roof could be held in place with ropes or folded over a spar.

"Four of these would use up the thirty metres or close to it, and if we go through the rest of what Patch and I have on the rack, we could make some simple screens, cut them at four metres, fold the top and bottom edge in 50 mm then bang some eyelets along each edge. Voila! No sewing! They're going to be perfect for Hells Beach."

The boys started making them up. The first job was to stand at either side of the cutting table and cut out all the components. The next part of the plan was for Jack to help get the screen on to the old Pearson sewing machine, and then for Dick to pedal like crazy as he sewed down the full length of the canvas. While he did that, Jack started folding and banging eyelets into the screens; they'd realised that they could also be used as walls, which would add a measure of privacy.

"It's a bloody long way down these joins Jack; especially when there's two runs to each join!"

"Yeah! Better you than me. That bloody thing looks like a bit of a beast!"

"Pity we couldn't fit it on the ute," said Dick, thinking about the possibilities.

Jack gave him one of those exasperated looks that needed no words.

"Just joking Jack! Joking! The thing weighs around 300 kilos."

The first tarp took forty-five minutes to sew.

"Lucky I'm not sewing all the way round mate ... we'd never get them finished!"

By the time they'd got to the fourth one, Dick had cut the time down to half an hour. After putting the last of the eyelets in they folded the canvas into as small a bundle as they could.

"There's a bloody lot of canvas here Dick!"

"I know," said Dick, massaging his overworked arm muscles. "I'm pretty sure everyone will appreciate what we've done."

Looking around his beloved workshop, Dick said with a sigh, "We'll take all the rope, some of the hand-sewing tools, as much leather as we can fit in, the saddlers clamps, scissors, knives, hammers, rivets, a box of knife blades and one box of cigarette lighters and whatever else we can fit in; you never know what we might have to repair or make."

They spent the rest of the day re-packing the Hilux; ending up deciding not to put the top on. The three double swags were laid flat on top, and then the canvas canopy went over the lot to hold it all on. The poles for the twenty-five-man army tent caused them some grief; in the end they punched some holes through the canvas along the side of the canopy where the cage was, so they could tie them on. Trying to get everything inside the canopy was a nightmare and some items had to be decanted from their boxes and packed in loose, but better to do that than to leave something behind.

"How do we get all the rope on Dick?"

"Mate, we'll have to take it all off the reels and stuff it in where we can. I want to take all of the laid rope, as well as all of the fids."

It was hard to work out exactly how many weapons and how much ammunition to take. There just wasn't enough room to take the lot, so in the end it came down to deciding what would be most useful to them. In the end they decided to take the 100 cartridges for the pump-action shotgun that Annie was carrying, a .22 rifle, a selection of machetes, and all the boning, skinning and hunting knives they could find. From Jack's original list they chose a .19 target rifle with two hundred rounds, a 9 mm pistol and a couple of boxes of ammo, the .45 pistol and fifty rounds that were already in the glove box of the Hilux, a .50 calibre sniper's rifle with ten rounds and various empty cases of mixed calibre, four bags of gunpowder and the reload press. Jack reminded him that the .243 deer rifle with 100 rounds had already gone with April.

From Dick's list they selected the two Bren guns with two boxes of .303 ammo, two SLR rifles with two boxes of 7.62 ammo, six Claymore mines, twelve high explosive grenades, the RPG attachment for the SLR, a box of dynamite, six 9 mm browning pistols with two hundred rounds, (everyone had been fitted out with these), one .22 rifle and fifty rounds, one cross bow and six bolts, a pump-action shotgun and fifty cartridges, two old .303 Lee Enfield rifles with ammo, a mixed bag of side arms, (most with no ammo), and fifty navy ration packs. The F1 sub machine gun with 100 rounds of 9 mm had already gone with Patch. On top of this arsenal, they had the silenced .22 sawn-off they'd acquired from up the road, so they were well-armed for such a small group of people. After re-organising the load more than once, they eventually fitted them all in. Some were behind the seat, and there was ammo on the floor and on the seat between them, but they managed it in the end. Standing back, they looked at the overladen vehicle.

"She's a bit low in the arse end Dick!"

"I reckon we can fix that!"

Dick grabbed three twenty-five litre plastic jerry cans, filled them with water and strapped them, along with Sarge's chainsaw fuel, to the bull bar. This successfully added more weight to the front of the vehicle, evening it up.

"I reckon that's about an extra hundred kilos Dick; looks better already!"

They couldn't be certain that they had enough fuel to get them to Barracouta, so they decided to go back up to Steve and Heidi's, just in case one of the thirty odd vehicles up there had a little bit of diesel left in it. They also had to honour Dick's promise to Patch to make sure they buried their poor neighbours before they left. Most of the vehicles used petrol, but in the end, they managed to get a five-litre can of the liquid gold out of an old BMW that Steve had driven for a while. The once loved vehicle now stood abandoned, covered in dust and junk; but the extra five litres it had given them would keep Sarge happy and it would add to his chainsaw fuel.

Digging a grave is not the nicest way to spend the afternoon but a promise was a promise. Once the deed had been done, Jack headed off along the track to the other end of the property, on a search for more fuel, while Dick continued to check the remaining three or four vehicles. There was only one diesel; an old Peugeot but it was empty of fuel.

There was a distant yell from Jack, who was running back down the track. "Dick, I've found some!"

"Great mate! What did you find?"

"An old backhoe. It looks like it's been broken down for years, but it's definitely got fuel in it!" It was a great find, yielding almost twenty extra litres. Dick was happy. "This will do just great! Now I can guarantee we'll make it all the way, at least we won't run out of juice."

They carefully poured it all into the Hilux, ending up with a little bit over half a tank again.

"I reckon we should eat around 1900 Jack, then leave around 2000."

"That gives us time for one last shower Dick."

"Too bloody right Jack! This time we won't flush the toilets! That will leave a welcoming odour for the new home-owners when they decide to move in."

Chapter 12

Anne Palmer (Annie)

Annie, who was to become Sarge's partner later in life, was born in 1987, and grew up on the family farm in Twaddle. Her father, Rod Palmer, was a prominent Lakeside bank manager. He was ten years older than his wife Anne and was a workaholic. After suffering a heart attack, he passed away at the age of 42. Her mother, Anne Palmer, pretty well raised their three children on her own following Rod's death. At that time, Annie's older sister Mary was ten years old, her brother Graeme was eight, and Annie was only six.

Anne did her best to try and give the kids a normal upbringing, unfortunately Mary ended up married to a drug dealer and both eventually ended up in gaol; their kids were looked after within the government welfare system, but nobody knew what had happened to them. Graeme left home at an early age, the last thing they heard was that he was living in outback Queensland with some local girl, bringing up a tribe of kids.

Annie was different, for the young girl, life was all about one thing, horses! Sure, she willingly helped her mother out on the farm, milking cows and taking on most of the chores that needed doing, but apart from that all she cared about was her horses. She was a great horsewoman, and Mary was pretty good too, Anne knew that, and whenever her girls wanted to show horses or enter competitions, she would move heaven and earth to make it happen.

They were always looked down on by other competitors because they couldn't afford the best saddle or the latest equine fashions in clothing. Anne did her best, being handy at the sewing machine, she was able to convert second-hand clothing bought at Vinnies into riding jackets, and she used to make the girls' jodhpurs herself. They couldn't afford riding boots, so instead rode in Blundstone boots, but they didn't mind. At least they were riding! Plus, they had one distinct advantage over many others, they could really ride! The more sophisticated riders, with their fashionable and expensive horse attire would point at them and laugh behind their backs whenever they'd turn up at the local shows in their tatty old saddles and handmade hacking clothes, they were the constant butt of many a joke. That was until they mounted up, after that the jaws did drop! In essence, they would simply beat everyone else, winning pretty well every event they entered. Whatever event or show they went to, on the return journey the car would be filled with blue ribbons.

Graeme, on the other hand, was at his happiest whenever his head was under a bonnet or inside an engine, he was constantly stripping down machinery on the farm to see how it worked. At the age of seventeen he scored an apprenticeship in Kings Town as an apprentice mechanic; he stuck it out for a while but was never really happy about having to work in the city. All he really wanted to do was stay on the farm and play with engines. They say that there is not much difference between brilliance and insanity; well Graeme was a great example of this. He had been known to get home from work, pull the engine out of his Holden

Torana, pull the head off, pull the cams out, replace them with different cams, and put the whole thing back together again, all before bedtime. He'd test the car out on the way to and from work the next day and if he didn't like the results, he'd do it all again the next night.

Annie attended Lakeside High School. The highlight of her first year there was when she attended a school camp at Dick and Patch's Motel in the Wilderness. In 2002, after Dick advertised the guides course again, Annie fronted up and announced that she wanted to take part. Dick wasn't so sure, the participants were supposed to be over eighteen years of age, and she was far too young. He turned down her application, thinking that would be the end of it. Well, he hadn't reckoned on the girl's stubbornness and determination! She used to ride her horse out from Twaddle to the motel most mornings, (most of the time bareback), and hang around helping to tack up, groom and feed the horses. Dick finally gave in and allowed her to do the course, setting up an arrangement for her to pay the fees back out of her earnings after she qualified.

This pleased Sarge no end; it meant he had another guide to potentially add to his list of conquests. Jan put up a strong fight to try and hang onto him but eventually Annie won. She saw the battle for his attention as a competition, much like any horse show and she loved to win! She put in the hours, just as she did when training a horse, and once she had the blue ribbon in her sights she went for the kill!

Annie went on to become one of their best guides, even in the early days the young girl was good with all the customers. There was a lot going on in Annie's life that she couldn't control, with her brother doing a runner, and her sister married to a criminal. To be able to achieve her dream and work with horses made all the difference. Mind you, there were quite a few nights when she'd have a little cry on Dick's shoulder as he drove her home after a ride; he filled the father-shaped hole in her life that had been empty for so long.

Annie worked for Dick and Patch in the trekking company from 2002 right up until the business folded. During the treks he would be in the lead, while Annie rode tail and Sarge drove the backup vehicle; they were the perfect team pretty much of all the longer rides from 2004 through to 2012. She enjoyed riding all of Dick and Patch's horses, and would occasionally bring along Chief, her own aging Quarter Horse. She had an infectious laugh and a warm smile, and the guests loved her.

Built like a rake, Annie never ate much; Dick reckoned that all he'd ever seen her eat were a type of sugar-laden cereal called Fruit Loops, which she'd cover with milk powder and drown in hot water; wherever possible she would eat this for breakfast, lunch and dinner! Even out on the treks, being not much of a meat lover, she would pass on the standard meal, instead opting for her favourite Fruit Loops. Despite her lack of a balanced diet, Annie never seemed to lack in energy. She was a hard worker, and rarely complained, doing pretty well any job that Dick asked her to do. Every now and then she would even ride solo for some of the smaller day rides, and she and Sarge could handle some of the overnighters on their own, provided the numbers were small. Mind you, this didn't always work, with Sarge tending to pay more attention to Annie than he did to the guests.

Early on, there had been one camp that could have brought them all undone. It was a holiday camp, the punters were mostly town kids wanting to get away from their parents for the holidays. Dick tended to think it was probably more likely that the parents were wanting to get the kids out of their hair for five days at a time during the school holidays. For the first time ever, Dick and

Patch decided to give the guides more responsibility than they usually did with this camp, leaving it up to Annie and Jan to plan the rides, organise the out-of-hours activities and supervise the kids. Annie, at sixteen years old, and Jan, at eighteen, weren't much older than the kids, so they should have realised it was potentially a disaster waiting to happen!

Unbeknownst to her parents, Tiffany, one of the younger camp kids, had bought along a can of beer, and decided to share it with a couple of her fellow campers during a bush walk. Then, to add to the situation, ignoring the rules completely, Jan decided to offer the younger kids a smoke. The kids, of course, thought that was great! For some reason, Tiffany decided to phone her mother that evening, and ended up telling her what was going on. Her mother, an overbearing, over-indulgent woman, who'd pampered the kid rotten all of her life, drove up to the motel at first light and demanded to see the owners.

Until that point, Dick and Patch were completely unaware of what had been going on, and were shocked when they heard about the cigarettes, beer, and other sordid goings on. Kids and guides alike denied it all when they questioned them, except for when they called in a boy called Peter, who'd never been able to lie without getting caught. Peter spilled the beans and told all, and Tiffany's mother threatened to call in the authorities; only backing down for a moment, when Peter had told them, in front of her, that it was Tiffany herself who'd supplied the beer. The mother wasn't going to have a bar of that, she kept carrying on with her threats until Dick produced the empty beer can. It was an unusual brand, not available in most parts of Taswegia, and it just happened to be Tiffany's father's favourite beer! That was a close call indeed!

After a while, Annie moved into Sarge's room at the motel, only going home to feed the animals and to see her mother. Her brother was still working in Kings Town and her sister was off with the drug dealer.

Nobody realised for a long time that Annie's mother Anne wasn't well, she didn't want to worry anyone, and with no kids living at home she managed to hide her illness for quite a while. Around the time that Graeme left Taswegia for the mainland, and Mary was locked up for the first time, her condition became much worse; possibly because of the stress. Too late, Annie realised how ill her mother was, and begged her to visit her doctor. The diagnosis was cancer, and poor Anne passed away not long after that.

Annie and Sarge moved into the farmhouse back in Twaddle in 2010. It was then that Sarge kickstarted his firewood business, while still helping on the treks with Annie whenever they were needed.

Chapter 13
Fred Webb's Hut

Wednesday 7th January 2015 ... Red Mountain.

Patch woke April at 2350, just in time for the French woman's turn at watch- keeping. Handing her a hot coffee, she said sleepily, "Here you go love ... something to wake you up!"

Crawling into her swag, Patch fell asleep before her head even hit the pillow.

Sarge, who'd been dreaming of better times, slowly emerged from a deep sleep. Opening his eyes, he could smell the familiar scents of a burning campfire, combined with a little whiff of eucalyptus and the dirt he had disturbed when he'd put the fire screen up the night before. He was warm in his swag, the only thing missing was the heat from Annie's body. They'd have to make do with singles until everyone regrouped at Hells Beach. He couldn't wait!

One of the problems with waking up in the middle of the night is your bladder tells your brain you need to empty it. Sarge had no idea what time it was, he'd left his wristwatch with Patch when she'd started her watch. He couldn't make up his mind about whether he should just roll over and try to get back to sleep, or maybe get up and relieve the tension in his bladder. Listening carefully, he could hear the others sleeping. Every now and then Annie would make the funny little whimper she'd always made as she slept, and he could hear Patch snoring away. Dick had always reckoned that his wife was a loud snorer; he could certainly detect that right now.

Rolling over in his swag, Sarge was suddenly wide awake. He let out an angry yell.

"WAKE UP APRIL!"

He wasn't in the mood for being polite!

"You'll get us all killed, you stupid bitch!"

As he'd rolled over, the first thing he'd seen was April, supposedly on watch, sound asleep, propped up against the wind break.

"Sorry!" the French woman blurted out, obviously upset at the ex-Sapper's blunt remark. "I didn't do it on purpose," she added tearfully.

Sarge picked up his wristwatch, realising it was already 0435.

"Fuck that tears it!"

Annie was stirring. "What's all the noise?"

"Nothing much," snapped Sarge. "We just need to be saddled up ready to go in twenty-five minutes!"

By now the commotion had woken Patch up.

"What time is it Sarge?"

"Don't ask Patch!"

April started to cry. Sobbing, she said that she'd never had to keep watch before in her life. Sarge ignored her completely.

Within twenty minutes the group had packed up the camp and saddled the horses. Patch dished out the cold breakfast.

"Not much this morning ladies and gent, just cold sausages, hard boiled eggs and muesli bars washed down with some good old H2O. Enjoy!"

April was quiet, they all knew how lousy she must have been feeling. As they started off down the trail Patch looked at Annie, nodding her head towards the French woman, hoping that maybe Annie would say something to April. Normally she would have broken the ice, but she didn't want to upset Sarge any further. Annie got the hint.

"Hey April. Don't worry about what happened last night, it could happen to any of us. Anyway, I'll cover you tonight seeing as I didn't get to keep a watch last night."

April gave the younger girl a shaky smile.

Moving up alongside of April, Patch gave her a hug. Turning towards Sarge, Patch and Annie both looked at him with that 'WELL???' look.

"All right. I give up! Sorry I went crook at you April."

"That's okay Sarge. It won't happen again!"

After following the track for around three kilometres along the top of Red Mountain, the group started to pick their way down the other side. In the dawn light the view over the Meed-Stead Valley was absolutely stunning.

As they rounded a sharp corner not far down from the beginning of the downhill descent, Annie, who was riding lead again, was confronted with what looked like a huge crater, which had been gouged into the side of the mountain. There was debris everywhere.

"Hey! Look at this!"

The group were stunned at the sight, it took a few minutes to work out what they were looking at. Sarge broke the silence.

"Looks like a plane wreck. It obviously fell out of the sky when the E1 hit, given the time of day that happened, and the type of debris it must have been a freight plane. They would have been the only planes flying at that time around here."

"That sounds about right Sarge. I remember Dick explaining the flight path to me, it used to take the planes straight over Red Mountain and right over the motel."

At the point where the plane had impacted with the mountain, the track had pretty well disintegrated, making it difficult to negotiate. Annie decided to take to the bush, starting off around a small stand of wattle trees.

The track eventually widened, and Sarge moved up into the middle of the group.

"Okay. Here's the heads up for today people!"

Annie looked at him. "What's this 'people' shit?"

"Sorry! Thought I was back in the army for a minute."

He went on to explain that within the next hour they would be crossing the main East Coast Highway at Meed-Stead, and this was where they could possibly run into trouble.

"The fire station and house are right on the road, so this is how I want us to proceed. Annie should be about one hundred metres out in front, leading the way. Then April needs to go next, leading Cowboy and then Patch with Bob. I'll tie the leads to the crupper bars on your saddles; that way you'll both have one hand free. If you need to, you'll be able to use that hand to shoot."

Ignoring their startled looks he kept going. "I'll be five hundred metres behind Patch, that way I can keep an eye on things. When you cross the highway, move to the left of the shearing shed that's there. This will mean it will be between you and the fire station; if it all turns to shit, take off up the paddock in a zig-zag pattern to make it harder for them to hit you. You know the way Annie, right up to the lone tree and across to the forestry gate. Don't look back under any circumstances ... I WILL catch up! Oh, and Annie, do NOT come back looking for me this time!"

"But I was worried about you Sarge!" said Annie defensively.

"Not this time Annie! We have too much riding on getting through this section."

"Do you think there will be Alliance troops there Sarge?" asked April.

Annie and Patch both looked at the solidly built ex-Sapper, waiting for his answer.

"It would make sense to put an outpost at Meed-Stead, which is halfway between Soothe and Barracouta. The junction with the Woodford Road's the perfect place. If I was in charge, that's what I'd do."

As they moved off again, he added, "Make sure your weapons are fully loaded and check that the safety's on; if anyone needs a refresher now's the time to ask!"

It was just before 0630. As they approached the junction, they followed Sarge's directions to the letter, with Annie on Tom taking a good hundred metre lead. Crossing the road, she disappeared around the left side of the shearing shed. As she reappeared from behind the shed, April on Fannie followed, leading Cowboy; then came Patch on Zen leading Bob. Crossing the road in turn they did the same. Sarge held Socks back and waited a couple of minutes to see if anything would happen.

His theory turned out to be correct! As the last two girls rode into the open and started up the hill, two Alliance troops appeared from the fire station, fumbling with their weapons as they prepared to fire upon the unsuspecting trio of women.

'Shit! Patch and April are sitting ducks at that range!' Sarge had to think fast.

"*True Grit*", an old John Wayne movie came to mind. His favourite part had always been where John Wayne's character, Rooster Cogburn, put the reins in his mouth and spurred his horse into a gallop while simultaneously firing two navy colt dragoon pistols: one in each hand.

Sarge didn't have the dragoons, but he did have his SLR. Putting the rope reins in his mouth, he spurred old Socks into a gallop. He crossed the road in a matter of seconds. As Socks' iron clad shoes hit the bitumen, the troopers spun around, not knowing who to shoot at first. That was all Sarge needed.

Boom! Boom! Boom! Boom!

The two of them dropped to the ground.

Sarge pulled Socks up and quickly dismounted, dropping the reins over the fence post. Bursting into the fire station he startled another pair of troopers who were coming down the stairs, obviously woken up by the noise.

Boom! Boom!

The L1A1 self-loading rifle sent the full metal jacketed rounds out at a staggering 2,700ft. per second. As the smoke cleared, he ran up the steep stairway. All was clear there, so he made his way back outside again.

His heart raced as he crossed the forty metres between the station and the house next door. Glancing up the hill he could see that the others had almost reached the top. He wasn't sure whether Annie could see him or not, but he gave her the thumbs up just in case.

As he opened the door to the house, he could smell the pungent remains of Asian spices from whatever they'd cooked the night before.

"Probably a bloody stir fry." Being a, 'meat and taters' man, Sarge had never liked this style of cooking.

His military training coming back to him, he scanned the room, keeping the SLR at the shoulder position. All clear there, so he went onto the bedrooms, and then what seemed to be an office. The desk was covered with paperwork, and there were weapons and ammo all over the floor. As he moved towards the desk to check out what was on there, he caught something moving out of the corner of his eye.

Sarge spun around quickly, but whoever had been there had taken off down the stairs and out the front door. As he raced downstairs, he could hear a truck door slam, then "Shit! Shit!" Someone was trying to start the diesel engine in a hurry, obviously they didn't realise that with no pre-heat trying to start the old Bedford look alike would fail every time, especially with an old Bedford!

He had just enough time to get to the front of the cab.

Boom! Boom!

Dropping the ten-round magazine out, he quickly loaded another.

Socks was becoming more and more agitated by the minute, he was a long way from his mates, and he didn't like the loud noises one bit. Sarge mounted up after packing the empty magazine in the wither bags.

"I'm sure glad I dropped the reins over the fence Socks! If I hadn't you would have been long gone and I would have had to fucking walk!" The old gelding just whinnied in reply, eager to get going.

Sarge rode over to the Bedford, digging in the wither bags for a grenade. Pulling the pin, he threw it into the cab. Convincing Socks they had to get a move on wasn't an issue; all his horse wanted to do was to catch up with his mates!

Whoomph!

The Australian-made F1 grenade did its job well, annihilating the old truck. Its 4000 steel spheres and 62 grams of RDX compound and the 5.5 second fuse only just gave him time to get out of range.

Sarge stopped halfway up the hill and surveyed the carnage behind him; he was more interested in checking whether or not there were any more troops coming.

"Looks good Socks!" The old nag tugged on the reins impatiently, more interested in catching up with the others than staying there any longer.

Annie, April and Patch were waiting anxiously at the forestry gate.

"Are you all right Sarge?" yelled Annie, as he rode into earshot.

"I am now!"

Annie was just pleased to have him back in one piece. "I'm sure glad they didn't get a shot off in your direction!"

Pulling up to give Socks a breather, Sarge told them all what had happened. All three were shocked to hear how close they'd come to being fired on.

Patch was in shock. "Fuck! Oops, sorry! We didn't have a clue!"

With tears in her eyes, April said to him, "You deserve a big hug Sarge, for saving our lives!"

"Save the hugs for Fred Webb's hut," replied Sarge.

They stopped for a quick lunch about halfway along the top track between the gate and the start of the bullock trail. They boiled water in one billy for a brew and filled the other with saveloys; although the bread was very stale by now, the savs still tasted good … especially once they'd been covered with tomato sauce.

"Well that's the last of the savs!" declared Patch.

"Believe me, they went down really well. I was starving!" said April, licking the last of the sauce off her fingers.

"You all performed brilliantly," said Sarge. "You don't know how proud I am of all of you for sticking to the plan!" This was directed at Annie, and she knew it.

As she enjoyed her coffee, Patch brought up another subject, one that was most likely on April's mind as well.

"I wonder how Dick and Jack are going. By now I'm hoping they'll be on the boat and well on their way."

"If I know Dick, they should be doing okay!" declared Sarge, who'd also been wondering how the pair was going, he knew that they were even more likely to run into Alliance troops because of where they were headed.

"Are there any other bad spots we have to go through over the next four days Sarge?" asked April.

Turning his thoughts away from his good mate and Jack, Sarge thought about the route they were going to take over the coming days. He told the girls that he was pretty sure the next day should be fine, they'd be camping at Mount Morris, and still in State Forest.

The following day was going to be pretty easy as well, although he still had to decide where to camp that night. In happier times they would have pulled up at Bulldust Peak; sleeping in the shearer's hut which overlooked the river. The property overlooked the outskirts of Bulldust, the problem was that he was almost certain there would be troops at the property so camping there was out of the question. If they made good time, he was pretty sure they'd be able to push on over the river and then skirt around the next farm; that way they could camp in the State Forest again. This would effectively shorten the next day, but it was a safer option.

They had choices as far as the short day went. They'd originally been going to camp on top of Willy Sugarloaf, then travel down the old bullock track through the remote shack area of Willy, before making the last push onto Hells Beach.

The bullock trail zig-zagged down some two hundred metres from the top track to the floor of the Pateena Valley. Back in the early 1900's it had been used to take the grain from the valley through to the flour mill at Meed-Stead, and you could still make out the rocks they'd used to line the pathway. The forest was old, with its overhead canopy entombing the track, protecting it from the outside world, as well as maintaining a constant temperature. It allowed just enough light in to make it passable. The ground was littered with gum leaves; over time the decaying leaves had destroyed all the weeds and small brush because of their acidic nature. This had left the forest floor quite open, and in places quite soft under foot wherever there was a build-up of leaves. Because very little sunlight could penetrate the canopy, the forest had a kind of dank smell to it, a little bit like when you leave something wet lying around.

With no signs of modern life, it was almost as if they had travelled back in time; their surroundings looked the same as they would have done back in 1905. The only sounds were the pant of horse breath, the call of the birds, the subtle tinkling of the hobbles in the saddlebags, and the occasional clatter of hooves as they hit old, hardened rocks.

Some of the horses weren't particularly enjoying the descent, especially Cowboy and Bob. Because both of them were being held closer to their lead horses than they would have liked, they were a bit uneasy on the loose leaves and shale rock. Sarge had been keeping an eye on them from the back, and realising what was happening, rode up alongside Bob. Reaching over, he unclipped the 16-hand Waler; and after doing the same to Cowboy he told the group, "They'll find it better now they can pick their own way down."

"Clever dick," muttered Annie, wishing she'd thought of it.

"Well, you're partly right," smiled Sarge. "It was Dick that taught me that."

They reached the bottom to find Bob and Cowboy patiently waiting as they munched on the green grass. From there they only had a four kilometre ride up the valley to reach the hut; Annie and Sarge weren't worried because they'd done it many times before. However, they were both aware of the toll that the mammoth ride was taking on the others, they'd ridden some fifty kilometres since camping on top of Red Mountain.

Fred Webb's hut had been built at the turn of last century. It consisted of four rooms, although only the two front ones were really useable. Dick and Sarge had built a brick barbeque in the front right-hand side room, the other had been used for those who preferred to sleep inside instead of spending the night outside under the stars. Fred Webb had built the hut, which was home to him and his wife and children. Fred was a contract thresher who, along with some of the other residents from the valley, operated a huge steam-driven threshing machine, which threshed the wheat that they grew in the valley. The grain was then bagged up ready to be sent to Meed-Stead.

The walls of the hut were hand-split hardwood frames covered with rough-sawn boards. The bare boards were then lined with newspaper for insulation, and then finished off by pasting wallpaper over the top. During the treks, Dick used to encourage the clients to take some time to read some of the articles out of the 1905 *Courier Mail* which still adorned the walls. It was amazing after so many years of neglect, that the print, although a bit faded in places, was still reasonably legible! The grass around the hut was very green and lush, so the horses were happy, very happy!

"With the hobbles on, I don't reckon they'll stray too far tonight," declared Annie. "How about I groom them all, while someone else cooks the tucker!"

April and Patch were more than happy to do the cooking. After thinking about what they had with them in the way of food, they announced that tonight's menu would be fresh veggies and reheated roast pork, washed down with a good cup of coffee! Despite the miserable start to her day, April was feeling a lot better by now. As they waited for the dinner to cook, the French woman went over and gave Sarge a peck on his stubbled cheek, and a hug.

"Thank you for what you did and said today Sarge. I promise I'll never fall asleep again when I'm on watch. Ever!"

Sarge blushed a little bit, not used to this kind of attention from April. Not wanting to miss out, Annie jumped onto his lap, declaring,"My turn!"

Patch was the last to give him a grateful hug, whispering as she did,"Dick would be proud of you mate!"

Annie went outside to tend to the horses, and Patch and April turned their attention to the chow, leaving Sarge on his own, thinking over the events of the day. His thoughts wandered back to times past, remembering the time when they'd taken the pupils from a prominent Kings Town boys' school on a trek. It had been part of the optional horse-riding stream; which participants could choose to undertake during the, *Duke of Edinburgh Awards* program. Those who chose it were first taught how to ride at a riding school south of Kings Town, and then tackled a three-day trek with Dick. If they survived that trek, they had to come back the following year and complete a four-day trek, and later on, a five-day trek. Their final task was to plan and lead a trek themselves. Dick always made sure either he or some of his staff tagged along with them to keep an eye on things, and to make sure they didn't come unstuck.

"Good times!" he said to himself, as Annie came back into the hut, happy that the horses were settled for the night.

"Watch keeping! Annie you take the first watch up to 0100. Patch, you'll be next till 0300, then I'll take over till we leave at 0600. Looks like you get a sleep-in tomorrow."

Chapter 14

Barracouta Here We Come!

Dinner for Dick and Jack consisted of a leg of lamb they'd found up the road in Heidi's freezer, roast spuds, zucchini and carrots out of Jack and April's garden. They washed it all down with a couple of wines which Jack had retrieved from his cellar.

Jack packed up the leftovers.

"I reckon these will be good for a snack to eat on the way Dick."

Both of them were kitted out in navy cargo trousers, black Mongrel boots, dark shirts, navy issue woolly pully's and a beanie; with the addition of the 9 mm in its webbing holster and belt they looked like a pair of covert operatives.

Even though they were in the Hilux, it was no simple task for Dick to work his way up through Steve and Heidi's farm and into the State Forest. With Jack keeping an eye out for smaller obstacles, he had to negotiate carefully around all the wrecks that Steve had left scattered around the place; it was a challenge at times, but they got through eventually. After heading to the back of the block and up the fire break they turned left, finally coming out into the State Forest. It would have been an easier drive if they'd taken the Old River Road, but they'd decided not to take the risk, figuring that by now at least some of the ten homes along that road would have been occupied by the enemy.

As they drove, Jack kept a constant eye out for any sign of trouble, with his SLR at the ready. Dick headed south first, under the towering presence of Poultry Hill, cutting left and then through the Myrtle Valley. The sky was clear of clouds that night, the moonlight meant they didn't need to use the NVG's.

Approaching a couple of small-holding weekenders, Dick slowed the ute down to a crawl, there were signs that both of them were occupied, and he let out a long sigh of relief once they were clear. After coming out on to the Old River Road they only had to pass two farms. No problems with the first one, they knew it was well-hidden from the road by huge pine trees. However, the second one would have a full view of the road.

Dick opted to cut the motor as they got close and allow the Hilux to coast past the second farm and down the hill. After crossing the Woodford Road, they emerged onto the M-road, this was a logging road, named using the same principle as the D-road system.

Both of them were glad of the opportunity to be able to relax for a while.

"Tell me about this boat Dick."

"The old fella that owned it used to fish with my old man. I first met him when I was a boy, he'd fished out of Barracouta all his life, and when I came across him, he was onto his second boat. He'd inherited his first boat from his old man, the one he was using when I met him was an old twenty-nine-foot carvel planked boat. There was no wheelhouse to speak of, just a wheel and an engine hatch down aft. Up forward there was a hatch to the forecastle, a tiny galley and a couple of bunks. Oh, and a wet well amidships.

"About twenty years ago, he had this boat built, it was a thirty-six-footer, made out of Huon Pine, and had an aft wheelhouse and a wet well. I remember there was a galley and a day-bunk in the wheelhouse, and a forecastle with four bunks in it. He was mainly fishing for crayfish, I know he held a forty-pot licence. Back when he paid for his, they were a darn sight cheaper than they are now, these days a pot licence will set you back around $40,000 for each pot!"

"Holy shit Dick! That's a lot of money!"

"Sure is! It means each pot has to make good money, although after forty years of fishing I dare say he would have been doing well in that department."

"What's a wet well?"

"It's a section of the hull that's blocked off from the rest of the boat, holes are drilled in the bottom to let it fill up with water. They keep the fish alive in there. It's a lot less costly than using holding tanks, which need water pumps in order to agitate the water. With the wet wells the sea does that naturally."

Dick went on to explain to Jack that, as part of the E1 modifications, all boats, both commercial and pleasure, had to comply. The only difference between boats and cars was that there was no buy-back scheme for boats. This had been tough on the old timers, and a lot of them simply could not afford it.

"Old Barry complied with the new power-plant by putting a modified main engine in, it was pretty much all he could afford. He simply, 'forgot' to tell the authorities that the *Cecil Jane* had an auxiliary. He knew he could disguise this by the fact that it was an inline motor that the drive shaft went through. Under the cowling it just looked like it was part of the gearbox. To make sure he'd get away with it, he put two new tanks in; one marked, 'fuel' (that fed the main engine), and the other marked, 'water' (that one fed the auxiliary). All you have to do is turn on the cock behind the tank."

Dick laughed, thinking how good it must have felt to the old man to have secretly defied the authorities.

"To the uninitiated it would look like it's just a water supply to the heads and showers."

"And you think this fishing boat will still be intact?"

"I guess time will tell Jack. Let's hope so! If it's no good, we'll have to find some other vessel. It's an awfully long swim to Hells Beach!"

As they travelled the fifteen kilometres of gravel road, they saw pretty well every form of wildlife imaginable; kangaroos, wombats, possums, devils, quolls, wallabies and owls. Coming to the end of the road, they turned right onto the sealed road to Bulldust, and made their way to within two kilometres of the first farm on that part of the road.

"It's lights off I reckon Jack!"

They steered the Hilux gingerly past the farm, across the little bridge, around a sweeping bend and into Bulldust. Driving with no lights had an eerie feeling, even though the NVG's helped, it still seemed strange.

They hit the first problem as they approached the main east coast highway; literally running over someone who'd been walking along the road. Obviously, they couldn't see Dick and Jack approaching, and didn't hear them until it was too late!

Bloop! Bloop!

At a speed of around twenty kilometres per hour, they ran right over him!

Hoping it wouldn't draw too much attention to themselves, Dick accelerated over the main bridge and quickly drove past the half-dozen houses in the main street of Bulldust.

"There's only one last house coming up on the left Jack!"

"Thank fuck for that Dick! My heart is racing like crazy!"

Dick knew there were no more properties for about the next ten kilometres, so he switched the lights back on and gunned the old Hilux; she was behaving quite well considering the load she had on the back.

So far so good! They were able to relax for now, but they knew their luck had to run out eventually.

As Dick had outlined to the group when he'd first mentioned his hair-brained scheme, the problem area was going to be between Bulldust and Oxford. This was where the road narrowed, following the Oxford River, there was absolutely nowhere to hide, with a sheer cliff on the right and a steep drop to the river on the left.

They were only a couple of clicks in when they saw the lights of a large vehicle coming towards them.

"Holy shit Dick! What are we going to do?"

Thinking fast, Dick answered,

"If they slow down Jack, we'll pull up alongside of them and open up with everything we have! You get ready to take the back of the truck and I'll do the cab."

Quickly pausing the ute, he retrieved the pump action from under the seat and put the 9 mm on his lap; moving forward again they slowly approached the moving truck.

As they drew closer, they could just make out someone riding on the running board, and realised he was flagging them down.

"Here goes nothing Jack!"

As they pulled up level with the cab of the truck, they realised that the person on the running board was dressed as an officer. The moment Dick stopped the ute, Jack flew out the door, firing the shotgun as he ran. Dick shot the officer first, and then the driver; while, with five more blasts Jack made quick work of the four troopers who'd been sitting in the back under the canopy.

After moving the Hilux just past the truck, Dick left it idling while they went to check out their options. They realised that the wire fence that was stopping vehicles from going into the river had finished just before the spot where they'd pulled up. After starting the truck, they wedged the accelerator with a stone while depressing the clutch with a stick and reached in to put it in gear. As soon as they released the clutch the truck moved forward, lurching over the bank and down the cliff into the river.

"If we run into any more trouble, I think we'll do the same thing!"

Dick was feeling somewhat overwhelmed with what they had just done.

"Are you okay Jack?"

"I'm still shaking, but I'll be all right. We're lucky the fence ended there; otherwise we'd never have been able to get the truck into the river!"

"You're not wrong mate," added Dick. "We're also, lucky the river is deep enough in that spot to hide the evidence! Mind you, for a minute there I wasn't sure whether or not to just gun it and keep going. They would have had a lot of trouble turning around in that tight space."

"Doesn't matter, it's done now Dick. I think we did the best thing. After all, we need to get some payback for the carnage they've been causing!"

They continued on towards Oxford, realising that things were going to get a lot hotter. They had plenty of houses to get past and a major bridge over the Oxford River to cross, then they had to drive right down the middle of what was normally a busy seaside town, passing the pub, the golf club and the Returned Serviceman's League along the way.

"Mate, I reckon we've got two choices. We can go in with our lights on, acting like we're meant to be there; just like the truck we just ditched. Thinking about it, I bet they thought we were one of their vehicles. With the canopy on the back we'd look a little bit like a Second World War jeep ... at least in the dark we might fool them! Or ... we can move slowly and stealthily using the NVG's and no lights."

"We're probably more likely to draw attention to ourselves if we go with no lights Dick. After all, it's not normal to travel around with your lights off unless you're up to no good."

"I tend to agree with you Jack. If we just drive through the town at the normal speed, we might just get away with it!"

Dick was thinking that if it worked here in Oxford, they'd do the same when they got to Barracouta.

"First house is coming up on the right Dick!"

Slowing the Hilux back to fifty kilometres per hour, Dick drove to the bridge, then turned left and continued on past the pub.

Jack whispered urgently, "Troops to the right Dick!"

The two men slouched down in their seats, with Dick especially trying to hide his height. Just as they passed the pub, the front doors opened, and a large group of men started spilling out on to the street.

"Hah! Looks like they have kick-out time as well," muttered Jack. "Hopefully, they'll be half blinded by the light from inside and our headlights as well!"

Someone called out to the pair, but not knowing what the hell they'd said, Dick just gave a little wave and kept moving. After passing the RSL and the golf club, the houses started to thin out a bit more.

"There's the turn off to Rascals Beach on the right, and one last house on the left Jack. Most of them seem to be occupied; there's been plenty of smoke coming from the chimneys. So far, so good, but don't let your guard down!"

"How much further do we have to drive before we get to the boat Dick?"

"Instead of taking the turn into Barracouta, I'm going to continue on past, then turn right and sort of scout around the town. The marina will be on our right; then just over the bridge we'll turn right again. From memory we'll be passing more boats and loading ramps, then another private marina. After that we should come to a little dirt track which runs down to a wooden jetty. There's usually a couple of fishing boats tied up there. I reckon we've got about twenty kilometres to go."

This part went off without a hitch, but when they got to the marina, they discovered that things weren't as Dick had hoped they'd be. What a bloody mess! Obviously once the Alliance had finished extracting the fuel from the vessels they must have tossed in a grenade or two; every single one of them was sitting on the bottom!

"Shit! Let's hope they didn't find Barry's boat!"

The private marina was usually kept locked up and secure behind a huge sliding steel gate, but as they approached, they could see the gate was open. A fuel retrieval truck was parked on the ramp, and they could just make out a number of hoses which were snaking out of sight on to one of the forty-foot Rivieras.

"What a fucking waste Jack!" said Dick in disgust. "Look at all those boats! There must have been two hundred vessels in this marina alone. Most of the squid boats are gone; they would most likely have been out fishing when the E1 hit. Looks like quite a few cray boats are out too, but most of the pleasure boats are still alongside, all of them useless, with their engines fucked! Makes you want to cry!"

"It doesn't sound like anyone's about Dick, maybe the Slopes have knocked off for the night."

Looking around, Dick realised that the Alliance was only targeting pleasure boats for destruction. All the commercial boats were left intact.

He pulled the Hilux up alongside the old wooden jetty around midnight, giving a bit of a shiver as he felt the chilly night breeze touch his face. To their relief it seemed that no-one had ventured this far along; the two boats tied up alongside were still in one piece. Barry's, which had obviously not been used for some time, was closest to the shore on the far side of the jetty, the other was a larger fishing boat which had that, 'I'm still working,' look about it. At least it would have been working up until the E1 had hit.

"Hey Jack! At least its sitting on the outside, it would have been a real pain if it had been on the inside of the jetty."

Dick was wondering what happened to all those fishing boats that had been out working at the time the E1 had hit. By his reckoning there were at least eight squid boats missing; they would have gone out to the continental shelf, and at the early hour of 0230 would have been right in the middle of their fishing run.

From what he remembered, it appeared nine or ten cray boats were missing. There was no way of working out what had happened to the crews, or whether they were maybe still floating adrift with no means to move apart from the currents. They wouldn't have been able to use the outboards on the tenders either, the only other thing they could have done was to try and row, and the shelf was just too far out for that.

Chapter 15
Mount Morris

Thursday 8th January 2015 ... Fred Webb's Hut, Pateena Valley. Through Sarge's eyes ...

Annie kept watch as the others slowly drifted off to sleep. For a while she sat alongside my swag, caressing my shaved head, it didn't take me long to drift off into sleep. She looked around at the familiar surroundings, conjuring up fond memories of her and I sleeping in our double swag during the treks. She smiled as she remembered my hardness as I entered her, and how she'd had to try and stifle her cries of pleasure so as not to wake the other sleepers. She allowed her thoughts to drift for a while, sifting through some of the hundreds of memories of the good times during her short but full-on career as a horseback tour guide.

She'd loved working for Dick and Patch, who were like second parents to her. After her mother had passed away, she'd come to appreciate their support and friendship more than ever. Annie knew she wasn't the easiest person to live with, she was known as a bit of a hard nut, and at times had to be brought back into line by Dick. She knew she'd been far too young to apply to be a guide. She had never forgotten that Dick had broken all the rules when he took her on board; her love and respect for Dick were beyond measure.

Annie shook Patch awake just before 0100. "Billy's hot Patch."

She gave the older woman a hug and said good night. Smiling to herself, Patch thought, "I'm never going to work that girl out!"

Patch couldn't help wondering what was happening to Dick, she was pretty sure he was okay, because if anything did wrong, she felt certain she would sense it. She tried to imagine where the pair of ex-divers might be and what they would be doing. She was missing him a lot right now; and as she thought about the great bear of a man that she'd fallen in love with, all those years ago on a beach, a little tear crept down her cheek and dripped into her coffee. "No time for crying," she reminded herself, thinking how ironic it was that they were all going to end up on a beach in just a few days.

Getting to her feet, Patch went outside to check on the horses. All was quiet there, their heads were down as they devoured the lush pasture without a care in the world.

"Better make the most of it," she said out loud, not sure whether there was going to be anything at all like this once they got to Hells Beach.

I must have slept like a log, waking to a gentle touch on my shoulder. Just for second, I thought it was Annie, and that I hadn't been asleep at all, but as I opened my eyes properly, I realised it was Patch.

"Morning Sarge. It's 0315. Sorry I forgot the time, I was thinking of other things."

"Hey, no problem Patch. You got Dick on your mind?"

"Who else would it be Sarge."

After an uneventful watch I woke everyone at 0600, reminding them that the day's ride was a relatively short one. We only had to go forty kilometres so we could afford a slower start.

"You'll get no arguments from me!" declared April, ruefully rubbing her sore butt. "I don't know what's worse, my back because of that damn swag, or my butt from the saddle! How do you do it day in and day out Annie?"

The young girl reckoned that you just got used to it. Mind you, she was only guessing. Over all the years she'd been riding, she'd never had any problems like that. As they saddled up Annie decided it might be a good idea for her to take Cowboy for the day to give April a break. This sure brought a big smile to the French woman's face.

"Ce serait merveilleux! Merci beaucoup Annie!"

"That means, 'That would be wonderful! Thank you so much Annie!'" Patch, always the peacekeeper, intervened before Annie could say anything. They had enough stress to deal with as it was; she didn't want any more bickering happening between the other two women. I had to quickly wipe the smile from my face before Annie caught sight of it. Time to change the subject!

"The ride today is going to take us down the valley to the access track back up onto forestry. We've got to pass pretty close to the main homestead, which could bring us trouble, so you'll all have to keep your wits about you at that point."

We were around eight kilometres down the track leading into the lush valley when we came across the family home that had belonged to Slick Brown. I remembered Dick running a couple of cattle musters for Slick a few years before they'd closed down. It had been hard work, but a lot of fun. I looked at my watch: 0730. After asking the others to stop and wait, I took Socks up to the house paddock on my own, staying out of sight as best I could.

After dismounting, I carefully made my way up to the house, and checked around the corner. More trouble! I was only a couple of metres from the patio where a family of four were enjoying breakfast in the morning sun. Sitting with them was an Alliance trooper.

"Shit!" I muttered under my breath. "Here we go again!"

I remembered seeing a trooper with the family at the Fly Marsh homestead as well; it looked like the Alliance were making sure the new residents would be well-protected. Retreating as quickly and as quietly as I could, I grabbed Socks and re-joined the group, explaining what I'd seen.

Patch was thinking out loud. "Can't we just kill the trooper and leave the family alone?"

She knew as soon as she'd said it that this was not possible, she hated the idea of killing, so it had been worth asking the question.

"Sorry Patch, no can do! We're going to have to kill them all or they'll alert the Alliance. If that happens, we're done for!"

There were solemn looks all round as I added, "You lot stay here. I'll sort it out."

Annie didn't like that at all. "Are you sure you don't want any help?"

I explained to the girls that I thought it would be better if I did the killing, their turn would come soon enough. I knew I'd be able to get pretty close to the group, so I borrowed the F1 from Patch, then rode back to the house paddock and after tying up my trusty steed I made my way back across the grass. I was thankful for the large hedge that hid me from their view. Although I had no issues with doing what had to be done, there was a part of me that longed for more peaceful times, I couldn't help thinking that there was something not quite right about killing people who were just relaxing and enjoying the time of day. Putting all thoughts like that aside, I focussed on the task at hand: making sure my aim was accurate.

Brert! Brert! Brert! Brert! Brert!

A wave of 9 mm rounds exploded from out of the thirty-four -round sterling SMG compatible box magazine; the F1s barrel making short work of the five occupants on the patio. With an effective firing range of one hundred and fifty metres and a rate of fire of over six hundred rounds per minute; it did the job it had been designed to do with ease. They didn't know what had hit them.

Realising there could possibly be more people in the house, I prepared myself for the worst, and went inside, finding myself in the kitchen. There was nobody there, so I started working my way around the rest of the house. Nothing! I was just about to head out the back door when I heard the unmistakable sound of a baby's cry! My heart sank.

"Shit! Damn! Fuck!"

After a more thorough search of the house, I found what looked to be a two or three-month old infant lying in a bassinet in the corner of the lounge room. I'd missed seeing it earlier because someone had draped a cover over the bassinet. After tossing up my options, I decided to simply leave it there; I'd done enough killing for one day! I decided it was best not to say anything to the others; after all they were all women and two of them were mothers. There was no way they would have been happy to leave the baby behind. I figured someone would eventually come to check out where the new occupants were ... so they'd be able to take care of it.

After riding back to where the others were waiting, I was bombarded with questions ...

"Who was there?"

"What sort of family was it?"

"Did they see you?"

"Were there any others in the house?"

I checked the clip before handing Patch back the F1 and re-claimed my SLR. I could understand their inquisitiveness, so I carefully filled them in about everything that had happened, well, almost everything!

Time to change the subject. "Looks like we're on the last clip Patch!"

After having a think about the best route to take, I decided to head up the valley wall instead of taking the dirt road we'd normally take. I figured we'd leave too many tracks if we used the dirt road. Once we'd reached the boundary fence, we all dismounted, working together to drop the boundary fence so that it looked like that spot was a dead end as far as hoof prints went. This was a common practise on treks, in places where the landowner was happy to allow access but did not have a regular gate in the desired place. After dismounting, we undid all of the wire strands on four of the steel pickets, and placed a sighter log on the ground in the middle of the four fence posts, then two of the girls stood on the wire on each side of the sighter log, which lowered the wires to the ground.

The horses were then led over the sighter log, each horse naturally lifted its feet to clear the log. The whole idea of doing things in this way was that it meant the horses wouldn't get tangled up in the wires. Once everyone was over the fence, we simply retied the wire, leaving the fence as we'd found it. The only tools required were either a small set of pliers or a Gerber/ Leatherman tool; mind you, you sometimes had to replace the tie wire, but this could usually be sourced from other fence posts nearby.

Upon reaching the top, we paused to give the horses a short break, and to admire the view over the way we'd come. We could pretty well see back down the whole of the Pateena Valley, as well as the farm; and away in the distance the township of Soothe.

"Bloody hell Sarge!" exclaimed Annie, "You can even see the bodies on the patio!"

"Let's get going, just in case anyone has their binoculars fixed on us!"

I didn't really want them to start dwelling on the dead bodies, and I was more than a little annoyed that Annie chose to remind me of the carnage I'd left behind. Killing didn't come easy to me. Sure, it was different when I shot a roo, then skinned and gutted it, that wasn't a problem. Killing people was something completely different! During my time in the military, my job had been more about engineering and blowing shit up; if any enemy happened to get in the way, well that was just how it was. It was going to take me quite a while to forget the young family I had to kill that morning. The parents couldn't have been more than thirty years-old, and I guessed the two kids would have been around nine or ten years at the most. Then there was the baby! I figured the trooper was probably ten or so years older. Time to stop thinking about it and move on!

As we made our way along the almost completely overgrown forestry tracks, it was obvious that the horses were feeling great. Tom was pulling like a train; he always seemed to be in a hurry to get where he was going. After a while April asked me where I was planning on stopping for lunch.

"There's an old drug runner's hut just around the corner April."

"Hut?" questioned Patch, "I can't see any hut Sarge!"

Annie responded before I could answer.

"Yeah, I know how you feel Patch. The first time Dick brought me here I was the same as you. Mind you, we used to be able to see the top of the hut above the trees, but they've grown a lot since then, so now you just have to know when to bust through the scrub."

And with that she turned Tom and punched right through a couple of bushes, yelling back at us, "Keep your heads down!"

The hut, an A-framed dwelling originally standing around twenty-feet high, was constructed from salvaged materials bought in by four-wheel-drive. It consisted of one large room, twenty by twelve feet in size, and a smaller loft, containing four bunks, which was above the main area. There was a kitchen at one end, with a sink and a tap plumbed up to the water tank, and around the room were scattered an eclectic array of furniture items. A steep ladder gave you access to the loft bedroom, and the toilet, which was some fifty feet away from the hut, had originally been a fishing boat wheelhouse. The cupboards were still half full of groceries, and there was even a half-full glass bottle of milk sitting on the sink! It looked like the animals had got in at some stage; the possums had made a right old mess of everything, even shredding the posters on the walls!

The remnants of a once flourishing garden, could be seen outside the hut. I explained that this was where the highly lucrative marijuana crop had been growing. I pointed out what was left of a sophisticated watering system, this had been used to keep the crop watered whenever the occupants had been away from the hut for a time. Dick had first come across the hut by accident; he'd been looking over the treetops and had been able to just make out the tip of the A-frame from where he'd been standing. After going to investigate, he'd found the crop in full bloom. Not being in favour of anything of that nature, Dick had contacted a mate he knew who worked in the Drug Squad; he'd given them the map coordinates, but they couldn't find the hut for some reason. In the end he'd had to take them in on horseback. They destroyed the crop, and then left their calling card, the main reason for doing this was to make sure that the drug growers knew that it was the Drug Squad, and not the local landowner, that had pulled the plants.

"Have we got time to boil the billy?" asked Patch.

"Sure. Plenty of time today, we're only around four hours from the camp site."

"Four hours! My butt is killing me already!" complained April as she rubbed her tender posterior.

"This will take your mind off it," sympathised Patch as she laid out cold meat, hard boiled eggs, and cheese and biscuits. "We'll wash it all down with a steaming hot coffee. What a feast!"

"I wonder what Dick and Jack are up to?"

It was April who'd asked the question, but I knew we were all thinking the same thing. April missed her busted up ex-CD, with his signature cowboy hat, Patch was craving the sound of Dick's voice, and the warmth of his hugs, and Annie was missing the man she wished was her real father. As for me, well I just missed my mate, deep down wishing it was me there with him instead of Jack.

The track to Mount Morris that we'd be taking once lunch was finished headed due north. To give the horses a chance to stretch their legs Annie suggested that she and I should hold back until Patch and April were about half a kilometre ahead of us, then let the two horses have a good run. The plan was for Bob and Cowboy to be handed over to Tom and Socks, so that April and Patch could hold back Zen and Fannie. Well that was the plan anyway!

What happened instead was that Tom and Socks decided not to stop, instead, galloping past Zen and Fannie at a great rate of knots, causing Bob and Cowboy to take off after our horses.

"Whoa, Fannie!"

Patch told me later that she'd realised that the French woman was having trouble holding the spritely Arab Quarter Horse Cross, but before she could say anything Fannie took off!

"Shit, Fannie! You're a bitch!" All April could do was swear and hold on tight as the little bay mare bolted up the track at the speed of light, eager to catch up to the others.

Patch muttered, "Don't you start Zen!" trying to hold the big chestnut Quarter Horse back as he moved restlessly back and forth. "Oh, what the hell!"

After a few seconds she let the big fellow have his head. As she flew past April on Fannie, she realised that the French woman was still trying to apply the brakes. Mind you, she didn't really have to worry, being a Quarter Horse she knew Zen would run out of steam pretty quickly. The Quarter Horse had the reputation of being the fastest horse in the world over a quarter mile, but they are sprinters, not stayers!

"What was the hurry?" asked Annie, laughing so hard she nearly fell off Tom.

"I just couldn't hold the bitch Annie!" puffed April.

"It was a good idea to let them have a bit of a run," I said to them. "Tonight's campsite is a bit restrictive and there's not much feed."

I knew we'd have to keep them hobbled, and contained in a small roped-off yard, that way they'd only need a small handful of feed each.

We arrived at the overnight stop at around 1700. Looking around, April and Patch could see the makings of one of Dick's campsites; there was a good-sized fireplace with a steel plate, a water hole and a nice number of trees to run the rope around. We soon had the windbreak up and the fire alight.

"You girls are getting quite good at setting up camp!"

Annie gave me a dirty look. "You know I didn't mean you love!"

While the others were grooming and feeding the horses, I prepared tonight's meal. There were new potatoes coming to the boil in the billy and a stockman's carrot casserole, (one of Dick's concoctions, on the go. The carrot casserole consisted of bacon, tinned mushrooms and onions, all cooked in the pan while the carrots simmered in the billy. Once the carrots were partly done, they were drained and added to the pan along with a tin of tomatoes. The whole lot was left to simmer while the rest of the meal cooked, which on this occasion was re-constituted dried peas and re-heated lamb chops which had been pre-cooked by the girls before they left.

"Yummo!" cried Patch with a grin.

"Thanks to your garden April, we have these tasty carrots and onions!"

"Growing it was my pleasure Sarge, but it's you who's cooking it for us!" April had always been proud of her vegetable garden and loved it when other people recognised her efforts.

The horses were more restless than they normally were. Well, it was mainly the mare, who wasn't used to being boxed up in such a small space with all those geldings!

"We might have to move Fannie April."

April agreed. "Yeah I reckon you're right Annie."

I took pity on them. "I'll do it girls. You just sit there and enjoy the coffee." As I got up and started walking over to the horses I added with a grin, "Oh, I've got a little treat for us all. Have a look in the wither bags sitting by my swag."

Annie thought it might be chocolate, and Patch was probably thinking the same. April didn't have a clue until she opened the bags.

"Well, Fuck me! Oops, sorry! Look, it's a bottle of whiskey!"

"Irish coffees all round!" I smiled.

I knew that Patch wasn't too fond of the taste of the fire water on its own; but I reckoned she'd probably find it more to her liking in her coffee!

"You're a sly old dog!" grinned Patch with a wink.

"Hey! Easy up on the 'old' bit Patch."

Thinking about the night ahead, I turned to April. "How do you feel about taking the first watch?"

"No problem Sarge!" she grinned. "I promise I'll do my best, and I WILL stay awake this time!"

"Annie, you take the guts watch and I'll take the morning. Patch, it's your night off this time."

April desperately wanted to not let her partners-in-crime down this time. In order to make sure she'd stay awake she downed quite a few mugs of coffee. The problem with this strategy was that, 'what goes in has to come back out', which meant lots of trips to the toilet, which in this case was not too far away, crouching down in the bush, just out of sight. She thought a lot about Jack and Dick, wondering how they were going, whether they too had come across any Alliance troops, and if they had, whether they'd had to kill anyone. It seemed surreal to be thinking about all this, only a couple of weeks back she would never have dreamed about killing anything, let alone another human being! Jack was the love of her life, she wouldn't know what to do if anything happened to him! She knew that Dick was a good man and would not let anything go wrong if he could help it, but even Dick might not be able to control the situation in the way he wanted to. As she sat there thinking about Jack, she couldn't stop the tears welling up in her eyes.

"Don't even think like that!" she scolded herself, as she went to wake up Annie.

The 'Guts Watch' was called that because it was simply the 'guts' or the middle of a night at sea. Some sailors loved it because they used to get, 'two sleeps', others hated it because they couldn't cope with the broken sleep. Annie loved the solitude, although she wasn't a great coffee drinker, with one cup a night being her limit. It seemed strange to be camping in a place which she had always known as a lunch stop.

She would pass most of her time while on watch with the horses, running the brush over all of them except Bob, she knew he hated the brush because of his sensitive skin. She smiled, remembering a trainee guide who'd been taking part in one of the courses. She'd been asked to prep all the horses for a ride but had come in crying because Bob had nearly bitten her ear off when she'd tried to groom him. Annie tried to remember her name but gave up in the end, it was obvious the kid hadn't stuck around for too long. There'd always been plenty of starters for Dick's horseback tour guide course, but only a few had stuck at it until the end. Too often they'd given up, having told themselves it would be a piece of cake; all they'd have to do was to have fun riding the horses! What brought most of them unstuck was learning the navigation and the other essential requirements of guide training, such as emergency procedures and tourism related shit.

As she gently whispered to Tom, she took a glance at Sarge's watch. It was 0300. "Time to wake him up!" she giggled to herself. "On the other hand, maybe I should just slide into Sarge's swag alongside him while no one's around!"

Chapter 16
The Boat

I t was 0025.

"Everything's nice and quiet Dick."

"Just the way I like it Jack!"

We climbed on board and after forcing the hasp and staple to the wheelhouse, opened the engine room hatch and descended into the eerie darkness. I switched on my torch, I didn't want to fall over anything right now!

"I'll go and unhook the house battery from the ute Jack, you start looking at the layout and work out what needs to be done."

Dick disappeared back up the ladder, then closed the hatch to block the light from my torch. I worked on disconnecting the huge battery, then turned on the fuel. After lifting the cowling of the auxiliary motor, I hooked up the wiring and started bleeding the injectors.

The E1 had sure made a huge mess of the main engine! Because of the internal parts, which were sticking out of the block, I realised that it was more than likely completely seized, meaning that the short coupling shaft between the main and auxiliary would have to be removed. Hearing Dick up top, I opened the hatch for him.

"I've got the battery Jack, you can replace the flat cne with this."

"There's a light switch there," I told him, pointing to the switch at the top of the ladder. "Just got to get the battery fitted so we can switch them on."

I explained what I had discovered and asked if he knew whether Barry had any tools on board.

"I think there should be a set of drawers over on the starboard side, Dick.

I wandered over to the drawers, it was a relief to find everything there that I'd need to do the job. Once I had fitted the battery, we'd be able to turn on the light. That would make things easier!

Dick started to transfer some of the load from the Hilux to the boat, putting food stuff in the wheelhouse and stacking the rest of the camping gear, weapons, and ammo on the deck. He'd removed some of the craypots that had been left on deck, figuring they were taking up valuable storage space; this left an area around the wet well where he could stack supplies. As he struggled with a particularly heavy box, he was startled by the sound of a vehicle that sounded too close for comfort, almost causing him to drop the box into the water.

"Shit!" Dick swore to himself, realising the noise was coming from the top road. "That was close!"

Dismantling the short shaft caused me no issues, and I quickly finished getting the auxiliary ready. At least I'd be able to bar it over now with no restriction coming from the main. Once I'd hooked up the battery, I heard the bilge pump start to cut in, the sound of water being pumped out and splashing into the water surrounding us was deafening! I quickly turned it off. We'd be able to turn it back on later when we needed to; after all the old girl wasn't sinking just yet!

Above me, Dick gave a tap on the engine room hatch, signalling me to turn off the light.

"I'll need a hand with the heavier stuff Jack."

"No problems Dick."

By now the night breeze coming off the water was bitterly cold, we both felt increasing pain in our hands after constantly exposing them to the just below zero temperature. Between us we managed to safely transfer the twenty-five-man army tent, along with its poles, on board, then did the same with the Bren gun and the boxes of other weapons, along with the last of the ammo.

"I think the best thing to do with the ute is to move it back up on to the road. If you take the drain plug out of the fuel tank, then drain the fuel and then put the plug back in, they'll most likely think we ran out of fuel. Hopefully, this will keep their attention away from the jetty!"

"I'm also hoping they won't realise one of the fishing boats has vanished Dick."

After clearing everything out of the cab of the ute we moved up to the road. I crawled underneath and drained the tank, mind you, it didn't take long! The fuel tank was almost empty.

"Oops!" Dick turned back and reached into the glove box. "Nearly forgot the NVGs!"

As we made our way back to the *Cecil Jane*, Dick told me about a time when he'd gone fishing with his old man. The vessel and the area had been very similar, and it had brought the memories of happy times flooding back. The freezing night breeze coming from the north-east looked like steam coming out of our mouths.

Dick checked the small dinghy which was swinging off the davits, it was lashed firm.

"Just right for our getaway Jack!" he exclaimed, explaining that the slight nor-east breeze would assist us to get away by only having to use the sail.

I thought I'd better remind him I was pretty well an amateur when it came to boats.

"I must tell you Dick that I know sweet-fuck-all about sailing or navigation or anything else to do with running boats."

"No problems Jack! All you've got to do is to keep that donk going. Do you think it's going to fire?"

"It should do. I know I've checked everything as well as crossed all the t's and dotted all the i's."

I looked at my watch. Time was going by way too fast, it was already 0410! After setting the ship's clock in the wheelhouse I went out on deck to see what I could do to give Dick a hand. After cutting the ties that held the mainsail to the boom, we dropped all lines, then I jumped back on board and helped Dick to pull on the main halyard that hoisted the sail.

We both held our breath, "Let's hope it's not rotten Jack!"

We had no need to worry. The old canvas sail looked to be in pretty good condition for its age, and when fully deployed we felt the old girl respond, as she started to move under the power of the wind. Dick guided the *Cecil Jane* out and away from potential danger. We were moving at a rate of about one knot; it wasn't fast, but it was certainly silent!

The creaking sound of the mast increased in volume as the wind took hold, shifting the thirty-six-footer along at nearly two knots.

"Hey Jack. I'm thinking if the donk doesn't fire, we'll just sail the whole way!"

I just shook my head and disappeared below to check how things were going in the engine room.

Dick was wondering whether he'd be able to find the channel which would take them out into the more open waters, it had been a long time since his early days as a boy going for a fish with his father. His memories carried him back to the story his father had told him about the first time the *Shirley Anne* had come into Barracouta. Dick's father and his Uncle Harry were making their way in from cray fishing. Not being sure exactly where the channel was, they'd run the boat up onto the sandbar, and had to wait almost twelve hours for the high tide to set them free again. They'd been the laugh of the town; almost every other local boat had passed them as they'd sat there high and dry! The next time the pair happened to visit the local pub they'd copped it from all the other commercial fishermen.

"Do you want the bilge pump on yet Dick?"

"No, we'll wait until the donk starts, we're going to need every bit of grunt we can get out of that battery!"

I focussed on sorting out the electrics and working out where to turn the navigational aids on when we needed them. Dick had decided not to use any navigational lights, just the radar. We were lucky that it was an old analogue set.

The spokes of the three-foot wheel felt good in Dick's hands as he manoeuvred the *Cecil Jane* close to the shore. There was just enough moonlight to allow him to make out the channel markers.

After turning off the light I emerged from the engine room.

"Crikey Dick! We're a bit close to the shore. What's that coming up in front?"

I was looking to the fish co-op wharf, which was looming up fast on our port side.

"It's the fish wharf Jack. It probably means trouble for us, but I can't get any further away from it because the channel runs right along the side of the wharf. I might get you to man the Bren gun on the port side just in case; I've mounted it on top of some craypots, and there's two magazines in the pot alongside of it."

"Roger that Dick!"

I realised how excited I was feeling about the thought of some real action again!

Dick joined me on deck and wished me luck as he handed the NVG's to me. As soon as I put them on, I realised there was movement happening on the wharf. We were taking machine gun fire before Dick even had time to warn me; I figured it was probably their type 73, which was based on a 1960s Russian knock-off. It could be magazine or belt-fed and used 7.62 mm ammo, same as our SLRs.

Thankfully their accuracy was not all that good, probably because they wouldn't have been able to get a clear look at us in the dark. However, they still managed to splinter the woodwork, with some of the rounds even passing through the wheelhouse! This was just a shade too close for Dick's liking!

Almost straight away I had them in my sights and opened up with the Bren. The slightly larger .303 rounds of my weapon, with its precise accuracy made short work of the two troopers who had drawn guard duty on the wharf. I held my breath for a few seconds but there was no return fire.

"Jack! You may as well get that donk started. Even if they hadn't heard us before now, they'd know we're here now for sure!"

I scampered down the hole and barred her over to the firing position. After making sure there was fuel available, I yelled out to my mate.

"Give that a go Dick!"

He hit the starter.

Whirr ... Whirr ... Whirr ...

Dick stopped and waited for a second, then tried again.

Whirr ... Whirr ... Whirr ... Nothing!

"It's not looking good Jack!"

"Bugger! Try one more time Dick."

As he put his finger on the starter again Dick said a little prayer. *Whirr ... Whirr ... Whirr ... Chug! Chug! Chug! Chug!*

"She's away!" yelled Dick in relief, quickly pushing the throttle lever forward into gear. The *Cecil Jane* surged forward like some prehistoric beast coming to life after a long sleep, she still wasn't going all that fast, but her bravado and speed was enough for what we wanted her to do.

"Time to drop the mainsail Jack. I think we're done with it for now."

"Roger that mate!"

I flew back out on deck and released the halyard holding up the sail.

"I don't know what we would have done without that bit of canvas!"

As I entered the wheelhouse I glanced at the clock, realising it was 0515. Finally, we were clear of civilisation, and for now at least, clear of danger. The last thing to slide by was the remnants of the old woodchip mill and its wharf.

"Feel like a brew Dick?" I grinned, fumbling around in the boxes for the coffee and the UHT milk; and of course, Dick's lemon juice.

"Might even shout you breakfast Jack!"

"Bloody good thing Dick. I'll have steak eggs and chips!"

"You'll get what I bloody give you sport," said Dick, laughing at me. We were both enjoying the respite from the stress and tension of the days leading up to this point.

Dick turned the boat to port, and as we rounded Home Spit, I started the bilge pump again and then swung back up out of the hole.

I was a bit confused, "Aren't we going the wrong way Dick?"

"Roger that Jack! I think we'll play it smart. I think we got away without being seen, but if anyone did happen to be watching us, they will have seen us heading north. We'll keep to that course and go about twenty miles up the coast; that way they'll think they know the way we're going. My plan is to turn out arcund the outside of Mary Island once we're out of sight ... then we'll start heading south."

This was smart thinking on Dick's behalf, I felt a ton of respect for the older ex-clearance diver. I was prouder than ever of my mate, and thankful to be on this adventure with someone who knew what he was doing!

Chapter 17
Buckle Peak

Friday 9th January 2015 ... Mount Morris.

It was 0500. "Wakey wakey! Hands off snakey!"

April groaned as she heard the cheerful awakening from Sarge as he wandered amongst the swags.

"Bloody hell! Where did that night go?" she barked, feeling like she hadn't had any sleep at all.

Patch yawned, "I must have dropped off as soon as I crawled into the swag."

Annie laughed, "Yeah, it didn't take long for you to be cutting wood like the rest of them!"

"I must admit that was the best night's sleep I've had in ages," admitted April, who was still not quite ready to get up and get going.

Annie gave a snigger, "It must have been the watch keeping!"

"I thought we might swap the horses around today," announced the ex-sapper.

Sarge had been giving it some thought; he didn't think that Dick or Jack would mind if someone else rode their horses for a while. He suggested that Annie ride Bob and he'd take Cowboy.

With Patch staying on Zen, and April with Fannie, Tom and Socks would be their new pack horses. It took a bit of mucking around, but they finally had the new arrangement in place.

"Geez. I could swim in this saddle of Dick's!" Annie slid her bum around the eighteen-inch stock saddle.

Sarge decided it was better to keep his seventeen-inch stock saddle instead of trying to fit into Jack's fifteen-inch western. He'd always hated the horn because it always seemed to get in the way, especially when cantering.

Tom seemed a little put out at first with no longer being lead horse. However, Bob was in his element; back where he knew he belonged.

Not long after they started off, they had to stop and drop another fence. This took them off forestry and onto the forty-thousand-acre property known as Black Marsh. They all enjoyed this part of the ride as they wound their way down through a valley of old forest eucalypt and then through a plantation of the same species of gum tree. The Cockatoo River flowed right through the middle of it all. Everyone felt good this morning, they were all enjoying the fresh air and the scenery, and the chance to think their own thoughts.

Bob was pulling like a train! Poor Sarge wasn't so lucky as he tried to get Cowboy to obey the most basic of commands. He almost wished he had a set of those really nasty spikey sours that some people wore.

"Bloody horse has no manners. Or for that matter, no brains!" muttered Sarge. "The stupid animal won't keep a straight line; he wanders around all over the place!"

The frustrated forty-five-year-old shook his fist as he continued his bitch.

"The problem with you Cowboy, is that bloody Jack lets you get away with murder! You need a few lessons quick smart. Look at Zen and Socks! They're quite happy moseying along as our newly instated pack horses, but you! You're a fucking pain!"

Of course, Cowboy took no notice of him whatsoever!

As Annie was approaching the traditional lunch stop, a nice grassy area near the river, an unexpected movement caught her attention. Quickly pulling Bob up, she whispered urgently, "Sarge!"

Sarge moved up alongside his partner, signalling to the others to stop where they were.

"What's up Hon?"

"Over there!" She nodded in the direction of the place she thought she'd seen movement. "I thought I saw someone near the lean-to-humpy."

Sarge tried to ride over to investigate, but Cowboy wouldn't respond to his signals.

"Shit! This fucking horse won't do anything I want him to do!"

Disgusted he dismounted, and after giving the reins to Annie, set off on foot.

The lean-to didn't look like it had been there very long; it consisted of brush which had been cut with a machete and then leaned up against a cross-member between two trees. It was obvious that someone was occupying the humpy, the food stocks, drink containers, freshly cut wood and a still-smouldering fire gave that away.

Sarge explored the area to the east, but finding nothing, he gave up the search and started to make his way back to the lunch stop. As he rounded the last bend, he pulled up short at the sight of a rough looking bloke who was threatening the girls with a .22 rifle. He was so focussed on what he was doing, that he had no idea that Sarge had come up behind him until the barrel of the SLR was jammed violently into the small of his back. The bloke nearly shit himself!

The old timer jumped, his face turning red.

"Hold it mateys! No need to get ya knickers in a knot!"

"Drop the weapon!" barked Sarge.

The stranger gingerly placed his aging .22 rifle on the ground.

"I didn't mean any harm, thought you were some of those Asian bastards!"

"Mate, do we look like we're Asian?"

Sarge was clearly not happy. The old timer had no idea how lucky he was that the ex-Sapper hadn't pulled the trigger without asking any questions.

Everyone was feeling edgy, and it took a while for their heart beats to settle down. They soon learned that the old fellow was the rouseabout from Black Marsh Farm; Graham had been hard at work cleaning a sheep carcass for the owners when he'd seen the old Bedford truck arrive and drive straight up to the homestead.

"They were bold-as-brass-like," he declared, shaking his head in disbelief. "I thought I was watching a movie."

As he heard the firing start, he stayed hidden until the troops had stopped spraying their ammunition around inside the homestead. Then, figuring they were all dead, he waited till they'd left, then high-tailed it out of there.

He had made the eight-kilometre trip back to the homestead a few times after that to scrounge food and other supplies, and had been there on the day the, 'new occupants,' moved in. He couldn't work out what was going on; it was a surreal feeling to be watching an Asian family going into and out of a house that not long before had been happily occupied by his employer and family. There were a couple of kids, and an older couple that he thought might have been grandparents. Although he hadn't seen anybody come back and clean-up the dead bodies, it was obvious that someone had taken care of it. Mind you, he swore he could still smell the stench!

Sarge filled him in with what had been going on since the invasion, although he was careful not to mention where they were going, or even that there was another two members in their party.

Graham turned and stoked up his fire.

"Do ya want a brew? It'll save ya having to light your own."

Patch whispered quietly to Sarge, "Do you think we can trust him? Do we invite him to join us?"

"He's not much use to us Patch; the bloke must be close to eighty! But I think we should at least ask him whether he wants to tag along."

While they finished off their lunches, Sarge went over and had a yarn with the old fellow, secretly hoping he'd turn them down.

"Nah. I'm going to stay here. I can survive out here for years livin' off the land."

Graham had a shitload of ammo, and by the look of the couple of bunnies he had dressed and ready for the fire, he could obviously shoot!

The group quickly downed their drinks and got ready to move on.

"You take care old man and don't let the bastards anywhere near you!"

It was kind of sad to watch the old fellow wave goodbye to them; they were all hoping he'd be okay.

Turning her thoughts to the ride ahead, Annie piped up, "It's five clicks to the river, we'd better get going!"

They'd have to cross the Cockatoo River again, but this time it would be three feet deep and twenty feet wide!

Patch was worried about leaving the old man behind. "Sarge, are you sure Graham didn't want to join us?"

"Quite sure Patch!"

The group rode along the isthmus of land that was enveloped by the Cockatoo River. After fighting their way through the dense underbrush, they rode out to the tip of the spit of land and pulled up facing the river. The sound of water running over the river boulders was deafening; and they could see a sheer cliff face on the other side, looming upwards for some 120 or so feet.

"How on earth are we going to get up there!" exclaimed April. Patch was thinking the same thing.

Annie explained what they were going to have to do.

"The only way up is to cross the river, then hop up on to the ledge on the other side. You'll then have to dismount then make your way on foot up the animal tracks zig zagging up the slope. The secret is to not walk on the tracks; let the horse use those. Your job is going to be to keep out of the way and pick your own way up alongside of the horses."

April's jaw dropped. "You have got to be fucking kidding!"

"No April, it's a piece of cake!"

"That's easy for you to say. Sarge how many times have you done it?"

"Three times, maybe four April. Annie has done it more than me, so she's the expert!"

Annie raised her voice, "Look April, just follow me and do exactly what I do. Patch, you too!"

She turned and waded through the river, the bank on the other side was quite high, which meant the ground was level with the stirrups, making it easy to dismount. After untying the lead rope from around Bob's neck, she started up the cliff, allowing Bob to pick his own way up the small winding animal tracks. Upon reaching the top, she looked back down on the group below her.

"Your turn next Patch. Leave Socks with Sarge, I'll come and get him in a minute."

Patch waded Zen across the Cockatoo River, with the icy cold-water lapping at her boots. After pulling him up alongside the bank, she dismounted and undid the lead rope, then followed Annie's lead. Although the cliff was even steeper than it had looked, the climb was much easier than she'd thought it would be. Zen kind of hopped up from one animal track to the next, in a random zig zag pattern; the same way that Bob had done.

Safely on top, she looked back over the edge, the 54-year-old exclaimed, "Fuck! Sorry! That's a long way down Annie!"

April went next, doing her best to emulate Patch and Annie. Although her progress was a little bit slower, it all went smoothly. Reaching the top at last, she collapsed in a heap on the ground, shaking in relief at being back on level ground again.

Shaking her head, Annie asked Patch to hold Bob; then carefully made her way back down. After grabbing Socks, she made her way back up the slope to join the others.

Sarge reckoned he'd be able to give it a go with both the remaining horses, so crossed the river and made his way up to the top. It was probably the best thing he could have done; he figured Cowboy would never have willingly made the climb without Tom! Sarge let them take a twenty-minute break, as he went through the next bit of the ride.

"It's going to get a bit hairy in about three hours, after we pass the last hill before Buckle Peak. From there we'll be in full view of the farm; all we can do is hope they're not looking our way!"

It was Sarge's intention to get them down off the hill and under the cover of a pine plantation; bypassing the shearer's quarters they usually used for a campsite. After that they'd cross the Cockatoo River one last time under the shadow of the town of Bulldust, before riding through another property and then into the State Forest.

He grinned, "Should be a piece of cake!"

The next section took them through an area that had been extensively logged; as they all settled into the rhythm of the ride,

Annie reckoned it looked more like a lunar landscape than the Taswegian forest.

They almost missed seeing a couple of vehicles that were lying dormant by the side of the track. They'd obviously been parked there for the night at the time the E1 had hit, rendering them useless. It was a strange thing to realise that the people who'd been camped there while they'd been clearing the plantation would have had to walk all the way back to Bulldust, totally unaware that the world had just shit itself!

After moving off the main track they cut around the back of a large hill, then through a farm gate and into the open, where they found themselves overlooking the Buckle Peak homestead. As they began to gingerly make their way down the hill, Sarge told them about the first trip Dick had done there. He and Bob had been on an exploratory ride on their own. All had gone well until they approached the last paddock; unbeknownst to Dick it was full of alpacas. Bob had pulled up without warning and snorted, then side-stepped ten paces, not quite sure what to think of the strange creatures.

The homestead was made up of two houses, various outbuildings, and the shearers' quarters.

Sarge felt uneasy, "There could be quite a few Alliance people here girls! Check your weapons and keep an eye out!"

Annie was in her usual place at the front. The gate between the machinery shed and the house belonging to the landowner's son was open, so she rode through and started working her way towards the shearers' quarters. Just as she drew level with the door, it was opened by an old Asian man who emptied the contents of his cup. He was so close that the liquid only just missed landing on Bob's feet! Annie acted instinctively, grabbing the pump action shotgun which was lying across her saddle and pulled the trigger, making Bob and the rest of the horses jump.

BOOOM!

It really doesn't matter how many times you fire a weapon off a horse, they are never ready for it. But to his credit, Bob recovered quickly, not missing a stride. The old guy was propelled backward, a large part of his chest missing where the shotgun blast had gone right through.

There was no time to think. Annie dug her heels in, heading for a little grove of trees which she hoped would provide some cover. April, still in shock, let go of the reins, but Fannie and Socks just followed Bob.

Patch, with Zen and Tom, started to catapult forward to catch up with the others; but pulled up short as she noticed movement out of the corner of her eye. More Asians had appeared, thankfully she realised that they hadn't noticed her, and instead were pointing to where they could see Sarge turning towards the doorway. Patch levelled the F1, slipping the safety forward and squeezed the trigger.

Brert! Brert! Brert! Brert! Brert!

The first Asian folded in half as he was hit by the blast, but there was another one right behind him! Struggling to keep her balance as Zen side-stepped around a rock, Patch pulled the trigger again!

Brert! Clink! Clink!

After dismounting, Sarge drew the 9 mm and kicked open the door, hitting the legs of the man inside, then had to duck as the door bounced back. He was still holding the reins, which didn't impress Cowboy one bit! Taking aim, he fired. With Cowboy still in tow Sarge entered the small hut, noticing that the fire was going well. He spied someone hiding under the table.

Bang!

Noticing a fresh loaf of bread on the table, still wrapped in its wax paper, Sarge grabbed it, thinking it would be good to have some fresh bread. Cowboy, who'd had enough by this stage, gave a mighty tug to the reins; nearly flipping Sarge back out the door. Sarge gave him a dirty look as he stowed the bread in the wither bags. He just started to mount up again and had one foot in the off-side stirrup when he heard the F1 run dry. Without pausing he twisted and fired.

Bang! Bang!

He dropped the attacker where he stood.

Zen didn't miss a beat; at Patch's signal he took off like a rocket! Cowboy wasn't about to be left behind! The 13-hand paint refused to wait any longer, galloping after Zen, with Sarge holding on tight as he desperately tried to get his other foot into the near-side stirrup!

Annie and April had pulled up in the trees, they could see Patch on Zen flying out in front, with Sarge and Cowboy just behind them, coming down the bank at full pelt! Annie held her breath, feeling like she was about to be sick, and certain Sarge was about to come off, but somehow, he managed to get the other foot in and regain control. Both horses reached the cover of the trees and skidded to a halt.

Sarge could see that Annie was upset and tried to make light of what had just happened.

"Well. That was fun!"

Annie's voice quivered as she fought back tears.

"Is he ... is he dead Sarge?"

Sarge knew that this was the first time Annie had killed anyone, he knew her emotions would be all over the place, but he didn't know what to say to make her feel better.

"Yep!" Better to keep it simple.

Patch looked at the ex-sapper. "Was anyone else in there Sarge?"

"There was one more Patch."

Sarge realised this would have been the first time for Patch as well. He wished Dick was here; he would have known what to say.

"You all right Patch?"

"Ask me later Sarge."

There was no way of knowing whether they'd alerted any more Alliance troops, so Sarge suggested they cross the river straight away, and get the next part out of the way.

"Lead on Annie!"

For once there was no response. Annie was white-faced and shaking. Sarge knew he had to take charge.

"We're changing horses Annie!"

He shortened Cowboy's stirrups and handed the reins to Annie; figuring that way she'd be able to concentrate on riding the paint instead of dwelling on what had just happened. After quickly mounting Bob, Sarge turned him towards the river and into the water. It wasn't all that deep in this spot, but it was about forty feet wide from bank to bank. Leaving the water on the other side, he started to move on, but after only five or six strides, stopped suddenly, holding up his hand as a warning to the others to wait. April, who was close behind him on Fannie, and towing Socks, almost ran up Bob's arse.

Patch was still reeling from the emotions running through her head. It had all happened so fast that she hadn't had a chance to think about what she was about to do; she'd never have thought she'd actually have the courage to kill somebody! It was no use worrying about it now. Shaking off the thoughts, she was in mid-stride, with Zen's front legs part-way up the bank, when she looked up to see Sarge giving the international signal to stop.

Annie, wondering what was going on, pulled Cowboy up behind Tom.

Two trucks and a jeep were making their way up the driveway to the homestead on the next property.

Sarge looked back at the others, "Shit! I reckon they're probably looking for us!"

"That's torn it" April blurted out. "What do we do now?"

Sarge thought fast.

"We'll cross the road and head into the plantation, then go around the homestead. I'm not sure how many clicks it will add, but we have no choice. We can't keep going this way now we've got company!"

They all nodded in agreement, then followed Sarge across the road and into a well-established eucalypt plantation. After leading the way in for about half a kilometre Sarge turred right again, continuing to maintain a course that was parallel with the driveway. Once he was sure they were out of earshot, he turned in the saddle saying, "Let's up the pace to a trot; if them bastards check out the river it won't take them long to discover our tracks!"

Sarge led them all at a trotting pace for well over two kilometres. April had finally had enough.

"Stop!" she yelled in desperation. "I can't take this anymore; my butt is killing me!"

Patch realised Sarge wouldn't have heard the French woman. She knew this was no time to go easy on anyone.

"We've got to keep going! Just concentrate on what you're doing ... not on your backside! If we stop, we'll all die!"

After what seemed like an eternity to April, Sarge felt it was safe to drop back to a walk and glanced back to see how the others were doing. He could already see an improvement in Cowboy's behaviour.

"Hah! I knew Annie wouldn't put up with his behaviour," he smiled to himself, still frustrated with the shitty little paint.

"Is everyone okay?"

With positive responses all round, Sarge asked Annie to take the lead again. Although Cowboy was reluctant at first to move to the front, the twenty-eight-year-old took no notice of his antics, in the end, realising that she was well and truly in charge, the paint gave in and did what she asked.

"Just stick to the track we're on for now," Sarge told her. "If my sense of direction is good, I figure we should come across the main track about a kilometre further on."

From his position at the rear of the group, he could see the other track leading off to the right; the only issue was that he could also see a number of trucks moving up and down. Both April and Patch were more than a little bit relieved when Sarge suggested that they take a short break while they waited to see whether the traffic would clear. The two women were glad to dismount and give their backsides a break from the constant riding.

Sarge scanned the area ahead.

"It's not looking good ladies!"

After giving things a bit of time to settle down, Sarge had another look back at the track. He could see the last truck as it headed back down the hill; this left only the jeep to have to deal with. Knowing he'd have to find out more, he whispered to Annie, "You take the girls and get moving again. I'll catch up to you in a while; I'm just going to do a bit of a reccy over there to see what's going on."

As the girls continued up the track Sarge peeled off to the right and wound his way through some three hundred metres of partially cleared track, eventually finding himself at the top of an old quarry. As he urged his mount towards the rim, the usually reliable Bob suddenly shied and backed up.

"Well old fellow, I know what that means!"

Sarge dismounted and carefully crept up to the steep cliff face. As he peered over the edge, Sarge could see the troops from the jeep tipping accelerant onto a large pile of rotting corpses. At least he now knew that they were dumping bodies and not looking for them! After backing away, he mounted up again, giving Bob a reassuring pat on the neck. As they moved off, he heard a familiar noise.

Whoomph!

Turning in the saddle, he could see a faint trace of lightly coloured smoke rising above the quarry; he knew this would have been caused by the accelerant as it ignited.

Sarge caught up with the others and told them what he'd seen. They were all glad to hear that they weren't being followed; at least for now!

"Mind you," added Sarge, "I don't think it will be long before someone finds our hoof prints. After that we're in trouble!"

It wasn't long before they came to the gate leading into forestry; after that they knew they only had around another four kilometres to go before they'd get to the usual lunch stop. They were all hoping it would be a good place to pull up for the night. It had been a long day; the ride from the lunch stop on Mt Willy to Buckle Peak was usually only a half-day ride; but it was now almost 2000 and light was fading fast. They ran the rope around some trees, creating a small clearing, and hobbled the weary horses. Annie was amazed at how they'd performed that day, and especially at the way Bob handled the loud shotgun blast just above his ears.

"You know Patch, if I'd been riding Tom, he would have put me on my arse!"

"I know Annie. He's one in a million. No wonder Dick thinks so much of him!"

After April and Sarge had put the wind break in place he broke the bad news to them.

"Unfortunately, we'll have to go without a fire tonight! We're just too close to civilisation to risk it. Dinner will have to be whatever you can rustle up cold."

He had a quiet word to each one in turn, making sure they were all right. It had been one hell of a day. April didn't say much; she was more than ready for bed. Deep down, she was more worried than ever about whether she was going to make it; her arse was more painful than it had ever been before.

Patch was still having trouble believing that when it had come to the crunch, she hadn't hesitated to pull the trigger! She'd certainly been scared and had even shut her eyes as she fired; but she'd still done what had to be done! Dick would be so proud of her! Trying not to think of how desperately she missed him, Patch gave Sarge a big hug, thanking him for saving her life.

Annie was still having trouble trying to come to terms with what she'd had to do, although Sarge was thankful to see that the bout with Cowboy had helped to take her mind off the evening's events.

Chapter 18
Sailing

Thursday 8ᵗʰ January 2015 ... Mercury Passage heading north.

It was 0700.

"Where's my fucking pill bag!" muttered Dick, realising it was, 'that time of day,' again.

"I put it in your Pussers grip Dick. You know ... the one you were issued with when you joined Pussers."

Dick found the pills he needed and washed them down with his coffee. Taking medication was something he still hated, but put up with, knowing it was the pills that kept him going.

"Let's see what we can rustle up for scran!"

"It's amazing that bloody bag is still in one-piece Dick!"

"Yeah, I know! I've had to replace the zip a couple of times and you can see where I had to do an emergency repair on one of the handles."

Finding the pre-cooked bangers that the girls had prepared before they'd left, Dick opened a couple of cans of tomatoes and mushrooms that he'd found in the cupboard in the galley.

"These will go together well. Sorry we don't have any bum nuts Jack."

"No problem," responded Jack, happy that they had something decent to eat. "Let's just hope the tinned stuff is okay!"

"Yeah this lot is good, the tins were still intact, and the contents looked okay once I opened them up."

"What the hell. I'm hungry!"

The *Cecil Jane* was heading due north, motoring along at about four or five knots. Dick knew that sticking to this speed would mean the trip would take longer, but figured it was safer that way. By his estimate they should be approaching the northern end of Mary Island in about five hours' time.

"Let's hope we don't have to outrun anything Dick!"

"I suppose if we see anything that's got Alliance written all over it, we'll just have to fight it out."

As the pair rounded the point, the sea state started to get a little worse; there were, 'white horses,' everywhere and the swell had built up to a couple of metres in height.

"We could be in for a lumpy one Dick."

"Just like old times Jack!"

They both laughed, they both loved being out on the water.

"Maybe we should secure the load on deck and prep the weapons before it gets any lumpier. You never know what we're going to come across, and we mightn't have much warning if it all turns to shit!"

Dick lashed the wheel and helped Jack as he started lashing the boxes down on the deck.

"At least there's a good supply of rope," smiled Jack.

"Well we are on a fishing boat Jack."

After successfully securing their cargo, the pair went back over the plan of attack.

"Jack, I was thinking you should man the Bren while I operate the SLR with the RPG attachment, which will give us a bit more firepower."

"If we do see a vessel, I reckon the best plan would be not to engage with them until we're at close quarters; just to make sure that we'll have a better chance of destroying them."

"Well let's hope they don't come chugging around the point in a bloody destroyer!"

The ex-CD specialist sniper grinned."If that happens, I guess we just go to plan B."

"Plan B? What the fuck is plan B!"

"While I was down in the engine room, I found two sets of scuba gear. They've been there a while but they're still full. You'll remember the ones ... they're a couple of old 72's with stainless steel hook harnesses, no BC's, aqua regulators plus weight belts, fins and goggles."

Jack continued, "I reckon if we end up facing a destroyer or the like, we should bail out and abandon the old *Cecil Jane* and disappear towards Mary Island or wherever we are at the time. We certainly won't be going anywhere in the dinghy!"

"Love it Jack! In the meantime, you may as well get your head down for a kip."

As Jack snored away, the *Cecil Jane* continued to head north, and rounded Point Bonaparte. Dick kept watch, wondering where the day would take them. After a while, his thoughts wandered, as he started thinking about Patch. He loved her with all his heart, hopefully, she was okay. He hoped all of them were okay. Boy, it was going to be one hell of a party once they all got to Hells Beach!

At 1230 he shook Jack awake. "Scran's up!"

Lunch was cold meat and a coffee. The sea state was still 2 metres, with the wind at 20 knots; the thirty-six-foot fishing boat was riding quite well, although there were a few times when Dick thought the old girl might break apart as she hit the next swell. To help her out he'd reduced their speed to around four knots.

"At this rate I reckon our ETA at Hells Beach will be around midnight tomorrow."

"I've got no idea what we'll find when we get there."

"Yeah," Dick agreed. "We can't even be sure whether the rest will be there by then. Let's see … they've been gone nearly four days now, it will be almost six by the time we get there. I reckon they'll arrive the day after we get there, but it depends on what, or who, they've come across along the way."

"How do you reckon they're going Dick?"

"We've got no way of really knowing. Annie is a good guide, but she's young, I don't know how she would stand up in a fight. I'm counting on Sarge, I know he'll do his best to look after them all. Patch has a cool head, so I'm hoping she'll be all right. How do you think April will fair?"

"I must admit, I'm a bit worried about her, she's never ridden that far in a day before, so after six or seven days her butt will be killing her by now. Mind you, mine would be doing the same. She's usually pretty level-headed but if there was a scrap she could go to pieces!"

"Like I said Jack, I'm sure Sarge will hold them all together!"

"Yeah. But what happens if Sarge takes a hit?"

"Let's not think of that mate."

Dick realised how tired he was. "I think I'll get some sleep Jack. Are you right with our course?"

"Roger that Dick! *Zero Five Zero.*"

Dick gave him a nod as he climbed into the day bed in the wheelhouse. It was still warm, and it didn't take him long to fall into a deep sleep.

It was around 1400, as the *Cecil Jane* rounded another point, Jack realised that they must be getting close to Bollards Beach.

Dick had been enjoying a rather pleasurable adult dream; reluctantly returning to reality at Jack's shout.

"We're coming about Dick. Plus, the radar's shit itself!"

"Better not get too close to Bollards Jack! There could be Alliance troops there."

Dick set their course towards Nod Isle, a little island off the northern end of Mary Island, then took the wheel while Jack got his head down again.

Dick found himself remembering the time he'd been on his first ship, *HMAS Sydney*. They'd been transporting troops to Vietnam, and as a young seaman he was required to do watch-keeping. The watches were a mix of deck watches, (as lookout) and tricks on the wheel, with each trick varying from one hour in good weather to half an hour in bad.

Bringing his thoughts back to their present situation, Dick knew they'd have to revise their operation now that the radar had shit itself. He should have known that it was just too bloody old, it probably hadn't been fired up in five years, so it wasn't any wonder that it had died. They'd have to keep their travel to daylight hours only, and lay-over close to shore in some of the secluded bays on Mary Island.

Around 1800, the *Cecil Jane* approached Cape Nod, which was the northern-most point of Mary Island.

"I don't know about you Dick, but I'm knackered!"

"You're not on your own there mate! I reckon the first inlet or small bay we come across will do us for today."

"The first bay is Dinosaurs Bay. It's pretty big and exposed to the north, but if we can get in close enough, we might be able to get into some calm water."

Just inside the northern end of Dinosaurs Bay was a rocky outcrop. Dick turned to starboard and headed in.

"The swell seems to be easing Dick."

"You could be right Jack," said Dick, switching on the depth sounder.

"62 feet … 52 feet … 47 feet … 30 feet … 20 feet … That will do us Jack."

Dick took the *Cecil Jane* back to neutral and then after a short burst astern he halted the aging fishing boat. Jack was already manning the anchor, as Dick gave the thumbs up signal, he let go, sending the chain rattling down the hawse pipe. Jack waited till it came to a stop then applied the brake to slow it down. After letting it out for another twenty feet he stopped the capstan.

"Just let her swing a little Jack; we'll see if she grabs!"

Caught by the anchor, the fishing boat swung bow into the swell.

"Grab the binoculars Jack, and have a squiz along the shoreline for visitors while I rustle up some scran."

Dick rummaged around in the esky and found some cooked corned dog, known to landlubbers as corned beef. Once he'd added a few vegies, spuds, carrots and cabbage, along with a mixture of herbs and spices, he soon had a nice little casserole going.

Once he'd finished scanning the surrounding area Jack turned his attention to the weapons on deck, double checking them before sauntering into the wheelhouse.

"Might see if the shower is operational Dick."

"That sounds like a good plan Jack," agreed Dick, "it seems like a lifetime since I last had one."

Jack went below and checked the fresh water supply, and then made sure that the twelve-volt breaker for the marine toilet and shower was switched to 'on'. Dick went out on deck and turned on the gas for the instant hot water system.

"It'll probably take about twenty minutes to heat up Jack."

"No problems. I'll test the heads first."

Dick suddenly realised that, with everything that had been going on, his usual trip to the toilet was running a bit late.

"Don't take too long mate. I'm right behind you!"

"That could be dangerous!"

In the half-metre swell the *Cecil Jane* (CJ) was riding well at anchor; the sound of the waves crashing on to the rocky beach was so loud that Dick was a bit worried they wouldn't hear anyone coming their way.

"I'll take the first watch Jack."

"I guess that means I get the guts?"

"Yep! And I'll do the morning. I'll give you a piss about first light, main engines will be required five minutes later, then we'll weigh anchor, and be under way ASAP!" Dick was laughing.

"Sounds like we're back in the Puss!"

"That was a great, 'pot mess' Dick."

Jack went forward to investigate the bunk arrangements.

"It's pretty cosy up forward Dick; I might just bunk down there."

"See ya at 2355!"

Dick poured his second cup of coffee and settled down in front of the radio, figuring he might as well have a bit of a play with it and see if he could get it going. He knew nothing was meant to work, but he also knew that the *CJ* had an old UHF set, as well as the standard fishing requirements of a VHF and HF. He found the breakers in the engine room, and switched on the three that were marked UHF, VHF and HF.

After unsuccessfully fiddling for a while with the VHF and HF, he turned his attention to the UHF, scanning all the channels in turn. Still no success! Giving up for now he left it on the repeater channel, channel 1.

Dick took another walk around the deck, scanning the horizon with his NVG's. All seemed to be clear, so he felt safe to make another trip to the heads. Thankfully, his body worked well this time. He flushed the old system, but it was noisier than he'd expected, and he hoped the din hadn't woken his mate.

After checking his 9 mm, and making sure he had a full clip, he put the kettle on again. The small brass ship's clock showed 2300. Dick hadn't realised just how much he'd missed the simplicity of life at sea; he allowed his thoughts to drift back again to the *HMAS Sydney* days. As a junior rating, with no real responsibility, it had been his job to go get the Kai or coffees for the other watch keepers, depending on their preference. Kai, which was pronounced 'Kye', was a thick hot chocolate drink enjoyed by the watch keepers; in the early days it was made from melted chocolate bars, and later on, from cocoa with tinned cow's milk.

This meant making his way to the galley and making up the drinks, placing them all on a tray, and then trying to get them to the watch keeper without spilling them. Even though the *Sydney* was a large aircraft carrier, this was no mean feat, it still had quite a motion at times, which meant that carrying up to ten tin mugs of drinks at a time often proved to be quite a challenge!

Dick had tried drinking Kai once, but he'd never taken to it. In fact, he'd never liked hot chocolate or cocoa, preferring coffee from the time he'd first been allowed to try it. These days he liked it black with a dash of lemon juice, but back then it had been the standard NATO brew of white with two sugars.

"It's 2350 Jack! All's clear and the kettle's on. I'm turning in ... give us a piss at 0350."

They were doing continuous watches, which meant hot bunking. Dick and Jack changed places, with Dick pretty well falling asleep before he hit the bunk. Jack felt he could have done with more than four hours' sleep, but figured it was better than none. After a long check through the NVG's of the uppers and the shoreline he felt happy they were safe. The whistle of the kettle told him the water was boiling, so he made himself a cuppa, and after finding some biscuits, settled in for his watch.

Friday 9th January 2015 ... Northern end of Dinosaurs Bay, Mary Island.

"Here is the news for Friday 2nd January 2015, Alex Brand reporting.

As I speak, we have reports that forces, calling themselves, "The New Alliance," have landed at all major ports in Taswegia ...

Troops are approaching the building! Stay tuned f... Shit! They're coming up the stairs! If we can get another ..."

Bang, Bang ... Schhhhhhhhhhh ... Only static!'

Jack just about had a heart attack. "Fucking hell!"
He realised that Dick must have turned the UHF set on earlier. This was obviously the broadcast Dick told them about, but why had it been repeated?
Jack looked at the clock, it was 0212.
"Do I wake Dick, or wait till there's another broadcast?"
Picking up the mic he transmitted, "Say again your last. Say again your last. Over."
Nothing but static. Resuming his seat in the corner of the day bed, Jack leaned up against the bulkhead, scanning the

surroundings through the NVG's. He found he could see the shoreline through the wheelhouse windows.

"Station on Channel 1. Do you copy?"

Jack nearly choked on his coffee, realising someone was trying to contact them. Time to get Dick!

Dick opened his eyes, woken from another deep sleep by Jack urgently shaking his shoulders.

"Is it that time already Jack?"

"Na! You're wanted on the phone mate!"

Dick pulled on some clothes while he listened intently as Jack filled him in about the repeated radio broadcast and the subsequent call.

"I wasn't sure whether it was a trap, so I figured it was better not to answer them."

"Wise move Jack, although I'm not sure they could track us. Can't be certain of that though, so we should keep it short and sweet."

The pair went back to the wheelhouse and Dick grabbed the mic.

"This is Bravo Zulu, Bravo Zulu. I have a copy."

"Who's Bravo Zulu Dick?"

"Just made it up Jack."

"Bravo Zulu on Channel 1. Glad to hear your voice. Where are you?"

Dick looked at Jack; they both knew it would be a stupid idea to give away their position.

"Station calling Bravo Zulu. Negative position. Who are you?"

"Bravo Zulu, we are survivors situated Benowa East Coast Taswegia. Following the Holocaust Taswegia has been invaded by troops from North Korea and Indonesia. They call themselves the Alliance. They are systematically killing everyone except for medical staff. Can you help? Over."

Jack looked at Dick. "What do you reckon?"

"Don't know. It could be legit mate, but I don't know that we're in a situation where we could help them even if we decided to try. Having said that, we can maybe give them a bit of hope. I don't even think they know where we're transmitting from, for all they know we might be in New Haka or Victoria. Mind you, that's a long shot because the repeater shouldn't work over those distances."

"Who knows Dick. Maybe the atomic fallout has done some weird shit to the atmosphere."

"That's quite possible mate. Quite possible."

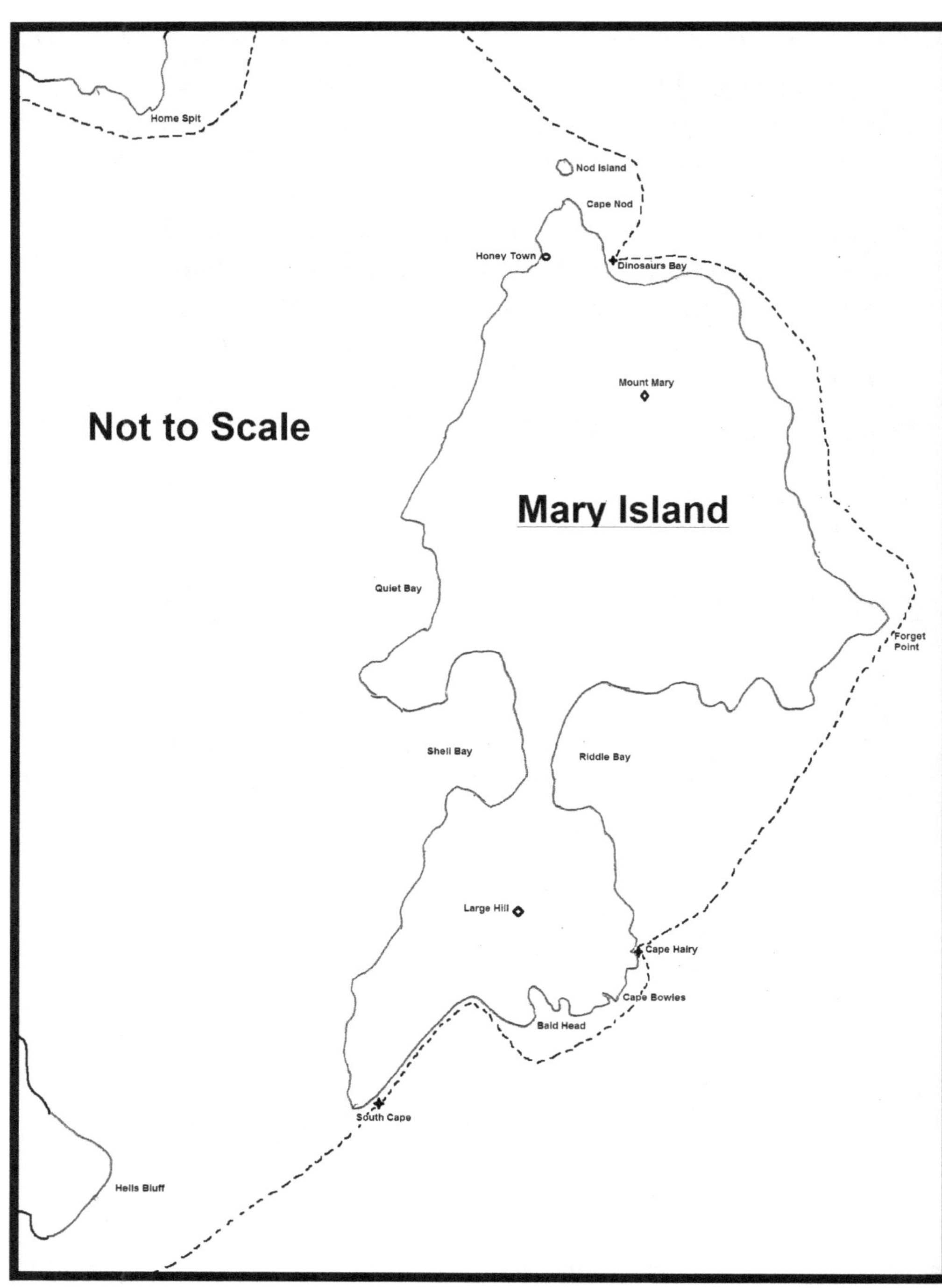

Home Spit
Nod Island
Cape Nod
Honey Town
Dinosaurs Bay
Not to Scale
Mount Mary
Mary Island
Quiet Bay
Forget Point
Shell Bay
Riddle Bay
Large Hill
Cape Hairy
Cape Bowles
Bald Head
South Cape
Hells Bluff

Chapter 19
Mt Willy and Beyond

Saturday 10th January 2015 ... Willy Town State Forest. Through Annie's eyes ...

It was 0400. I'd woken Sarge an hour ago by sliding into his swag with nothing on but my tee shirt. Rain had started to fall, we could hear it on the canvas swags. It got heavier by the minute, in the end Sarge decided it was time to wake up the others.

"Sorry ladies! There's no point in us letting everything get soaking wet. May as well break camp and start the day."

"What? In the dark Sarge?"

"You're darn right April."

He explained that if they stayed where they were all the camping gear would get saturated, including the swags. It would be much easier to keep everything dry once it was rolled up and stored under the protection of the rain sheets.

By 0430 we were saddled up and moving off. We were all wet through and appreciated the warmth of our mounts under us as the rain started to pour down even harder.

"All this rain's good for one thing girls," said Sarge. "At least it's going to wash away any hoof prints we might have left behind us."

It didn't take long for our eyes to adjust to the moonlight, or at least what there was of it. As daybreak approached the rain started to ease, well it was either that, or else we were moving away from it. By now we'd been travelling for almost three hours.

"We should be starting to descend soon Annie."

"Yep! Got ya Sarge. I can see the entrance to the track coming up."

As we descended out of forestry, the memory of Sarge in his swag made me smile. I felt kind of guilty about our 'bang', which was how Dick would have described it. Geez those navy boys had some strange sayings!

The rain had almost stopped altogether as we rode past an old boiler which had long been embedded in the forest. This was a remnant left over from the old steam-driven sawmill that had been the main industry for this area back then.

We made our way down to the sleepy hollow of Willy Town. Although this was mainly a shack area, we weren't sure what we'd find there, what we did know was that the last thing we wanted to do was to leave any sign we'd been there. If the Alliance followed us from this point on it would be a disaster, this was the, 'last frontier,' so to speak before we'd reach Hells Beach.

We'd changed back to our regular mounts the night before, so I was back on my champion. Tom pushed up to the stream.

"We'd better travel for about a click up through the water," called Sarge. "Even if the trackers did get a whiff of our scent, the water might confuse them for a while."

"Good thinking Sarge!"

The stream ran along the back of three properties. We all kept a sharp eye out but didn't see any movement, and eventually drew parallel with the last little shack.

Sarge dismounted and called out,

"Stay put girls! I'll go for a look see."

All he found were bodies. After quickly scanning the area, the ex-Sapper reported back to the group.

"Looks like we've got here in between the kill and clean-up squads. I suggest we should get the hell out of here."

"How many bodies Sarge?"

"About seven or eight Patch," said Sarge sadly, "it was hard to tell. It looked like a few families had holed up together."

"Were there any kids?"

"It looked like there were a few April, but like I said, it was hard to tell without getting any closer."

Sarge remounted and motioned to me to lead off. After making our way up the stream for another three hundred metres we finally emerged and crossed the road.

"Looks like no vehicles have been on this road for a while. The kill squad truck must have stopped at the last house, they haven't even checked to see whether there were any more houses further down the road."

"Are they going to see our hoof prints Sarge?"

"Yes, I reckon they could. I figure the best thing we can do is to get clear by going further through the bushes, then go back on foot and do the old brush-off trick."

"What about up further Sarge? You know, the place where we'll come out on to the old firebreak before climbing the bluff."

"Yeah, we'll have to do the same thing there too Annie," he replied.

Once we were all successfully over the road and hidden from view, Sarge told us to dismount and wait there for him. After finding a suitable branch, he went back to erase our tracks, making sure he backed up and erased his own as he went. This can't have been easy, given that the ground was more like mud than dirt!

As he remounted Socks it started to rain again.

"Ah well. At least that means a double-dose of disguising!" muttered Sarge.

April, thankful that today was the final leg, was hoping we didn't have far to go. "How much further?"

"Good question," I replied. "I can't remember."

Sarge answered the French woman.

"I think I can answer that one. It's about fifteen kilometres to the firebreak, that will make it about midday by the time we get there. After that we've got another twelve kilometres to go before we reach the top of the bluff. We might have to stop for lunch half-way up. It's terribly steep and will be hard on the horses, especially when we're towing pack horses."

"So, lunch about 1230 then Sarge? Will we be able to light a fire so we can dry out a bit?"

"It should be all right April, but it depends on whether the rain eases and whether we can get one lit!"

April wasn't happy with his answer.

"I suppose all the wood will be wet."

I laughed. "Don't worry, I know a trick that Dick taught me. We should be able to find some dry twigs on the old trees. Those ones will be dryer because they're off the ground, so they'll be easier to light."

"Now I know why someone invented fire lighters Annie!"

As the rain eased, we all started to feel a bit more comfortable.

"Geez, I'm bloody proud of these horses!" I boasted.

Sarge waded into the conversation. "You know, I don't think most horses could have coped with what we've been through over the past week."

He looked at us, and continued,"And I'll tell you what girls, I'm bloody proud of you all for the same reason. As a matter of fact,

I don't know whether some of the diggers I served with back in Iraq would have done as well as you have."

We were all silent for a while, just thinking about what Sarge had said. We knew he'd meant every word, he was not one to give praise lightly. In fact, I couldn't remember him ever giving that sort of accolade before, to anyone!

I knew April was feeling sore again, she was probably wondering whether she'd ever get used to that dammed saddle, but at least she kept her mouth shut this time.

As we made our way towards the firebreak we rode in silence, all of us were thinking about other places and other times.

Saturday 10ᵗʰ January 2015 ... Willy Town State Forest. Through April's eyes ...

I was remembering my hometown of Chevaigne-du-Maine, and my favourite baker; the one who'd had a little shop just down the road from our home.

My parents used to take me to his shop in the mornings, and we'd each select a croissant. I was allowed to have a milkshake while my mother and father enjoyed a coffee, this was a real breakfast treat.

I really missed those long-gone days, and I wondered what it was like there now, and how much devastation there'd been after the blasts. I remembered the trip Jack and I had made back there, when I'd showed him the house I was brought up in, as well as the house that I lived in with the monster. I shuddered. Not all memories were good.

I often wondered what had happened to my daughter, it had been six months since I'd last spoken to her on the phone. After many years of having no contact with each other, Rachel had finally found me through email, and since then we'd tried to stay in touch.

Jack and I had been planning a trip to France to catch up with her when everything had gone crazy. I had no way of knowing whether Rachel was alive, or if not, how she'd died. I knew Jack hated it when I started thinking like this, but I guess, like most other mothers, I couldn't help worrying.

Saturday 10th January 2015 ... Willy Town State Forest. Through Annie's eyes ...

As I negotiated the track in front, I found myself thinking back to the days on the farm with mum, getting ready for a horse show.

"Come on Mary! We'll be late if you don't get a wriggle on!"

Mary was always late, usually she was at her boyfriend's place and had to sneak back into the room early in the morning so mum wouldn't know.

"Your sister is always ready before you. What's wrong with you girl!"

Mary was two years older than me. She'd met Toby at school, and they'd been sweethearts from the age of six. Mum couldn't stand the boy, she knew he'd come from a bad family, and he was always in trouble with the law. But the more she tried to persuade Mary not to see him, the more Mary wanted him!

She'd filled my head with all the gory details about how, when she was thirteen years old, she and Toby had slept together for the first time. I didn't want to know, it was all water off my back. I didn't like Toby anyway, and besides, all I cared about in those days were the horses.

Saturday 10th January 2015 ... Willy Town State Forest. Through Patch's eyes ...

My mind took me back to the day I'd met Dick. I could still clearly remember that day at the beach, and all of the antics that had gone on with my sister and the moron who ended up getting smashed by one of Dick's mates.

I thought about our second date. Dick had rung up the very next day and we'd arranged to meet at the same coffee shop on the beach. I remembered thinking that the handsome man was built like a 'brick shithouse,' he was a couple of pick-handles wide across the shoulders, and the first man ever to make me feel petite. I'd never had that happen before!

We'd spent the day enjoying each other's company and had eventually ended up at an Italian restaurant for dinner.

I remembered telling Dick, "Well if you're going to shout dinner, I'll buy the wine!"

Not being a big wine drinker, I had no idea that you didn't have to spend a fortune on a bottle in order to get a good one, so I ordered a forty-nine-dollar bottle of Shiraz! It was horrible!

We'd laughed about it later while sitting in Dick's car overlooking the town of Carnarvon; I remembered we'd talked for hours about our upbringing and our families.

I remembered the first time Dick had kissed me. Not sure whether he'd offend me, he'd asked in a kind of old-fashioned way, "Would you mind if I kissed you?"

This was a novel approach, and one that I liked, after I agreed we shared our first, a very passionate kiss. Wow! I'd known from that moment on that he was the one. Later that night, after he'd driven me back to my flat, it seemed only natural to invite him in.

It was obvious that he was more experienced than I was in the art of love making, I remembered experiencing a kind of pleasure I'd never experienced before.

The snap of a fallen branch in front of me brought me back to reality. Blushing at my thoughts, I asked Sarge what time it was.

Saturday 10th January 2015 … Willy Town State Forest. Through Sarge's eyes…

I was miles away, lost in thought, and didn't hear Patch's question at first. I was thinking about the days I'd spent in Iraq. After deploying in April 2005, I'd been part of the 2nd Combat Engineer Regiment based in Brisbane, for the purposes of the jump into Iraq, we'd been attached to the 4th Battalion Royal Australian Commando Regiment.

The Australian government had announced that the Australian Army would deploy a battle group to Al Muthanna Province to provide security for the Japanese engineers deployed to the province, as well as to help train the Iraqi security forces. This force was around five hundred strong, and was equipped with armoured vehicles, including ASLAV's and Bushmasters. Known as the Al Muthanna Task Group, it commenced operations in April 2005.

My first tour was for six months. I remembered going home on leave in November and how proud my dad had been of his little boy's achievements. My girlfriend at that time wasn't supportive of what I did, all she wanted was for me to get out of the army! It wasn't a good relationship from the beginning, and after it ended badly while we were living in Brisbane, I'd volunteered for a second tour.

Following the withdrawal of the Japanese force and the transition of Al Muthanna to Iraqi control, in July 2006 the Australian battle group was relocated to the Tallil Air Base in the neighbouring Dhi Qar province.

From that point on we became known as the Overwatch Battle Group West, or OBG(W); a title that reflected the unit's new role. Al Muthanna and Dhi Qar were the westernmost of the four southern provinces, and OBG(W) became the prime coalition intervention force in the western sector of the British multi-national Division

(South East) (Iraq) (BMND-SE) area of operations, with BMND-SE based in the southern port city of Basrah.

Responsibility for Overwatch in Dhi Qar was subsequently assumed from the withdrawing Italian contingent in late October 2006, after which the OBG(W) continued to train the Iraqi security forces. By late 2006, the overall numbers of personnel committed to Operation Catalyst (Iraq) had risen to 1400.

My main roll was that of Engineering Support and I'd quite enjoyed working with the British, I didn't even mind the Japanese, although I wasn't too happy with the Yanks!

After returning home again at Christmas 2006, I went back to Brisbane, but after the excitement of Iraq, I just couldr't settle into life back in Australia, so I volunteered again in late 2007.

The Australian combat forces began withdrawing from Iraq on 1 June 2008, and the OBG(W) and Australian Army Training Team formally ceased combat operations on 2 June 2008, after having helped to train some 33,000 Iraqi soldiers.

Approximately 200 Australian personnel remained in Iraq undertaking logistical and air surveillance duties. I was keen to have my deployment extended, but my boss reckoned he couldn't justify my request, so my third deployment ended in June 2008.

Saturday 10th January 2015 ... Willy Town State Forest. Through April's eyes ...

Jerking back into reality, the ex-Sapper blurted out, "It's 1200 Patch, and I'm bloody hungry!"

"I agreed, me too! What's for ... you know ... what do you call it in the army Sarge? I know in Pussers Jack and Dick called it scran?"

"Chow April! We called it chow, among other things." Sarge answered.

I wasn't sure how Patch had ended up being the custodian of the scran, chow, tucker or whatever; mind you, she reckoned she didn't really mind.

"We've got some snags ... we can heat them up in a billy. Plus, there's still some cheese, carrots and biscuits, we can wash it down with our usual coffee. I'll just fire up the old coffee machine that I have hiding in my wither bags!"

"Sounds like marvellous chow to me Patch!"

"What does scran mean again?" asked Annie.

"I'll tell you after we eat Annie," said Sarge. "Speaking of food, I think we should give the horses a handful of grain, then try and find them some sweet pickings at lunch time. The poor bastards have been working hard today."

After finding a small patch of grass, we decided to break for lunch where we were. Sarge and Annie de-tacked all the horses and hobbled them.

"Don't want the buggers to get excited and run off now do we."

I snorted. "If they do, Annie, it won't be me chasing them!"

"That's fine by me April. You can walk!"

"Now, now girls. Be nice!"

Sarge was aware of the continual conflict between me and Annie. I tried not to react, but sometimes I just couldn't help it; the younger girl had such an attitude at times.

Patch prepped the lunch, while I went searching for dry twigs; the fire was soon well under way.

Patch decided to boil the cooked snags; she reckoned they'd be nicer hot.

She was watching the horses as she worked, they were happily munching away on what looked like a very good selection of native grasses.

"You know, I wonder what they think about all this killing."

"I hadn't really thought about it Patch. What do you reckon Annie?"

"I reckon all they want to do is eat and try and do what we ask."

Sarge grinned ruefully. "Well, maybe not Cowboy!"

The next two hours went by pretty quickly. With full bellies, we were all feeling content; even the horses were stepp'ng out a little, so we rode in silence for quite a while.

After rounding a large boulder, we were greeted by a magnificent view that fair took my breath away! The scene from the top of the bluff was amazing! From what I could see, we'd come to a dead end, after the huge boulder the track just stopped. I couldn't see anything to my right or to my left, it was pretty scary being this high above the sea, which was way down below us.

I looked at Annie. "You're the expert. Where to now?"

"You'll see!"

From the top of the bluff we could see all the way to Mary Island in the north east, and if we used the binoculars, we could just make out the entrance to Barracouta in the far distance.

"Might be able to see Jack and Dick!"

"Now there's a thought Patch!"

Sarge slowly scanned the section of water between Mary Island and the coast, shaking his head.

"Nothing yet Patch."

As we looked south, we could make out the peninsular, and if we carefully leaned out over the edge as far as we dared, we could just make out a strip of sand a long way below us.

"Is that Hells Beach?" I asked.

"Well it's what you can see of it from here April; it's kind of tucked in underneath us," explained Sarge.

I shuddered at the thought of what I was fairly sure we were going to have to do next.

"How on earth are we going to get down there?"

"Ah! This is where it gets tricky! We'll have to get a move on, otherwise we'll still be trying to climb down there when it gets dark, and that's just plain dangerous."

Sarge explained that what we were looking at was, in fact, an illusion. From the front it looked like a dead end, just boulders and a cliff. He pointed to an even larger boulder to our right.

"Once you squeeze around the back of that one, you'll find there's a small but passable animal track about twelve inches wide. It will be scary because the drop on your left is a long way down, but after about twenty feet the track widens out and cuts back towards the cliff. After that it's just a matter of zig zagging our way down to the beach below. Oh, and once you get to the bottom, you'll find the track turns into a stream."

"We're not mountain goats Sarge!"

"No, we're not April. Look, I realise it's a bit scary, and in places a bit dangerous, but it acts as a natural barrier to anyone who might be following us, but who won't know where the track goes."

"You got that part right Sarge! No one in their right mind would go down there."

"Except us," whispered Annie, as she moved Tom around the boulder and disappeared out of sight.

"You've got to trust me April. If it will help you and Patch, I'll take the pack horses down."

"That's very kind of you Sarge."

I was still terrified, but I trusted the ex-Sapper, and I knew I had no choice.

"I'll have a go Sarge. I reckon I can handle Bob too."

"Good on ya Patch."

If Patch figured she could do it, I wasn't going to stay behind, before I could change my mind, I started off on Fannie, carefully making my way around the boulder and trying hard not to look down. It was definitely scary at first, but just as Sarge had told us, once I got around the boulder the track widened out.

I could hear Patch following me on Zen, with Bob walking along behind. As we reached easier ground Patch exclaimed,

"Bob has obviously done this before!"

Sarge, on Socks, and towing Cowboy, laughed out loud.

"Only about ten times Patch, but that's more times than anyone else!"

We zig-zagged down the narrow, but surprisingly safe track, for what seemed like an eternity, and, just as Sarge had said we would, ended up at the bottom in a fresh-water stream.

Annie had stopped there to let Tom have a drink while they waited for us to catch up. She yelled back up the line, "Give them all a drink here, everyone needs to wait until they've had their fill."

Only another half-kilometre further down the stream we came upon the beach. It was unexpectedly beautiful, reminding me of the sort of tropical scene you might find on a post card from a tropical island. I drank in the sight of the pure white sand, and the gentle surf rolling onto the half-kilometre stretch, framed on both sides by high cliffs overlooking a small area beyond the dunes. Towering over these I could see even higher cliffs, which seemed to stretch right up to the sky itself!

Turning back in her saddle, Annie threw her hands in the air and triumphantly declared, "Welcome to Hells Beach!"

Chapter 20
Fishing

Friday 9th January 2015 … northern end of Dinosaurs Bay, Mary Island.

It was 0230.

"Station at Benowa East Coast Taswegia. This is Bravo Zulu. Over."

Jack and Dick had decided that, just in case there really were survivors, it was better to give them some incentive to live. They planned to tell them they'd also survived, but that was all.

"Bravo Zulu this is Benowa receiving 20/20."

"Benowa, we have also survived. Nice touch to replay the broadcast. It's too dangerous to give place names; you never know whether the bad guys are listening. Suggest you use Bravo Echo. How many in your party? Over."

"Bravo Zulu, this is Bravo Echo. There are twelve of us, made up of five families. How many of you?"

"Bravo Echo there are six of us. Over."

"BREAKER! BREAKER! DO NOT TRANSMIT! THEY ARE LISTENING!"

"Bravo Zulu how far are you away from us? Over."

"Bravo Echo too far. Repeat too far. Will try to keep in contact. Out!"

Dick looked at Jack.

"Who the fuck was the **other station!** It sounded like they were trying to warn us."

"Boy. That was a turn up for the books Dick!"

"Yeah. Not sure I fully trust them. The silly bastards gave their position away and if the Alliance was listening, they'll now know there are still more people at Benowa that they'll have to get rid of!"

Jack shook his head. It was hard to know what to believe.

"You'd better go and get your head down for an hour or so Dick. You didn't get your full kip before."

"Yeah, I feel stuffed Jack. Give us a piss at daybreak."

Jack went back to his seat and daydreamed of April. He remembered vividly the first time he'd slept with her, with her long flowing hair that went well down past her waist. She was like Lady Godiva, with those huge breasts! The week he spent with her after his wounding. What a time that was!

All he could hear was the gentle slapping of the waves against the timber hull, the creaking of the rigging, and the occasional sound of a piece of kit as it moved and knocked against something else; he had reached that half-dazed, half-asleep mode brought about by sleep deprivation and physical exhaustion, which he remembered well from his time in Pussers. It could be a dangerous time, especially for someone supposed to be on watch.

Shaking himself awake, Jack got up and did the deck rounds, scanning the horizon with the NVG's. Satisfied that all was well he put the kettle on.

"It's 0500 Dick! All's good and the kettle's boiling."

"Great mate! And thanks for the extra hours."

Jack flashed up the engine. The sound of the rumble below decks gave Dick a great sense of wellbeing.

"The fuel state is at ninety-per-cent mate."

Dick moved the *CJ* forward up on the pick, while Jack fired up the capstan.

"Chain vertical!"

Then, a few moments later, "Pick clear!"

With the anchor finally stowed away, Dick put the old girl into gear and swung the wheel to head southwest, gently chugging out of the bay.

"I reckon the sea state is lighter today, less than half a metre," smiled Dick.

Jack was thinking about the distance ahead. "Where do you reckon we'll get to today?"

"With a bit of luck and a fair breeze so to speak, we should get as far down as Hairy Cape or maybe even Bald Head."

"What's for scran?" Jack was hungry.

"Thought I might rustle up train smash Jack."

After downing his breakfast Jack went forward to get his head down again. Dick sat back in the skipper's chair, thinking about how good it would be to make love with Patch. After a time, his thoughts wandered back to Pussers, CDAT, and his time with CD Team 1; and then on to his quick trip to Nam, and his attachment to CDT3, a special CD team put together to assist the US Navy Seals with explosive ordnance disposal units and specialist insurgency work in late 1971 to 1972.

The Yank Seals were different to the general army guys, they were more professional and not as blasé in the way they looked at things in general. He'd made quite a few good friends from among their number; one in particular had meant a lot to him.

Lee and his wife Carol were now retired and happily living in Texas on their small ranch outside of San Angelo. Lee was the mate who bred Quarter Horses, including Zen, the one he'd bought for Patch. He'd often wondered what had happened to Lee following the Holocaust; he had a real fondness for the 'Old Curmudgeon and Wanna-be Indian', as he'd called himself. Lee had been brought up by an Indian family and absolutely loved their culture, their customs, and the people themselves.

After the war, he had become a professor of literature and had taught in Japan for many years before returning to Texas. After that he'd taught at a university in Houston for many years; eventually moving to San Angelo and teaching at a university there. Carol was his second wife, they'd met while he was in Houston. She'd ended up working at San Angelo as the university's student liaison officer.

Dick and Patch had visited them twice over the years, he was a true mate, and he sure did miss the old bugger.

He remembered another mate, an ex-pat Australian, who had moved to Los Angeles with his wife Katherine. After the war, Ed had run his own security business, taking care of some pretty high-profile customers. Dick had lost touch with him but figured he would have almost retired by now ... maybe ... Nah! The man was a workaholic! He'd never retire. Dick guessed that was all out the window now, all he could hope for was that they didn't suffer too much.

After giving Jack a shake at 1150 he served up lunch, compliments of old Barry. Tinned bollocks in blood, known more commonly as meatballs in tomato sauce.

The afternoon watch was uneventful, and they passed Forget Point in good time.

"It's 1620 Dick! I let you sleep in a little. All's good, it looks like we're halfway across Riddle Bay."

Dick felt better for the sleep and appreciated what his mate had done for him. It was common practise, when only two people were on board, to bend the rules sometimes during watch keeping.

"I'll return the favour mate!"

Dick peered over the navigation chart, confirming their position.

"We'll head for the bay between Cape Hairy and Cape Bowles; I reckon our ETA will be around 1900."

Jack went below to do his engine room rounds. It wasn't totally necessary, the space was too small to even swing a cat around in there, which meant he could do the rounds from half-way down the ladder, but it was an old habit he wasn't ready to break.

Jack seemed to be taking longer than usual. Dick called down the hatch, "Everything okay Jack?"

Jack popped his head up out of the hole, looking like some sort of genie rising up in a cloud of smoke.

"Had a bit of a problem," he reported. "The fuel state's eighty-per-cent, and the water level's sixty-five-per-cent. We had a small leak coming from the gearbox housing; I've tightened that one. The stern gland is also leaking a bit."

"How bad is the stern gland leak mate?"

"It's not too bad. I've got the bilge pump going, and it's managing to keep up with it. It's probably just a product of the old girl's age, along with that pounding she got yesterday!"

Dick pointed off the port bow, where a pod of dolphins was playfully frolicking in what there was of their bow wash.

"It's 1840. We've made great time mate!"

"Yeah! I reckon the wind and sea up our arse have helped us along too."

As they rounded the point of Cape Hairy, Dick yelled out, "Vessel off the starboard bow! Action stations!"

Jack, who was in the heads, swore loudly to himself.

"Can't it wait till I finish my shit Dick?"

Dick slowed the *CJ* down to half throttle and waited until Jack had finished his business.

After checking the vessel out with the glasses, he handed them to Jack, saying, "There's no sign of life mate. To me it looks like a Conquest."

After scanning the boat Jack agreed.

"Can't see anyone either Dick. Do you reckon it's a fishing boat?"

They idled the boat up on the port side of the *Carnivore*. She turned out to be a sixty-five-foot Conquest; the fibreglass boats that had ushered in a brand-new way of fishing. They were fast boats, with a top speed of forty-five knots. Instead of slowly chugging out to the fishing grounds, laying their pots, then lying up in a bay for twelve hours or so then having to go back out to pull the pots, the fishermen could simply zip out and drop the pots then zip back in. They'd then repeat the process twelve hours later; they used more fuel, but the whole thing was far less stressful for the crew.

Jack and Dick weren't taking any chances. Jack first slipped a few fenders over the side and then manned the Bren on the starboard side, keeping a close eye on the fibreglass vessel as Dick bought the old single-screwed boat alongside. After giving it a burst astern, and then neutral, Dick made for the line amidships and made it fast to the main bollard on the *Carnivore*.

"I'll leave the donk going for a bit Jack; just in case we need to exit fast!"

"Good idea! I'll check the engine room Dick."

With his 9 mm Browning high-power drawn and at the ready, Dick jumped the guard rail and quickly made his way into the forward wheelhouse, and then down the stairs to the sleeping quarters.

Jack appeared through the engine room hatch.

"All clear aft!"

Dick reported, "All clear forward too. Looks like the ship's dinghy is missing. Better keep an eye on the shore mate while I look around and try to work out what happened."

"The engine's fucked Dick! The E1 made a real mess of it!"

Jack lowered himself into a seat and kept his eye on the rocky beach, which was only some 500 metres away, while Dick went through all the stuff in the wheelhouse, the storage lockers and cool room. He handed his mate a beer.

"Looks like they were cray fishing at the time the E1 hit. My guess is that they anchored overnight, then stayed on board for a while and exhausted all the fresh food. They've left some tinned stuff and a shit load of grog behind; looks like they've just taken some of their clothing, and some of the tinned stuff and scarpered in the dinghy. And they're armed! Looks like they were packing some weapons in the gun safe, but it's empty now."

"Interesting Dick. Why do you reckon they left the grog behind?"

"Don't know. Maybe they just took as much as they could carry. All we know for sure is that they're not here at the moment. My guess is that they're probably ashore somewhere on Mary Island, it's even possible they might not even know what's been going on. If it was me, I would have gone over to the settlement on the other side of the island, there's usually a couple of park rangers living there."

They both knew they didn't have time to go and search for the missing men, as far as they were aware the Alliance didn't have any vessels in the area, but they couldn't be certain of that. Their best bet was to stick to the plan. They both agreed that, with possibly two crew members missing, this would mean there were either two extra people on the island now, or possibly two more locals dead!

Watch keeping was as normal, except for Dick taking the guts and Jack the first and the morning watches; they also enjoyed a change of menu selections from their newly found pantry pot mess.

Watches were a little more interesting now that they had a second vessel to look around, as well as mooring lines to check. They spent a fair bit of watch time going through the *Carnivore* more thoroughly, extracting anything they thought might prove to be even remotely useable.

*Saturday 10*th *January 2015 … Cape Hairy, outside Mary Island.*

"It's 0530! We'd better load whatever we've found that's useable!"

They'd added a fair bit of booty to their stores; two boxes of tinned food, mainly consisting of ten tins of HITS (Herrings in Tomato Sauce), one carton of tinned cow (condensed milk), twelve cartons of beer, six cases of wine, three litres of rum, three litres of whiskey and two cartons of Coke.

Added to the loot were quite a few fishing rods along with tackle, cutlery, crockery, pots and pans, two full gas bottles, twelve fenders, four twelve-volt batteries and last, but not least, a large bulkhead-mounted first aid kit.

Jack called out from the engine room. "Do you want me to drain the diesel out Dick?"

"Have you got any containers mate?"

"Yeah … there's about eight twenty-five litre water containers below which are full of water."

"Shit! We don't need the water, so if you think it's possible, we'll take the diesel."

They worked together, with Jack filling and Dick carting the containers to the *CJ*, while maintaining a constant eye on the coast just in case the crew happened to come back. They were just about to leave when Dick grabbed a bin full of buoys and pot rope coils.

"You never know when we might need this!"

"Should we blow her up Dick?"

Jack was grinning, hoping his mate would agree.

"No Jack. I reckon it would make too much noise and draw attention to us. If you can think of a different way to sink her though, go for it!"

Jack thought long and hard.

"Too easy! I could simply chop a few holes in the hull with the fire axe!"

"Way to go mate!"

Jack was off like an excited schoolboy about to blow up his first mailbox on cracker night! Loud noises came from the engine room, followed by the sound of rushing water. Jack eventually re-emerged from the hatch and quickly jumped the rail, smiling like he'd just touched his first pussy.

Dick put the old girl into gear, and they started to move away from the *Carnivore*, which by this time was slowly but quite definitely sinking.

"There's fifty foot of water under us mate! Nobody will realise it was here."

Dick headed the boat back out to sea, realising he was famished.

"Shit, I'm starving! With all that excitement we completely forgot about brekkie."

"I'll get something together mate while you take us out," said Jack, starting to search for tins of spaghetti bol.

Dick turned in his seat to check what was happening with the *Carnivore*. He could see the wheelhouse still showing above the waterline.

"Bugger! I forgot about the floatation devices!"

Boof!

Dick heard the sound of a muffled explosion coming from the Conquest; and watched it quickly sink out of sight. Puzzled, he looked over at his mate, who was whistling nonchalantly, and looking in the other direction.

"What the fuck was that Jack!"

Jack was laughing. "I couldn't help myself! I accidentally left a grenade wedged against the hull with a buoy attached to the pin; when it flooded it must have pulled the pin. Who'd have thought that would happen. Good thing it was nice and silent!"

"Good one mate. Remind me never to get on your wrong side!"

Still chuckling, Jack went forward to lash down the booty they'd acquired.

By lunchtime they found themselves level with Bald Head and heading straight for Hells Bluff. They were making good progress; in another four hours they'd be clear of Mary Island. Then they could turn southwest.

"ETA Hells Beach! 2300!" declared Dick, after double checking his calculations on the little chart table alongside the wheel.

Their discussion that afternoon centred around what they were going to do with the *CJ* once they'd arrived at Hells Beach. Dick suggested they should drop the pick and wait till first light; then let more chain out, allowing the boat to run back until it was about twenty feet from the beach.

Depending on how rough the surf was, they should then be able to unload. By Dick's reckoning, the water should only be three or four feet deep at the stern at that point; he didn't want to let her in too much closer than that because he didn't want to damage the prop.

The other way would be to use the dinghy and ferry the goods ashore; this would be a lot slower but definitely safer.

"You never know when we might need her again Jack!"

"I dunno. She's a bit slow for my liking Dick."

"But she's all we have mate."

Deciding where to keep the *CJ* was proving to be a problem. One option was to simply moor her off the beach and use the little dinghy as a tender; but that would leave her, and them, pretty exposed. If the Alliance ever did arrive in a war ship the, *'Cecil Jane'* would stick out like a sore thumb!

"Maybe she would fit in the gulch just south of the beach. I discovered it while exploring on one of the treks; it looked to be about one hundred-and-fifty-feet long and maybe twenty-five-feet wide. I don't know for sure, but I'm guessing the depth is plenty deep enough; it looked like it was about thirty feet straight down. There was good access via a pathway from the beach, we used to take the clients swimming there sometimes when the surf was too rough."

"That sounds perfect Dick!"

"Almost, but not quite mate. We'll need to work out how to tie her off, or else the surge will smash her to pieces! The gulch has got sheer rock sides, and one of them is flat on top, a bit like a wharf. It's certainly worth looking at, especially now we have plenty of fenders and mooring lines."

"Thanks to the *Carnivore!*" added Jack.

Dick, after scouring the horizon through the binoculars, suddenly turned the vessel hard to starboard.

"Hands to tea, starboard 30!"

This had been a regular event at sea when the skipper wanted to test the ship's manoeuvrability at the start of the second dog-watch, which just so happened to coincide with scran! The crew, of course, just reckoned it was the old man's way of getting back at them, with all their meals sent skating across the tables, accompanied by the clatter of plates hitting the deck in the scullery.

Jack had been halfway through making the brews!

"What the fuck Dick! I nearly lost them!"

"Sorry mate! I just noticed something in the water, if my theory is right, we're in for a treat!"

He reminded Jack about the bin of buoys and spare ropes that he'd grabbed as they'd left the *Carnivore*.

"See those buoys in the water off our starboard bow? They're the same shape and colour as the ones I picked up. Fetch the gaff Jack; we're going cray fishing!"

Dick skilfully brought the *CJ* up on the outside of the first buoy under the shadow of Mary Island's southern coastline.

"Tell me which way the rope is lying Jack. I might have to come up on the inside; if we do it wrong the pot will be under the boat!"

Dick remembered his father drilling this into him whenever they'd been out fishing together.

Jack, who'd moved over to the starboard side near the pot hauler, was ready and waiting.

"Rope's lying away from the buoy and away from us Dick," he yelled.

Swinging the boat to port, Dick yelled out, "We'll come around again! Better make sure the breaker is onto the pot hauler, and to give yourself more room, you can open that section of railing alongside the hauler."

Jack disappeared down the hole then re-emerged, with thumbs up.

"Better give me the run around on the pot hauler gizmo mate. I haven't used one of those before!"

"You'll have to hook the pot line with the gaff, then run it over the lead and around the hauler, then hit the hydraulic lever. The line should run out the other side and wind the pot up. Once it hits the table, it'll stop. The table will swing up and become level; at that point you'll need to stop the hauler, lift the pot down onto the deck then remove the crayfish. Put the rope in the pot and buoy on top; then just flip the catch to let the table go for the next pot."

"Sounds easy enough mate. What do we do with the crays?"

"Ah yes! I forgot that part Jack. Just throw them in the well!"

Dick explained that he had no idea what they'd find in the pots; they'd been in the water since the E1 had hit. They could be full of dead crays if an octopus had got into the pot and killed them all.

Crayfish are cannibalistic and will eat their own kind, so it's even possible that more crays could have moved in to eat what was already in there.

"Shit! It all sounds a bit barbaric!"

As they came up on the first buoy, Jack hooked the line, following Dick's instructions to the letter. Dick went out on deck to help his mate.

The pot was just visible, about forty foot down.

"Looks heavy Jack!"

"I can see red, that means there are crays!"

The pot hit the stop and the table levelled out.

"Fucking Hell mate! Looks like it's chockers!"

"It sure does Jack!"

Both of them grunted as they strained to lift the heavy pot onto the deck.

"Got your gloves on?"

Jack quickly put on the good shooting gloves he kept in the side pocket of his cargo pants.

"Make sure you grab them on the back; and be careful not to get your fingers in the way of those claws! You can use the antennas to hang on to them, but it's risky, if they flap their tail the antenna might snap right off!"

As Jack started picking up the first cray, Dick lifted the starboard lid on the wet well.

Splash! Splash! Splash!

One by one Jack threw the crays into the well. Dick stopped him a few times, explaining the dead ones were no good.

"Just throw them in the piss mate!"

"Shit! We're getting a bit close to the shore."

The ex-navy CD ran to the wheelhouse, kicking the old girl astern just in time, and backing her away from the dangerous rocks. After he was happy that they were well away he went back and helped Jack push the empty pot to the port side of the boat.

"Did you count them mate?"

"Yep sure did! Do you want me to keep a tally?"

"That would be a good idea; that way we'll have some idea how long we can survive on them."

After moving up to the next buoy, Jack powered into it like a man possessed.

After Dick helped him lift the second pot down onto the deck he asked,"Are we going to pull them all?"

"Might as well mate!"

"But there's got to be twenty of them!"

"Yep! I reckon this is half of the *Carnivore's* pots. I'm guessing she would have had the same as Barry; a forty-pot licence."

"This could take a while."

"You're probably right. We should drop the pick after we finish just inside Southern Cape, then do the dash across to Hells Beach tomorrow morning. It wouldn't be much fun doing it in the dark with no radar; those sheer rock faces are nasty!"

Pots three through to twenty went pretty much the same way, with the exception of a few light ones in the middle. Then there was the pot from hell! Number seventeen! You couldn't have squeezed another cray into the damn thing, no matter how hard you tried! Lifting it up almost broke both their backs! All in all, it took them almost four hours, working flat out, to pull the twenty pots.

"I don't know about you Jack, but I'm buggered, and I didn't do half as much work as you did."

"I don't know about that mate. I couldn't have lifted the fucking things on my own. Do you want a brew?"

"Nah ... I reckon its beer o'clock instead. We've certainly earned one! I'll head to the point and we'll lay over just inside, it looks like a good night sea-wise. How many did we end up with mate?"

Dick lashed the wheel and turned to grab the beers, while Jack headed back out on deck with a pad and pencil in hand.

"It'll only take a second to add them up Dick, I scratched the tallies into the timber hand-rail."

Jack closed the well hatch and made it back inside just as Dick ripped the top off a partially chilled beer.

"Guess what! We've scored a grand total of over five hundred crayfish! Five hundred and eighty-eight to be precise!"

"Fuck me mate! That's phenomenal! I knew we had a good tally; even though we had to throw quite a few back. Of course, a lot of them are runts that couldn't get out of the escape hatches because there wasn't enough room to move around, but no one is going to prosecute us for undersized crays are they!"

Jack had a grin from ear to ear.

"We make pretty good fishermen don't we Dick."

"You bet Jack. Do you realise that if each cray weighed even one kilo, what we have in the well is worth over fifty-eight thousand dollars!"

"You've got to be fucking joking mate! Some of those crayfish are more like one and a half kilos apiece!"

"Yeah! But if we work on the average, it's still one hell of a catch!"

"We're rich Dick!"

"Maybe Jack, but who are we going to sell them to. The Alliance?"

Jack laughed.

"Well, I guess we've got no choice. We'll just have to eat the fuckers!"

"I reckon so. Go grab a couple out of the well for scran. I've got a hankering for curried crayfish!"

Chapter 21

Dr Roger Johns (Doc)

Roger Johns was born in Kings Town in 1950, and was the son of a prominent Kings Town doctor. After completing his early education at the exclusive Kings Town Boys Grammar School, Roger continued to follow in his father's footsteps, excelling at university, where he studied medicine. At some stage during his studies he was given the nickname of Doc; the nickname stuck, and from that point on he was only referred to as, 'Roger' in legal documents, on the electoral roll or by his mother!

During his school years, Doc took part in all the normal non-curriculum activities, although he wasn't keen about competing in contact sports. His reluctance in this area was overlooked by both masters and fellow students because of his enthusiastic and skilled participation as part of the sailing team.

Just like his father before him, Roger loved all aspects of sailing and became a regular and successful competitor, representing the university in all on-water-based competitions. His potential came to the notice of the Commodore of the Kings Town Royal Yacht Club, and he was eventually persuaded to race under their banner as a master yachtsman, even competing in several Jackson to Kings Town races.

Doc joined the Naval Reserves in 1968, and as a seaman midshipman studied navigation with the ultimate goal of becoming a navigation officer.

He first came across Dick at HMAS Waterhen; Dick was there as a member of CDT1, while Roger was there with the *HMAS Bass*, which was the reserve boat from the Kings Town Port Division. They discovered early on that they were both Kings Town born and bred, and quickly became friends.

After becoming an Officer in 1974, Doc worked his way up the promotion chain, eventually making Captain just before the Navy pushed him out in 2010.

Doc's specialty was navigation, he always found himself drafted onto Royal Australian Navy ships for extended stays as their Nav Officer, or in later years as Captain of their patrol boats and landing craft. Being self-employed meant he had the freedom to do this; Dick was one of the few who realised that being on the water was the life Doc truly loved.

Whenever he was at home, he'd ring up Dick and say, "Going for a sail for a couple of days mate, want to come?"

If Dick could manage the time away, Patch would tell him to 'go for it,' realising how important their mateship was to both of them. If for some reason Dick wasn't available, Doc would simply go sailing on his own.

Eventually Doc qualified as a doctor, choosing to become a surgeon like his father. However, after a few years he became disillusioned with all the non-essential elective surgery he was performing and decided to specialise in the area of ear, nose and throat diseases. Rising quickly through the ranks, he was at one stage invited to act as President of ASOHNS, the esteemed Australian Society of Otolaryngology Head and Neck Surgery.

In his university days, his peers would have described him as a quiet man who usually stuck to his own company; although for some reason the women seemed to like him, and he never lacked for female company.

Being a prominent ear nose and throat specialist in Kings Town meant there were always plenty of beautiful women waiting in the wings, hoping to catch the eye of the very eligible bachelor, but much to everyone's surprise, in the end it was a girl from the sticks who ended up getting her hooks into Doc.

Millie Johnson came from down the peninsula, growing up in the sleepy seaside town of Sand Alley. After meeting Doc in a night club, she made up her mind, she knew what she wanted and went after it. He didn't have a chance!

They became man and wife in 1975, and soon afterwards had one child, Ebony, who was her mother's pride and joy.

Doc loved his sailing and had always owned a yacht, and whenever possible Dick would go sailing with him. Doc didn't have many close friends apart from Dick; over the years a unique mateship had developed between the two men, and they'd joined forces in quite a few projects.

The Motel in the Wilderness had been one of them. Doc had not only helped to finance the project; he'd also put in more than a few hours helping to build the motel. Dick and Patch had investigated the cost of putting in a landline, but they just couldn't afford it.

In the end Doc gave Dick an analogue mobile phone, also known as a brick phone; it was the only thing that would work in the remote area where they'd built the motel. Even back then, Doc was adamant in his belief that one day the digital system would fail; so much so that he kept an address book of all his mates who still owned a brick phone. He'd even lobbied strongly for the Telco giant to keep it going, eventually they half gave in, leaving the satellite pathway open, although most people found the analogue system too restrictive, and opted instead for the modern digital one.

Dick and Patch used the brick phone for many years, only giving it up when the analogue system was superseded by the digital one.

In their early days together, Millie had been Doc's receptionist, but once married and living in the prestigious Kings Town suburb of Chook Point, she lost interest in performing her receptionist duties, preferring to play, 'Lady of the House' instead. Over the years they simply drifted apart. Doc buried himself in his work, and Millie became a recluse, preferring to stay at home playing, 'Lady of the House' instead of spending time with him.

She put all her energies into spoiling her only daughter. If there was anything Ebony wanted, all she had to do was to put on a teary tantrum in front of her mother, and her every wish would be granted. This was always a sore point with Doc, who resented the fact that all his wife and daughter seemed to see him as was a, 'cash cow'. In the end there was only one main topic of 'conversation' between them.

"Make the girl go out and get a part time job so that she can earn her spending money, instead of fleecing me for all I've got!' was his catch cry.

Ebony could have ended up as a spoilt brat, but at some stage during her high school years, somebody must have given her some good advice, because she turned her attention to her studies; eventually moving into the field of medicine, and qualifying as a paediatrician. Eventually Ebony moved to Brisbane, where she ended up marrying a lawyer.

Millie, who'd been a pack-a-day smoker for most of her life, was diagnosed with terminal cancer in 2014, and was given six months to live.

Even though their relationship had been rocky for years, Doc took it pretty hard when in December 2014 Millie was admitted to the General Hospital in Kings Town.

Chapter 22
At Last!

Sunday 11th January 2015 ... Hells Beach.

Because they'd reached Hells Beach after dark, all they'd had time to do was to run a rope across the small canyon the horses would call home from now on. They'd watered the horses one more time in the stream at the end of the beach, and then hobbled them and let them happily munch away at the abundance of grass in their new home.

The group rolled out their swags and were soon fast asleep, not even bothering to eat. Sarge had elected to not post a watch, saying, "If they find us now, well stiff shit!"

Patch loved waking to the sound of the surf, although she hadn't had much of a chance to do this over the years. Sleepily looking around, she could see that Sarge, always an early riser, had already started a fire and had the billy on.

"What's the time Sarge?"

"You're as bad as Dick, he doesn't wear a watch either!" Sarge was giving her a hard time, he didn't really mind being asked. "It's 0710 Patch. Did you sleep well?"

"I slept like a log! It must be all this salt air."

April stirred. "What's on the agenda for today boss," she asked, smiling at the ex-Sapper who was concentrating on making a brew.

"I figure today we'll take it easy … just do a bit of housekeeping."

He explained that they needed to get everything set up properly. They'd be digging the latrine, fencing the horses in properly, setting up the water troughs, and segregating the grass in the canyon so the horses wouldn't eat it out all at once. Once all that was done, he was happy for them all to chill out for the day and enjoy a swim and a well-deserved rest. It looked like it was going to be a great day as far as the weather went.

"How's scran coming along Sarge?"

"This morning's grub is freshly heated bread with butter and vegemite Patch."

"Yummo!" The fifty-four-year-old loved her vegemite!

They all set about making the most of the morning by getting their camp set up. Sarge dug the latrine and sorted out a couple of logs to use as a makeshift seat. Annie groomed the horses, giving them a little grain feed and worked out the water problem. For now, she decided to use an old twenty-five-litre drum which had been left behind after a past trek to make two water troughs. Sarge gave her a hand by cutting it in half. April and Patch spent the morning gathering a supply of firewood.

Patch reported the wood situation to Sarge.

"There's plenty of wood. Look at it all! I reckon there's about two tons of the stuff that's been washed up at the other end of the beach."

Sarge fetched some more water and put the billy on again, warning them not to put too much driftwood on the fire at once. He'd found it tended to spit out sparks more than bush logs did; probably something to do with the salt content.

"Is there time for a dip before lunch Sarge? April and I are definitely in need of a wash!"

"No problems Patch. Go for it! Lunch will be up in about an hour."

Annie looked at the two older women. "Is it okay to join you two?" asked the perky twenty-eight-year-old.

"Get your togs on Annie. We'll meet you down there!"

Sunday 11ᵗʰ January 2015 ... South Cape, Mary Island.

Dick gave Jack a piss at 0500.

"Time to move mate," he said, shaking his mate awake. Don't be too long, I'm almost done heating up the left-over curry from last night."

After downing a quick breakfast, they made the *CJ* ready for sea.

"Main engine ready for sea, Sir!" said Jack with a wicked laugh.

"Roger that Number One!"

Dick smiled as they started the windlass and recovered the anchor, moving the vessel ahead and out into the channel. Swinging the wheel to port he headed south west, then took a quick look at the chart.

"Looks like ETA Hells Beach is still around 1150!"

The sea condition was dead calm.

"On second thoughts, we just might make even better time Jack."

"Let's hope there's a reception party waiting for us Dick."

"Any kind of party will do me Jack; well maybe not a necktie party!"

Making around 4.5 knots, the *CJ* steamed towards Hells Beach.

The entrance could be difficult to see, especially coming from the north, that's because it was hidden by the rocky outcrop known as Hells Point.

Seeing they were getting close to where they'd been heading, Jack checked the little ship's clock again. It was dead on 1100.

"I think I can see the entrance Dick!"

Jack was pointing in the direction of what might have been a break in the seemingly endless rock formations.

"It's just a little colour difference, but I think it might be what we're looking for."

Dick nodded in agreement and swung the wheel to starboard. "Yep! You're right Jack."

It looked as if the *Cecil Jane's* course was going to take her straight onto the rocks at the foot of the sheer cliffs ahead.

"This is scary Dick! I wouldn't have wanted to be doing this at night; especially with no radar!"

By now they were only about a quarter mile out. The white sand was becoming visible, and Jack was thankful to see that the closer they got the wider the opening appeared to be.

Sunday 11th January 2015 ... Hells Beach.

As the aging fishing boat entered the bay, Dick pointed out the rocks that hid the gulch off the port side. Once they were inside the bay, the swell all but disappeared. The pair scanned the length of the beach.

"Bugger, no reception party Dick. What do you want to do?"

"I reckon we should come about and drop the pick, then go astern until we're in about four feet of water and tie off. After that we'll be able to start unloading."

Jack manned the windlass as Dick swung the CJ a full one-hundred-and-eighty degrees, heading back out towards the entrance.

"Drop anchor!"

Jack released the brake on the windlass and the chain rattled down the hawse pipe.

"Once it's on the bottom Jack, just allow for a bit of feed while I go astern."

"Roger that!"

As the anchor dug in, they could feel the boat straighten, slow astern. Jack watched the chain slowly run out.

"I reckon that will do Jack. It looks like there's only three or four feet under the stern."

As they stood in the doorway to the wheelhouse the pair looked longingly towards the sand dunes.

"Shit! I'm a Dickhead!" Dick swore, as he leaned over and hit the boat's horn.

Honk! Honk! Honk!

Patch and April had been climbing the steep dunes. As they heard the sound of the horn, they both spun around, Patch grabbing hold of April as the French woman stumbled and almost slid back down again.

"Bloody hell April! We've got visitors! Sarge! Annie! They're here!"

Patch ran down the sand towards the boat and headed straight into the water. The lanky brunette, being a competent swimmer, didn't take long to reach the boat.

Dick and Jack had seen her dive in.

"Looks like she's in a bit of a hurry Dick!"

As Patch reached the fishing boat, Dick reached down, grabbing his wife's arm, and pulled her aboard.

"Honey! Boy did I miss you!"

He held her close, sharing a passionate kiss. Out of the corner of his eye he could see Jack in the water wading in to greet April, who was wading out to meet him.

By the time they'd stopped hugging each other; Sarge and Annie had reached the boat and were climbing on board.

Sarge was relieved to see Dick was still in one piece. "Mate! Am I glad to see you!"

"Likewise, Sarge! You too Annie!"

Annie gave the big man a hug, receiving a kiss on the forehead in return. Jack helped April to climb on board, and together they showed the foursome around the little boat.

"Well I reckon we should eat, then get this lot ashore. After that I want to hear all about your adventures!"

"No problems Dick. I've got some soup on back at camp; I bet you two have quite a story to tell as well!"

The unloading went well … Jack stayed on board, and handed the stores down to April, who stowed them on the dinghy before pulling ashore. Annie and Patch helped her unload, then carried the boxes to the campsite. In the meantime, Dick was busy unloading the weapons and ammo; handing them to Sarge who carefully waded ashore with them held high above his head. They all helped to unload the larger items, transporting the tent, poles, and tables ashore in the dinghy.

It took them just over three hours to unload, which was all the time they could spare. By the time they'd finished the tide had started to come in, which meant towards the end they'd had to constantly let out a bit more chain so that they could bring the boat closer to shore.

After pulling the dinghy up on to the sand, they worked together to erect the twenty-five-man army tent.

"I'm glad you remembered to leave enough space free for it Sarge!"

Sarge grinned at Dick, glad to be back with his old mate again.

"Yep! I was pretty sure you'd want to keep the same layout going Dick."

The girls erected the toilet tent and sat the seat frame over the long drop that had been dug by Sarge earlier that day.

Three of the trestle tables had been placed inside the tent; they'd agreed to leave the fourth one outside so that they could use it for prep work.

"What do you feel like for scran Dick?"

"Crayfish!"

Patch looked at Dick, wondering whether the sun had got to him.

"What crayfish?"

Dick was giving her that, 'I know something that you don't know,' kind of look.

"Dick! Don't tell me you've got crayfish! How many? Where? When?"

"It's a very long story darling! I'll fill you in later, over a wine or two!"

"Wine. What wine?"

"Yuk, I don't like crayfish Dick!"

"How would you know that Annie? You've never eaten it before."

"Shut up Sarge! You know I don't eat much seafood!"

They all longed to take time to sit and relax and catch up on what had been happening, but the time was ticking on.

"Where do you want to move the CJ to Dick?"

"I reckon we should move it into the left side of the bay. That way it won't be as visible to any others who wander this way. That should work until we can work out how to tie her off to the gulch Jack. Once we've got her in the right place, remind me to bring some crays ashore."

Jack and Dick set off in the dinghy, and after tying it to the stern, moved the CJ, as they now called her, to a spot well out of sight.

"You know mate, it's amazing how we Taswegians seem to shorten the names of pretty well everything!"

"I think Aussie's are just lazy with their English, that's all. Don't forget to give her a fair bit of chain Jack."

After placing the beer and the full bladders of the cask wine into the canvas bags that Dick and Jack had made up out of what was left in the workshop, they lowered them into the stream at the other end of the beach; that way they could be sure the cold water would keep them all chilled. They stored the rest of the booty in the tent, by now it was starting to look rather full in there!

At last they had it all done and could finally relax around the fire. The fire screen around the outside helped to trap the fire's warmth, and for the first time in over a week they were able to enjoy a well-earned drink together.

As always, Dick was hungry, he prepared an old kerosene tin for cooking the crays in, by filling it with water. After adding a bit of sugar and salt he waited until the water came to the boil. Jack had helped him to drown the fish earlier, knowing how much the girls hated the idea of boiling them alive! They were so large that the ex-CD could only fit three in at a time.

"It looks like we'll be cooking them in two batches."

Dick looked around the group, thinking of all they'd been through.

"I'd like to raise a toast to us all! I must say I'm incredibly proud of every one of you. You've already told me a little bit about the ride over, and I know it hasn't been an easy time for any of you. You've all been through so much! I'd like to say a special thanks to Annie for guiding you all here, and also to Sarge for making sure you all arrived in one piece. I have no idea what's going to happen from here on in, so let's just take it one day at a time."

Jack told the group about the adventures he and Dick had shared, there were lots of questions, and a few, 'oohs' and 'ah's,' and more than once they remembered things they'd forgotten, but eventually they had talked it all out. After another toast, they discussed the plans for the coming day.

"The first thing we need to work out is how to secure the CJ in the gulch. We have plenty of fenders and rope, we just need to work out what to tie her off to."

"I was thinking we should maybe tie her to the flat wall. If we pull her in tight against the fenders, she should be safe from the surge."

"It's a good thing you and Jack brought all that rope from the workshop Dick!"

"Well there was no sense leaving it for the slopes Love! We're just lucky we could fit it in. Mind you, we also picked up a shitload more from the *Carnivore* as well."

Sarge had been thinking about what to do in the event of there being any unwanted visitors. He shared his thoughts with the group.

"I reckon we should set up a booby trap at the start of each of the entrance tracks ... just in case!"

"How many Claymores have we got?"

"Six Sarge."

"Aren't the roos going to be a problem Sarge?"

"Nah ... there's not too many around here April. I think it must be too sandy for them, they tend to stick to forestry."

"We'll have to do a reccy ride south and survey the area, that way we might be able to find out how far the Alliance have got to. It would be better to get to the farm before them if we can."

"What if old John and his missus are there Dick?"

"Well Sarge, I guess we'll just have to cross that bridge when we get to it."

Dick went through the ride plan with the group.

"We need to gather as much food as we can, but I really don't want to pack it back. If anything goes wrong, we'll have to move fast, so it will have to be saddlebags only."

"Who's going Dick?" asked Patch, secretly hoping it wasn't going to be her.

After the long ride she was in constant pain, although she hadn't told anyone else. The thought of more riding right now was not something she wanted to think about. Mind you, if Dick really wanted her to come, she would have done so.

Dick had been thinking about the best way to go about it.

"Patch."

Patch's heart sank, although for her man she'd do it.

"I've been thinking. Are you happy to let Sarge ride Zen?"

What a relief! "No worries Honey! That's the least I can do for the man who saved my life!"

"Okay then. Sarge if you'll ride Zen, Annie can take Tom and I'll take Bob. Those three are our strongest horses and will stand the best chance of carrying a bigger haul.

"It would be great if you're happy to stay here Jack, that way you can look after April and Patch. The fire will need to be kept going as well. If you want to do some fishing while we're away, that would be great!"

Annie was excited at the thought of being included in the raiding party.

"While we were on the CJ, Jack and I worked out a good warning system; if there's any trouble while we're away, you know what to do Jack!"

"Yep, set off a flare. Dick and I discovered a shitload of them on the boat, it seems old Barry had been keeping them for the last ten years!"

Dick nodded. "That's right ... as a professional fisherman he would have had to get new ones each year to stay in survey.

Usually you have to hand your old ones back in, but by the look of it, I'm guessing the old fellow didn't care much for the rules!"

By now the crayfish were cooked; served with a few spuds, along with some seafood sauce and tinned veggies, it was quite a feast! Annie was game enough to try a taste, but really didn't like it, so she opted for tinned sausages instead.

"How many crays did you catch again darling?" asked Patch, not sure Dick hadn't been making the numbers up.

Jack piped up with a grin, "Believe me, there were heaps ... five-hundred-and-eighty-eight of them altogether. Dick reckons if we could sell them, they'd be worth around fifty-eight thousand dollars!"

"They should last us quite a while! All we have to do now is convince Annie to like them. Do you like scale fish Annie?"

"Only flake Dick, oh and maybe a bit of flathead!"

"I'll teach you how to use a handline to fish Annie ... there should be plenty of flathead in the bay."

Patch licked her lips. "Yummo! I love flathead, especially the way you do it, skinned and boned, and crusted with lemon pepper!"

They spent a few memorable hours just listening to the sounds of the night; the waves gently lapping at the beach accompanied by the murmur of the wind through the trees. The only other sound was an occasional whinny from the horses. Thoughts of the Alliance were far from their minds that night as they spent time laughing and talking and enjoying each other's company.

Eventually slipping into the swag alongside of Patch, Dick realised he had never felt quite as contented as he did right now. The head of their swag faced away from the fire; Dick didn't have to do too much to persuade Patch to take off her underwear. It was good to feel her warm body close to his again. Later, as they lay there together, they whispered about possible outcomes, both wondering whether the brick phone would prove to be the answer they hoped it would be.

"That reminds me Hon," murmured Dick, drifting off to sleep. "Don't forget to remind me I need to look at charging the bloody thing tomorrow."

Chapter 23
Invasion Force

0900 Wednesday 31ˢᵗ December 2014 ... on board 'Emily Maersk', South Tasman Sea.

General Jun Lee Sung, Supreme Commander of the invasion fleet, stood on the bridge wing of the *Emily Maersk*; currently one of the largest containerships on the seas. She had been designed to carry more than 11,000 six-metre containers at any one time: with 144 containers on deck, and with the rest below in the cargo hold.

The *Emily Maersk* had undergone a massive conversion to ready her for this mission. Loaded into her containers were one-hundred-and-forty-four vehicles: forty-four jeeps in the containers on deck and one hundred trucks in the ones down in the hold. The area below deck had undergone an extensive conversion, and now housed 275,000 personnel. 75,000 of these were troops; the rest were NK Nationals.

The *Emily Maersk* was 397 metres long and 63 metres wide and was powered by an engine that produced the equivalent output of 1,156 cars. The anchor alone weighed in at an impressive 29 tonnes.

The plan had been born over two years earlier. That was when the President, Gin Gum Kim, decided it was necessary to set up another secret Alliance with Indonesia and India. The design of the ships was paramount to the success of the operation. To be able to transport the massive numbers of personnel from North Korea, India, and Indonesia to Taswegia was going to be no mean feat.

It had been a slow voyage so far, taking forty-two days at an average rate of five knots to cover 9,000 nautical miles. The brief from the President had been simple and non-negotiable.

"Kill everyone!"

The General had been especially hand-picked to lead the invasion force; the President held him in high regard because of his family connections. Jun Lee's father had also been a General; the proven track record of his family meant that President Gin Gum Kim expected nothing but excellence from him during this mission.

As they travelled down the east coast of Taswegia, Jun Lee felt prouder than ever before, although his pride was tempered with a fair amount of sadness. He was proud because he was the chosen one, but also sad because his wife and smaller children could not be with him, held up in the north of Korea because of a family matter, they had not been able to make it back in time to sail with the first convoy.

He was thankful that at least one of his children was with him, his eldest son was an expert in the art of threshing wheat, Jun Lee's plan was to put him in charge of the wind-driven mill at Lakeside.

They were only forty nautical miles from Kings Town.

"Eight hours until we dock General!"

Jun Lee acknowledged the officer.

He thought back to the design of the super ships. They'd built a total of twenty-three vessels in an amazingly brief amount of time. Ten were to travel to Taswegia and another ten to New Haka, that left three. Two of these were going to India and the last to Indonesia.

The official notification advising the order of departure for the four convoys undertaking the voyage had been very precise. The General was fully aware of the need for such precision. It was imperative that all ships in the first convoy arrive on the same date, and as near to the same time as possible. This would give the invasion force occupying the small island state the advantage of surprise, allowing them to catch the Taswegians totally off-guard, with no time to regroup and retaliate.

Official Orders. North Korea to Taswegia, Convoys 1 to 4

Convoy Number 1			
Ship	**Departure Date**	**Destination**	**ETA**
Emily Maersk	5th November 2014	Kings Town	1st January 2015
Louise Maersk	5th November 2014	Kings Town	1st January 2015
Lindy Maersk	5th November 2014	Devonshire	1st January 2015
Julie Maersk	5th November 2014	Bull Bay	1st January 2015
Convoy Number 2			
Joan Maersk	12th November 2014	Kings Town	6th January 2015
Kim Maersk	12th November 2014	Kings Town	6th January 2015
Convoy Number 3			
Sonya Maersk	17th November 2014	Kings Town	11th January 2015
Jessi Maersk	17th November 2014	Kings Town	11th January 2015
Convoy Number 4			
Julia Maersk	23rd November 2014	Kings Town	18th January 2015
Elizabeth Maersk	23rd November 2014	Kings Town	18th January 2015

President Gin Gum Kim, North Korea.

The decision had been made to send all medical staff with the third convoy; upon their arrival in Taswegia, the local staff would be considered no longer necessary, and would be dealt with accordingly.

The fourth convoy was to include among its passengers the President, his family, and the Presidential Staff.

No less than eight naval escort vessels, all of a suitable size for the task, were selected to accompany the series of convoys. These were two Najin Class light frigates, built in North Korea and refitted in early 2014 for the voyage, four Sariwon Class corvette's, also NK built, and two new Nampo Class light frigates.

Jun Lee and all the area commanders had visited Taswegia some months prior to the departure of the first convoy, under the guise of being a visiting tour group of senior citizens. Their true objective had been to gather information considered vital to the success of the planned invasion.

This had included precise mapping of all military installations, police stations, and major buildings of interest, as well as port control in Kings Town, Bull Bay and Devonshire. They'd spent a pleasurable three weeks openly travelling around the state, gathering all the information they needed. No one had any idea of what they were really doing. Who would have thought that the polite group of visitors could have had such a sinister ulterior motive.

The days leading up to their departure hadn't been easy, and there had been many times the General had doubted that the super tankers would be ready in time. Then there were other issues, such as when the workers had finally realised what was happening and that there had been no plans for them to go along. Naturally, they'd wanted in on the plan, this had created a huge headache for the government, who'd placed all responsibility for getting everything sorted out squarely on to Jun Lee's shoulders. Failure was not an option, and the consequences of failure were something he didn't want to think about!

Despite his sadness at not having his wife and younger children with him, for the main part the General had felt nothing but relief when they'd started to move away from the docks.

He did not anticipate any issues as they landed in Taswegia on the 1st. These types of ships had been delivering goods to Taswegia for well over a decade, so the sight of them shouldn't cause any alarm. There would be no unloading facilities because the E1 had destroyed all unloading machinery, so this work would be done by using the aging onboard Derricks.

The plan was first to unload the 144 containers holding the vehicles from both of the super tankers, and to place them onto the wharf. Once it was dark the seventy-five thousand troops from each of the vessels would disembark and gather in the now unused cruise terminal.

At 0500 on 2nd January all invading troops throughout Taswegia were to act together and disperse throughout the different communities within the state.

The first step was to isolate the threat by quietly taking over police stations and military installations, followed by the next part of the plan; to walk in on parliament and demand their surrender. It would be essential not to alert the general public to what was happening, that way the locals would continue to believe that nothing untoward had happened.

Kings Town port control, which these days only kept basic office hours, would simply log the ship as per usual practise. Its presence might raise a few eyebrows, because the port had been pretty well void of all traffic since E1, but there should be nothing in particular to alert officials that anything was actually wrong.

The finishing touches to the invasion plan had come together well, although, as General Jun Lee now realised, it was obvious that the plan to delay the arrival of the NK medical staff until the third convoy was going to cause some problems. The directive from the President had been to, 'kill everyone.' However, with none of their own medical people there in the beginning, this would be too risky, so they would have to keep the local hospital staff alive.

The General was secretly hoping that there would be at least some medical staff on the other two super tankers arriving up north; or that those in charge of the two vessels would realise the issue just as he had done, and have the foresight to keep the local staff alive, for now at least.

He had wanted this command so much! He missed the world of military action and combat; the war with South Korea held no real excitement for him these days, with only the occasional skirmish happening, things had become downright boring. He craved some real action!

Having said that, he really didn't expect much resistance from the Taswegians; most of them wouldn't even realise what was happening, and by the time they did, they would all be dead.

As he often did, Jun Lee examined his feelings about this intently, trying to identify any potential weaknesses within himself. He wasn't exactly sure how he felt, maybe a little uneasy about it all, because it was not like conventional warfare. After all, the cold-blooded plan was to systematically kill innocent citizens.

The General sighed heavily, knowing that President Gin Gum Kim saw these sacrifices as necessary in order to guarantee the survival of his own people.

He knew that the President and his family would be joining the fourth convoy, this would sail with a full naval escort. He hoped, by the time they arrived in Taswegia, that the state would be under the full control of the Alliance. Jun Lee would be proud to display the state, in all its glory, to his leader!

He thought about the nuclear strike itself. It had been automated, with all key targets pre-selected, thus minimising the potential for human error. The thousand-strong arsenal of ICBM's, (or as they are now known, multiple independently targetable re-entry vehicles, or MIRV's) had ten warheads on each rocket, meaning a force of approximately fifty mega-tons. This was approximately 2500 times greater than what was dropped on Hiroshima or Nagasaki, and meant, in effect, that they would be sending out ten thousand warheads!

These would target all of the Western world's major cities and population centres, as well as the middle east conflict zone. Some parts of China would be hit as well. Even though China initially joined the Alliance, North Korea had never fully trusted its old foe; the formation of the smaller Alliance presented the perfect opportunity to annihilate them.

Once the invasion had taken place, Jun Lee was almost certain that President Gin Gum Kim would look favourably upon him and was secretly hoping that he might even be allowed to take one of the many luxury maxi-yachts in Kings Town Marina as a trophy. This would fulfil one of his long-held dreams; in the limited spare time he did have, the General filled many hours fantasising about the possibilities.

Once the order to proceed had been given on 2nd January, a number of different vehicles would be deployed into the local community, and out into all areas south of Kings Town for up to two hours' driving distance. They would use a number of different vehicles; varying from truck and jeep combinations, carrying thirty troops at a time, to single trucks, such as the 3-ton Bedford-like trucks with canvas canopies, built by Kia Motors in the 1950's, and capable of carrying twenty-two troopers, or single Mercedes-like jeeps, some with hard-tops, and some with canvas canopies, each carrying eight troopers. The plan was for these to progressively spread further out into the countryside, like ripples made by a pebble thrown into a pond.

The far-southern townships of Dove, Geeves and President, along with Apples, Maggot, Queens and all the little towns in between would be invaded simultaneously, and their police stations overrun. At the same time, the same scenario would be played out in the northern suburbs of Kings Town. It hadn't taken long for the earlier reconnaissance team of, 'tourists' to realise that, for the most part, Taswegia's police force lived in houses alongside or not far from their stations; meaning it would be easy to quickly track them down and kill them.

In the days following the initial invasion, the Alliance planned to continue to increase their hold over out-lying areas; it was anticipated that eventually the entire island state would be covered, and the three forces would meet up in the middle of Taswegia.

The most critical part of the plan was that it was crucial for everyone to start the invasion at the precise time of 0800. The sight of military trucks travelling around shouldn't be an issue, the troops would be dressed in their fatigues and, with no weapons on display, it would just look like any other, 'normal' exercise within the state. In fact, the general public might even think they'd managed to finally get some vehicles going!

As they turned into the river and began the final approach to Kings Town, Jun Lee went over the brief again with his Officers. They were to instruct the troopers to kill everyone, with one exception only: the white coated hospital and medical staff. The General was well aware that every community had a small medical centre. To ease the burden on the Kings Town hospital, he would allow the staff of these smaller centres to live, at least for the moment.

After docking at Governor Wharf No. 1 dead on 1700 on 31st December, the *Emily Maersk* immediately began the task of unloading the 144 containers. The port control staff had finished work for the day just before their arrival; with 1st January being the New Year's Day public holiday, they were assured of not seeing any of the local officials until 0800 on 2nd January.

Having docked at Governor Wharf No. 2, the *Louise Maersk* did the same. Unlike a lot of ports, Kings Town held the advantage of being a natural deep harbour; if it hadn't been for this, the large super tankers would have been unable to get alongside.

Friday 2nd January 2015 ... Kings Town.

By 0630 all the troops were ready and waiting in the deserted cruise terminal. After loading into the vehicles, they sat patiently, awaiting their designated times to disperse.

At 0700 Jun Lee made his way to the terminal and mounted his jeep. It felt good to know that at this precise time there were over one hundred teams making their way to various targets throughout the isolated state.

After arriving at Parliament House, they made their way into the building, and to the shock of all members present, declared their intentions, demanding that the Premier surrender Taswegia to their control.

Premier Mick Sheehan was in total shock at first, then horrified, as he realised the gravity of the situation. As he and the members were directed outside, they were joined by the Governor and his wife, who had been escorted from Government House on the domain ...

Upon witnessing the shock beheading of Mick Sheehan, some members of Parliament fainted, and some vomited, but most tried to run. The Alliance troops made short work of killing them all.

As he watched the action unfold, General Jun Lee noticed a man who'd been with the gathering in Parliament House speaking into a radio as he backed away around a corner of the building.

"Kill him!"

The troops followed the man into an old Marine Board building; closing in on him as he disappeared up the stairs.

Chapter 24
The Hospital

Friday 2nd January 2015 ... on board *Footy*, Chook Point Marina.

Doc was on *Footy*, his beloved yacht. He could be found here on most mornings, before heading off to the hospital to visit his patients. He was thinking about his estranged wife; she was still hanging on some four weeks after being admitted. Even though their marriage was pretty well over, Doc still went in most days to see how she was going.

His daily routine was simple; he'd spend time on his beloved boat first up, taking care of a few minor repairs. Even though the E1 had left him with no engine he was still able to sail the thirty-three-foot steel mono hull whenever he got a chance. Some mornings he'd just sit there soaking up the scenery, and sometimes he'd take her out for a bit ... as long as he could spend some time on her he was happy.

Then it was off to the hospital until lunchtime, and then back to his rooms for afternoon appointments. After finishing up around 1600, he'd head back to the boat and enjoy a couple of hours sailing on the river.

He hadn't heard from his daughter in months. All he'd been able to do was to leave a message on her phone, telling her about Millie.

Stores of available diesel were dangerously low, which meant the use of power at the hospital had been severely restricted. They only fired it up these days if they had to perform essential, or life-threatening surgery.

The number of patients he had to take care of had gradually dwindled over time; nobody could drive around, so it was really only people who lived within walking distance that could come to see him. Nobody had much money these days, so most of the time he'd see his patients for free.

He missed life with the navy reserves more than he'd ever realised he would. Once they'd given him the flick, the only pleasure he'd found in life was whenever he could spend time on his boat. He'd walk from home to the marina, and then to the hospital, and then back to the marina, then home again.

Doc looked at his watch, noticing that the time was 0959.

"Might as well have a listen to the news through the UHF."

"Here is the news for Friday 2nd January 2015, Alex Brand reporting.

As I speak, we have reports that forces, calling themselves, "The New Alliance," have landed at all major ports in Taswegia …

Troops are approaching the building! Stay tuned f… Shit! They're coming up the stairs! If we can get another …"

Bang, Bang … Schhhhhhhhhhhh … Only static!'

Doc stared at the radio for a second, stunned at what he'd heard. Quickly recovering, he ran up the cabin stairs and out of the cabin and took off on foot towards the hospital. Normally he'd take his time, but today he ran most of the way.

In the distance he noticed a couple of huge tankers berthed at Macquarie No. 1 Wharf. Doc pulled up and stood for a minute, trying to work out whether they'd been there before. He was pretty sure that space had been empty yesterday.

"Shit!"

Tempted to take the shortcut through the Parliament House lawns he started to run in through the gates, but changed his mind, realising it was probably too big a risk to be worth taking.

There was panic everywhere he looked. People were shouting, and then literally running for their lives a few seconds later at the sound of gunfire. Doc heard a vehicle screech to a stop and looked around to see an old Second World War jeep stop just up the street from where he was standing. Eight troopers jumped out and disappeared into the building.

He could hear shots, then the sound of women screaming in terror.

"Shit! Shit! Shit!"

Doc headed for the hospital, pulling his white coat out of his briefcase as he ran, and putting it on as he made it safely inside the double front doors. Out of breath, he stopped and leaned against the wall, trying to come to terms with whatever was going on outside.

Inside the hospital, insulated from the outside world by its clean white walls, high ceilings and echoing corridors, was like being in another world; it all seemed quite surreal, considering the chaos he'd just witnessed, but then he realised they wouldn't have a clue about what was going on.

"What's all the noise from outside about Doc?"

Doc thought quickly, trying to work out how to answer that question in one sentence without frightening the young intern to death. He couldn't think of a way, so just blurted it all out.

"The Alliance has invaded us! They're killing everyone! I don't even know whether the hospital will be safe, although they reckon they're not killing the doctors. Run for your bloody life!"

The young kid's jaw dropped, he looked at Doc as if he was a fucking nutter.

"Yeah right! Pull the other one Doc!"

"Suit yourself!"

Doc raced up the stairs to Millie's ward, literally running into one of his peers as she opened the door. Doc apologised as he picked Sue Millar up off the floor.

"What's going on Doc?"

Doc repeated it all again.

"The Alliance has invaded us! They're killing everyone! Only the doctors will be safe, although there's no guarantee of that. Run for your bloody life!"

Sue laughed at him.

"You're ever so funny Doc!"

He grabbed the blonde and almost bent her in half as he planted a strong tongue kiss on her.

"What do you think you're doing!" she complained. "Well I never!"

"And if you don't get a fucking move on you never will!"

Doc grabbed her arm and dragged her over to the window.

"Look for yourself!"

What she saw made her hair stand on end! Being on a corner, she had a clear view down two streets; she could see the Alliance troops advancing on foot, shooting everyone they came across. The sight of dead and dying bodies sprawled on the roads and footpaths for as far as she could see was horrible!

Some of the wounded were trying to crawl away, and almost got clear, only to be gunned down by specialist snipers.

Sue whimpered in fear.

"What's going to happen to us Doc?"

"If you do exactly as I say you'll be all right. Put your white coat on. NOW!"

Sue was a midwife, not a qualified doctor. She'd always wanted to become one but had never been able to find the money to go to medical school. Instead she'd started life in the medical world as a nurse's aide, qualifying as a nurse after completing her training part time. After deciding to specialise in midwifery, she was eventually appointed to the position of Sister-in-charge of the midwifery ward at the General Hospital.

"Whatever you do, you've got to tell them you're a Paeciatrician, specialising in childbirth!"

"I can't do that! What will the other staff say!"

"Fuck them! I'm pretty sure people will keep their mouths shut once they start to understand how serious this situation is!"

Doc left the middle-aged woman standing in a daze, just staring out the window, and made his way to the cancer ward.

He was wondering whether he should have just dropped the lines *on Footy* and sailed away. Nah! They would have come and got him, or maybe shot him out of the water! *Footy* didn't move that fast; and even in the stiffest of stiff breezes she could only manage about five knots. She was just too dammed heavy!

Millie was asleep, sedated by the medication, and completely unaware of the carnage outside. Maybe that's the best thing for her, he thought, as he sat on the bed holding her hand.

Listening intently, he could hear the rumble of vehicles outside in front of the hospital. Before the E1 had hit this would have been perfectly normal, but hearing the noise now felt surreal.

Through the open door to the ward Doc could hear distant shouting, then more gunshots, followed by screaming.

"It's probably that little upstart downstairs on the front desk."

The sounds of heavy boots clattered across the lino floors, and the gunshots and screaming came closer and closer. Doc swung around just in time to see a nurse start to run past the door. She screamed as she was shot in the back, and blood started to spurt out of a massive hole that had appeared in her chest. The 7.62 round must have gone straight through!

A short man dressed in an officer's uniform appeared in the doorway. Doc wasn't certain what his rank was, possibly a General. He was surrounded by half a dozen troopers, with their rifles, complete with fixed bayonets, held at the, 'present arms' position.

The officer looked at Doc, then spoke in reasonably fluent English with a heavy Korean accent.

"I am General Jun Lee Sung, Commander-in-Chief of the Alliance! You are Doctor Roger. No?"

"I am Doctor Roger Johns."

"Ah yes. You will please come with me. I wish to hold a meeting in the staffroom."

The General motioned the closest trooper towards Millie. Doc took a step sideways, placing himself between the trooper and Millie.

"N ... No!" he stuttered, "Th ... th ... this is my w ... wife, Millie!"

"Of course, Doctor," smiled the General reassuringly. "No harm will come to her. Please be certain that family of doctors are safe."

Doc recognised that sly smile. It was the type of smile that said, "Fuck you, you jerk! As soon as you leave, we'll put a bullet in her head."

Doc moved to the doorway, then stopped, first looking back at Millie, then up and down the corridor as the troopers systematically worked their way through each ward. The executions were, for the most part, silent, apart from an occasional muffled cry; the blood dripping from their bayonets was a clear indication about how they were going about their grizzly work.

"Please, Doctor. The staffroom. Now!"

"Wait!" replied Doc wearily. "She's dying of cancer, I was about to give her something for the pain, I will be along in a minute."

Jun Lee nodded curtly, and angrily motioned to one of the troopers to remain at the door, before marching off in the direction of the staffroom.

Doc turned to Millie, thankful that she was none the wiser about what was going on. She'd gone through enough pain and suffering already. Fumbling in his bag, he found the vial he was looking for and loaded a syringe.

Doc gently held Millie's hand in one of his, and with the other he carefully injected the entire contents of the syringe into the IV drip above her head. He waited for a minute, just to make sure the medication did what it had to do. There were no electronic machines these days, so he checked for a pulse manually. Nothing.

He double checked for a pulse through the carotid artery and was satisfied that there was nothing. She was gone.

Leaning over, he gently kissed her forehead, tears welling up in his eyes as he left the room. The guard looked at him and gestured in the general direction of the staffroom. Doc nodded and headed off, preparing himself for what he knew would happen next.

He wasn't even twenty paces down the corridor when he heard the sound of a type 54 handgun.

Bang!

"Goodbye Millie," he whispered, "at least you're finally out of pain."

The staffroom door was open, as Doc entered the room he bumped into Sue, who was standing just inside, isolated from the others.

"Sorry Doctor Millar."

Doc turned to close the door.

"Leave it!"

Jun Lee was on the other side of the room, with his troops lined up behind him. Looking around Doc could see about twenty white coats huddled together on his side.

"Doctor Roger! You know this person?"

"Who?"

The General pointed to Sue.

"Of course! I know everyone in this room."

"Is that so Doctor."

Doc explained to the General that he had worked there for the last forty years; in fact, he'd probably helped train most of them. He knew some better than others, but he assured the General that he definitely knew who they all were.

"Ah ... if that is so Doctor Roger, please be so kind as to introduce everyone in the room, along with their specialty."

Doc thought fast, realising what Jun Lee was up to. He was trying to work out who were genuine doctors, and who were just people pretending to be doctors in order to avoid being shot!

It was true that Doc knew most of them by sight, and around half of them by name; but some were only vague acquaintances, and he wasn't certain of their role within the hospital. He'd have no trouble identifying the bona fide doctors, but the others ... well, all he could hope for was that he might at least remember which department they were from.

"I am waiting Doctor Roger!"

Jun Lee was obviously getting angrier by the minute.

"Ah yes." Doc started with Sue. "Well, you already know Doctor Sue Millar, I mentioned her earlier."

"What department Doctor! I am losing patience!"

Doc nervously cleared his throat, thinking, 'What the hell! Here goes!'

"Doctor Sue Millar, Paediatrician," he began, then continued, looking each one in the eye as he moved around the room, hoping they would all play along with him. He began with the white coat standing furthest to the right.

"Introducing Doctor Phil Brown, Surgeon; Doctor Ted Green, Anaesthetist; Doctor Les Solomon, Cardiology; Doctor Helen Smith, Diagnostic Imaging; Doctor Henry Swain, ENT; Doctor Alex Wallace, Endoscopy, and Doctor Rob Simpson, Gynaecology."

"And the others?"

Doc continued. "Doctor David Benson, Haematology; Doctor Lynda Browne, Nephrology; Doctor Bruce Charles, Oncology; Doctor Bob Silver, Orthopaedics; Doctor Patricia Collins, Radiotherapy; Doctor Dave Reddy, Renal and Doctor Reginald Miles, Urology."

The first fifteen had been easy, he knew them all really well. Apart from the pork pie he told the General about Sue, the rest really were doctors. Well, except for Helen Smith, you don't normally refer to a radiographer as a doctor.

"And!!!!!"

The General was becoming impatient. Jun Lee was red in the face; you could almost see the steam coming out of his ears.

Knowing that the last four weren't doctors, Doc was almost certain they'd be shot immediately if the Alliance found out. Clearing his throat, he kept going, hoping beyond hope that he was placing these people in an area that they at least had some knowledge of.

"Okay! Doctor Julie Smith, Paediatrician; Doctor Michael Bane, Gynaecology; Doctor Christine Simmons, Haematology and last, but not least, Doctor Ian Walters, Intensive Care."

Doc was extremely nervous, although he tried not to show it. He was almost certain the last four were all nursing Sisters, and he was pretty sure he'd seen them in the departments he'd matched them with. All he could do now was pray he'd got it right.

"Hmmm!" said Jun Lee. "Are you quite certain of this Doctor Roger?"

"Yes, I am quite certain."

Doc was pretty sure the gook General didn't believe him; he had no idea what he was planning next.

"We shall see!"

With that, he beckoned one of his troops to come forward.

"Bring the whore in!"

The man scurried off. Doc could hear a muffled conversation coming from the corridor. One voice was male, probably the trooper; the other was definitely female. Jun Lee's eyes narrowed as he looked Doc up and down.

"Indeed! We shall see!"

Doc was starting to get nervous, recognising the threat within the General's comments.

Nari Kim entered the room, escorted by the trooper. His bayonet was held out in front of him, pointing at Nari as she was paraded up and down in front of the others as if she was some kind of offering.

"Nurse Kim will now tell me who has been lying!"

The General glanced over at Doc with a knowing look on his face, and then looked the other white coats up and down, one at a time. The tension in the room was so thick that one could almost have cut it with a knife!

'Holy fuck!' Doc hadn't expected this.

He'd come to know Nari quite well. She was a South Korean triage nurse, who'd been visiting Taswegia on a working holiday, and had joined the out-patients department at the hospital in order to add to her nursing experience.

His brain was going a hundred miles an hour as he ran through all the possibilities. The fact that she was still alive was, in itself, a miracle. This might have been because she was Korean by birth, or maybe because she was useful to the Alliance as an interpreter. Jun Lee himself spoke pretty good English, but Nari could be used in other areas. On the other hand, it was possible she'd been part of the plan all along; and had been planted there at the hospital as a spy. If this was the case, the game was definitely up!

She'd obviously been told to stand just outside the room, listening to him as he'd run through his fellow doctors. Now he understood why the General had wanted the door left open.

Doc looked at the guard behind Nari, wondering if he could overpower the man; although the trooper was short in stature, he still looked pretty strong.

"Come girl! Is the doctor correct?"

Nari looked absolutely terrified.

"Y ... y ... yes," she stammered.

"No! I mean are these people exactly who he says they are?"

Nari shot a glance at Doc, knowing that he hadn't told the absolute truth.

"Yes! This is all correct!"

"Good! Good! Now we can get down to business."

Jun Lee walked around the room, constantly shifting his semi-automatic type 54 pistol from his left to his right hand, and eyeing each of the white coats off in a menacing manner that made each of them wish they could disappear down through the floor. Finally coming back to Doc, he stopped right in front of him. Doc's fists were clenched as tightly as they could be clenched, and it was obvious he was only about five seconds away from doing something they might all regret.

"Well done, Doctor Roger! Well done!"

Doc breathed a sigh of relief.

The General nodded to the trooper again and motioned him to take Nari away.

"Where are you taking her?"

"Do not worry Doctor Roger. We will not kill the whore. She will come in handy for us as we get established, and she will also be something for the officers to play with."

Although, Doc remained calm on the outside, inside he was seething in anger at the thought of poor Nari being abused by these monkey-faced heathens! He had always enjoyed their chats in the staff canteen, and at times had found himself manipulating his timetable to make sure his coffee breaks coincided with hers. It hadn't hurt that she was an extremely attractive young woman, with a beautiful smile!

"You doctors will continue to operate this hospital. You will treat my men and members of the Alliance. If you fail to agree with this, you will be shot!"

Sue Millar was having trouble coming to terms with everything that was happening. "But what about nursing staff? You've murdered all of ours!"

"Ah yes, Doctor Millar, but we have nurses arriving on the next transport. They will be here within the week. In the meantime, you will nurse for each other as required."

"How are we going to operate without power?"

"We will take care of that Doctor Roger. As our troopers collect the unwanted diesel from your useless vehicles, we will top up the tanks and run the generators. And yes! There will be power to the hospital and a few other important buildings around the town."

The General was obviously relishing the fact that he was in charge. He arrogantly strutted up and down the room, looking a bit like an overstuffed peacock! Under different circumstances Doc might have burst out laughing.

"You and your families will be safe. An Alliance trooper will escort you to your homes and register your family members. You will only be permitted to travel between the hospital and your home; if you are caught outside that area you will be shot! Have I made myself quite clear!"

It was a statement, not a question! Everyone in the room nodded in unison.

"Oh, and one last thing! I would advise each of you to wear your white coats. We don't wish to shoot any of you by mistake. Do we?"

The General seemed satisfied that he had made his instructions quite clear.

"Now go! Troops are waiting at the front door of the hospital, ready to escort you to your homes."

"But what about our patients General?"

"What patients? Doctor ... Brown wasn't it? The hospital will be cleared, and you will return here to start work at 6 a.m. sharp tomorrow! If any of you are found to be missing, we will find you and kill you. And then we will kill all of your families!"

The General was obviously done with them, turning his back to them as they solemnly left the room. As they walked towards the stairs, Sue grabbed Doc's arm.

"Why do you think Nari didn't give us away?"

"I'm not sure Sue. At first, I thought she might have been working for them, but maybe she is on our side after all. We'll just have to wait and see."

"But she's Korean Doc! Like them!"

Doc was startled at the hatred in her voice; she was almost spitting the words out!

"No. She's not like them Sue. Nari is from South Korea; I'm guessing the Alliance are North Korean. Those two countries have been at war for many years."

The ex-midwife, recently elevated to the position of Paediatrician, wasn't so sure. "Well I still don't trust her Doc!"

As they left the hospital a junior officer paired each of them with a trooper. Obviously, they were meant to go straight home.

"Shit! I thought it was only lunch time."

His assigned escort was a young man of around twenty years of age. As he wandered off in the direction of his home, Doc couldn't help wondering whether the troopers had been given alternative orders. What if they'd been ordered to annihilate the families of the hospital staff, eagerly waiting to welcome their loved ones home from work. He wasn't too worried about his own situation; in his case there was nobody waiting at home. His daughter had left years ago, and now Millie was gone too.

Doc groaned out loud, finally starting to allow himself to think about what he'd had to do earlier. He remembered the Hippocratic Oath he'd taken all those years ago, and his solemn oath to save lives, now he'd just done the opposite to his wife! He smiled ironically to himself; at least he'd been able to beat them as far as Millie was concerned.

Doc shook his head, knowing that all the normal rules were out the window now. It was obvious that the invaders were not complying with any kind of Hippocratic Oath.

"I killed my wife!"

His escort gave him a puzzled look.

"Eh?"

"Shit!"

Doc gave himself a bit of a shake, realising he'd voiced his thoughts out loud!

Home was an old sandstone house on the waterfront at Chook Point. It overlooked the Chook Point Marina, where his beloved yacht *Footy* was moored. After pouring himself a scotch he collapsed into his favourite chair.

His escort, who'd gone off to search the rest of the building, returned after around ten minutes or so; he seemed most surprised to have found no-one else living there. Giving Doc a suspicious look, he extracted a hard-covered book from an inside pocket of his tunic, opening it at what was obviously a section about Doc's house. After scribbling something down on the first page, he gave Doc a quick bow, and left.

Doc sat there, sipping his scotch, and thought back over the day's events, realising it hadn't even been a full day yet! It was only 1400! Realising how hungry he was, he grabbed some cold meat, before returning to stand in front of the large window that overlooked the marina and the port of Kings Town.

From where he stood, he could clearly see Macquarie No 1 wharf, where the two huge Alliance ships were both unloading. Doc couldn't get over how large they were; until now he hadn't taken much notice of them. They each had to be at least four hundred metres long!

He frowned as he thought of all the innocent people who'd been systematically slaughtered today, as well as all those who would be slaughtered tomorrow.

"Maybe even tonight!" Doc spoke his thoughts out loud again, thinking about the other doctors and their families, and hoping his theory would be proved to be incorrect!

Realising his escort wasn't going to come back, Doc waited until dusk, and then made his way carefully down to the marina and slipped aboard *Footy*. He'd always loved the tranquillity of the waterfront. As he sat alone in the cockpit with a hip flask of his favourite scotch and a huge cigar, he reminisced about earlier days spent sailing with his mate Dick.

"Shit!" I wonder what's happened to Dick and Patch!"

He thought briefly again about simply slipping the lines and sailing away. After all, there was a light Nor-Easter blowing; perfect for running down the channel. But then what?' Where would you go, you silly bastard! Hide? Where! And for how long?'

He switched on the UHF, but there was nothing but static.

Saturday 3rd January 2015 ... General Hospital, Kings Town.

It was 0545 by the time Doc walked through the front entrance to the General Hospital. He was feeling just a little bit worse for wear; the previous night's scotch possibly had something to do with it.

Something was different. After looking around, he realised that guards had been posted in the spot where the information booth and front counter had been yesterday. Before he could stop himself, Doc went up to visit Millie's ward; stopping and cursing to himself as he remembered she wasn't there anymore. Old habits!

The building was eerily quiet. In normal times it would have been full of the sound of voices and machinery noises, but now there was nothing. No sign of the carnage from yesterday, all the rooms he walked past had been hosed out.

He made his way down to the staffroom, reaching the door at the same time as Sue Millar.

"Is everything okay Sue? How did it go last night when you got home?"

"Oh Doc! It's horrible! I don't know where my husband is, he wasn't at home when I got there. There was shooting coming from the house next door. I'm not sure, but I think they might have found the old lady hiding in her wine cellar. I could hear someone yelling, and then she started screaming, the noise sounded like it was coming from that direction. Then there was a loud bang, and the screaming stopped. What about you? Is Millie home yet?"

"Millie died yesterday Sue ... in hospital."

Sue looked at the older man in shock.

"Don't tell me she was shot by those monkeys!"

"No, thank God! It was the cancer that got her."

"I am so sorry Doc."

"I'm not Sue. I'm glad she doesn't have to witness all of this! Have you seen anyone else this morning?"

"No, not yet."

The power came on as they entered the staffroom.

"Might as well fill the urn. Could do with a strong coffee!"

A few minutes later the others started to file in through the door. There was plenty of muttering about the early start, and most people had a similar story to Sue's to share. They all reported finding no one at home when they'd got there.

The only exception was Ted Green. Obviously still traumatised, he told them how he'd returned home to find that his wife and two daughters had been raped and mutilated, their naked bodies left sprawled out where the intruders had finished with them.

One of the other doctors gave him a hug as he started to sob loudly, struggling to continue. He'd discovered his wife staked out on the island bench in the kitchen, her bruised and battered body had suffered multiple stab wounds from the many kitchen knives that were now scattered around her body, still covered in blood.

He'd made a dash upstairs, desperately hoping his two daughters were somehow still alive, or maybe hiding under their beds. His oldest daughter, fourteen-year-old Sara was lying naked on her bed; it looked like she'd been gutted, with a gaping knife wound running from her vagina to her throat.

The younger girl, twelve-year-old Honey, had obviously tried to make a run for it, he'd found her in the back yard, gagged and naked. Between sobs he told them he thought she'd been sodomised before they'd broken her neck.

Sickened, Doc did a rough head count. It looked like everyone was there except for Julie Smith, the former nurse whom he'd said was a Paediatrician. Thinking to himself that the stupid girl had probably done a runner, he shook his head sadly.

Li Chun, one of Jun Lee's officers, marched into the staffroom, carrying a sword. Li Chun stood at around five foot nothing tall; Doc thought the little Runt was probably in his early fifties, although it was difficult to be sure of their ages. He tried to guess the man's military status. Not being all that familiar with NK badges of rank he couldn't be certain; but if he was to hazard a guess, he would have thought Captain.

"My name Captain Li Chun! You come with me!"

They followed him out to the corridor and along to one of the windows facing the main road. Li Chun gestured toward the street below. They crowded around the window, trying to see what he was pointing to.

"You look!" They were confronted by the sight of a flatbed truck, standing in the middle of the now-empty street. Thrown onto the back was the lifeless body of Julie, along with those of her husband, her mother, and probably her kid.

"You look!" Li Chun was furious as some of them tried to back away from the window.

"You look good! You no come to work hospital; you die!"

Nodding in satisfaction, the Captain turned and marched away; knowing he'd made his point.

Patricia Collins collapsed sobbing to the floor. Reg Miles, after helping her up, led the way back to the staffroom, where Doc poured her a comforting cup of tea. They sat in silence, waiting to see what would happen next.

Sue was the next to give into her fear. Howling in terror she sobbed, "I don't think I can take any more of this!"

"Shut up!"

Doc checked the corridor quickly, knowing they wouldn't have much time before the Captain returned to the staffroom.

Looking each of them in the eye, he spoke to them quietly, but firmly.

"I'm sorry to be blunt, but there's no choice! These guys aren't mucking around, and they don't care about what happens to us. You all need to toughen up! It's either that, or you're all dead!"

The door flew open, and the Captain entered the room. His orders were short, but clear.

"You go work! Now!"

Ian and a few of the others made their way to the out-patient department, where they found a mixture of patients waiting for them. There were a couple of heavily pregnant women, (obviously Alliance wives), a few older Asians with varying illnesses, and a number of troopers who'd obviously been caught in the crossfire with the local police the day before.

Doc spent most of the day in surgery, helping Phil Brown to extract bullets from Alliance troops. Even when working on shitheads like these, Doc was surprised at how good it felt to be doing surgery again. The Hippocratic Oath was the Hippocratic Oath after all, and for the first time in a long time he felt some of the old pride in his surgical skills return.

It was a long morning, and by lunch time Doc was famished. He went to investigate what, if anything, would be on offer in the canteen; he was fairly sure they wouldn't let them starve; their work was considered essential, at least for now.

North Korean (NK) nationals were standing guard behind the counter; the food was definitely not the type of cuisine normally served up, but at least, with the power back on, it was hot and smelled delicious. Doc filled his plate with some sort of a stir-fry.

Wandering over to the tables he spotted Nari sitting in the corner on her own. The other workers seemed to have ostracized the Korean girl; Doc approached her table, feeling sorry for the young girl, who looked exhausted and quite dazed.

He touched her on the shoulder, not wanting to frighten her.

"How are you fairing Nari?"

Nari jumped at his touch and looked up into his face, feeling comforted by the sight of the sixty-five-year old smiling kindly at her.

"Oh! Hi Doc. I'm all right. I was sorry to hear about Millie."

"Where have they got you working? In triage?" asked Doc, who felt genuinely concerned about how she was doing.

"Oh, they've got me working all right!"

Doc was shocked at the bitterness in her voice.

"When I'm not working, I'm being made to sleep with that stinking General or one of his subordinates. They treat me like a dog, and they call me a stinking whore! They made me stay in one of the rooms here last night; I was constantly molested by his officers. He says I have to gain his trust, or he will kill me!"

Doc was horrified. He tried to speak but nothing came out; his mouth was extremely dry. Taking a sip of his coffee, he said, "Maybe I can speak to him and talk him into letting you come home with me. I am on my own now, so I'd appreciate your company."

"That would be a life saver Doc! I don't think he would agree though; he is a hard man. I have overheard some of his orders; and I truly believe he is a madman!"

Nari sighed, and left, telling Doc that she didn't dare turn up late.

The afternoon dragged by, but at last it was 1800; knock off time.

Before Doc left for the day, he asked to see Captain Li Chun.

"What you want!"

The Captain had a look of arrogance about him, but that didn't faze Doc, who just glared back at the Runt.

"I need to speak to the General!"

The Captain was taken aback by the request; Doc even wondered whether he might not be a little bit scared of his Commanding Officer.

"Why! What you want! Is this about the way I treat you?"

Doc sensed he was right, the Runt was more than a little bit worried.

"No, it's nothing like that. A personal matter."

The Captain, feeling reassured that it wasn't about him, smiled and nodded his head.

Doc followed the Captain as he led the way out of the hospital and down the main road towards the dock. They eventually arrived at Parliament House; Doc realised that this must be where the General had established his headquarters. He'd obviously commandeered the best office in the building; that of the former Premier. The ornate office was lined with the best of Taswegian timbers, and was filled with beautiful pieces of furniture made from Tas Oak, Myrtle, Huon, King Billy Pine and Sassafras.

"You stand here!"

Tapping on the former Premier's door, the Runt announced,

"Doctor Roger to see you General."

"Ah! Yes, the good Doctor Roger! How are you? I am told you had no one waiting at home for you?"

Doc tried his best not to sound too sarcastic. "You don't miss a trick General."

"I cannot afford to Doctor Roger. Now, what can I do for you?"

"Well, it's a little sensitive General. You see, I have a girlfriend, although nobody knows about us. I would like to take her home with me, now that my wife has died."

"Ah yes! Your wife in hospital. Yes. I remember. So sorry!"

Doc looked at the obvious smirk on his face, knowing that the General was fully aware that Millie had been murdered, just like all the other patients. What he wasn't aware of was the part that Doc had played in her death.

"Yes, the cancer got her. She died just after you left the room."

The look of surprise on Jun Lee's face made Doc feel just a little bit better about it all. It was a small triumph, but it had made a difference to the way Millie's life had ended.

"Oh! That's too bad!"

The General was not at all impressed that he had not known the truth about how Millie had died. He changed the subject abruptly, smiling suddenly, and reminding Doc of an adolescent who'd been caught masturbating over a dirty magazine. He could see that same kind of stupid grin on Jun Lee's face.

"What is your friend's name Doctor Roger? Would it be ... Doctor Millar perhaps? Doctor ... Sue Millar?"

"Of course not!" the sixty-five-year-old ENT doctor replied. "No, it's Nari. Nari Kim."

The General was clearly amused at this new turn of events.

"I like you Doctor Roger. Because of this I will let you have the South Korean whore. She was beginning to bore me anyway."

Turning away, the General lit a cigarette; obviously finished with the conversation.

Doc didn't want to lose his chance, he wanted to get Nari out of there tonight if he possibly could. After taking a deep breath, he calmly responded, "Thank you. Can I go and get her now?"

"No! Tomorrow Doctor Roger. Tomorrow!"

There was nothing he could do for now. As he walked home, Doc couldn't help wondering whether Nari would last the night.

Later that evening he went back down to *Footy*. As he sat in the cockpit, he tried playing with the UHF set again. Nothing!

He wondered how long all this was going to go on for. Surely, he wasn't meant to end his days working as a lonely slave for the Alliance! He wondered about what would happen when the transport ship carrying the nurses arrived; he had no doubt that they would have their own doctors on the vessel as well.

Doc was almost certain that, once the NK National medical staff had arrived, he and the others would be of no further use to the General; after all, he'd already seen the ruthless way they disposed of anyone they didn't want to keep around.

Chapter 25
Settling in

Patch opened her eyes, thinking about how much she loved being able to wake up to the sound of waves breaking on the beach, and realising that this was going to be one of the nicest things about living here.

It had been one of the best night's sleep she'd had for some time. Once Dick had finally drifted off she'd laid there for a while, quietly looking up at the multitudes of stars far above her. She'd been a bit worried about having to get up during the night for her usual 3 a.m. toilet stop, but was amazed to find that she'd slept right through.

Once scran was finished, Sarge and Annie went off to work on some booby traps. It had been agreed that the best place to set up the first one was at the top of the track coming from the north, at the spot where they'd carefully made their way around the rocks two days earlier.

It was a long slog back up the sandy path, but once they got there, Annie helped Sarge to set up the Claymore mine with a catgut trip wire running across the track. From this position, the mine would be facing any oncoming threat and would make short work of anyone who happened to show up.

Sarge then moved a little way back down the track, around ten feet away from the mine, then placed a long stick across the path at knee height.

Annie was puzzled. "What's that for Sarge?"

"It's a reminder to any of us that happen to be climbing back up the track, we don't want to forget about the trap!"

"You're a smart cookie!"

While Sarge and Annie attended to the security side of things, April and Patch gathered their daily pile of firewood and tidied up the camp then went to join Jack and Dick, who'd headed over to the gulch.

Dick felt happy it would be suitable for their needs.

"It certainly looks ideal for what we want. Just got to find something we can tie off to."

Jack was investigating the rocky wharf.

"There's a fissure here that might do the job Dick. What do you reckon?"

"Looks good. Just have to think of something we can drop in there to use as a tie off point."

"What about the spare pick?"

"That's a great idea Jack. The CJ doesn't need a second anchor. Maybe if we can wedge it into the crack, we can use it as a shackle to tie off to."

At least that was a start. They'd need to find another one on the other side, as well as one at the stern and one at the bow. Patch scanned the area at the other end of the gulch.

"See that tree over there," she said, "do you think that would do the trick?"

Dick laughed. "You know Patch, it just might! It's a fair way away, but it's not like we're short of rope!"

They managed to set up a tie off point at the other end by dropping in a length of steel that Jack had found down in the engine room. They had no idea why it had been there, and Jack was pretty sure it wouldn't be needed on the CJ. All they had to do now was get the old girl into the gulch and test out whether their plan was going to work.

The surge wasn't too great, Dick reckoned he should be able to go in astern once all the fenders had been secured on the starboard side.

After heading in a southerly direction for about four hundred metres up the track, Sarge and Annie set up the second claymore, using the same method as they had on the other side.

Annie was a bit worried about what would happen if any of the locals happened to come up the track, but Sarge wasn't too fussed, knowing that, even before the invasion, very few people had ever used that track to get down to the beach.

"I reckon it's like this... 'no invitation, no entry', and to quote Forest Gump, 'that's all I have to say about that!'"

Straightening his back, Sarge added the sighter branch to make sure they wouldn't put themselves in danger.

Annie figured he was probably right, and it wasn't like they had much choice. Shrugging off her worries, she remembered something Dick had promised her.

"Let's get back. Dick promised to show me how to fish! I've never done that before."

After a late lunch, Dick, Patch and Annie rowed out to the CJ. The others were happy to stay behind, April had volunteered to clean up before taking a bit of a walk along the beach, while Jack and Sarge were going to investigate the best places to set up the camo tarp shelters that Jack and Dick had made.

Sarge pointed out the spot where he knew Dick had always liked to set up his swag.

"I know Dick would want his over here. It's probably a good idea to keep the 'Boss' happy!"

Once they'd got Dick and Patch's shelter set up over their swag, they did the same with Sarge and Annie's, only closer to the fire.

"I always like to be close to the fire; I'm always first up anyway, and that way I can keep an eye on it."

Jack looked around, trying to work out the best place for his and April's shelter. He knew how much April liked her privacy, she would be really embarrassed if anyone caught a glimpse of her getting dressed or undressed, and he knew she'd probably prefer to be closer to the heads. Well, not too close, but definitely well away from the others.

Out on CJ, Dick set Annie and Patch up with handlines, and then started to splice a few eyes in the mooring lines they were going to use in the gulch. Each one that was to be shackled to the anchor and the steel bar would need an eye, and to help with attachment, he'd need to splice one into the line going around the tree as well.

He'd also decided to rig up a couple of spring lines using the same anchor points. His plan was to run one of these from the crack astern to the bow of the boat, and the other from the stern of the boat to the crack up forward; that way they'd act as a spring.

Annie started squealing like a teenager.

"Shit! Dick! I've got a bite! What do I do!"

"Pull it up girl!"

Dick couldn't help laughing as he helped her to pull the fish in. She was grinning from ear to ear; like a cat that had just bagged a mouse. After carefully taking the hook out of the flathead, Annie showed her catch to Patch before proudly placing it in the bucket.

"That's great Annie! All we have to do now is catch a dozen more!"

Dick had picked a good spot, it didn't take long before both Patch and Annie started pulling them in thick and fast.

Once they had just over half a bucket-full of fish, Dick decided it was time to move; after firing up CJ he set the windlass going. Annie was fascinated by everything Dick was doing.

"I've never seen you on a boat Dick. This is great! How did you learn all this stuff?"

"Come on Annie, you knew I was in the Navy!"

"Yeah. But I thought you were a diver and that you just killed people and stuff like that."

"Yes, but I was still in the Navy. We were trained to use all kinds of vessels. It wasn't just about, 'killing people and stuff'!"

He manoeuvred CJ to the entrance to the gulch and gave a 'honk' to let Sarge, Jack and April know he was ready. Dick showed Annie and Patch how to set the fenders over the side and tie them off to the handrail with a clove hitch.

The swell wasn't too bad, he wanted to make this look good, knowing how embarrassed he would be if he stuffed it up!

As he came slowly astern on his first attempt, Dick realised it wasn't going to work this time. The vessel simply wasn't coming astern straight enough, and because it was only a single screw, the CJ just wasn't responsive enough when they were so close to the rock walls.

Trying again, he pushed the old girl ahead; giving her a lot more throttle so that they'd come in faster and not get pushed against the rock wharf. Once they were well in the middle, it wouldn't matter so much if they touched. That time it worked well.

Dick threw the lines to his shore crew and watched as they tied off, first around the tree and back through the eye and onto the stern bollard, then shackled to the anchor and steel bar, then forward to the rock outcrop. With the springs in place they stood back to survey their handywork.

"Think it will hold Dick?"

"Well Sarge, I guess that will depend on the sea conditions. If it's as sheltered in here as I'm hoping it will be, we'll be okay. If not, unfortunately, she could break loose and be smashed to smithereens! But this is the best option we've got, so we'll just have to wait and see."

Dick gave Annie a lesson on how to skin and bone the flathead in one go, while the others headed back to camp.

"It will make them easier to cook and eat Annie."

After making a mess of the first few, Annie wasn't too keen on ruining the rest.

"Catching them is one thing Dick, but I'm not so good at this part. It might be better if you did them, at least that way they won't get so mashed up!"

Dick agreed, happy to take over.

"It looks like it's flathead for scran then!"

After scran everyone helped to finish off the tarp shelter for Jack and April. Standing back to survey their efforts, they all agreed the camp was looking good.

Chapter 26
The Girlfriend

Sunday 4th January 2015 ... General Hospital, Kings Town.

Doc got to the staffroom first. The others joined him soon after, gathering in small groups as they waited for their daily orders. Knowing it wouldn't be long before the Captain arrived, Doc quickly called them together.

"Hush up for a minute, before the Runt gets here. I've got something to say. I wanted to let you know that Nari is going to come and live at my house; I know she is being abused, so I've offered her this alternative, and I'm hoping I'll have your support."

There were murmurings amongst the group, he could see looks of anger on some of their faces, as well as shock on others, and surprise on a few. He wasn't surprised to hear mutterings about 'traitor,' and 'General's whore,' he knew that most of them hadn't taken the time to get to know Nari, and after everything that had happened, to most of them she just looked like another Korean.

He knew it wouldn't be too long before the Runt joined them. Raising his voice above the others, he continued.

"Now just fucking remember this! She had the power to get us all shot the other day, and she chose not to say anything. Surely you all realise she's not the enemy!"

"What will the General say Doc?"

"I don't give a shit about what he thinks Ted. Anyway, I've cleared it with the General already, and just so you know, I've told him she's my girlfriend."

The quiet voice of Bruce Charles came from the back of the room. Bruce was one of the only other senior members of the faculty and was everyone's favourite oncology doctor. Doc had always had a lot of time for the older oncology doctor.

"Well, I think what you are doing is a noble thing Doc!"

"I appreciate your support Bruce," Doc nodded his appreciation, then turned to the others. "Now has anyone seen Nari this morning?"

Before anyone could answer, the door opened, and the NK Captain made his entrance.

The Runt finished his pep talk; it was the usual shit that they were coming to expect from him. "Do this!" "Do not do this or you will be shot!"

As they all headed off to their various departments, Doc turned to the Captain, asking if he'd seen Nari.

"Doctor Roger, why do you trouble yourself with this whore?"

"Because that whore, as you call her, is my girlfriend!"

As he saw the look of amusement on the Captain's face, Doc had to hide his hatred.

"And she will be coming home with me tonight!"

The Runt didn't know which way to look, at first he thought that Doc was joking; but then realised that the stern look on Doc's face meant that he was deadly serious. He wasn't sure what to say, other than to blurt out,

"The General will not like this!"

Doc knew he had the upper hand and stood his ground, towering over the five-foot tall Captain.

"The General has already approved it."

The Runt wasn't willing to risk incurring the wrath of the General. Grudgingly he led the way down to the basement level of the hospital, pointing to a room at the far end of the corridor on the left-hand side. After informing Doc that he would be checking with the General, he turned his back and left.

Doc opened the door and found Nari on the bed, her face was covered in bruises, and she was dressed in nothing but her triage top. She looked like she had just done fifteen rounds with Mike Tyson.

She clung to him, sobbing as she told him what had happened.

"The bastards came for me last night! Three of Jun Lee's officers. They took it in turns to rape me, then beat me before leaving me here. They were laughing the whole time. It was horrible! They just didn't care!"

Doc felt terrible.

"I'm so sorry Nari! All this was probably my fault. I wanted to come and get you last night, but the General said I had to wait until today. Now I know why!"

The twenty-five-year-old looked up at Doc, clinging to the bit of hope he seemed to be offering her.

"What did the General say Doc? Is he going to let me come and live with you?"

Doc smiled grimly.

"He said 'Yes.' Now let's get you cleaned up!"

Doc pulled some swabs out of the drawer alongside the bed as Nari stretched out so that he could clean her wounds. As he turned her over, he flinched, realising she had been anally raped. He didn't say anything about what he saw, knowing how traumatised she would be.

He looked at Nari, the look of sadness in his eyes was mixed with compassion, and he felt a tremendous sense of respect for the young woman because of the terrible ordeal she'd just been through.

Doc turned away as he felt the tears start to well up in his eyes, telling her, "Stay there for a minute. I'll try and find you some scrubs."

After reassuring Nari that he wouldn't be away for too long, he headed off along the corridor to find a clothing cupboard. After choosing something in what he hoped was the right size for the girl, he went back and helped her to put on the uniform.

He was concerned about the pain she must be in.

"Do you think you can last the day down in triage?"

Nari managed a smile. "I'll make sure I do!"

Doc spent most of the morning patching up troops; secretly amused to see many of their injuries had been self-inflicted. One trooper had managed to shoot himself through the shoulder when he'd been skylarking with his rifle held the wrong way around, and another been shot in the stomach when he'd taken hold of his mate's weapon by the muzzle. At one stage Doc had even assisted with delivering a child. At least the morning in surgery hadn't been boring!

He caught up with Nari at lunch time, and was relieved to see her smiling as she told him about all the triage patients they'd been handling in emergency. Apparently, some of the local people, who'd been holed up in their house since the day before, had fought back after seeing their wives and one of their children executed in front of them; they'd managed to shoot four troopers with a .22 rifle before being killed themselves.

Nari told Doc that the groups of troopers going around the houses were known as, 'jug-eum-ui-bundae,' or 'Death Squads'. It was their job to travel around the community, inspecting every house and eradicating its inhabitants in whichever way they chose.

At the end of the day Doc made sure he got to triage half an hour before knock-off time, just in case they played a dirty trick on him and took Nari away. As he walked home with her, he was reminded of the time when he'd first taken Millie home to meet his parents. He held Nari's hand tightly as they made their way down the main road towards the docks, calling into her flat on the way, so that she could grab her suitcase and some of her clothing. Doc was surprised when he saw how little food she had in her pantry.

"There's nothing here Nari. Haven't you been eating at home?"

Nari was slow to answer, obviously embarrassed to tell him that she'd been surviving on the food from the hospital, usually whatever the patients had left on their plates.

"Bloody hell girl! We'll have to change that!"

Nari liked Doc, she'd looked up to him ever since her first day of work at the hospital. She'd sat alone at one of the lunch tables, drinking a coffee and watching the other staff laugh together as they ate their lunch. Doc had made a real difference that first day, when he'd come and sat with her while he ate.

Once they'd arrived home, Doc showed Nari his daughter's old room, telling her that it was hers now. Doc boxed up some of the stuff that Ebony had left behind.

"I should have done this years ago. If anything fits you, you are welcome to use it."

Doc emptied some of the drawers, folding the various items of clothing before storing them away neatly.

"Have you not heard from her Doc?"

"No, not since the E1."

Once Nari had settled in, they enjoyed a dinner of home-made mutton soup and fresh bread, then moved into the lounge. Away from the pressures of the hospital, they were both able to relax, as Nari told Doc about some of the other patients she'd worked on that afternoon.

"I think most of them were victims of the local resistance."

"Were they from the death squads Nari?"

"No, these were from the, 'bundae leul jeongli,' I think you'd call them, 'clean up squads.' Their job is to collect all the bodies and take them up to the old South Kings Town tip to burn them."

"Humph! Hopefully the Alliance will have an effective hygiene policy in place."

For the most part, the pair just sat there in companionable silence. Normally he would have been anxious to go down to *Footy* for the evening, but Doc realised that this was the first time in a really long time that he'd actually enjoyed someone else's company.

Monday 5th January 2015 ... Doc's home, Chook Point.

At some stage during the night, Doc had woken to the sound of Nari crying. He'd laid there for a while, wondering if he should go and see if she was all right, but must have drifted off again, because the next time he opened his eyes he realised it was 0500.

Doc spent the main part of his workday with the midwife, helping with two difficult deliveries. Both of the heavily pregnant women he'd seen two days earlier decided it was time to give birth that day. Between them and a constant trickle of patients with gunshot wounds, the hospital filled up quickly. The triage department was run off its feet and had to call in five additional doctors.

On top of everything else, the generator ran out of diesel, which did nothing to help the triage team. Frustration levels mounted to the extent that Doc and Phil were delegated to go and see the Runt and find out exactly what he was doing about the power.

"We are fully aware of this unfortunate situation Doctor Roger. You may be assured that we will be rectifying the problem. We have teams out as we speak, who will collect more fuel."

Doc found out later, that the Alliance had a team of troopers who had been allocated the task of driving around in an old Bedford look-alike truck with a fuel tank on the back. Their task was to stop and investigate the thousands of vehicles which had been abandoned after the E1 had hit, and to secure all the leftover diesel fuel they could find.

It was a laborious task, and meant they had to check every driveway and garage, to ascertain whether the vehicles there were diesel or petrol driven. One NK trooper had made a disastrous mistake, which almost resulted in him being added to the bodies being burned at the tip. Not being able to tell the difference between petrol and diesel, he had pumped a half-full tank of unleaded petrol into their almost full diesel tank. The mistake had been discovered just before they'd begun to transfer the fuel to the generator tank at the hospital.

When the Captain found out he was furious. Knowing that he would bear the brunt of the General's rage once word of the incident filtered through to him, he had totally lost his temper, yelling and screaming at the team for almost an hour before dismissing them in disgust.

Nari spent most of the evening filling Doc in about all the information she had been able to gather from the various conversations she had overheard between the troopers.

"I'm not sure what we're going to do with all this intel Nari, but I know we will be able to use it at some stage."

"I am just happy to be able to help Doc. The more I learn about the Alliance perhaps means that maybe you will be able to defeat them!"

He smiled at her, feeling quite honoured at knowing how much trust the young girl had placed in his abilities.

"I think it will take a little more than just me Nari!"

Tuesday 6th January 2015 ... Kings Town.

The walk to the hospital took Doc and Nari around forty minutes, which gave them plenty of time to take notice of what was happening along the way. The town was slowly being cleaned up, and there was now almost no sign of the pools of blood and piles of body parts that had originally been left in front of almost every house. The clean-up crews were thorough; if they happened to notice any signs of new bloodshed during their walk home, by the next morning there was no sign of it.

Every morning they were lined up in the staffroom again, just like school children. This morning was no exception to the rule, everyone was there.

Li Chun entered to hear most of them complaining about the fact that they'd been at the hospital working since Friday with no break.

"You work every day! 6 a.m. to 6 p.m!"

Michael Bane, the gynaecologist, had heard enough! Marching up to the Runt, he yelled at him, "That's not fucking fair! You can't work us seven days a week!"

The Runt calmly drew his type 54, 7.62 mm or 38-calibre pistol, and aimed it directly at the infuriated doctor.

BANG!

The soft-leaded hollow point round blew the entire right side of Michael's head away as it exited, the plopping sound of the contents of his head as they hit the wall was sickening!

Christine Simmons had been standing immediately to Michael's left, and vomited, breaking down and sobbing as his blood and brain matter sprayed all over her.

The Runt drew himself up to his full height, satisfied that they had understood his point.

"You work every day! 6 a.m. to 6 p.m!"

As he left the room, he shouted back at them, "You go work! Now!"

As Nari and Ian started to clean up the mess, Doc suggested they should get to triage before they found themselves in the shit.

"Reg and I will take care of that."

Reg, still shaking, went to find a trolley. As they lifted the body on board, he asked, "What the fuck was that about Doc?"

"Mate, it was just a show of power."

"But if they keep going like this, there will be none of us left to run the place!"

"I'm not sure that will worry them one-bit Reg!"

Disposing of a body was now part of their normal routine, they simply pushed it through an old laundry chute, leaving the body to slide down to street level and onto the back of one of the clean-up trucks.

"Talk about unhygienic! Look at all the blood in the chute; within a week it will be rife with bacteria!"

"I know Reg, all we can do is to take the necessary precautions to protect ourselves. I really don't think they're at all worried about hygiene."

Doc picked up Nari at 1750, before starting the walk home together. Nari was worried about their food stocks.

"We will have to scrounge some food from somewhere soon Doc, we're getting very low on supplies!"

"That's okay Nari, we'll get some tonight. Just got to wait until it's almost dark."

"Where are we going to get it from Doc?"

"*Footy!*"

She looked up at him with those big brown eyes of hers but said nothing. Doc was aware of the risk he was taking, if Nari did turn out to be a spy, taking her to the marina could prove to be a real problem for him.

There was something about her that made him fairly confident that he could trust her. After all, she'd proven herself already, and had certainly taken a beating! There was no disguising the state her body had been in when he found her yesterday.

Besides, she seemed to have no issues with filling him in about any intel she'd gathered during the day. Her latest news had been gleaned from a conversation she'd overheard between the Runt and the General. She told Doc that the next Alliance convoy was expected to arrive today.

Maybe she was a spy after all ... but working against the Alliance, and not for them!

Nari had never been this close to a boat before.

"Is this your boat Doc?"

"Yep! She's all mine Nari. I used to come down every right and just sit and enjoy the night air."

With an innocent smile, she asked, "Can we still do that Doc?"

Nari held out her hand so that Doc could help her to climb on board. After leading the way below, Doc opened one of the many stowage compartments, revealing enough tinned and dry food to last the pair a month.

"Holy shit Doc! You save a lot up!"

Doc grinned, "For a rainy-day Love."

His use of a term of endearment had really only been a slip of the tongue, probably because he was in female company, but once he realised what he'd said, Doc also realised he hadn't minded saying it.

Nari was still holding his hand.

"I like you Doc."

They cooked up a feast on the boat's gas stove and finished off the meal with tinned plum pudding and custard.

"I REALLY like you now Doc!"

Wednesday 7th January 2015 ... General Hospital, Kings Town.

The following day Doc worked with Phil in surgery, patching up wounded troopers who'd been sent up from triage. Once again, their injuries were, for the most part, gunshot wounds.

They smiled to themselves, knowing that every bullet they extracted had come from a Taswegian weapon. They'd heard that the kill squad was now operating in the Glen area; by the looks of it, they'd come across some pretty fierce resistance from the local people!

Horrible stories were filtering back to them, about local people who'd been discovered and killed. There were no exceptions; from small children, to babies, to old women, nothing escaped the wrath of the, 'jug-eum-ui-bundae'.

From what the two surgeons could make out, there must have been at least six of these squads. Their orders were obviously simple but deadly; kill everyone, destroy everything if that proved necessary, mark the property for diesel removal, then clean up and get on to the next place.

They had heard constant explosions throughout the day, some seemed to be quite close, while others were a long way away. They'd been told these were caused by the troops blowing up any vehicles, boats or any other form of transport the locals might use to escape.

As they walked home that evening, Doc pointed to the harbour.

"Look Nari, two more tankers. Do you know what that means?"

The ex-South Korean triage nurse replied, "Yes! More nationals, more troopers and more work for us!"

That evening Nari reported to Doc that she had heard two troopers talking about the UHF station in Kings Town and how it had been fixed. It seemed that they were not very happy with the initial squad who'd shot up the place; killing the broadcaster was fine, but they had been instructed not to damage the equipment. This had now been repaired and was now monitored constantly."

"Well done Love! This is a real piece of Intel we can use, we now know for certain that the UHF is not a secure way to broadcast."

"Oh, and there was one other thing. It seems that the General is not happy that the convoy arrived late."

Nari leaned over, and after lighting the cigar Doc was fondling between his teeth, snuggled into his side. Doc felt an unexpected stirring in his loins; something that hadn't happened to him for at least the past seven years!

Thursday 8th January 2015 ... General Hospital, Kings Town.

In the staffroom that morning the Runt advised that there were a large number of wounded waiting in triage. One of the problems with having no communications was that they never knew when patients would be turning up. Doc, Christine and David were instructed to assist Nari and Ian in triage until the wounded were sorted out.

The First Officer was shot up pretty badly and had to be taken straight off to surgery. Unfortunately, he had died on the operating table.

That evening, over another meal on *Footy*, Nari, who'd been unusually quiet since leaving work, asked, "Why did you call your boat *Footy* Doc?"

"That's a good question. I think it started as a joke. I wasn't very good at sports when I was a kid, the furthest I could kick a football was about thirty-three feet. Somebody stupidly mentioned that I should call my boat *Footy* in honour of my football prowess, because it was the same length as my maximum kicking ability. Cheeky sods!"

Doc settled down to enjoy his accustomed after-dinner cigar.

"I've been thinking we should move some of the food up to the house, just in case anything happens to *Footy*."

"That sounds like a good plan Doc."

Nari was silent for a while. Doc was pretty sure she had something important she wanted to tell him, but didn't say anything, knowing she'd talk about it when she was ready. Eventually she broke the silence.

"Doc … I … I have some b … bad news; I don't know how to tell you."

"What's up?"

"After the trooper died in surgery today, I heard the General telling the Runt that he wouldn't have to put up with our incompetence for much longer. He said that he hoped the third convoy would be here any day now, and that their own medical staff would be on board."

Taking a deep breath, she continued bravely.

"Doc, they are going to execute all of us after that; maybe all except for just a few specialists."

Nari was crying. Doc held her tightly, placing his arm around her shoulders.

"I think I'd already guessed this was how it was Nari. I suspected we were only fill-ins. We need a plan, if the ships arrive, we will need to move quickly!"

Holding Nari, he wiped the tears away from her eyes with his thumb, thinking how innocent she was. 'What a fucked-up world we live in,' he thought, still looking at her eyes, so wide and brown.

She leaned up and kissed him ever so softly on the lips. Doc felt his body respond as he gently returned her kisses, remembering to be careful not to aggravate the bruises.

Feeling his heart start to race in anticipation at what was happening, he picked Nari up and carried her half stooped to the double forward berth, laying her down on the soft mattress before climbing in beside her.

"I think we'll both be more comfortable up here," he smiled at her.

Time passed as they both became lost in the excitement and wonder of their new found intimacy, eventually finding themselves lying in each other's arms in a kind of contented drowsiness, oblivious to the world around them, and finally drifting into a deep sleep, the sort of satisfied sleep you fall into only when you are physically and mentally exhausted.

Friday 9ᵗʰ January 2015 ... on board Footy, Chook Point Marina.

"Here is the news for Friday 2nd January 2015, Alex Brand reporting.

As I speak, we have reports that forces, calling themselves, "The New Alliance," have landed at all major ports in Taswegia ...

Troops are approaching the building! Stay tuned f... Shit! They're coming up the stairs! If we can get another ..."

Bang, Bang ... Schhhhhhhhhhhh ... Only static!'

Doc woke suddenly, dazedly thinking he was trapped in some kind of ground hog day! The replay had woken Nari as well.

"What was that Doc?"

"It's the UHF broadcast they put out when the Alliance invaded. Someone has replayed it!"

"Say again your last. Say again your last. Over."

The pair sat there in disbelief.

"There's someone else on the radio Nari!"

"Station on Channel 1. Do you copy?"

Silence …

Doc's thoughts were all over the place! He was wondering if he should grab the mic. No! Not likely with the bloody Alliance listening! Or were they? After all it was … 0130 by the ship's clock above the bed. Maybe they're not listening. But what if they were?

"Shit Nari! Do I warn them?"

Nari cuddled her naked breasts into his back.

"Maybe we see who they are first? They might talk some more."

"This is Bravo Zulu, Bravo Zulu. I have a copy."

"There it goes again Doc!"

"It was a different voice that time."

"Bravo Zulu, on Channel 1. Glad to hear your voice. Where are you?"

"Station calling Bravo Zulu, negative position, who are you?"

"Bravo Zulu, we are survivors situated Benowa East Coast Taswegia. Following the Holocaust, Taswegia has been invaded by troops from North Korea and Indonesia. They call themselves the Alliance. They are systematically killing everyone except for medical staff. Can you help? Over."

Doc and Nari just looked at each other. They were both bewildered by what they'd just heard, and what the consequences might be. What they did know was there was a distinct possibility that someone else had survived!

Doc sighed. He wished he knew for sure what was happening.

He looked at Nari, marvelling that a beautiful girl like her genuinely wanted to be with someone like him. Gathering her into his arms he gave up thinking about everything else that was happening for now.

She returned his kisses passionately, and they quickly became lost in the discovery of each other's love.

The urgent crackle of the UHF shocked them both back to reality.

"Station at Benowa East Coast Taswegia. This is Bravo Zulu. Over."

"That was well timed Doc!" declared Nari, sitting up and cuddling the aging doctor.

"Bravo Zulu, this is Benowa receiving 20/20."

"Benowa, we have also survived. Nice touch to replay the broadcast. It's too dangerous to give place names, you never know whether the bad guys are listening. Suggest you use Bravo Echo. How many in your party? Over."

"Bravo Zulu, this is Bravo Echo. There are twelve of us, made up of five families. How many of you?"

"Bravo Echo, there are six of us. Over."

"Enough is enough Nari! I have got to warn them!"

Doc kissed her forehead. Running to the cockpit he grabbed the mic, blurting out,

"BREAKER! BREAKER! DO NOT TRANSMIT! THEY ARE LISTENING!"

"Bravo Zulu, how far are you away from us? Over."

"Bravo Echo, too far! Repeat too far! Will try to keep in contact. Out."

Doc looked at the clock, surprised to see it was already 0300. Looking down, he still couldn't believe what he saw, this beautiful woman lying on his bed and truly wanting him, a sixty-five year old crony, who hadn't had sex of any kind in seven years!

'Hell!' he thought to himself. 'If this is how it ends, I'm happy'

In the end they'd drifted back to sleep in each other's arms and didn't wake up again until 0530! The pair had to run to get to work by 0600! Thankfully, they got there just ahead of the Runt.

As they entered the room together, they realised there was someone missing.

Li Chun entered, and stood in front of them, glaring at each one in turn.

He turned to Phil Brown, the surgeon.

"Why Officer Kim die yesterday?"

"He was too far gone by the time we got him! He died from internal complications; there was nothing we could do!"

"I see!"

The Captain turned and drew his type 54 pistol, then swung back and shot Phil in the head. The 7.62 mm round left a neat 8 mm hole as it entered, but upon exiting it tore out the back of Phil's skull.

"It is unacceptable to lose a trooper! Incompetence! You will not do this again!"

The Runt marched towards the door, turning back to give one final command.

"Go work! Now!"

After he'd gone, Doc looked around at the others; noticing how exhausted they all looked.

"He was obviously too upset to notice we were a man short! Does anyone know where old Henry has gone to?"

It was obvious that the Alliance troops, or at least their officers, were getting jumpy; Doc wondered if the main reason for this was the increased pressure that was being imposed on them by the General to meet his deadlines. He was aware from Nari's intel that the next convoy should have been here by now, so it was obvious that Jun Lee's plans were possibly not going as well as he would have liked.

Work had started to slacken off, which meant for the first time most of the doctors did not have much to do. However, instead of allowing them some time off they'd been ordered to turn their attention to general nursing duties.

"I don't know about you Doc, but you can shove emptying bed pans and sponge bathing Slopes!"

"Well Ted, given the alternative if we refused to do it, I suggest you just shut the fuck up and wear it!"

"Good point!"

Both Doc and Nari enjoyed their time away from the stress of the hospital that evening, as they spent a good couple of hours moving some of the supplies from *Footy* up to the house.

Finished at last, they sat down in some comfortable chairs while Nari shared the Intel she had gathered that day.

"I don't have much to report Doc, other than a couple of troopers saying they had drawn home duty. I don't know what that means. One of them asked the other one what area he'd been given. He told him that he was to head down Soothe way. What do you think?"

"I'm wondering if the Alliance are planning to send a trooper or two with each family they place in our homes. They know there's been some insurgency from some of the local people, so they'd want to make sure their own people were protected."

"That's an awful lot of homes Doc!"

"Yes, it could spread them thin, especially with all those who've been injured. No wonder they're a bit jumpy ... they must be desperate to see those reinforcements turn up!"

Saturday 10th January 2015 ... Kings Town.

Doc, Ted Green the anaesthetist, Les Solomon from Cardiology and Helen Smith from Diagnostic Imaging had now been designated as the permanent surgery team. As they scrubbed up Helen muttered,

"I hope you know what you're doing Doc! I don't want to end up like poor Phil."

"It's not going to matter one way or the other Helen. I've heard that as soon as the next convoy gets here, we're all going to be on the chopping block anyway. Sorry to be so blunt, but there's no point in hiding it."

The others looked at him in shock; they'd had no idea of what was coming.

"You sure Doc? What'll we do?"

"When's the convoy due?"

"How long have we got?"

Doc wished he had some better answers.

"What the fuck are we going to do people? Stand around grizzling or fix these patients! We'll just have to keep going and try and think of a plan. I think the first cab off the rank this morning is a ruptured hernia!"

As he put on his surgical gloves he added, "Oh, and just so you know, the missing convoy was due last Tuesday!"

As they walked home that evening, Nari held Doc's hand, and asked how his day had gone.

"At least no one died!" he said with a twisted grin. "And yours?"

"You know Doc, the usual cuts and bruises, gunshot wounds, and a hernia, we sent that one up to you."

They decided to eat dinner at the house that night.

"You know Doc, we're really lucky to be able to grab a hot shower at work each day. I guess it's one of the benefits of working at the hospital."

"Yes! I was getting sick of having to make do with cold washes here or having to boil the kettle fifteen times so I could have a shallow tub bath."

Getting up from the table, Nari sat on Doc's lap, with her face turned to his. He kissed her hard, realising how much he'd missed being with her that day. As he wrapped his arms around her slight body, he thought about what their daily life was like now. It was just like being in a war; they never knew which day was going to be their last! Not for the first time, Doc reminded himself how good it was to have someone like Nari living with him, at least in the evenings they were both able to forget what was happening for a time.

After removing both of their lower garments he gently pushed her back onto the kitchen table. Doc remembered with a shudder how he'd actually been daydreaming about this earlier today while he'd been in theatre. He'd been thinking of Nari, and not concentrating on what he was doing, and had almost snipped in the wrong place as he'd sutured up the patient!

Their lovemaking came to a violent climax; it was so intense that Doc thought for a minute he was having a heart attack!

"You all right Doc?" Nari sounded worried.

"I'm okay Love; I'm just an old man who's enjoying himself immensely."

They wandered down to visit *Footy*, and sat there contentedly together in the cockpit, enjoying the silence. It was a dark, still night.

Nari lit Doc's cigar.

"Is that your last one Doc?"

"Yes, I'm afraid so!"

He caressed her hair, knowing he hadn't felt this good in a long time. Neither of them spoke too often about how they felt towards each other, they just enjoyed the time they had. There was no point in making plans, it could all literally change tomorrow.

"Have you thought of a plan Doc?"

Doc kissed her gently on the lips.

"Oh, I've thought of plenty of plans my love, but most of them are fruitless!"

Nari wasn't familiar with the term.

"What do you mean?"

"Well, it's like this. I'll think of an idea, like setting sail one night and sailing down the channel. But that's as far as I can get with it. Where would we go? And how would we survive? It's most likely that eventually we'd be hunted down and killed. The only hope might be if we could join some of the others out there, that way we might have a chance to fight back."

"Like the people on the radio Doc?"

"Yeah. Maybe."

"I heard some news today Doc, but it wasn't that good. They went to check on Doctor Henry because he didn't turn up at work today; and they found him hiding at home. They killed him and his family as well."

"Shit! The way things are going it won't be too long before you and I will be the only ones left!"

Doc thought back to his conversation with the rest of the surgical team earlier that day.

"While I was getting ready for theatre today, I had to let the others know that we could all die once the next convoy arrives!"

"How did they take that Doc?"

"Well, it didn't go down all that well. Pat Collins had a hissy fit; and all the others could do was ask when, and why."

"You know they look up to you Doc! You're the man!"

Nari looked at him, smiling. Pulling her top over her head and letting her pants drop to the floor, she added,

"You're my man!"

There was one thing about sex that always intrigued Doc. The more you have it, the more you want it! And what's more, the more you used your love muscle the better it seemed to work.

As they lay in bed later on, with Nari snuggled into his arm, Doc looked around the cabin. His eyes suddenly fixed on a bag which had been stuffed into a compartment on the starboard side aft. It had been there for quite some time, and it took him a while to work out what was in it. Suddenly the penny dropped.

"Of course! It's the bloody brick phone!"

He didn't realise he'd spoken out loud. Nari woke in shock as he jumped out of bed, excited at his discovery.

He gave her a reassuring hug.

"It's okay Love. Sorry I scared you! I've just realised that the old analogue mobile phone network might still work; at least it might if there are still some of the old satellites up there. I was a real techie nut with these things in the early days, I'd forgotten I'd hung on to that one."

"What makes them so different?"

"Maybe you shouldn't have asked me that," he said, playfully squeezing one of her nipples.

"I told you I was really into this stuff. The first analogue system was called advanced mobile phone system or AMPS, and it hit Australia in 1987. AMPS technology was a real pioneer in its field; in its day it was considered the leading edge in driving mass market use of cellular technology. Mind you, it had a few issues, especially when you compare it to today's standards!"

Nari frowned, trying to keep up with what he was saying.

"Like what Doc?"

"Well, it was encrypted, and made it easy to eavesdrop or listen in on other people's conversations, especially if you had a scanner. So that was all good. However, it used a frequency division multiple access scheme and needed lots of wireless spectrum for support, which made them really very restrictive, and not all that secure. The first ones only gave you thirty minutes of talk time and took twelve hours to charge. Not only that, they weighed a bloody ton, hence the nickname of, 'brick phone'. From memory, most of the ones sold in Australia were the Motorola brand."

Doc laughed at the look of concentration on Nari's face, suddenly remembering that he had a long list of analogue phone numbers tucked away somewhere. He just had to remember where he'd put it!

Sunday 11th January 2015 ... General Hospital, Kings Town.

As Doc entered the theatre, Pat noted that he'd had a definite spring to his step lately.

"Someone's in a good mood," she smiled. She was quite fond of Doc and had been pleased at the difference she'd seen in him since he'd, 'got a girlfriend'.

"Nari's good for you!"

Ignoring her comment, Doc looked around, wondering where Ted was.

"That's not good, he's playing with fire if he doesn't turn up. If he HAS done a runner, let's hope it was a good one!"

Pat started crying.

"Not like poor Henry, who was hiding under the bed when they found him. I just wish it would all go away."

Pat's sobs grew louder, Doc was pretty sure she was about to have a complete breakdown. He could hear footsteps coming down the hallway, quickly realising they were the sound of the hobnailed boots worn by the Alliance. Slapping her face hard, he pushed her into the scrub room.

"Get a hold of yourself! If the Runt sees you like this, he might just pop one in your pretty head!"

Pat, although reeling from the slap, quickly came to her senses.

"Sorry Doc, but thanks!"

As Li Chun entered the room Doc changed the subject, hoping he wouldn't focus on Pat's red face.

"Well Pat, where's the first patient. Should be here by now. Oh! Good morning Li Chun."

"Come Doctor Roger! Bring your bag! You too Doctor Patricia! Come!"

Li Chun led them downstairs to a waiting jeep, informing them as they walked that they were to go and assist at the scene of an accident in the northern suburbs.

"Why not send the triage team? Surely they would be more suited to do this Li Chun."

"No! General says Doctor Roger must go!"

After driving through North Kings Town, the driver took the road to the river community of Bridge, about thirty kilometres away. Eventually they turned onto a farm a few kilometres outside Bridge.

Doc and Pat were confronted by the sight of a farmer, whose hand had been caught in the workings of a hand-operated threshing machine. At least that was what Doc thought it might have been.

"I've never seen anything like this before Pat!"

"Me neither Doc! We'd better see what we can do for the poor chap."

After giving the Asian an injection of morphine, they tried to reverse the workings; his hand had been caught in between some cogs and was stuck fast. It soon became clear that they weren't going to be able to free it. They were left with no choice.

"I'm afraid we're going to have to amputate Pat! Better give him another one to knock him out!"

The pair worked together to amputate four fingers from his left hand. Despite the less than ideal surgical conditions they managed the operation as best they could. Once they had him free of the machine and safely in the jeep, they nodded to the driver to get them back to the hospital as quickly as he could. During the return journey Doc took note of everything he saw; it was obvious that the Alliance forces were now well and truly integrated into the homes left vacant by the murdered locals.

As they drove up Fifteen Mile Hill, he saw NK Nationals on almost every property. It seemed they'd had to get used to cooking outside because of the lack of power; there was a fire going in most of the house yards they passed.

After arriving back at work, the pair returned to surgery, working quickly to get the NK farmer's hand cleaned up. As they scrubbed down, they were startled by the sound of screams coming from somewhere on the floor above. They made their way carefully up the fire escape stairs to the oncology ward, both taking a step backwards as they came across Bruce, who was lying in the doorway of one of the rooms.

On the other side of the room they could see the body of Lynda Browne tied to a bed; her underwear had been removed, and her skirt was up over her head.

Pat went to move forward, to check the two bodies for any signs of life but stopped with a jerk as Doc grabbed her by the arm. He pointed to the floor, where a pool of blood had formed, oozing from Bruce's body.

"Oh fuck!" Pat gasped, looking over at Lynda. "What about her … is she … still alive?"

Telling her to stay put, Doc stepped over the gathering pool of blood. It was obvious that Bruce was dead; after checking Lynda's pulse, and looking at her wounds he knew she was the same. It looked like both of them had been bayoneted to death.

"Let's get the hell out of here Pat!"

Nari cooked dinner for them while Doc started rifling through the linen cupboard in the hallway, looking for his brick phone list. Nari called out from the kitchen.

"I heard there was some trouble on the oncology ward today Doc!"

Doc was curious to know what she'd heard.

"What sort of trouble Love?"

"There's a rumour that one of the ward guards has been collecting money from the others. Kind of like a ... what do you call it ... a pimp! They were paying to take it in turns to rape one of the doctors. Someone said it was Lynda Browne. Someone else was saying that Doctor Bruce saw the troopers lined up at the door and tried to stop them. They killed him first, and then did the same to Lynda to stop her from telling."

Doc nodded with satisfaction as he found what he was looking for and came back into the kitchen.

"That's terrible Love, I hope they catch the bastards!"

"I know one of our guards told me that Li Chun was furious when he heard what had happened. He's been interrogating our guards, trying to find out if they were involved as well."

Doc thought it better not to tell her what he'd seen, he figured she'd seen enough lately.

Making love to Nari had become the pinnacle of his day. Their passion for each other was unbridled, no sooner had they arrived home when she'd unzip his trousers, eager to get started. That evening he'd bent her over the back of the couch, and made passionate love to her.

Later that evening, back on *Footy*, they sat in companionable silence, soaking up the moonlit view and the unmistakable smell of the saltwater, accompanied by the gentle sound of water lapping against the yacht's steel hull.

Nari disappeared down below to get a drink of water, leaving Doc looking around the marina. He couldn't help thinking about all the boats that were now going to waste. Some of them were worth millions of dollars, their former owners had been prominent Kings Town businessmen and women, most of them would be long dead by now.

He looked at a seventy-five-foot maxi yacht which was moored on the next walkway over. He knew her well, having sailed on her in numerous Jackson to Kings Town races over the years. Doc shook his head sadly, wishing there was some way of travelling back in time to those far better days.

"Guess what!"

Nari had a grin from ear to ear as she held out a handful of cigars.

"I have a present for you Doc!"

"Where on earth did you manage to find those?"

Nari told him about a trooper that had died on the way to hospital. She'd discovered them in his pocket while she was disposing of the body.

"Don't worry Doc! He didn't die in our care! He was already dead when the truck arrived."

Doc gave her a grateful kiss.

"Thank you Nari. I guess they're no good to him now."

Nari giggled, pleased to have been able to surprise him.

"Doc, you're such a funny man!"

Doc had resigned himself to no longer being able to enjoy his nightly cigar; Nari's gift really lifted his spirits.

Getting to his feet he retrieved the brick phone and showed Nari how to set it up and plug in the handset. The battery pack had been on charge since the night before; after sitting the phone down on top of the pack, Doc rifled through the small address book that had been hiding in the hall cupboard, looking through the lists of names and numbers.

"Ah! That's the one I was after!"

Doc turned to Nari. "Remember that radio broadcast we heard early Saturday morning? I thought I recognised one of the voices, but I wasn't sure until now. I think one of them was my old mate, Dick Mann!"

"Who is this Dick Mann, my man?"

Nari giggled like a schoolgirl, pleased with her joking play on words.

Doc laughed, kissing her on the forehead before telling her about the friendship between Dick and himself. Switching on the brick phone, he dialled Dicks number.

Br … Br … Br … Beeep!

"Bugger! It looks like it's switched off Love. I'll try again later."

Reaching out, he drew Nari in close to him, his mouth searching for hers. For the time being, their worries faded away as they made passionate love again.

Monday 12th January 2015 … on board *Footy*, Chook Point Marina.

A loud rumbling from the direction of the harbour woke Nari from a deep sleep. It sounded a bit like a large tractor, only from underwater! Playfully she bit Doc's left nipple. He was confused by the noise at first.

"Hey! What gives!"

Nari pointed towards the harbour. Doc could hear the noise clearly now.

"Shit! That sounds like a fucking F-Boat!"

Clearing the bed in a single leap, he made it to the cockpit just as the wake of the boat hit *Footy*, making her rock violently.

"W … what was that Doc?" Nari sounded worried and frightened.

"It's a fucking Fremantle Class Patrol Boat!"

She joined him at the cowling.

"Is it one of ours Doc? Maybe they've come to kick ass!"

"No such luck my little lovely!" said Doc grimly. "We sold them to the Indo's around 2005!"

"What's Indo's?"

"Sorry, the Indonesian Navy! I can't quite make out the number. The bloody thing hasn't changed much; the paint job's just a little bit darker, but there's still a number on the bow. We were supposed to scrap them, but some lowlife did a backhanded deal and we ended up selling four of them to Indonesia; *Fremantle, Warrnambool, Townsville* and *Wollongong!*"

Doc did a double take.

"Shit! She's doing a lap of the harbour and heading this way! I can see the number ... it's ... it's 204! It's *Warrnambool!*"

Once again, they only just made it to work on time. Doc had asked Nari to find out what she could about the new arrival. They found they were short another doctor this morning. This time it was Bob Silver from orthopaedics who hadn't showed.

"Stupid bastard!" Doc mumbled to the group as they each went off to their respective work areas.

Pat and Doc were joined by Dr Dave Reddy from renal.

"There's nothing like a change! I've always wanted to be an anaesthetist!"

"Well it seems like Ted might have done a runner, and we need someone to do his job, so we're glad you're here!"

The day's surgeries included an appendix removal, a tooth removal, and another delivery.

As they walked home that night, Nari and Doc could see the *Warrnambool* berthed at Queens Pier. The sight of her brought the memories of Doc's navy days and the countless days of sea time he'd done on the F-boats flooding back. While he hadn't actually served on the 204, he'd served on two of her sister ships, the *Cessnock* and the *Dubbo* as their Navigation Officer.

Nari cooked a stir-fry and headed to bed early, she was in the early days of her period, and as always, she found the first couple of days pretty painful.

Doc lit his cigar, savouring the moment as he thought of Nari and the strange life that had now become the 'norm'. Before the appearance of FCPB 204 *Warrnambool*, he'd started to think about doing a runner with Nari, on *Footy*, but now he was having second thoughts.

He turned the UHF radio on. Nothing! Hitting 'scan' again, he waited through the full scan of all forty channels, but there was still nothing. Next, he tried dialling Dick's number with no response, and finally selected a number at random belonging to some bloke he couldn't even remember. Nothing!

Giving up for now, he thought about the changes they'd seen as they walked to and from work. Big changes had taken place in Kings Town. Apart from the occasional shop that had been re-vamped into a guard station, most shops were now boarded up, and the inner-city hotels had been converted into living quarters for the troopers. Apart from what Doc had seen of the surrounding suburbs on the journey he and Pat had taken out to Bridge, they had no idea what else had changed.

He'd tried without success to come up with a way he and Nari could leave before it was too late, he kept running into dead ends. The only new Intel Nari had been able to gather was that the boat had come down the west coast, and that there was meant to be another one coming down the east coast. However, because of the lack of communications they had no way of knowing when it was expected to arrive.

Doc sighed and headed off to bed. After stripping off and sliding in between the sheets, he cuddled up to Nari, feeling her warm body snuggle up close to his. She was starting to feel much better, especially now that her man was beside her. Unable to sleep, they talked about possible plans of escape.

Doc still reckoned the best solution to the problem was to set sail in *Footy* and head down south. There were many small bays down that way which might provide a good place to hide in, they'd just have to find somewhere with no vehicle tracks in from the main roads.

They both agreed this was probably their only chance. All they had to do now was to wait for the *Warrnambool* to leave on patrol.

"Did you have any luck with your friend on the brick phone?"

"No Love. Not yet."

Tuesday 13th January 2015 ... General Hospital, Kings Town.

Following the morning muster, the Runt ordered them all outside. Just like a class of children on an excursion they were herded up Drum Street and into the pedestrian mall, where they were ordered to stand and wait.

Looking around they could see a group of Alliance troopers, headed by six officers, and standing to the right of these, a group of NK Nationals. The General, who had been conversing with the officers, turned and approached the doctors as he saw them arrive.

Appearing to be in a jovial mood, he addressed his comments to Doc.

"Good morning Doctor Roger. So glad of you to come!"

"Well General, I guess we didn't have much say in the matter. What's going on?"

"You have come to witness an execution!"

The group looked at each other in consternation, hoping it wasn't going to be one of them. Both Pat Collins and Christine Simmons were terrified; Doc glared at the two women, silently pleading with them to calm down so as not to draw the General's attention.

"Ah Doctor Roger! You will see that I am a fair man. I show you that we believe in justice where it is warranted. I show you that we are prepared to punish our own when they have done wrong!"

As one of the senior troopers led the condemned man out from inside one of the buildings, Doc realised he must be the trooper who had committed the heinous crime against Lynda and Bruce. The man was bound, with a hood covering his face. After leading him to one of the benches in the mall, he was bent over the back rest and his hood removed.

The General called Nari to his side, and then made an announcement in the Korean language.

"Nari Kim! You translate in English. Now!"

"The General said, '*This soldier of the Alliance has committed a crime against two members of the Hospital Staff and will be punished accordingly!*'"

Jun Lee nodded his approval, motioning to Nari to stand back.

Li Chun emerged from among the group of officers and saluted the General, then stood behind the bound man. Drawing his sword, he raised it far above his head, and then brought it down hard on the back of the condemned man's neck.

Whoosh!

As the sharp blade bit cleanly, the prisoner's head and body parted company. Blood spurted out of the now headless body, spattering the pavement, the head rolled over to the side of the road, and the body simply dropped down behind the seat. After cleaning his sword on the dead trooper's tunic, Li Chun saluted again, then stepped back into position among the other officers.

Sickened, Pat whispered to Doc, "What did you make of that?"

"I think it was really just a propaganda stunt, laid on for our benefit. We all know they've committed far worse crimes than that!"

After being escorted back to the hospital, the doctors were ordered to continue their duties. Doc and Pat found themselves back in theatre, patching up some NK farmer who'd been shot by troops as they'd attempted to take over a farmhouse. Even though the farmer had taken up residence two days earlier, somehow the troopers had got their wires crossed; believing the place was occupied by locals.

As they made their way back to Chook Point that night, Doc noticed what appeared to be a fuel truck siphoning fuel out of vessels in the marina.

"Shit! That doesn't look good Love!"

From the main window of the house, Doc and Nari watched the truck stop at each vessel in turn as it made its way along the pier. Deciding it was too risky to go down to the marina that night, they stayed where they were; the only thing on Doc's mind that night was his hope that they wouldn't find anything untoward on *Footy* if they happened to go on board to have a look!

Chapter 27
High Head

It was 1900. Ernie and Belle Flood were doing what they'd always done, even before the E1 hit. The pair had been married for thirty-eight years, most of the time they could be found sitting outside on their verandah, smoking and drinking endless cups of coffee, and taking in the view of the entrance to the beautiful Ramat River in northern Taswegia.

Prior to E1, Ernie had worked as a crane driver at the Bull Bay terminal just outside of Gary Town, only 10 minutes' drive from the High Head lighthouse, which was the place they called home. Belle had been a housewife for the whole of their married life, managing all of the chores associated with their home.

The lighthouse had become automated quite a few years before, and before E1, had still played an important role as the main navigational aid for vessels entering the river. Bull Bay was the main shipping terminal for Lawn, from that point on, the narrow channel up the river was too narrow to allow safe passage for the larger ships. The terminal hosted an aluminium smelter, a manganese alloy smelter, and two working power stations. and was the docking and unloading point for most of the ships bringing wood chips, containers, alumina, petroleum and other bulk materials into that part of the island state. These days both the river and the terminal were pretty well deserted.

"Bugger, someone must have drunk my coffee while I wasn't looking."

Ernie stood up, stretching his back as he asked, "You fu-ck-offee?"

Belle nodded her head, smiling at the old family joke as she lit up another cigarette. As Ernie bent down to pick up her empty cup, he suddenly turned and stared back at the river, it didn't seem possible, but he was almost certain he'd seen the tail end of a ship as it disappeared from view.

"What the fuck was that!"

"What was what? I didn't see anything Ernie."

"Not sure Love! I might take the bike down to the terminal in the morning and check it out."

After another coffee, Belle called it a day and headed off to bed around 2030. Ernie disappeared down to the cellar and made his way through the old tunnel that connected the light house with the High Head Pilot House, which was the home of their daughter Nic Walt, who lived there with her husband, Smokey, and their two sons, Gaz and Boz. Smokey had been the head shipping pilot and was in charge of all shipping movements in and out of the Ramat River, while Nic ran the Pilot House's tourist information centre. Baz and Boz were both pilots like their father.

"Well! Look what the cat's dragged in, Howdy Ernie."

Ernie got on well with his son-in-law.

"Did you see the ship Smokey?"

The forty-eight-year-old was wondering whether his father-in-law had finally lost the plot.

"What ship mate? There's been no traffic since E1."

"I'm telling you, I definitely saw something, and I swear it was a ship!"

Ernie dragged his son-in-law all the way out to the breakwater, from there the pair could just see the stern of a large ship as it disappeared into the Bull Bay wharf.

"Holy shit Ern! You weren't kidding! What do you suppose is going on? I thought all ships had gone, 'kerplunk' after the goings on last December."

"I'm not sure mate, but I'm planning on riding the old bike to the terminal in the morning to check out what's going on. You up for a ride?"

"Sure, why not. I've only got the missus's bike, but I wouldn't mind tagging along. What time?"

Friday 2nd January 2015 … Bull Bay Shipping Terminal, Security Gate E.

The pair left High Head around 0545, and after a twelve-and-a-half-kilometre ride along the back road, they found themselves at Gate E around 0700, overlooking the main wharf. Accessing Ernie's old work site wasn't an issue, there'd been no need for security since the E1 had hit, and it didn't take them long to push aside the loose cyclone fencing at the side of the gate.

The pilot grinned as the pair made their way over to the short rock wall separating the security gate and the road leading down to the wharf.

"I bet this is just like old times mate, sneaking into work and late for a shift."

"Many times, mate. Off the record of course!"

The super tanker's on-board crane was in full swing, unloading the deck containers. Smokey was about to start moving towards the wharf when Ernie tackled him, dragging him to the ground.

The forty-eight-year-old struggled to escape Ernie's grip.

"What the fuck Ernie!"

"Use your eyes mate! Can't you see they're military."

Ernie let go of Smokey once he was certain he'd got his point across. Looking towards the main gate, he could see a familiar group approaching the wharf.

"Look! Isn't that Ron and a couple of his workers? Looks like they're trying to find out what's going on as well."

Ernie's old boss and two of his team drew level with the first container just as a truck was unloaded out of it and onto the wharf. Ron yelled something to the driver, pointing at the other ten or so containers that were already on the wharf, obviously asking what was in them. A young officer stepped out from behind the container, and aimed his service pistol at Ron, firing once and shooting him in the head. Ron's co-workers tried to attack the officer but were also shot and killed as other troopers appeared from nearby.

Smokey couldn't believe what he was seeing. "Did you see that Ern?"

Ernie watched as the troopers unloaded more trucks and a number of jeeps.

"Mate, this smacks of some sort of invasion. The bastards must have been organising this for months ... all of these vehicles have to be pre-2000, otherwise they wouldn't be able to work,

Smokey frowned. "Nah, surely that's not possible mate, Why? and who?"

From their hiding place behind the rock wall the pair witnessed hundreds of armed troops moving around the wharf before climbing into the vehicles.

"Think it's time to skedaddle Smokey, looks like they're getting ready to move!"

After exiting through the fence, they started peddling back the way they'd come. As he took a quick look back, Ernie realised that most of the trucks had turned right towards Lawn. At first it looked like they were in the clear, but then he saw a few trucks turn left towards Gary Town, before starting to head in their direction.

"That's not good mate! We'd better step on it!"

As they cycled through the outskirts of Gary Town, they could hear gunshots behind them as the troopers riding in the trucks dispersed into homes and started shooting the occupants. Sheltering behind a thick stand of tea tree, they waited for a gap in the traffic.

Ernie whispered urgently, "Looks like nearly all of them are heading up the main street, we'll have to make a run for it past the roundabout and hope none of them see us. Once we get past that we'll be able to get off the road and take that bush track of yours up the river to High Head."

The words were barely out of his mouth when shots started flying over their heads, one of the troopers had caught sight of the pair and started firing.

"Struth Ern!"

Smokey knew the river front like the back of his hand; they dashed for the river, and then cycled like mad up the single lane bush-track walk. Smokey led the way, giving a warning shout to Ernie whenever there was a bend in the track; hoping the older man would be able to keep up with him. The sounds of revving trucks, gunfire and screaming sounded surreal, but certainly made them pedal faster!

After stopping at the old Gary Town retirement village, they burst into a relatively new house in front of the navigational lead light, this was home to their friends, Charlotte and Henry Platt. Charlotte and Henry, both Senior Constables, were the town's sole police force, although Ernie knew they were supposed to be enjoying their holidays right now.

"Charlotte! Henry! Where the fuck are you?"

A voice came from round the back of the house.

"In the garden Ern!" The forty-two-year-old police officer greeted them with a smile. What brings you this far south?'

His smile soon turned to a look of disbelief as Ernie and Smokey told them about what they'd seen.

"There's no way! Are you sure you haven't been drinking you two?" Charlotte calmly turned back to what she'd been doing, levering the weeds out of her neat veggie patch.

Smokey yelled, "Shut up and listen! You'll hear better from out the front!"

They followed the river pilot down the drive, looking at each other in shock as they heard the sound of distant gunfire.

"They're killing everyone they come across, and it's not going to be too long before they start coming in this direction!"

Finally realising the urgency of the situation, Henry sprang into action.

"Get some gear together Charlotte! You'll need your sidearm and all the ammo!"

Charlotte was in tears, pointing to the retirement village.

"We need to go and warn the residents!"

"There's no time for that, if what the boys are saying is correct, we've got to get out of here now! There are too many of them to handle on our own. Once we've had time to re-group, we can work out a plan."

It was 1030 by the time the four of them got to the High Head Pilot House. Ernie went back through the tunnel to warn Belle, while Smokey filled Nic and the boys in about what they'd seen. There was a military museum attached to the information centre; Boz and Baz took the two police officers into the locked storerooms to have a look at the armoury.

There was a fair bit of gear there that might prove useful: twenty-four .303 rifles and four boxes of ammo, ten Browning pistols and two thousand rounds of 9 mm ammo to suit, one .303 Bren gun and another two boxes of ammo, various flare guns and flares, and also three Colt .45 revolvers with one hundred rounds of ammunition.

Gaz wasn't certain whether it would all be in working order.

"We don't even know whether any of this still works, or even how old it is. I know there's some stuff here that dates back to WWII."

Henry replied in his usual dry manner, "Well, it's better than nothing, and I guess we'll find out soon enough whether it's still useable."

After loading it all into a trolley, the team pulled it into the tunnel system and secured the entrance.

The High Head tunnel system had been put in place at the time the lighthouse had been built, the extra access was deemed necessary because of the really bad weather that often hit that part of Taswegia's coastline. The tunnel enabled clear access from the lighthouse to the pilot station, and to the two other empty houses on the point. Anyone using the tunnels was assured of a good supply of fresh air through the numerous vents in the tunnel ceilings; these had been kept hidden from prying outside eyes by carefully placed rocks and smaller stones. The various entrances to the tunnel were also well hidden, most people had forgotten they were even there. Ernie and Belle's daughter Nic had spent many enjoyable weekends and holidays exploring the tunnel system; she was certainly the current resident expert about what was down there.

As children, Nic and other local kids had converted one of the side tunnels into a rough shack and Ernie had later helped them fit it out as a kind of retreat, complete with half a dozen beds and some old couches that had been headed for the local tip. During their teenage years, Nic and her friends had used it as an escape from their parents and from the world in general; many a drunken party had taken place down there, and it was rumoured that this was the spot where young Nic had lost her virginity. These days it was all looking a bit sad and grubby but was still a good place for a hide-away.

By 1800 they had the food and weapons stowed away, and the other tunnel entrances had also been made secure. Charlotte, Nic and Bell got a pot of coffee going on the metho stove, and then started putting something together for dinner, while Smokey, Ernie, Gaz, Boz, and Henry started working on getting things cleaned up. They all agreed that, for now at least, this was the safest place for all of them.

Boz had been thinking.

"I reckon we ought to go and take a look, we need to find out how far up they've made it so far."

"It might pay to wait till after dark Boz," said Henry, "then I'll come with you."

Over dinner the main topic of discussion was about what they'd seen and heard, as well as tossing about the many unanswerable questions they were all thinking about, like why, and how, and who?

Just after 2300, Henry re-opened one of the unused entrances that came out near the house opposite the pilot station, and went to investigate, taking Boz with him as a guide. As they emerged from the tunnel, they looked around, thankful for the faint moonlight that helped to break the darkness of the night. They could see a jeep pulled up outside the station, and a number of bodies lying in the street and strewn on front lawns. It looked like the locals had tried to make a run for it.

Carefully, they made their way over the back fence of the place next door, trying to move as stealthily as they could. Finding themselves in the next street over, they moved silently from house to house, checking each one as they went. They were shocked to find the local inhabitants had either been shot at close range or bludgeoned to death. Some of them had even been bayonetted. The women had all been mutilated, and many of them raped as well. Boz had always considered himself to be pretty hardened, but threw up after leaving the third house. Even Henry, who had some twenty-four-years of service under his belt, was finding it hard to comprehend what they'd found.

"This is horrific Boz! It might pay not to mention too many of the gory details to the women."

Saturday 3rd January 2015 ... High Head Residential Sector.

Around 0124, Henry and Boz saw a jeep pull up outside the corner house of the street they were searching at that time.

"If we move fast enough Boz, we might be able to at least save one person's life,"

As they approached the back of the house the sound of two gunshots rang out, followed by screaming. As Henry carefully peered through a sliding door, he saw two troopers in the act of raping a young girl. He quietly slid the door open, and stepped through, levelling his service Glock 17 38 revolver at the first male, and firing as he went. He got the young trooper in the back, making him slump forward over the girl. The second trooper, who'd been holding her arms, let go of them and tried to grab his rifle. Boz had never fired a handgun before, but didn't hesitate, pushing the safety off the 9 mm Browning pistol and pulling the trigger. The kick of the weapon testified to the fact that it wasn't a toy!

The young girl was distraught, sobbing with fear.

"It's all right Love, we're here to help. What's your name?"

Henry's calm voice helped her to calm down. Her name was Kylie, she'd had no warning about what was going to happen until the troopers had burst in through the door. He helped the young lass back into her clothes while Boz went to check whether there were any others close by.

Boz was still shocked that he'd actually killed somebody!

"It looks all clear Henry."

It was 0300 by the time they got back, thankful to find Nic and Belle still up, with coffee on the boil. As they enjoyed the hot brew, Henry introduced Kylie to the two women before telling them about how things had gone while they were away. Although they'd agreed to spare them some of the worst details, that proved a bit difficult in the end, Kylie made no bones about sharing all the gory details with Nic and Belle.

Sunday 4th January 2015 ... High Head Tunnel System.

It was 0830. Belle woke her sixty-four-year-old husband with a fresh coffee and filled him in about the previous night's escapades.

"Is the girl all right?"

"She's still sleeping Ern. I've been thinking how traumatic it must have been for her to see her parents killed, and then to be almost raped and killed herself. I'm worried she might never get over it. Mind you, I'm having trouble myself, trying to take in everything that's happened over the last two days."

The accommodation area had been divided into six double bedrooms, with curtains for privacy; each of these opened into the common area, which boasted four large couches, a couple of armchairs and a large table with ten chairs. Set off to the side were a couple of kitchen benches, which had been fitted out with metho burners, a sink, and water taps. A gas unit had been placed halfway between them and the lighthouse, which meant there was plenty of hot water, and a shower had been built alongside the gas unit.

By 1200 everyone was up. All of them were seated around the large table, with the exception of Smokey and Gaz, who were out on the bikes, riding around the river track and checking the homes in High Head. Their objective was to find out as much information as they could about the troops. Henry recounted his and Boz's reconnoitre of the night before and made sure that everyone was introduced to Kylie.

Earlier that morning, Nic and Boz had made a trip back to the pilothouse, only to find that someone had already taken up residence there. Boz had to hold Nic back in order to stop her from bursting in and giving the intruder a piece of her mind! Although they'd managed a stealthy retreat, Nic was definitely not in a good mood.

Belle and Charlotte had checked out the lighthouse but had found it was still empty.

By 1600, Smokey and Gaz were back.

"They're just stowing the bikes now," reported Boz, eager to find out what the pair had discovered.

"Smokey and I made it all the way to Gary Town. It seems we're dealing with a group called the Alliance. We came across a couple of them who were practising their English, they were talking about the ten ships that the Alliance had sent after the nuclear holocaust happened. Apparently, they don't actually know for sure whether all of the ships made it out safely ... it seems that some are running late and might have been caught up in the blast."

Smokey continued the story. "Looks like what Ernie and I saw a couple of nights ago is happening in Devon and in Kings Town as well! It all got a bit sketchy after a while. They kept mixing the English up with their own language, but it sounded like they were talking about being press-ganged into, 'bundae leul jeongli', or something like that. We also heard something like, 'jug-eum-ui-bundae.' Gaz and I think that what they're doing is placing their own families in our homes, with a trooper at each place for protection. It looks like we've definitely been invaded."

Nineteen-year-old Kylie raised her hand. "I've been learning to speak Korean at University, from what you heard, it sounds like our invaders are from there."

Henry agreed, telling the group he thought they were most likely from North Korea. He'd heard through official channels that they'd pushed the button.

"It looks like they've chosen us as their base for world domination, probably because there's little or no fallout here."

Gaz continued the story.

"Every home we visited was the same; all the locals were dead! What Henry and Boz told us was gruesome enough, but there was some stuff we saw that was even worse!"

Smokey nodded, continuing, "Everywhere we looked we could see trucks, with bodies being loaded onto them. It looked like they were heading for the Gary Town tip. We could see a heap of black smoke coming from that direction; if I was to hazard a guess, I'd say they're cremating them there."

Kylie interrupted, "I've just worked out what they were saying … the two phrases you heard … one means, 'clean up squads', and the other one means, 'death squads.' Yes! They're definitely from North Korea!"

Charlotte gave Belle a hug, the reality of what they were hearing was hard to take in.

Charlotte shook her head.

"This is terrible. Why all the killing? Surely that's not necessary."

"Based on what Smokey and Baz have told us, with ten ships we're talking about a huge number of NK Nationals, maybe more than 2.5 million! That's five times our population!" Looking around at the group, Henry continued, "There just isn't enough room for us and them. The only logical answer to them would be to simply kill us all."

Nic was furious! "Not fucking likely! They're going to find out they've just unleashed a hornet's nest! I know I'm not very big, but there's no way I'm going to let some gook just move into my home!"

Ernie nodded. "We're going to need to add to our number! Smokey, did you see any signs of survivors in Gary Town?"

"There were about three or four homes that were empty, I'm guessing the clean-up squads hadn't got to them yet; I'm hoping the locals might have got wind of what was happening and scarpered."

Boz agreed. He'd just remembered that one of the empty homes was usually rented by a mate of his who'd served in the reserves with him. Ron was no fool, it wouldn't have taken him long to work out what was going on.

Monday 5th January 2015 ... High Head Lighthouse.

It was 1000. Boz and Gaz had drawn the short straw and had been sent to the lighthouse by their grandparents to check if it was still clear, and to retrieve any tinned food they could find there. While they were there, they also gathered some fresh vegetables from Ernie's garden.

"Looks like it's all clear Boz. I don't reckon anyone's been here since the last time we checked."

Gaz agreed. "Maybe they don't think the place is liveable."

After storing the food inside the tunnel, they sealed the entrance, and decided to take a trip along the eight-kilometre walking track heading towards East Beach. The track, which ran all the way to Cimitiere Creek, was part of the track system they all used to get to Gary Town undetected.

About half-way there, they found evidence of someone camping on the foreshore.

"The question, Bro, is whether this was from before the gooks got here, or after."

"That's a really good question Boz. Let's hope it was after; maybe that way we can invite whoever it is to add to our ranks."

As they walked, the brothers talked about everything that had happened. Boz told Gaz about how he'd shot the trooper with the 9 mm Browning. Gaz was curious to know how that had felt; sure, they'd done a lot of training in the army reserves, but they'd never actually deployed overseas.

After a while their discussion shifted to fantasising about the next move, or more to the point, what they thought this move should be.

Boz was after blood, especially now that he'd had a taste of what that was like. He raised his voice, "I think it's about time we started killing the fu … !"

Gaz stopped him by clamping his hand over Boz's mouth.

"Shhhh! Quieten down! There's voices around the next point mate."

Dropping to the ground, they withdrew their 9 mm Brownings from their waistbands, and crawled forward on hands and knees to where they could see what was happening. Two males and a female were sitting around a campfire trying to cook a fish which had been speared onto a stick.

Gaz whispered, "I think I know a couple of them. It looks like the Smith kids, you know, Claudia, and I think it's Chris, from East Beach. I think they're both around twenty years old, although it's hard to tell."

"The other one used to work in the Gary Town fish and chip shop, I don't know his name. Do you reckon they're armed?"

"I wouldn't think so, but we probably shouldn't take any chances!"

The brothers crawled forward to within twenty metres of the trio. After waiting until Boz had moved around to their right, Gaz stood up and yelled, "You're lucky we're not gooks!"

The trio dropped their fish and turned to run, but Boz cut them off. By this time the brothers were both brandishing their weapons, and with nowhere to go Claudia fainted.

"Please don't hurt us!" yelled Chris.

Boz saw the other kid start to move towards a clump of bushes.

"Don't be a fool mate. We're on your side!"

Gaz came in close and removed the aging .22 rifle from its hiding place. After making sure the girl was okay, he introduced his brother and himself to the group. It turned out that two of them were indeed Claudia and Chris Smith, the other was their mate, Bill Gates, all of them were from East Beach. The trio told the brothers that on the day of the invasion they had been doing what they'd always done since the E1; trying to catch a meal. Cimitiere Creek was their favourite place, they usually ended up with a feed of flathead, and very occasionally some salmon. They'd been almost back at Bill's house when they'd heard shots and screaming. Hiding in the bushes, they'd felt helpless as they'd witnessed the terrible butchering. After carefully making a retreat, they'd then rushed the two blocks to the Smith residence, just in time for Chris and Claudia to see their mother cut down as she'd tried to run away.

"It was horrible! All those people, our neighbours, murdered by the heathens; and we just sat by and did nothing!" The nineteen-year-old was obviously upset.

Gaz said sadly, "There was nothing you could have done Claudia."

The brothers told the trio what they'd learnt about the invasion and invited them back to the tunnel.

Boz whistled the all clear signal as he led the way into the common room.

Henry and Smokey had been busy fitting telescopic sights to three of the Lee Enfield .303 rifles; they'd found the sights in amongst the ammo and cleaning gear. As the five young people entered the room, they nodded a brief "hello".

"Look what we found at Cimitiere Creek guys."

Claudia was welcomed by everyone, especially the women, the boys found themselves sitting with the men as they learned more about the little band of, 'Resistance Fighters'. Ernie had started calling them by this name as a joke at first, but they'd all liked the idea, and the title had kind of stuck.

Smokey, Boz, Gaz and Henry gave the group a lesson on how to load and use the Browning,s and the .303's, as well as how to clean them. It was agreed that the three Army reservists would carry the scoped rifles, while Henry, Bill and Chris would use the plain .303's. Everyone else was issued with a Browning. They all felt better, now that their number had started to increase.

"So," said Nic, "what's our next move going to be?"

Wednesday 7th January 2015 ... East Beach.

It was 0200, probably the best time to attempt a reccy. Claudia, Bill and Chris, along with Gaz and Ernie, went off to investigate whether they could get anywhere near the former Smith and Gates residences. If possible, they wanted to fetch some of their clothing, and also some more food to add to their stores. Smokey warned them not to use the rifles because they'd be too noisy, even the 9 mms would be too loud, unless the blasts could be muffled somehow.

Gaz and Bill quietly entered Bill's bedroom through an unlocked sliding glass door. The twenty-year-old was furious to find three NK Nationals in his double bed; they were kids, aged between ten and twelve. The ex-fish shop worker shoved a pillow over the head of one of the kids to try and suffocate him, but he made so much noise that he woke the others. Pushing the 9 mm into the pillow, Bill pulled the trigger.

Dooff!

That worked! Bill did the same to the next kid, while Gaz took care of the other one. The pair moved quietly through the house, systematically and cleanly despatching the other occupants. Once they were certain all was clear, they motioned to Claudia, Chris and Ernie to join them inside, where they worked on collecting the supplies and clothing they were looking for. After rummaging through a wardrobe in one of the rooms, Bill produced a hunting rifle, another .22 and a carton of bullets, adding these to their haul with a grim smile.

By the time they got to Claudia and Chris's home it was 0345. The two-storey brick and tile house was set back off the road. Bill and Gaz told the others how they'd managed to silence the noise of their 9 mms, warning them they might have to be ready to do the same.

Claudia volunteered to stand guard, not certain that she'd actually be able to make herself pull the trigger if she needed to. Chris and Ernie quietly made their way upstairs to the bedrooms that used to be his and his sister's. A trooper was in his room, snoring loudly; without giving himself time to think, the twenty-year-old shot the man through a pillow. The sound was more of a loud *Thud* than a *Dooff!*

They found two kids in Claudia's room: a girl about fifteen years old, and another aged about ten. Ernie had seen action in East Timor, once he reminded himself that this was the enemy, he didn't have to struggle too much about having to kill the young pair. Bill and Gaz took care of the couple who were sleeping in the downstairs master bedroom.

They quickly filled their rucksacks with all the food they could carry, while Claudia gathered up some of her clothing.

Gaz was wondering about the Alliance weapons.

"What do we do with the trooper's weapon? I don't think their ammo's the same as ours."

Ernie replied, "The way we're going we'll soon have a fair collection of theirs, don't forget, we don't have much ammo of our own ... it's going to run out long before theirs will."

Chris, who'd gone off to check the place next door, reappeared, pushing a pram.

"I thought this might make it easier to carry all the gear we've found."

In the meantime, Henry, Smokey, Boz, Nic, Charlotte, Belle and Kylie had made the trip to the old RSL building in Gary Town; this was alongside the house rented by Boz and Gaz's reserve mate, Ron. Henry checked his watch: 0210.

Boz went off to check the house, finding it empty, he checked out his mate's bedroom. As he'd thought, some of his clothing was missing, along with his army pack. Boz reported back to the group.

"I reckon Ron's survived okay, looks like he's been back to get some more gear."

"Think mate! Where do you think he'd be likely to hole up with all this going on?"

While the twenty-seven-year-old pondered over Smokey's question, Henry and Charlotte, together with Belle, made the short journey to their old place of work; the Gary Town Police Station.

Leaving Belle to keep watch, the two police officers entered the old station by the side door after retrieving the hidden spare key and approached the front desk area with their weapons drawn. They stopped as they heard voices, realising that one of the cells was occupied.

Henry pointed in the direction of the three cells. "Looks like they might have a bad boy locked up!"

Charlotte used her small makeup mirror to look around the corner at the desk sergeant's spot, holding up one finger to her husband and indicating that there was one Alliance trooper there. After waiting until the guard had his back to her, the feisty senior constable moved up behind him and belted him over the head with the butt of her service revolver.

"Nice work Love! We'd better check out the rest of the place."

There was nobody else there, apart from the occupant of the cell, who was calling out to whoever was there. After they'd emptied the armoury of all weapons and ammunition, and loaded them into a PVC carry bag, Charlotte looked at Henry, nodding to the cells. After waiting till Charlotte had disappeared outside, he opened the cellblock door. The NK National had no idea what hit him. Henry shot him in the chest, killing him instantly; as he went back past the main desk, he also put a bullet into the guard, just to make sure he was dead.

"I reckon I know where Ron would have gone!" exclaimed Boz, remembering where they'd all used to gather after Reserves on a Tuesday night.

It was 0525 by the time they reached the old Gary Town Sailing Club. The dilapidated building had been condemned some years ago; the only people who ever went in there these days were a few locals. Beneath the building was an old wine cellar, which housed an odd assortment of various bottles of alcohol, this was where the budding young soldiers used to take the girls, to try and get them drunk. Boz approached the old building, indicating to Smokey and Henry to stay behind him. He knocked on the wine cellar wall, nodding with satisfaction when a door opened opposite the place where they were standing.

"Boz! You bugger! What gives! What's happening? Oh, hello Mr Walt; you too Constable Platt. You'd better come inside before you get seen."

Inside they found six males and two females, ranging in age from ten to twenty-five. It looked like they were well set up; looking around they could see a gas stove, water from an old line above them, plenty of food, and some mattresses on the ground.

"You lot been here long?"

"Most of us have been here on and off for about two days now Constable Platt. Some longer. We go out at night to find food, as well as look around and check if there are any survivors. It's a bit hard, not knowing for sure what's happening."

Smokey and Henry told the group what they knew.

Henry added, "Are you guys happy to stay here for a while; at least until we get a bit better established?"

The ex-army reservist looked at him. "We could, but it would help if we were armed, Sir?"

Smokey and Henry looked at each other and nodded; telling the group they might be able to help as far as weapons went. The senior constable handed Ron his 9 mm Glock automatic, along with a box of rounds; quickly explaining how to use it.

Thursday 8th January 2015 ... High Head Tunnels.

"What do you reckon about that lot we've just met?"

Smokey wanted to make sure they could be trusted. The group were just finishing lunch, they'd all slept late following their late-night escapade into Gary Town.

Henry had been thinking the same thing.

"What do you really know about Ron, Boz? I know you were in the reserves with him."

"I've known him for about three years now, we used to hang out together after parade on a Tuesday night, and we also did a couple of training weekends together down near Bulldust. I think he might have worked for the Hydro Electric Company in Lawn."

Charlotte asked, "Do you think we can trust this guy? And what about his mates?"

"I reckon he's like the rest of us" said Boz. "We're all just trying to survive. I don't think he's going to dob us in or anything stupid like that; if he did, he'd just end up exposing himself! As for the others, I think they're all just shit scared."

"A lot like us!" murmured Kylie.

Ernie agreed, stubbing out his cigarette. Time to tell the rest of the group about the plan he and Belle had come up with. They both reckoned the only way they were going to survive was to fight back as best they could. They also needed to start looking for other pockets of survivors; banding together would give them the strength and numbers they'd need in order to kill the enemy. One thing they were going to need more of, and quickly, was weapons, and ammo.

Ernie turned to Henry.

"What was the result of your raid on the old police station mate?"

Pulling a small notebook from his top shirt pocket, Henry reported their haul.

"We didn't do too badly. Six Glock 17's and two thousand rounds of 9 mm x 20 mm case ammo, eighteen 17-round magazines to suit, two crowd control pump action 12-gauge shotguns with twenty teargas shells, and twenty of the older Smith and Wesson 38 calibre revolvers with three hundred rounds of ammo. We've also started gathering a few of their type 68 assault rifles and ammo; we figure it's no good leaving them behind!"

Ernie nodded. "That's great, although I'm a bit concerned that we don't seem to have anything except the Lee Enfield's and the type 68's for long-distance killing. Mind you, from what we've learnt recently, keeping things up-close and personal seems to be the best way to go."

Claudia thought about everything she'd heard.

"So, what do we do now? You know. When do we start to fight back Ernie? You said you and Belle had a plan; let's hear the rest of it!"

Ernie smiled at the nineteen-year-old. "Things aren't set in concrete yet, but we do need to discuss it. My idea is to split up into three groups and do a reccy or a raid every night. The best time is probably going to be between 11 p.m. and 5 a.m. ... that way we'd be back here before daylight."

Ernie looked around, and seeing no disagreement in their faces, continued on.

"I was thinking that Group 1 should be me and Belle, along with Boz and Kylie. Henry, Charlotte, Claudia and Chris, you four should be Group 2. That leaves Smokey, Nic, Gaz and Bill to make up Group 3.

Ernie paused to light up another cigarette and take a sip of his coffee.

"I suggest that Group 1 should cover Gary Town, out as far as the football ground, as well as everything between here and there along the river track. Group 2 can cover East Beach and out as far as Cimitiere Creek; you'll also need to keep an eye on the Gary Town Airport. Group 3, your area will cover from the Gary Town roundabout to Bull Bay."

Ernie expanded on the operation. It was going to have to be twofold, they'd have to kill as many gooks as they could, as well as find local survivors, arm them and make sure their hiding places were secure.

"Now has anyone got ideas about where some of the locals might be hiding? We already know about the sailing club."

Chris spoke up. "What about the old RSL building, opposite the college. It's been empty for about a year now, and the windows have been boarded up, but it would make a good place to hide."

Henry was doubtful. "I reckon it could be too exposed. It's right on the main road, so there's a heap of traffic that goes past that spot, but it would be a good place for Group 3 to check out first."

Charlotte had been thinking. "I remember when we used to do patrols, the go-to-place for a lot of teenagers was the Gary Town wreckers; there's lots of old derelict car bodies to hide in there, and I don't think this Alliance mob would give it a second thought. Looks like that's another one for Group 3."

Nic collected the cups. As she started to wash them in the small camp sink, she suggested, "What about the airstrip? I seem to remember there's a couple of old bunkers on the perimeter of the strip, sunk into the concrete."

Smokey laughed. "Yeah, I remember those. They built them during the Second World War, just in case we got bombed!"

Chapter 28
First Raid

Tuesday 13th January 2015 ... somewhere south of Hells Beach.

After pulling Zen up, Sarge dismounted and disabled the Claymore, laying the catgut to one side. The morning air was crisp, and there was evidence of a slight morning dew. Dick had wanted an early start to what could be a very long day, so they'd left at 0645, after enjoying a quick coffee. The ride would take them up out of Hells Beach along sandy tracks no wider than an animal track for around ten kilometres through dense bush, followed by an eucalypt plantation and finally past numerous out-buildings scattered across the open paddocks to the farmhouse.

Dick and Sarge had been there once before, around ten years back, when they'd been trying to find a way to drive down to Hells Beach. They'd heard a rumour that the farm had a track leading all the way down to the beach, and that the owner was charging a fee before letting people go through. Sarge and Dick met with the man, and after a long discussion had found out that, while he was charging a fee for people to traverse his property, the track was only good for walkers. This was no good to Dick and Sarge, who'd been looking for a way to get the trekking backup vehicle down to the beach.

"You lead Annie, just follow your nose."

Tom was full of beans after enjoying the rest day and plenty of good grass.

"How are you getting on with Zen, Sarge?"

"Pretty good mate, he's not at all like Socks!"

Zen sidestepped an echidna that had buried himself in the sand as he'd seen the twelve long legs coming his way. It was slow going through the sand track, in this spot the bush track was virtually non-existent.

"Doesn't look like there's been any traffic coming this way for quite a while!"

"You're right Annie. Backpackers used to come here for a while, but I figure the owner was probably charging them too much, because they stopped coming. I was trying to remember his name. Sarge, do you remember?"

"Sure do!" said Sarge with a laugh. "It was Johnny Badman, Dick!"

"How apt Sarge!"

Just before they started to move out of the shelter of the plantation, Dick asked them to check their weapons. Annie had the 9 mm and one spare magazine, while Sarge and Dick were carrying the SLR's with two speedy loaders each, along with their own 9 mms and spare magazines strapped to their hips. They had around a kilometre of open ground to cover before reaching the first outbuilding.

"Let's move it up a couple of gears boys and girls!"

Dick spurred Bob into a canter, forcing Tom and Zen to follow; after covering the click in no time at all the trio pulled up behind the machinery shed.

"I'm thinking we should leave the horses here."

After dismounting and tying up their four-legged friends, the trio made their way across to the farmhouse, some fifty metres away; constantly scanning their surroundings as they went. After reaching the back door, Sarge entered first, and keeping his head low, moved to the left. Dick went high and to the right, while Annie waited just outside the back door. After quickly checking all the rooms they gave the all clear.

"All looks good Annie!"

It was a typical farmhouse, with a large kitchen at the rear of the house, and with a huge table in the middle of the room. The lounge was in the middle of the house, and the bedrooms were at the front. Opposite the lounge room, a lean-to had been added on, this had been used as a dining room.

Sarge did a quick check out the front door and up the street.

"All clear guys."

As he cleared the rubbish off the table, the aging CD looked at Annie.

"Can you go through the pantry and start moving all the food onto the table; we can then work out what's useable and what's not."

"Sarge can you have a look for any ammo that John might have left lying around. I'll check the shed for anything we can use."

Annie started going through the pantry shelves, as Dick and Sarge went off in opposite directions. A few minutes later they both heard a yell from the house.

"Dick! Sarge! I've found something!"

As the pair came back into the house, they were greeted by Annie waving a note in their faces.

"I found it on the floor, it must have fallen off the table. It's one of those notes from Australia Post ... *'To Whom It May Concern, we have mail to deliver.'*

Annie was out the door like a shot, leaving the two mates looking at each other in bewilderment.

"What's she up to mate?"

"Buggered if I know Sarge!"

There was the sound of running footsteps, then Annie burst back into the kitchen, clutching a letter she'd found in the mailbox at the end of the drive.

"You open it Dick!"

Sarge laughed at the excited look on her face, knowing she'd always loved to be the one who got to empty the mailbox first. Things were different where they lived, most farms were a long way away from the post office, so if you ever wanted to post a letter, you'd place it in your mailbox and display a flag or a piece of cloth so that the postman would know there was something to pick up.

Dick opened the envelope, and extracted the letter, which was dated Monday, 12th January 2015.

"Just hoping the right people find this note!

Rode the treddly up to visit my cousin Sid in Bronze last night. As I got there, I could see some kind of foreign troops. They were killing everyone in the house. Looked like they might have been Chinese or something, From where I was standing, I could see some of the other houses ... looked like the same thing had happened there.

Luckily, they didn't see me!

I got back here pronto. I've packed up the family, (baker's dozen less five) ... we're heading to canal ... dinghy across the channel 27 and making way to (Fortescue) being cryptic I know, will gather as many people I can with weapons ... J."

Annie was trying to work out what 'J' had meant. "So, there are seven of them?"

"Not quite Annie. There's eight."

"But twelve less five is seven Dick! Right?"

"Yep, but there's thirteen in a baker's dozen, so that means there are eight. Old John would be hoping the slopes wouldn't know that!"

"Where's Fortescue?"

"Don't know that name Annie. It sounds French, better get April to decipher it!"

Annie grinned. "Yeah the French bird has got to be good for something!"

All Dick could do was to give her the look! "The channel 27's simple enough; UHF channel 27. It looks like he's got a hand-held, they're only useful when you get to within a couple of hundred metres of them."

There was plenty of tinned stuff, as well as an open ten-kilogram bag of rice, herbs, spices, and jars of pasta sauce. Dick had found a few useful items in the shed; fishing tackle, hand lines and a set of fins and goggles. Unfortunately, Sarge hadn't been able to find any ammo.

"Looks like old John must have taken it all with him!"

"Better not take the rice Annie,"

"Why not? It's only just been opened Dick,"

"Yeah, just opened, but looks like nothing's been taken out of it! If I was going to set a trap for the Alliance, this would be an easy one to do, poison the rice! After all, he would have known they'd eat it."

They all agreed it wasn't worth the risk. They'd just got the rest of the food loaded into the saddlebags when they heard shots coming from up the road.

"How far to the next house Dick?"

"From memory Sarge, it's about four kilometres away."

"Sounds about right for the gunshots!"

"I think there might have been three or four .22 rifle shots, the heavier one would be the trooper's 68."

"Do we go and help?"

"I reckon by the time we got there it would be all over, although I do have an idea! Annie, Sarge, drop your saddlebags over there and mount up again. We'll head up the road and I'll explain on the way."

As they rode up the dirt road the aging CD explained his idea.

"See that hay shed on the right, Sarge? You and I will set up an ambush there."

"What do you want me to do Dick?"

"Well Annie, it's like this; if you're game enough, you're going to be the bait. Sarge and I will position ourselves on either side of the track leading into the hay shed, I'll be waiting behind some of the round bales, and Sarge will take his position behind the silage on the other side of the track. What you have to do Annie, is to walk up the middle of the road on Tom until they see you. Then just turn tail and get back here fast."

Sarge was worried. "They'll nail her when she stops to open the gate!"

"Normally I'd agree Sarge, but not this time, because she's going to jump the gate! Is Tom going to be all right with that height Annie?"

"Hell yeah! You know he can jump six feet Dick! Although I might have to give him a sighter on top of the gate, can't really see the top rail!"

Sarge cut some bright yellow plastic tarpaulin material up and wound it around the top of the gate.

"Is that better?"

"That's perfect Hon!"

Realising they'd heard no rifle fire for some time, Dick took up his position behind a large round bale of hay. After tying Bob and Zen up to an equally large hay bale around the back, Sarge hopped down behind a roll of silage. From where he was sitting, he had a good view of Annie, she only got four hundred metres away before she saw the top of a vehicle appearing over the ridge.

Annie hesitated, wondering whether she should wait until she was certain they'd seen her. Her heart was pounding!

"Shit!"

The jeep suddenly accelerated towards her, the passenger leaning out the window as he fired his pistol. Annie quickly turned Tom and gave him his head. This was what the huge seventeen-hand thoroughbred was waiting for. At full gallop he veered to the right to give himself a better approach towards the gate, and then left as he lined up with the wooden slatted gate.

Jumping in a stock saddle is not as easy as it is in a jumping saddle; you can't get your legs up high enough because of the huge knee pads. Annie and Tom weren't worried though, they'd done this many a time before. They were up and over, without Tom missing a single beat. The astonished looks on the troopers' faces said it all. They skidded to a halt at the gate and sat there dumbfounded at the sight of Annie and Tom riding away from them. Cursing, the passenger got out to open the gate; yelling at the driver to move on through.

Simultaneously, Dick and Sarge stood up, their SLR's sending bursts of ammo in the direction of the jeep. Sarge took out the driver, while Dick took care of the passenger. Hearing some return fire coming through a slit in the canvas on the back of the jeep, the two boys emptied the rest of their magazines into the canopy, figuring that would bring an end to it.

After slipping a couple of re-loaders into their magazines, they both ran towards the jeep, only to see one of the troopers taking off back up the road after somehow managing to climb out of the back. Although he was limping and obviously wounded, he'd made good progress and was almost out of sight by the time Dick managed to take aim and fire. His gun was waving all over the place, and his normally excellent aim was well off; all he succeeded in doing was to bust up the dirt at the runner's feet.

"Sorry mate! No fucking good," puffed Dick.

Sarge vaulted into the jeep, kicking the dead driver out, and reversed into the street. Revving the old beast hard, he dropped the clutch and took off up the road after the wounded man. By now Annie had managed to catch up with Dick.

"Where's he going Dick?"

Dick gave Annie a reassuring kiss on the forehead.

"You'll see! I'm proud of you my girl, and I know your mum would be too."

She'd always liked it when he called her his girl.

Flooring the accelerator, Sarge soon had the wounded trooper in his sights. It was obvious the wounded man was really struggling as he desperately looked around for somewhere to hide.

Bloop! Bloop!

Sarge ran right over the top of him, then reversed back to where the trooper was lying. Opening the door, he leaned down and shot him in the head with his 9 mm Browning, before turning the jeep around to drive back to where Dick and Annie were waiting. Sarge made a mock bow as they heartily applauded his efforts.

"What do we do with the jeep?"

"I reckon we should throw the bodies in the back and drive it back up the road to the other farm; we can then set the scene to look like there's been a gun battle. If we set the jeep alight, that will take care of the bodies. It will mean it's a long way from here, which might help to cover Johnny's escape."

Annie led the way on Tom, leading Bob and Zen the four kilometres back up the road to the previous farm. Dick and Sarge followed close behind in the jeep.

What they found there was similar to what they'd seen everywhere else. It looked like the old woman had been shot where she stood when she'd answered the door. They found the husband lying on the ground near the back door, with his .22 rifle still in his hands; it was pretty obvious that one of the troopers had circled round behind him and shot him in the back!

Dick and Sarge had a look around the house while Annie waited outside with the horses. They decided against taking any more tinned stuff; both agreeing that they had more than enough to carry, although Sarge decided they could do with more .22 ammo if there was any lying around. After checking a couple of the rooms, he realised Dick had disappeared.

"Where are you Dick?"

"Out here Sarge! Now we know what the old fellow was doing when they disturbed him!"

Dick had found the old man's kill house.

"Spot on Dick! Looks like he's had a pig hanging up. He must have just started cutting it up with the hand saw when the troopers arrived. It looks like some of it has already been bagged up; do you reckon we can fit it in?"

"Mate! We'll just have to make room; I love porker!"

Dick found a couple of hessian bags in the corner of the room; after soaking them in water he started filling one of them up with the bagged meat. Sarge cut the shoulder and leg off the other side, placing them in the other bag.

"Reckon we should get going," said Dick, heading off to where Annie was impatiently waiting for them to finish so they could get out of there.

"Just want to get rid of the jeep before we get going; we'll meet you in the plantation Annie."

Annie nodded as she moved off on Tom. After taking care of the jeep, Dick and Sarge remounted, and headed off to the plantation by a more direct route, reaching the shelter of the trees well ahead of her.

Dick said to Sarge, "You know, I'm bloody proud of her mate!"

"Yeah she's some woman mate!"

As he watched Annie riding towards them through the trees, Sarge thought about what his mate had said.

"You know, I am proud of her Dick, and I just love her to bits!"

"Mate that's great! You just need to remember to tell her that more often!"

Annie had a wide smile on her face. Dick noticed an extra bag that had been slung over Tom's shoulders.

"What's in the bags boys?"

"You first," said Sarge, "what's in yours?"

"The garden was full of veggies! I kind of just helped myself! We've got new spuds, sweet corn and tomatoes; probably enough for about four feeds! Now it's your turn Sarge ... what's in your bags?"

The old Sapper just smiled, "Crayfish dear!"

Annie snorted, and handed the boys a few muesli bars. By now it was almost 1400; they'd been so busy they hadn't noticed how quickly time was flying by.

Dick realised that Bob was moving a lot slower as they began to make their way back.

"You poor old bugger Bob, I keep forgetting how old you are! Are you happy to carry my half of the booty Sarge?"

Sarge nodded, helping Dick to tie the two hessian sacks together using some baling twine. Bob was much happier, now that his load had been lightened, while Zen didn't ever blink an eye at the extra weight. After that, they made good progress back to camp.

Before making their way down the final track, Sarge dismounted and gave Zen to Annie to lead, while he took care of the booby trap. Once they were safely past, he brushed out the tracks again and re-set the Claymore mine.

As the trio rode back into the camp, they felt like soldiers returning from a war zone. Patch, April and Jack de-tacked the horses for the weary riders and unpacked their booty.

Jack grunted as he carried the heavy wet hessian sacks over to the stores area.

"Bloody hell mate! These are heavy!" As he looked into the bags a huge smile lit up his face, as he exclaimed, "Where the fuck did you get this!"

Annie's eyes widened as Jack extracted a huge leg of pork and held it up in front of her.

"You bastard Sarge Michaels! I'll get you for that! Bloody Crayfish! You had me fooled that time!"

Sarge grinned, saying, "Hey, you can beat me up when we get to bed doll!"

Over a hot coffee, the trio told the others about the events of the day. April's mouth was already watering in anticipation as she thought about how they could make the pork last longer.

"We can cook the belly for bacon, and the leg can be roasted tomorrow night. The water's pretty icy cold here, so I was thinking that if we keep the hessian bags wet, we'll have something like an old-fashioned meat safe." The French woman was in her element. "And," she said, looking at Sarge, "someone might even build us a smoker!"

"That's a great idea," agreed Dick. "Shit! I almost forgot!"

Dick pulled the note they'd found at Julie Bay out of his pocket and handed it to April.

"I think that some of this might need your interpreter skills April."

April studied the piece of paper. "I get the, 'Bakers dozen' thing ..."

"Yes, well so did we. But what does, 'Fortescue' mean?"

"'Fortescue!' That word is from old French, Dick. The meaning is, 'Strong ...' I'm just trying to think what the other part was ... 'Strong ...'" April frowned, then laughed as she recalled the meaning. "Ah yes, I remember! It means something similar to 'Strong Armour', or 'Strong Fort'!"

That made sense! Dick shared his thoughts with the others.

"I think they might have been going to Strong Fort Bay. It's way out on the tip of the peninsula, nearly all the way to Mans Island! It's not all that well-fortified, well not like we are here, and it's a bigger bay. I know you can drive into the place, and there's a ranger station and an accommodation bunkhouse there, with around thirty beds. It was the base camp for at least three well-known bushwalks."

Sarge wasn't thinking about bushwalking right now, His stomach was rumbling.

"I reckon it will be pork chops for scran tonight!"

Chapter 29
Not a Nice Day

Wednesday 14th January 2015 ... Hells Beach. Through Dick's eyes ...

I lay in the swag, letting my thoughts wander wherever they wanted to go. There was no wind, just the birds chirping along to the slow rumble of light surf as it rolled onto the beach. It had been good to enjoy a full night's sleep at long last, a welcome break from the previous twelve days of constant stress as we'd had to fight for our lives, watch our friends and neighbours get killed, and deal with constant scenes of death and destruction everywhere we went.

It was hard to believe we'd finally made it to our safe haven. 'Hells Beach,' a strange name for such a safe refuge.

I'd always considered sleeping outside under the stars to be an experience that was almost divine, I loved sleeping this way. Even when at times the temperatures were a bit cool, inside the swag it was comfortable and warm, and sleeping in the double swag and being able to cuddle up to someone I loved, was especially good. I loved being able to wake naturally, allowing the early light to slowly and gently awaken my senses.

The first thing that usually kicked in was my sense of smell, the heavy scent of the Australian bush with its eucalyptus and the wattle, and the whiff of the slight dew on the grass was unmistakable. Next came the sounds of the birds, the movement of the wind in the trees overhead, and the gentle snoring of people as they slept. The best part of all was to be able to slowly open up my eyes and just lie there for a time, soaking it all in.

I folded back the swag's weather flap, although it wasn't fully light yet, it looked like it was going to be a pretty reasonable day as far as the weather went. Alongside me I felt Patch starting to stir as I leaned on one elbow, looking around our campsite. About twenty feet away on the other side of the now-smouldering campfire, I could just make out Jack and April's swag. No sign of movement there.

As I looked in the other direction, I could just see someone moving towards the fire. As usual, Sarge was up before anyone else, kick-starting his day by collecting some dry kindling to get the fire going for the billy. Annie was still sitting in their swag, wincing a bit as she struggled to brush the knots out of her long golden locks.

Fully awake now, I sat up, checking out the rest of the campsite, the twenty-five man army tent which held our provisions, then, further towards the west, the canyon housing our horses, with its temporary fence across the entrance, allowing them to roam free of hobbles within the safety of the canyon.

I watched Sarge strike a match to a rolled-up piece of paper, after inserting this under the smouldering timber there was a satisfying, *whoosh!* as it ignited. After pulling on my trousers, I filled the billy out of one of the clean water containers and slung it onto the iron hook on the tripod above the fire.

As I cleaned off the steel plate with my trusty paint scraper, I looked forward to eggs and bacon for breakfast. April had packed plenty of eggs, and we had to use the last of the bacon before it went off. April missed her chooks, she'd become quite excited when we'd mentioned that we'd seen a bunch of chooks the previous day while we'd been at old John's place. She'd already talked Jack into erecting a chook run and had suggested more than once that we should do something about procuring a live hen or two during the next raid.

Jack and April stirred, asking sleepily if there was anything pressing to do. Together with Patch, they'd spent a productive day yesterday, apart from the normal clean-up duties, they'd collected a huge pile of firewood and re-organised the stores. Jack had also dug a new, fully functional drop-toilet, and filled in the temporary one we'd used until now.

Figuring they'd earned the right to take things a bit easier today, I headed off down to the beach to get a bucket of salt water to clean the barbeque plate with. I remembered an old stockman teaching me this hygienic method of sterilizing a cooking plate; once it was red hot, all you had to do was to stand back and hit it with the salt water. The plate would be rendered sterile, and ready for use, with just a slight crust of salt on top. All you had to do then was to add a bit of cooking oil and start cooking.

The campsite was situated well down below the sand dunes, and about fifty feet away from them. As I sauntered nonchalantly through the slight cutting between the dunes, I suddenly pulled up short!

"Holy Shit!"

Sitting right in front of me, about half a mile offshore, was a Fremantle Class Patrol Boat! There was no mistaking the muffled sound of the underwater exhaust, and I could hear the anchor cable still rattling its way down the hawser pipe. My gaze shifted to a spot in the water, about half-way between the boat and the beach, my heart sank as I spied a RHIB slowly making its way ashore!

"Shit! That's not good."

I spun around as I detected movement out of the corner of my eye, realising it was April, on her way down to the surf for an early morning wash. This was her favourite time of the day, she'd already taken her waist-long hair out of its usual braid, ready to enjoy a good swim in the salt water.

I opened my mouth to warn her, but I couldn't get the words out. I couldn't even get to her in time, the combination of an aging body, tired limbs and the soft sand over such a distance made it impossible! Catching sight of the boat, and assuming it was full of good guys, the sixty-one-year-old French woman started waving to them, hoping to get their attention.

The bowman on the RHIB opened up with what sounded like an AK47!

Boom! Boom!

I got to April too late. As I reached out to pull her cown and out of sight, the first round hit her in the right shoulder, closely followed by the second in her right thigh.

Smack!

I hit the dirt, landing on top of April's limp body. By this time the bowman had spent his full clip, and the second crewman had started to engage the beach with rapid fire. Alerted by the noise, the others had run to the beach, it didn't take them long to realise what was going on. Jack got to us first, between us, despite the rounds from the 7.62 spitting up the sand all around, we somehow managed to drag April back over the dune and out of sight.

"Holy fuck!" declared Sarge, as Annie desperately tried to stem the flow of blood.

"She's bleeding like a stuck pig!"

"Good one Annie!" I yelled, "Straight to the point as always! Just do what you can to help her."

Carefully I peered over the dunes, trying to keep out of sight. Through my binoculars I could make out six people on the RHIB; I knew by their uniforms that they were definitely not Aussies! By now they were only four hundred yards from the beach. Seeing movement from the Patrol Boat, I knew what was coming next.

"Jack! Get that bloody canon of yours and see if you can stop those bastards from opening up with the 40-60!"

Their uniforms had fooled April into thinking that they were Australian sailors, the problem was that she hadn't noticed the different shade of camo. That had been the first warning to me that something wasn't right, my hunch was quickly confirmed once I saw the Fremantle Class Patrol Boat's number on the bow. It was 203! I knew we'd sold that one, along with three others, to the Indonesian Navy, which meant that it now belonged to the Alliance!

By now they'd come a fair way in, and were only about fifty yards away, approaching our camp from the left. The first of the salvos almost reached our observation post,

"*Va-Boom! Va-Boom! Va-Boom!*

Three craters, all around six feet in diameter, appeared just in front of us, as the 40-60 Bofors gun on the forecastle let fly. Sand went everywhere!

Just behind the top of the dune, Jack had been quickly digging in with his Barrett M107A1 .50 calibre sniper's rifle ready in hand. With its bolt action, muzzle suppressor and powerful scope, it was Jack's perfect choice of weapon for such a distance. Pulling his cowboy hat firmly over his eyes to shield the morning sun, Jack took his time as he re-loaded.

Thump! Click, Click!

The loading rating who was manning the Bofor had no idea what hit him, his head simply disintegrated! I was pretty sure Jack would have been using his own cartridges. I knew he always liked to add an extra dose of powder whenever he reloaded them, he'd always reckoned it gave him that extra punch!

Thump! Click, Click!

The operator behind the controls didn't even have time to get out of his seat before a big hole appeared in his chest.

Patch and Annie had acted together as triage team, managing to stop the blood which had been flowing from April's wounds. They concentrated on looking after April as they tried not to think about what might be happening on the beach.

After gathering together some more firepower, Sarge brought the Bren and the two 9 mm browning pistols over to where Jack and I were crouched down behind the dunes. Unfortunately, we were low on ammo for the military hardware and restricted to some 7.62mm ammo, but it would have to do.

We quickly discussed our options, realising if we wanted to stay at Hells Beach, we'd have no choice but to kill all of the Alliance personnel on the boat. This wasn't going to be an easy task, seeing there were only six of us, or five, now that April was out of action.

I thought of an idea, it was a long shot, but we didn't have many other options.

"I'm thinking we should try and lure them into the camp. If we stay hidden, they might let their guard down, thinking we've done a runner! That will give us a chance to ambush them. If we can do it without making too much noise, once we've been able to deal with the ones on foot, we could then spray a lot of their ammo around, hopefully those left on the boat will think they've done us all in."

I paused to take a breath. "All we have to do then is impersonate them and take the RHIB back to the boat. If we hold up some fresh food high enough for them to see it we might just be able to pull it off! Easy!"

I was not all that confident it would work, but none of us could think of anything else; so that was our plan.

By now, the RHIB had almost reached the beach, meaning we only had five minutes to get ready!

"Jack! I need you to disable that bloody 40-60; otherwise as soon as they get another crewman out on deck we're fucked! Can you see the front cowling covering the operator?"

"Yep! Got it in the scope now! Where do you want me to hit it?"

Thinking back to my weapons mechanic days, I knew that the Bofor was fired with a simple firing cable, a bit like the brake cable on a bicycle. This was controlled from a trigger on the joystick and ended up on the firing plunger on the gun.

"Okay Jack, I reckon if you aim for a spot, say, around twelve inches down from the top and six inches to the left of centre you'll be about right!"

Thump! Click, Click! Thump! Click, Click!

Jack's two rounds hit exactly where he intended them to, easily puncturing the alloy cowling and smashing right through the joystick and trigger assembly, completely disabling the gun!

A quick look through the binoculars confirmed that the hole was right where we'd wanted it to be.

"You could have waited until the operator got in! That way we would have had another kill!"

Jack grinned. I found myself grinning too. It seemed strange to be able to find a glimpse of humour at such a horrifying time, but we all knew that nothing was normal anymore!

Upon making our way back to the camp, we found that the girls had managed to get April into the entrance to the horse canyon. It was a good spot, being hidden behind some really large boulders which formed part of the natural entry point. Now that the bleeding had stopped, April seemed to be doing much better, even complaining that her hair was still out and covered in blood. She was certainly a tough old frog!

I looked at the girls, wondering how they'd go with whatever would happen next. Noticing my questioning look in their direction, Patch gave me a thumbs up; knowing this was going to be tough whichever way it went!

Annie had loaded the .303 and found half a box of ammo, wanting to be prepared if it all went pear-shaped. As she propped the weapon against a boulder, she gave Patch a reassuring smile.

"It will be okay Patch, we're going to nail the little yellow bastards!"

Jack, Sarge and I quickly shared our plan with the girls and set about preparing the ambush. The first job was to convince them that everyone had scarpered, all of us except April ran together towards the narrow trail that led to the only access from above, then moved back down from the rocky cliff face, being careful not to disturb the clean set of prints we'd left in the sand.

Jack crouched down behind the army tent with his knife drawn and ready for action, while Sarge concealed himself with his pig sticker in the bushes behind the dunes. I holed up on the other side of the track, with a baseball bat in hand.

Jack whispered, "Do you reckon this is going to work?"

I just nodded, "Remember, you're first up mate!"

Jack would have to make the first move. We'd left the flap of the army tent open and had moved some of the stuff to where it could be easily seen from outside. If the plan worked, the first man would hopefully think we'd all disappeared, and have a look in the tent to see what he could find. Jack's plan was to despatch him at that point, hopefully the rest wouldn't be too far behind him.

The plan was for Sarge to then take out the second man while I took care of the third. We didn't have time to worry about the other three; if all went well, two of them would stay with the RHIB, and we were just going to have to wing it as far as the 'floater' went!

From where we were hiding, Jack, Sarge and I could clearly see Patch and Annie; knowing that they would get the first glimpse of the approaching enemy as their heads appeared above the sand dunes. It wouldn't be long now!

My heart started to beat faster as I saw Annie give the thumbs up signal, as she and Patch moved further back behind their rock fortress.

Although we'd all seen action in the past, this was different. I knew Jack's and Sarge's hearts would be racing as fast as mine was right now! I wasn't sure whether it was because our loved ones were with us, or whether it was because it was a, 'do or die' moment, not only for ourselves but for the entire Taswegian community, (whatever was left of it) as well.

We were well aware of the wholesale slaughter that had been going on over the past few weeks, as the Alliance had tried their hardest to rid themselves of the local people, with the intention of taking over our homes. There simply was not enough room for them and us to co-exist!

The first crewman appeared from the direction of the dunes. A short man, with monkey-like features, he was brandishing what looked like something similar to an AK47. Coming to an abrupt halt, he scanned the campsite carefully, paying particular attention to the footprints we'd left behind. Then, looking at the tent, he jabbered something in his own language.

'Shit!' For a moment I thought we were going to have to deal with them all at once, but then realised he must have been talking out loud to himself!

The man made his way into the tent, talking as he went. As he pulled the front flap out of the way, he could obviously see all the food stored on the trestle table, alongside the eskies full of grog, and as he worked his way through the boxes alongside the far side of the tent, Jack made his move. With all the force he could muster, he whacked a long piece of wood against the side of the tent, knocking the crewman to the ground, then after dragging him through the bottom of the tent, decorated his chest with his blade; embedding it up to the hilt, The whole thing took less than five seconds!

Totally unaware of what was waiting for him, the second bloke crept forward into the campsite. Without hesitation, Sarge moved in behind him, and, using the familiar manoeuvre of clasping his hand over the man's mouth, drove his blade up under the ribs from the back and into the heart.

Two more of them were right behind him but were slow to react, giving me time to give the head of the fourth crewman a mighty *thwack* with the full swing of my bat. At the same time Sarge managed to knock the weapon out of the hand of the third man, after drawing my bat up to full height above my head I brought it crashing down on the unlucky man's head.

After dragging the bodies out of sight, I started to straighten up, but froze as Jack hissed at me to stand still! His knife only missed me by an inch, coming to a neat stop in the chest of a fifth snoozer, who'd just appeared from the direction of the beach.

"Fuck that was close! Thanks mate!"

Patch and Annie's grinning faces appeared above their rocky barrier, they were both obviously awestruck by the spectacle they'd just witnessed.

I did a quick head count, this should mean there was only one more. Moving quietly back to the beach I went to check what was happening on the boat, but there appeared to be no movement there. We'd all suspected that the nuclear blasts had crippled all VHF and HF radio transmissions, which would have meant they probably didn't have any communications with them. We had the advantage of knowing that it was only the old UHF and analogue mobile phones that might be able to work, and even then, there was only a very small window from this latitude where they'd be able to get a clear shot at the satellite.

I wondered how long it would take for the last crew member to come looking for his mates. We didn't have too long to wait, Annie whistled as he appeared over the dunes, calling out to his mates. We couldn't understand what he was saying, but it didn't really matter, he only made it ten feet inside the camp before I despatched him in the same way as I had the other two.

Voila! We had our six-pack!

"Glad that's over! What's our next move?"

"Well Sarge, I guess we're going to have to try and work out how we're going to be able to fit into their uniforms!"

This could be a problem! I was six-foot-five and weighed one hundred and twenty kilograms! Sarge was shorter, but he was still built like a brick shithouse, Only Jack, the smallest of the three of us, had any real hope of fitting into their uniforms.

Taking a deep breath, Annie said, "I'll do it,"

Sarge nodded, giving me one of those, 'You know what she's like Dick' looks.

To put them off the track, Jack picked up the AK and let off a burst above his head, then screamed out loudly before letting off a few more. I added to the fun by firing the 9 mm a few times above my head, then Jack repeated his actions ... a few more screams, followed by a few more shots, and then ... silence!

I looked at the others, there was no time to waste.

"They're probably trying to work out whether they've lost any of their men, or maybe whether they've been wounded. Annie and Sarge, see if you can fit into some of the uniforms. Jack, can you grab the fins and goggles. I'll try and pull on a shirt as best I can ... I've got a bit of a plan that just might work."

As Annie and Sarge changed their clothing, I explained what I was thinking about.

"Okay, here's the plan! First, we carry two of the bodies down to the RHIB; we'll need to make it look like they've been wounded by supporting them between two of us. Once we've placed them into the bow of the RHIB we'll need to get in ourselves. Jack, you'll need to lie down behind us in the water and hang on to the tow rope. If we tow you about ten feet behind the motor, they won't be able to see you from the boat because of the wash."

After looking around at the group to make sure they were following me, I continued. "Now, things could get a little hectic as we approach. It's possible we'll get away with it at first, but as we get closer, they're going to realise we're not who they thought we were. Jack, you're going to have to make your move as soon as I stop the RHIB. Your job is to dive under the patrol boat and swim to the port side, they probably won't notice you because they should all be preoccupied with what's happening on the starboard side."

"Yeah!" muttered Sarge, "they'll probably be shooting at us!"

"About twenty yards out I'll stop the RHIB; by then I reckon we'll be engaging them, unless they happen to all be on the piss below, in that case it will be a piece of cake!"

We knew we had to be ready for anything, so we checked and re-loaded our weapons, and after making sure Annie knew how to use hers, picked up the two bodies still wearing uniforms, and headed off to the RHIB. There was no time for long goodbyes; I kissed Patch hard on the lips, and reminded her how much I loved her, before following the rest down to the boat.

The twenty-two-foot RHIB was standard navy issue, with a centre consul aft, and a nav light frame over the top. With her twin 150's, and solid floor with eight seats facing forward, she was familiar to both Jack and myself.

We placed the bodies of the two crewmen up forward in the forecastle, facing aft, and sitting well below the gunwale. Annie sat in the forward starboard chair, with Sarge just in front of the consul and me behind the controls. We'd passed a line astern for Jack, who was being towed along behind the boat.

I didn't want to give it too much stick because this would have been too uncomfortable for Jack and might possibly have made him let go. I figured they wouldn't be too worried about our slower pace; after all, as they'd come ashore they hadn't been moving too fast, and on this return journey, they'd think it was because we were carrying the wounded with us.

I was hoping they weren't too good with the maths, otherwise they'd realise we were missing a crewman!

By this time, we were two hundred yards out. There was still nobody visible on deck, maybe our luck was holding!

I whispered loud enough for Sarge to hear me over the noise of the engine. "So far so good!"

One hundred yards! There was still no one on deck. Same at fifty yards out.

Bringing the throttles back to, 'slow ahead,' I called out softly, "Get ready!"

We all had our weapons pointed in the general direction of the patrol boat, although we tried not to make it look too obvious.

Now that we were closer, I realised that the Indonesians hadn't made too many changes to the old girl. She was looking pretty much the same as when we'd sold her to them. The only real change was the retro fitting of four sets of torpedo tubes.

We were close enough to hear the muffled exhaust of the running generators, as well as various, 'people noises,' coming up from below. Only twenty yards out now. We were travelling so slowly that the little sound we were making was covered by the noise of the generators.

Jack let go of the rope and disappeared, making his way to the side of the boat under the surface of the water. We saw his fins surface just in front of the hull, then disappear again as he swam under the boat and over to the far side. Our plan was working perfectly. Still seeing no sign of life on deck, I manoeuvred the RHIB right up to the boarding ladder; the RHIB nudged the hull ever so lightly as Sarge sprang up the ladder, startling the watchman on deck, who'd been sound asleep at his post.

Before he had time to sound the alarm, the luckless watchman found himself upended and flying through the air, landing in the RHIB on top of his mates. Annie gave him a good knock on the head with the butt of the AK.

Leaving Annie to tie up the RHIB to the boarding ladder, I was hot on Sarge's trail, joining him on deck. With our 9 mm Brownings cocked and at the ready, we entered starboard side amidships, finding the engine room hatch on our left, and the electrical room in front.

As we turned to move forward, we found ourselves in a passageway. I remembered the layout well, the xo's and the skipper's cabins would be on the port side, while the officers' heads and showers and the wardroom would be on the starboard side. I motioned to Sarge to make his way up the half dozen steps forward to check out the bridge, while I went downstairs, past the comms centre to the crew's mess deck.

There they all were, lined up for scran. As I came in through the door the first bloke in line looked at me and nodded, then turned away again. Suddenly realising something wasn't right, he turned back, doing a double take; but it was too late!

Bang! Bang! Bang! Bang!

Just like that! Four dead crewmen!

I could hear noises coming from somewhere above me, Sarge's 9 mm.

Bang! Bang!

Hearing a noise behind me I swung around to see a sleepy junior sailor coming through the hatch, he'd obviously been woken from a deep sleep by the noise of gunfire. He stopped dead in his tracks as he saw me standing over his mates, brandishing the Browning.

Bang!

He was only ten feet away from where I was standing, so I couldn't miss, shooting him clean between the eyes! After taking a quick reccy forward through the mess and into the junior sailors' heads and showers to make sure there were no more, I went back up to the bridge. Sarge was in the middle of dragging the bodies from there out on to the deck. I helped him to pile them on the quarterdeck before doing a quick head count.

"That makes two in the wheelhouse, the five from below, the six that were in the RHIB, plus two on the Bofor! That makes fifteen in total."

"That's not enough! We've got to find the rest of them!"

Sarge was wondering whether their manning levels might be different to ours.

"That's a good point," I admitted, "but we'll have to make sure! Where the fuck is Jack? Hope the bastard hasn't drowned! April will never forgive us!"

As we started moving aft back down the main passageway, we met Jack as he emerged from the engine room. The bayonet attached to his SLR was dripping with blood, and after looking at the glint in his eye, Sarge grinned,

"Well I think we both know what you've been up to!"

"Yep! I got the two who were below. They didn't even hear me enter because of the noise of the gen sets! They were good little Vegemites. Even had their earmuffs on and all!"

"We'd better check the senior sailors mess Jack. Just in case!"

As I helped Annie up on board, I could see Patch standing on the beach; obviously worrying about us. I gave her the thumbs up before giving the others a quick run-down on the layout of the Fremantle class patrol boats. I sent them off in different directions to check each compartment; feeling relieved as all returned, reporting nothing amiss. The boat was clear! Phew!

Sitting down in the mess, we talked about what we should do next.

"It's pretty obvious. I'll go back and get Patch and April and bring them on board. We need to make the most of the hot lunch that someone has kindly prepared; it should be good grub, even if it IS slope food! After that we can get April's wounds dressed in sickbay, and then reccy what's on board."

After climbing back down to the RHIB, I was off like a cut cat, doing 40 knots all the way to the beach. Patch came running to meet me, and we exchanged a long bear hug and a lingering kiss.

Patch was beaming. "You have no idea how relieved I am that you're all okay!"

Although we had to half-carry April to the RHIB, we were soon on our way back to the patrol boat. Once April had been patched up a bit better and our bellies full, the coffee pot was set to boil as we took stock of our position.

"It looks like the torpedos are twenty-one-inch American. All four tubes are full; they were surplus from the second world war and still made in the 80's. I think they were originally fitted to the P.T. boats; like in the television series, *'McHale's Navy,'* that type of Patrol Torpedo boat."

"Weren't they made of plywood Dick?"

"Everyone thought so Sarge. What most people don't know is that they were really made out of mahogany; double diagonally planked and sheathed with canvas. They were really light and strong; and easy to repair. Launched by compressed air, each torpedo had its own engine and a direct-action warhead, as soon as it hit anything solid, it would simply explode!"

Jack had been waiting impatiently to report the engineering status.

"The fuel capacity's 10,000 litres and water capacity is 6,000 litres. Both engines are good to go back on a single generator to save fuel. She's also carrying four hundred litres of unleaded fuel for the outboards!"

Sarge had checked the Armoury.

"I've got good news Jack! There's plenty of rounds for that cannon of yours, forty boxes of 50-cal, twenty boxes of 7.62 mm plus numerous boxes of 40-60. Mind you, that's not much good to us now that you've fucked the gun! Plus, there's twenty old self-loading rifles, a couple of F1s, two Armalites, ten 9 mm Brownings, and a shit load of 9 mm ammo. Oh, the Indonesian stuff, 20 x Pindad P2 Semi Auto pistols and 12 x SS1 R5 Raider Assault Rifles, a shit load of 5.56 and 9mm ammo and the usual flare pistols and flares, two hundred grenades, a special SLR with sniper sight and silencer and what looks like about fifty 80 mm mortar bombs! What would they want them for Dick?"

"Well Sarge, the Fremantles were originally set up with a mortar on the quarter deck. Maybe it's still floating around somewhere!"

Annie wanted to know what he'd meant by a 40-60.

"Good question Annie! The number means the size of the bore. In this case, the bore is 40 mm x 60, this gives you the length of the barrel: 2400 mm."

Annie and Patch had checked out the stores. Looks like we had a pantry stocked full of enough dry provisions for a couple of months, and a couple of freezers full of meat. They hadn't been able to find any fresh fruit or vegetables, although none of us were surprised by this. The boat had just completed quite a journey, which meant they would have run out long before reaching Taswegia. Since the Holocaust, all fresh food had been confiscated by the Alliance, who were hoarding all that they could get their hands on for their own people.

April lay patiently on the operating table in sickbay while Patch and Jack re-dressed her wounds. Sticking my head around the corner, I asked how she was doing.

Patch was worried. "It doesn't look good Dick, The thigh wound was through and through, although the artery was nicked ever so slightly. We don't want to move her too much, there's too much risk of her bleeding out. Plus, she's still got that round in her shoulder. The bullet really needs to come out of her shoulder; but it's a bit close to vital organs for my liking!"

"Shit! Shit! Shit!"

All the girls could do for poor April was to take advantage of the luxury of having hot water. After washing her hair and giving her a sponge bath, they got to enjoy their first real hot tubs in a couple of weeks.

Sarge used the wardroom heads and showers, while Jack and I used those belonging to the senior sailors. Sarge got a big head after using the, 'Captain's' shower, so of course, we all got great satisfaction out of pulling the piss out of him. It was good to see them all smiling again.

I fired up the radar so that I could check if anything was within range. Even though it was a bit antiquated, and probably still used valves, it was a powerful set, and much stronger than the old 916 they used to use on the A-Boats, even though we were well inside the bay I was fairly confident it would have picked up anything that had been anywhere too near to us.

We ended up having a, 'round table' meeting over a bit of supper before heading to bed. Even April was there, propped up on the settee and enjoying a bit of a nibble. Patch was feeling really worried about her friend, but April reassured her that she was feeling much more comfortable now.

"My hair's been washed and I'm feeling clean, and I'm with the people I care most about. What more could a girl want," she laughed.

Everyone fell silent, deep in thought. Breaking the silence, I touched on the topic I knew we were all thinking about.

"We really need to get April some proper medical support. And we need to get it as quickly as possible."

Seeing nods of agreement all round, I continued, summarising the position we'd found ourselves in at this time.

"We've already decided the best place to be right now is here in Hells Beach. The place is a natural fortress, with only one real weak link, we know now that any threat we face is most likely going to come in by sea. We did well today, although we were lucky not to have suffered more injuries than we did. At least, if there's a next time, we'll be better prepared!

"We've agreed we should stick to the original plan; to try and get a signal out by using the brick phone whenever the narrow window of opportunity presents itself. I know we're all keen to see if we can make contact with any other pockets of resistance throughout Taswegia, or even possibly in New Haka.

"I guess there could be a very small possibility that one or two allied ships might be okay still, if any of them have been able to get far enough south to escape the radiation, their passengers might be alive. However, as far as we can tell, it's most likely that mainland Australia is done for, same with the rest of the world. The only other possible places that might still be fallout-free could be some of the more remote areas of the northern hemisphere, maybe around Greenland and the like.

"I'm pretty sure I can speak for us all in saying that, if we can find enough people who are willing to join forces with us and fight back, we might have a chance to beat the Alliance. After all, they're in no better position than we are as far as electronics and communications go; and we have the added advantage of being on our own home soil!"

I paused, trying to get my thoughts together.

"Hmmmm ... " said Patch, "we all know whenever Dick goes quiet like that, he's busy coming up with some kind of a plan!"

Annie agreed. "Come on Dick, let's have it! What do you reckon?"

I took a deep breath. "All right! Here goes nothing! I'm thinking that Sarge, Annie, Patch and April should stay here and guard the fort. The name of this old tub is *Fremantle*, HMAS *Fremantle*, 203; the number is nearly worn off, but I'd recognise her anywhere. She was the first of the Fremantle class patrol boats; built in the UK and commissioned around 1980 if I remember correctly.

Anyway, I'm suggesting we unload most of the supplies and ammo from the boat; although it might be a good idea to keep the 40-60 shells on board and try and repair the firing cable on the Bofor. Jack, how's your powder supply?"

"Well Dick, I reckon I've only got enough to reload about one hundred rounds of .303 cal specials; I think there's about four boxes of .303 cases left. Based on Sarge's report, the .50 cal shouldn't be a problem now, there's a fair bit of 7.62 among all the other stuff."

Nodding in agreement, I continued.

"I think the RHIB should stay here, along with plenty of fuel, just in case it's needed. In the meantime, my plan is for Jack and myself to take the *Fremantle* well out to sea and around Man's Island, and then make our way up into Kings Town. It could be dangerous, but if the Alliance happens to have a few of these old rust buckets moored there we won't look too much out of place. If we can manage to get alongside up around Chook Point at night, without being seen, we can go and get the Doc!"

"What Doc is that?" asked Jack.

Annie was shaking her head. "Yeah! They're not going to let you just go ashore and grab one of theirs!"

"I'm talking about my mate, Roger... Doc! He lives in Kings Town at Chook Point. There's plenty of small boat jetties around there; if I can raise him on the brick phone, we might be able to get him and his missus out safely!"

Patch was thinking. "You might be on to something Dick, I'm pretty sure the Alliance will have kept him alive, he'd be needed because of his skills!" Her face fell as she added, "But isn't he only an ear, nose and throat man, Dick?"

"You're right about that Patch, but he's still had the basic training. In fact, I think he might even have been a surgeon before he decided to specialise in ENT. He only changed over because of the money."

Looking around at the group, I continued.

"Look. If anyone has kept their old brick phone it will be Doc! He's a typical bloody Pom! The old Scrooge never throws anything away! Anyway, even if we can't raise him on the analogue, we can take a chance and just drop in for a cuppa!"

The End ... or is it?

Author page with 'Website'

hope you have enjoyed TOAST Book 1, 'The Ride to Hell.'
To visit my Authors page and view all of my other books, just type the following link into your browser.

www.rickallenbooks.com
TALES OF A SADDLETRAMP
SADDLERY CARE AND MAINTENANCE

Glossary

AEST:	Australian Eastern Standard Time
AMPS:	Advanced Mobile Phone System
Bangers:	Sausages
BMND-SE:	British Multi-National Division South East
Brekkie:	Breakfast
Broken Arrow:	Descriptive term for when the enemy has overrun the base
Bum Nuts:	Eggs
CDAT:	Clearance Diving Acceptance Test
CD:	Clearance Diver
CDT 3:	Clearance Diving Team 3
CDTs:	Clearance Diving Teams
Chow:	Army Food
DDG:	Guided Missile Destroyer
Dob:	Tell tales on, report to the authorities
ENT:	Ear Nose and Throat
EOD:	Explosive Ordnance Disposal
FCPB:	Fremantle Class Patrol Boat
Fid:	Tool for splicing rope
Fo'c'sle:	The Forecastle, forward part of the upper deck forward of the mast

GSW:	Gun Shot Wounds
Heads:	Toilet
HF:	High Frequency
HITS:	Herrings In Tomato Sauce
Hot Bunking:	As one sailor gets out of a bunk another one climbs straight into the same bunk
ISIS:	Militant group (Islamic State of Iraq and Syria)
IT:	Information Technology
Kai:	A thick hot chocolate drink, pronounced 'Kye'
Kip:	Sleep
Local Bike:	Woman of loose moral standards, 'ridden' by everyone
MCM:	Mine Counter Measures
MHC:	Mine Hunter Coastal
MIRV's:	Multiple Independently Targetable Re-entry Vehicles
MTO:	Maritime Tactical Operations
NK:	North Korean
NVGs:	Night Vision Goggles
OBG(W):	Overwatch Battle Group West
Pit or Rack:	Bunk, Bed
Pongos:	Army (wherever the Army goes the pong, or smell, goes)
Pot Mess:	Scran rustled up out of whatever could be found in a tin
PTSD:	Post Traumatic Stress Disorder
Pussers Grip:	Canvas carry bag issued when you joined
Pussers:	Royal Australian Navy
RAA:	Royal Australian Army

RAE:	Royal Australian Engineers
RFDS:	Royal Flying Doctor Service
RHIB:	Rigid-Hulled Inflatable Boat
Roger:	Received
Roo:	Kangaroo
ROV:	Remote Operated Vehicles
RPG:	Rocket Propelled Grenade
RSL:	Returned Serviceman's League
Runt:	Someone of small stature
SAS:	Special Air Service
Scran:	Shit Cooked by the Royal Australian Navy (food)
Snag:	Sausage (Australian slang)
Shake:	To wake someone up
Slope:	Derogatory term for Asian (no longer considered appropriate)
SLR:	Self Loading Rifle
Standard NATO Brew:	Coffee with milk and two sugars
TAG(E):	Tactical Assault Group (East)
Tinned Cow:	Condensed Milk
TPI:	Totally and Permanently Incapacitated
UBDR:	Underwater Battle Damage Repair
UHF:	Ultra High Frequency
VHF:	Very High Frequency
WM:	Weapons Mechanic
Woolly Pully:	Thick, navy-issue jumper
WWI:	World War One

Weapons

NORTH KOREAN ALLIANCE WEAPONS

Type 54 Pistols

Chinese-made Tokarev batches, the 54 pistol has a 7.62 mm x 25 mm or 38 calibre super rounds. This is a knock-off of the Soviet Union made TT semi auto pistol and was issued with an 8-round magazine. Short recoil, actuated locked breech, single action, and semi-automatic. Muzzle velocity 420 m/s (1378 ft/s). Effective firing range: 50 m.

Type 68 Assault Rifle

Commonly called an AKM semi-automatic rifle with a 7.62 x 39 mm round. With a M43 30 round magazine it fires 600 rounds a minute gas operated 350 m effective range

Type 73

Light Machine Gun, which was based on a 1960s Russian knock-off, Indigenous design based on the Vz. 52 machine gun and the Kalashnikov PK machine gun design. Either magazine or belt fed, it used 7.62 mm ammo, same as the SLR.

INDONESIAN ALLIANCE WEAPONS

Pindad P2 Semi-automatic Pistol

Standard issue sidearm, a local copy of the Browning Hi-Power. Approximately 2000 P2s manufactured. Firing a 9 x 19 mm Parabellum round, it is a firearms cartridge that was designed by Georg Luger and introduced in 1902 by the German weapons manufacturer, Deutsche Waffen-und Munitionsfabriken (DWM) for their Luger semi-automatic pistol. The name, Parabellum, is derived from the Latin, *Si vis pacem, para bellum*, which was the motto of DWM.

'A *semi-automatic pistol is a type of pistol that is semi-automatic, meaning it uses the energy of the fired cartridge to cycle the action of the firearm and advance the next available cartridge into position for firing. One cartridge is fired each time the trigger of a semi-automatic pistol is pulled; the pistol's, 'disconnector,' ensures this behaviour.'*

The SS1-R5 Raider

Assault Rifles are used by the Indonesian Military. Designed for Special Forces operations such as infiltration, short distance contact in jungle, mountain, marsh, sea and urban warfare. SS1-R5 can be attached with bayonet and various types of telescopes. It has Safe, Single and Fully Automatic firing options. The weapon fires a 5.56 x 45 mm NATO round and is a rimless bottlenecked intermediate cartridge family developed in the late 1970s in Belgium by FN Herstal. The 5.56 x 45 mm NATO cartridge family was derived from, but is not identical to, the .223 Remington cartridge designed by Remington Arms in the early 1960s.

TASWEGIAN RESISTANCE FORCE WEAPONS

Browning 9 mm Semi-Automatic Pistol

9 mm Hi Power pistols have a magazine capacity of 13 cartridges plus one in the chamber, for a total capacity of 14 cartridges. It was based on a design by American firearms inventor, John Browning, firing a 7.62 x 21 mm Parabellum round. Short recoil operated. Rate of fire Semi-automatic. Muzzle velocity 335 m/s (1100 ft/s) Effective firing range 50 m (54.7 yd) Feed system Detachable box magazine; capacities 13 rounds.

The Bren Gun

Usually called simply the Bren, is a series of light machine guns (LMG) made by Britain in the 1930s and used in various roles until 1992. Effective firing range: 550 m (600 yd) Maximum firing range: 1690 m (1850 yd). Designed in Czechoslovakia. When the British Army adopted the 7.62 mm NATO cartridge, the Bren was re-designed to 7.62 mm calibre, and fitted with a new bolt, barrel and magazine.

SLR

Australian L1A1 is also known as the, 'self-loading rifle' (SLR), and in fully automatic form the, 'automatic rifle' (AR). Cartridge 7.62 x 51 mm NATO round. Action: Gas-operated, tilting breechblock. Rate of fire: Semi-automatic. Muzzle velocity: 823 m/s (2700 ft/s). Effective firing range: 800 m (875 yds) (Effective range). Feed system: 20- or 30-round detachable box magazine. Sights: Aperture rear sight, post front sight.

F1 Sub Machine Gun

9 x 19 mm Parabellum F1 was a standard Australian submachine gun manufactured by the Lithgow Small Arms Factory. First issued

to Australian troops in July 1963, it replaced the Owen machine carbine. Like the Owen, the F1 had a distinctive top mounted magazine. Sights: Offset iron sights, Feed system: 34-round Sterling SMG compatible box magazine, effective firing range: 150 m. Maximum firing range: 100–200 m, Rate of fire: 600–640 rounds/min. Calibre: 9 mm

Barrett .50 calibre Sniper's Rifle

The Barrett M82a1, standardized by the U.S. military as the M107, is recoil operated. The Barrett M107 A1 is a .50 calibre, shoulder-fired, semi-automatic sniper rifle. The A1 means it is fitted with a Muzzle Suppressor. Like its predecessors, the rifle is said to have manageable recoil. Effective firing range: 1800 m (1969 yd) Designer: Ronnie Barrett. Cartridge: .50 BMG.

The Winchester Model 70-243

A bolt-action sporting rifle. Introduced in 1936, earning the moniker, 'The Rifleman's Rifle'. The .243 produces a velocity of 902.21 m (2960 feet) per second with a 100-grain (6.6 gram) projectile commercially loaded, fired from a 24-inch (610 mm) barrel.

12-Gauge Shotgun

A shotgun, also known as a scattergun, is a firearm that is usually designed to be fired from the shoulder, which uses the energy of a fixed shell to fire a number of small spherical pellets, called shot, or a solid projectile called a slug. Shotguns come in a wide variety of sizes, ranging from 5.5 mm (.22 in) bore up to 5 cm (2.0 in) bore, and in a range of firearm operating mechanisms, including breech loading, single-barrelled, double or combination gun, pump-action, bolt, and lever-action, revolver, semi-automatic, and even fully automatic variants.

M16 Armalite

Commonly called the M16 rifle, officially designated an Assault Rifle, Calibre 5.56 mm, M16 is a family of military rifles adapted from the Armalite AR-15 rifle for the United States military. The original M16 rifle was a 5.56 mm automatic rifle, limited twist rifling in the barrel to enable the rounds to tumble literally chopping through the jungle and with a 20-round magaz ne, later modifications included a 30 round curved magazine, it had a rate of fire of 700-950 rounds per minute and a Muzzle velocity of 960 metres per second.

Browning .50 Calibre machine gun

It is a heavy machine gun designed toward the end of World War I by John Browning. Cartridge .50 BMG (12.7·99 mm NATO) Action Short recoil-operated, Rate of fire 450–600 rounds/min to 1,200–1,300 rounds/min (AN/M3) Muzzle velocity 390 m/s (2,910 ft/s). Effective firing range 1800 m Maximum firing range 7,400 m Feed system Belt-fed (M2 or M9 links).